ß

THE FOUR LAST THINGS

Suffer the little children to come unto me . . .

Little Lucy Appleyard is snatched from her child minder's on a cold winter afternoon, and the nightmare begins. When Eddie takes her home to beautiful, child-loving Angel, he knows he's done the right thing. But Lucy's not like their other visitors, and unwittingly she strikes through Angel's defences to something both vulnerable and volatile at the core.

To the outside world Lucy has disappeared into a black hole with no clues to her whereabouts . . . until the first grisly discovery in a London graveyard. More such finds are to follow, all at religious sites, and, in a city haunted by religion, what do these offerings signify?

All that stands now between Lucy and the final sacrifice are a CID sergeant on the verge of disgrace and a woman cleric – Lucy's parents – but how can they hope to halt the evil forces that are gathering around their innocent daughter?

The Four Last Things is the first novel in Andrew Taylor's Roth Trilogy, a gothic psychodrama set against the changing face of the Church of England.

THE FOUR LAST THINGS

BOOK ONE OF
THE ROTH TRILOGY

Andrew Taylor

HarperCollins*Publishers*

Collins Crime
An imprint of HarperCollins*Publishers*
77–85 Fulham Palace Road, London W6 8JB

First published in Great Britain
in 1997 by Collins Crime

1 3 5 7 9 10 8 6 4 2

Copyright © Andrew Taylor 1997

The Author asserts the moral right to be
identified as the author of this work

A catalogue record for this book is
available from the British Library

ISBN 0 00 232557 8

Set in Meridien and Bodoni

Photoset by Rowland Phototypesetting Ltd
Bury St Edmunds, Suffolk
Printed and bound in Great Britain by
Caledonian International Book Manufacturing Ltd, Glasgow

For Caroline

'. . . nor can I think I have the true Theory of death, when I contemplate a skull, or behold a Skeleton . . . I have therefore inlarged that common *Memento mori*, into a more Christian memorandum, *Memento quatuor Novissima*, those four inevitable points of us all, Death, Judgment, Heaven, and Hell.'

Sir Thomas Browne, *Religio Medici* (1642), Part I, Section 45

PROLOGUE

'In brief, we all are monsters, that is, a composition
of Man and Beast . . .'

Religio Medici, I, 55

All his life Eddie had believed in Father Christmas. In childhood his belief had been unthinking and literal; he clung to
it for longer than his contemporaries and abandoned it only
with regret. In its place came another conviction, another
Father Christmas: less defined than the first and therefore
less vulnerable.

This Father Christmas was a private deity, the source of
small miracles and unexpected joys. This Father Christmas –
who else? – was responsible for Lucy Appleyard.

Lucy was standing in the yard at the back of Carla
Vaughan's house. Eddie was in the shadows of the alleyway,
but Lucy was next to a lighted window and there could be
no mistake. It was raining, and her dark hair was flecked
with drops of water that gleamed like pearls. The sight of
her took his breath away. It was as if she were waiting for
him. An early present, he thought, gift-wrapped for Christmas. He moved closer and stopped at the gate.

'Hello.' He kept his voice soft and low. 'Hello, Lucy.'

She did not reply. Nor did she seem to register his use of
her name. Her self-possession frightened Eddie. He had never
been like that and never would be. For a long moment they
stared at each other. She was wearing what Eddie recognized
as her main outdoor coat – a green quilted affair with a hood;
it was too large for her and made her look younger than she
was. Her hands, almost hidden by the cuffs, were clasped in

9

front of her. He thought she was holding something. On her feet she wore the red cowboy boots.

Behind her the back door was closed. There were lights in the house but no sign of movement. Eddie had never been as close to her as this. If he leant forward, and stretched out his hand, he would be able to touch her.

'Soon be Christmas,' he said. 'Three and a half weeks, is it?'

Lucy tossed her head: four years old and already a coquette.

'Have you written to Santa Claus? Told him what you'd like?'

She stared at him. Then she nodded.

'So what have you asked him for?'

'Lots of things.' She spoke well for her age, articulation clear, the voice well-modulated. She glanced back at the lighted windows of the house. The movement revealed what she was carrying: a purse, too large to be hers, surely? She turned back to him. 'Who are you?'

Eddie stroked his beard. 'I work for Father Christmas.' There was a long silence, and he wondered if he'd gone too far. 'How do you think he gets into all those houses?' He waved his hand along the terrace, at a vista of roofs and chimneys, outhouses and satellite dishes; the terrace backed on to another terrace, and Eddie was standing in the alley which ran between the two rows of backyards.

Lucy followed the direction of his wave with her eyes, raising herself on the toes of one foot, a miniature ballerina. She shrugged.

'Just think of them. Millions of houses, all over London, all over the world.' He watched her thinking about it, her eyes growing larger. 'Chimneys aren't much use – hardly anyone these days has proper fires, do they? But he has other ways in and out. I can't tell you about that. It's a secret.'

'A secret,' she echoed.

'In the weeks before Christmas, he sends me and a few others around to see where the problems might be, what's

10

the best way in. Some houses are very difficult, and flats can be even worse.'

She nodded. An intelligent child, he thought: she had already begun to think out the implications of Santa Claus and his alleged activities. He remembered trying to cope with the problems himself. How did a stout gentleman carrying a large sack manage to get into all those homes on Christmas Eve? How did he get all the toys in the sack? Why didn't parents see him? The difficulties could only be resolved if one allowed him magical, or at least supernatural, powers. Lucy hadn't reached that point yet: she might be puzzled but at present she lacked the ability to follow her doubts to their logical conclusions. She still lived in an age of faith. Faced with something she did not understand, she would automatically assume that the failure was hers.

Eddie's skin tingled. His senses were on the alert, monitoring not only Lucy but the houses and gardens around them. It was early evening; at this time of year, on the cusp between autumn and winter, darkness came early. The day had been raw, gloomy and damp. He had seen no one since he turned into the alleyway.

Traffic passed in the distance; the faint but insistent rhythm of a disco bass pattern underpinned the howl of a distant siren, probably on the Harrow Road; but here everything was quiet. London was full of these unexpected pools of silence. The streetlights were coming on and the sky above the rooftops was tinged an unhealthy yellow.

'You look as if you're going out.' Eddie knew at once that this had been the wrong thing to say. Once again Lucy glanced back at the house, measuring the distance between herself and the back door. Hard on the heels of this realization came another: perhaps she wasn't afraid of Eddie but of outraged authority on the other side of that door.

He blurted out, 'It's a nice evening for a walk.' Idiotic or not, the remark seemed to have a relaxing effect on Lucy. She turned back to him, peering up at his face.

He rested his arms along the top of the gate. 'Are you going out?' he asked, politely interested, talking as one adult to another.

11

Again the toss of the head: this time inviting a clash of wills. 'I'm going to Woolworth's.'

'What are you going to buy?'

She lowered her voice. 'A conjur—' The word eluded her and she swiftly found a substitute: 'A magic set. So I can do tricks. See – I've got my purse.' She held it out: a substantial oblong, made for the handbag not the pocket; designed for an adult not a child.

Eddie took a long, deep breath. Suddenly it was hard to breathe. There always came a point when one crossed the boundary between the permissible and the forbidden. He knew that Angel would be furious. Angel believed in careful preparation, in following a plan; that way, she said, no one got hurt. She hated anything which smacked of improvisation. His heart almost failed him at the thought of her reaction.

Yet how could he turn away from this chance? Lucy was offering herself to him, his Christmas present. Had anyone ever had such a lovely present? But what if someone saw them? He was afraid, and the fear was wrapped up with desire.

'Is it far?' Lucy asked. 'Woolworth's, I mean.'

'Not really. Are you going there now?'

'I might.' Again she glanced back at the house. 'The gate's locked. There's a bolt.'

The gate was a little over four feet high. Eddie put his left hand over and felt until he found the bolt. He had to work it to and fro to loosen it in its socket; it was too stiff for a child of Lucy's age, even if she could have reached it. At last it slid back, metal smacking on metal. He tensed, waiting for opening doors, for faces at the windows, for dogs to bark, for angry questions. He guessed from her stillness that Lucy too was waiting. Their shared tension made them comrades.

Eddie pushed the gate: it swung into the yard with a creak like a long sigh. Lucy stepped backwards. Her face was pale, intent and unreadable.

'Are you coming?' He made as if to turn away, knowing that the last thing he must seem was threatening. 'I'll give you a ride there in my van if you want. We'll be back in a few minutes.'

Lucy looked back at the house again.

'Don't worry about Carla. You'll be back before she notices you're gone.'

'You know Carla?'

'Of course I do.' Eddie was on safer ground here. 'I told you that I worked for Father Christmas. He knows everything. I saw you with her yesterday in the library. Do you remember? I winked at you.'

The quality of Lucy's silence changed. She was curious now, perhaps relieved.

'And I saw you at St George's the other Sunday, too. Your mummy's called Sally and your daddy's called Michael.'

'You know them too?'

'Father Christmas knows everyone.'

Still she lingered. 'Carla will be cross.'

'She won't be cross with either of us. Not if she wants any Christmas presents this year.'

'Carla wants to win the Lottery for Christmas. I know. I asked her.'

'We'll have to see.'

Eddie took a step down the alleyway. He stopped, turned back and held out his hand to Lucy. Without a backward glance, she slipped through the open gate and put her hand in his.

One

'Who can but pity the merciful intention of those
hands that do destroy themselves? the Devil, were
it in his power, would do the like . . .'

Religio Medici, I, 51

1

'God does not change,' said the Reverend Sally Appleyard.
'But we do.'

She stopped and stared down the church. It wasn't that
she didn't know what to say next, nor that she was afraid:
but time itself was suddenly paralysed. As time could not
move, all time was present.

She had had these attacks since childhood, though less
frequently since she had left adolescence behind; often they
occurred near the start of an emotional upheaval. They were
characterized by a dreamlike sense of inevitability – similar,
Sally suspected, to the preliminaries to an epileptic fit. The
faculty might conceivably be a spiritual gift, but it was a very
uncomfortable one which appeared to serve no purpose.

Her nervousness had vanished. The silence was total,
which was characteristic. No one coughed, the babies were
asleep and the children were quiet. Even the traffic had faded
away. August sunshine streamed in an arrested waterfall of
light through the windows of the south-nave aisle and the
south windows of the clerestory. She knew beyond any
doubt that something terrible was going to happen.

The two people Sally loved best in the world were sitting
in the second pew from the front, almost directly beneath
her. Lucy was sitting on Michael's lap, frowning up at her

mother. On the seat beside her was a book and a small cloth doll named Jimmy. Michael's head was just above Lucy's. When you saw their heads so close together, it was impossible to doubt the relationship between them: the resemblance was easy to see and impossible to analyse. Michael had his arms locked around Lucy. He was staring past the pulpit and the nave altar, up the chancel to the old high altar. His face was sad, she thought: why had she not noticed that before?

Sally could not see Derek without turning her head. But she knew he would be staring at her with his light-blue eyes fringed with long sandy lashes. Derek disturbed her because she did not like him. Derek was the vicar, a thin and enviably articulate man with a very pink skin and hair so blond it was almost white.

Most of the other faces were strange to her. They must be wondering why I'm just standing here, Sally thought, though she knew from experience that these moments existed outside time. In a sense, they were all asleep: only she was awake.

The pressure was building up. She wasn't sure whether it was inside her or outside her; it didn't matter. She was sweating and the neatly printed notes for her sermon clung to her damp fingers.

As always in these moments, she felt guilty. She stared down at her husband and daughter and thought: if I were spiritually strong enough, I should be able to stop this or to make something constructive out of it. Despair flooded through her.

'Your will be done,' she said, or thought she said. 'Not mine.'

As if the words were a signal, time began to flow once more. A woman stood up towards the back of the church. Sally Appleyard braced herself. Now it was coming, whatever it was, she felt better. Anything was an improvement on waiting.

She stared down the nave. The woman was in her sixties or seventies, small, slight and wearing a grubby beige raincoat which was much too large for her. She clutched a plastic bag in her arms, hugging it against her chest as if it were a baby.

On her head was a black beret pulled down over her ears. A ragged fringe of grey, greasy hair stuck out under the rim of the beret. It was a warm day but she looked pinched, grey and cold.

'She-devil. Blasphemer against Christ. Apostate.' As she spoke, the woman stared straight at Sally and spittle, visible even at a distance, sprayed from her mouth. The voice was low, monotonous and cultivated. 'Impious bitch. Whore of Babylon. Daughter of Satan. May God damn you and yours.'

Sally said nothing. She stared at the woman and tried to pray for her. Even those who did not believe in God were willing to blame the shortcomings of their lives on him. God was hard to find so his ministers made convenient substitutes.

The woman's lips were still moving. Sally tried to blot out the stream of increasingly obscene curses. In the congregation, more and more heads craned towards the back of the church. Some of them belonged to children. It wasn't right that children should hear this.

She was aware of Michael standing up, passing Lucy to Derek's wife in the pew in front, and stepping into the aisle. She was aware too of Stella walking westwards down the nave towards the woman in the raincoat. Stella was one of the churchwardens, a tall, stately black woman who appeared never to be in a hurry.

Everything Sally saw, even Lucy and Michael, seemed both physically remote and to belong to a lesser order of importance. It impinged on her no more than the flickering images on a television set with the sound turned down. Her mind was focused on the woman in the beret and raincoat, not on her appearance or what she was saying but on the deeper reality beneath. Sally tried with all her might to get through to her. She found herself visualizing a stone wall topped with strands of barbed wire.

Michael and Stella had reached the woman now. Like an obliging child confronted by her parents, she held out her arms, giving one hand to Michael and one to Stella; she closed her mouth at last but her eyes were still on Sally. For an instant Michael, Stella and the woman made a strangely

familiar tableau: a scene from a Renaissance painting, perhaps, showing a martyr about to be dragged uncomplainingly
to the stake, with her eyes staring past the invisible face of the
artist, standing where her accuser would be, to the equally
invisible heavenly radiance beyond.

The tableau destroyed itself. Stella scooped up the carrier
bag with her free hand. She and Michael drew the woman
along the pew and walked with her towards the west door.
Their shoes clattered on the bright Victorian tiles and rang
on the central-heating gratings. The woman did not struggle
but she twisted herself round until she was walking sideways.
This allowed her to turn her head as far as she could and
continue to stare at Sally.

The heavy oak door opened. The sound of traffic poured
into the church. Sally glimpsed sunlit buildings, black railings
and a blue sky. The door closed with a dull, rolling boom.
For an instant the boom didn't sound like a closing door at
all: it was more like the whirr of great wings beating the air.

Sally took a deep breath. As she exhaled, a picture filled
her mind: an angel, stern and heavily feathered, the detail
hard and glittering, the wings flexing and rippling. She
pushed the picture away.

'God does not change,' she said again, her voice grim. 'But
we do.'

2

Afterwards Derek said, 'These days we need bouncers, not
churchwardens.'

Sally turned to look at him combing his thinning hair in
the vestry mirror. 'Seriously?'

'We wouldn't be the first.' His reflection gave her one of
his pastoral smiles. 'I don't mean it, of course. But you'll
have to get used to these interruptions. We get all sorts in
Kensal Vale. It's not some snug little suburb.'

This was a dig at Sally's last parish, a predominantly
middle-class enclave in the diocese of St Albans. Derek took

a perverse pride in the statistics of Kensal Vale's suffering.

'She needs help,' Sally said.

'Perhaps. I suspect she's done this before. There have been similar reports elsewhere in the diocese. Someone with a bee in her bonnet about women in holy orders.' He slipped the comb into his pocket and turned to face her. 'Plenty of them around, I'm afraid. We just have to grin and bear it. Or rather them. We get worse interruptions than dotty old ladies, after all – drunks, drug addicts and nutters in all shapes and sizes.' He smiled, pulling back his lips to reveal teeth so perfect they looked false. 'Maybe bouncers aren't such a bad idea after all.'

Sally bit back a reply to the effect that it was a shame they couldn't do something more constructive. It was early days yet. She had only just started her curacy at St George's, Kensal Vale. Salaried parish jobs for women deacons were scarce, and she would be a fool to antagonize Derek before her first Sunday was over. Perhaps, too, she was being unfair to him.

She checked her appearance in the mirror. After all this time the dog collar still felt unnatural against her neck. She had wanted what the collar symbolized for so long. Now she wasn't sure.

Derek was too shrewd a manager to let dislike fester unnecessarily. 'I liked your sermon. A splendid beginning to your work here. Do you think we should make more of the parallels between feminism and the anti-slavery movement?'

A few minutes later Sally followed him through the church to the Parish Room, which occupied what had once been the Lady Chapel. Its conversion last year had been largely due to Derek's gift for indefatigable fund-raising. About thirty people had lingered after the service to drink grey, watery coffee and meet their new curate.

Lucy saw her mother first. She ran across the floor and flung her arms around Sally's thighs.

'I wanted you,' Lucy muttered in an accusing whisper. She was holding her doll Jimmy clamped to her nose, a sign of either tiredness or stress. 'I wanted you. I didn't like that nasty old woman.'

Sally patted Lucy's back. 'I'm here, darling, I'm here.'

Stella towed Michael towards them. She was in her forties, a good woman, Sally suspected, but one who dealt in certainties and liked the sound of her own voice and the authority her position gave her in the affairs of the parish. Michael looked dazed.

'We were just talking about you,' Stella announced with pride, as though the circumstance conferred merit on all concerned. 'Great sermon.' She dug a long forefinger into Michael's ribcage. 'I hope you're cooking the Sunday lunch after all that.'

Sally took the coffee which Michael held out to her. 'What happened to the old woman?' she asked. 'Did you find out where she lives?'

Stella shook her head. 'She just kept telling us to go away and leave her in peace.'

'Ironic, when you think about it,' Michael said, apparently addressing his cup.

'And then a bus came along,' Stella continued, 'and she hopped on. Short of putting an armlock on her, there wasn't much we could do.'

'She's not a regular, then?'

'Never seen her before. Don't take it to heart. Nothing personal.'

Lucy tugged Sally's arm, and coffee slopped into the saucer. 'She should go to prison. She's a witch.'

'She's done nothing bad,' Sally said. 'She's just unhappy. You don't send people to prison for being unhappy, do you?'

'Unhappy? Why?'

'Unhappy?' Derek Cutter appeared beside Stella and ruffled Lucy's hair. 'A young lady like you shouldn't be unhappy. It's not allowed.'

Pink and horrified, Lucy squirmed behind her mother.

'Sally tells me this was once the Lady Chapel,' Michael said, diverting Derek's attention from Lucy. 'Times change.'

'We were lucky to be able to use the space so constructively. And in keeping with the spirit of the place, too.' Derek beckoned a middle-aged man, small and sharp-eyed, a balding cherub. 'Sally, I'd like you to meet Frank Howell. Frank, this is Sally Appleyard, our new curate, and her husband Michael.'

'Detective Sergeant, isn't it?' Howell's eyes were red-rimmed.

Michael nodded.

'There's a piece about your lady wife in the local rag. They mentioned it there.'

Derek coughed. 'I suppose you could say all of us are professionally nosy in our different ways. Frank's a freelance journalist.'

Howell was shaking hands with Stella. 'For my sins, eh?'

'In fact, Frank was telling me he was wondering whether we at St George's might form the basis of a feature. The Church of England at work in modern London.' Derek's nose twitched. 'Old wine in new bottles, one might say.'

'Amazing, when you think about it.' Howell grinned at them. 'Here we are, in an increasingly godless society, but Joe Public just can't get enough of the good old C of E.'

'I don't know if I'd agree with you there, Frank.' Derek flashed his teeth in a conciliatory smile. 'Sometimes I think we are not as godless as some of us like to think. Attendance figures are actually increasing – I can find you the statistic, if you want. You have to hand it to the Evangelicals, they have turned the tide. Of course, at St George's we try to have something for everyone – a broad, non-sectarian approach. We see ourselves as –'

'You're doing a fine job, all right.' Howell kept his eyes on Sally. 'But at the end of the day, what sells a feature is human interest. It's the people who count, eh? So maybe we could have a chat sometime.' He glanced round the little circle of faces. 'With all of you, that is.'

'Delighted,' Derek replied for them all. 'I –'

'Good. I'll give you a ring then, set something up.' Howell glanced at his watch. 'Good Lord – is that the time? Must love you and leave you.'

Derek watched him go. 'Frank was very helpful over the conversion of the Lady Chapel,' he murmured to Sally, patting her arm. 'He did a piece on the opening ceremony. We had the bishop, you know.' Suddenly he stood on tiptoe, and waved vigorously at his wife. 'There's Margaret – I know she wanted a word with you, Sally. I think she may have found you a baby-sitter. She's not one of ours but a lovely woman, all the same. Utterly reliable, too. Her name's Carla Vaughan.'

3

On the way home to Hercules Road, Michael and Sally conducted an argument in whispers in the front of the car while Lucy, strapped into the back seat, sang along with 'Puff the Magic Dragon' on the stereo. It was not so much an argument as a quarrel with gloves on.

'Aren't we going rather fast?' Sally asked.

'I didn't realize we were going to be so late.'

'Nor did I. The service took longer than I expected, and –'

'I'm worried about lunch. I left it on quite high.'

Sally remembered all the meals which had been spoiled because Michael's job had made him late. She counted to five to keep her temper in check.

'This Carla woman, Sal – the child minder.'

'What about her?'

'I wish we knew a bit more.'

'She sounds fine to me. Anyway, I'll see her before we decide.'

'I wish –'

'You wish what?'

He accelerated through changing traffic lights. 'I wish she wasn't necessary.'

'We've been through all this, haven't we?'

'I suppose I thought your job might be more flexible.'

'Well, it's not. I'm sorry but there it is.'

He reacted to her tone as much as to her words. 'What about Lucy?'

'She's your daughter too.' Sally began to count to ten.

'I know. And I know we agreed right from the start we both wanted to work. But –'

Sally reached eight before her control snapped. 'You'd like me to be something sensible like a teacher, wouldn't you? Something safe, something that wouldn't embarrass you. Something that would fit in with having children. Or better still, you'd like me to be just a wife and mother.'

'A child needs her parents. That's all I'm saying.'

'This child has two parents. If you're so concerned –'

'And what's going to happen when she's older? Do you want her to be a latchkey kid?'

'I've got a job to do, and so have you. Other people manage.'

'Do they?'

Sally glanced in the mirror at the back of the sun visor. Lucy was still singing along with a robust indifference to the tune but she had Jimmy pushed against her cheek; she sensed that her parents were arguing.

'Listen, Michael. Being ordained is a vocation. It's not something I can just ignore.'

He did not reply, which fuelled her worst fears. He used silence as a weapon of offence.

'Anyway, we talked about all this before we married. I know the reality is harder than we thought. But we agreed. Remember?'

His hands tightened on the steering wheel. 'That was different. That was before we had Lucy. You're always tired now.'

Too tired for sex, among other things: another reason for guilt. At first they had made a joke of it, but even the best jokes wore thin with repetition.

'That's not the point.'

'Of course it's the point, love,' he said. 'You're trying to do too much.'

There was another silence. 'Puff the Magic Dragon' gave way to 'The Wheels on the Bus'. Lucy kicked out the rhythm on the back of Sally's seat, attention-seeking behaviour. This should have been a time of celebration after Sally's first service at St George's. Now she wondered whether she was fit to be in orders at all.

'You'd rather I wasn't ordained,' Sally said to Michael,

23

voicing a fear rather than a fact. 'In your heart of hearts, you think women clergy are unnatural.'

'I never said that.'

'You don't need to say it. You're just the same as Uncle David. Go on, admit it.'

He stared at the road ahead and pushed the car over the speed limit. Mentioning Uncle David had been a mistake. Mentioning Uncle David was always a mistake.

'Come on.' Sally would have liked to shake him. 'Talk to me.'

They finished the journey in silence. In an effort to use the time constructively, Sally tried to pray for the old woman who had cursed her. She felt as if her prayers were falling into a dark vacuum.

'Your will be done,' she said again and again in the silence of her mind; and the words were merely sounds emptied of meaning. It was as if she were talking into a telephone and not knowing whether the person on the other end was listening or even there at all. She tried to persuade herself that this was due to the stress of the moment. Soon the stress would pass, she told herself, and normal telephonic reception would be restored. It would be childish to suppose that the problem was caused by the old woman's curse.

'Shit,' said Michael, as they turned into Hercules Road. Someone had usurped their parking space.

'It's all right,' Sally said, hoping that Lucy had not heard. 'There's a space further up.'

Michael reversed the Rover into it, jolting the nearside rear wheel against the kerb. He waited on the pavement, jingling his keys, while Sally extracted Lucy and her belongings.

'What's for lunch?' Lucy demanded. 'I'm hungry.'

'Ask your father.'

'A sort of lamb casserole with haricot beans.' Michael tended to cook what he liked to eat.

'Yuk. Can I have Frosties instead?'

Their flat was in a small, purpose-built block dating from the 1930s. Michael had bought it before their marriage. It was spacious for one person, comfortable for two and just large enough to accommodate a small child as well. As Sally opened the front door, the smell of burning rushed out to greet them.

'Shit,' Michael said. 'And double shit.'

4

Before Lucy was born, Sally and Michael Appleyard had decided that they would not allow any children they might have to disrupt their lives. They had seen how the arrival of children had affected the lives of friends, usually, it seemed, for the worse. They themselves were determined to avoid the trap.

They had met through Michael's job, almost six years before Sally was offered the Kensal Vale curacy. Michael had arrested a garage owner who specialized in selling stolen cars. Sally, who had recently been ordained as a deacon, knew his wife through church and had responded to a desperate phone call from her. The apparent urgency was such that she came as she was, in gardening clothes, with very little make-up and without a dog collar.

'It's a mistake,' the woman wailed, tears streaking her carefully made-up face, 'some ghastly mistake. Or someone's fitted him up. Why can't the police understand?'

While the woman alternately wept and raged, Michael and another officer had searched the house. It was Sally who dealt with the children, talked to the solicitor and held the woman's hand while they asked her questions she couldn't or wouldn't answer. At the time she took little notice of Michael except to think that he carried out a difficult job with more sensitivity than she would have expected.

Three evenings later, Michael arrived out of the blue at Sally's flat. On this occasion she was wearing her dog collar. Ostensibly he wanted to see if she had an address for the wife, who had disappeared. On impulse she asked him in and offered him coffee. At this second meeting she looked at him as an individual and on the whole liked what she saw: a thin face with dark eyes and a fair complexion; the sort of brown hair that once had been blond; medium height, broad shoulders and slim hips. When she came into the sitting room with the coffee she found him in front of the bookcase. He did not comment directly on its contents or on the crucifix which hung on the wall above.

'When were you ordained?'

'Only a few weeks ago.'

'In the Church of England?'

She nodded, concentrating on pouring the coffee.

'So that means you're a deacon?'

'Yes. And that's as far as I'm likely to get unless the Synod votes in favour of women priests.'

'A deacon can do everything a priest can except celebrate Communion: is that right?'

'More or less. Are you –?'

'A practising Christian? I'm afraid it's more theory than practice. My godfather's a priest.'

'Where?'

'He lives in Cambridge now. He's retired. He used to teach at a theological college in the States.' Michael sipped his coffee. 'I doubt if Uncle David approves of the ordination of women.'

'Many older priests find it hard to accept. And younger ones, too, for that matter. It's not easy for them.'

They went on to talk of other things. As he was leaving, he paused in the doorway and asked her out to dinner. The invitation surprised her as much (he later admitted) as it surprised him. She refused, but he kept on asking until she accepted, just to get rid of him.

Michael took her to a Chinese restaurant in Swiss Cottage. For most of the time he encouraged her to talk about herself, either evading or returning short answers to the questions she lobbed in return. She told him that she had left her job as a careers adviser in order to go to theological college. Now she was ordained, she had little chance of finding a curacy in the immediate future, all the more so because her father was ill and she did not want to move too far away from him.

26

'Besides, a lot of dioceses have no time for women deacons.'

Michael pushed the dish of roast duck towards her. 'If you're a deacon – or a priest – well, that has to come first, I suppose? It has to be the most important thing in life, your first allegiance.'

'Of course.'

'So where do people fit in? I know you're not married, but do you have a boyfriend? And what about children? Or would God be more important?'

'Are you always like this?'

'Like what?'

'So pushy.'

'I'm not usually like this at all.'

She bent over her plate, knowing her thick hair would curtain her face. In those days she had worn it long, and gloried in it.

'You're not celibate, are you?' he asked.

'It's nothing to do with you.'

'Yes, it is.'

'As it happens, no. But it's still nothing to do with you.'

Three months later they were married.

5

It was ridiculous, Sally told herself, to read significance into the malicious ramblings of an unhappy woman. To see them as a portent would be pure superstition. Yet in the weeks that followed Sally's first service at St George's, the old woman was often in her mind. The memory of what she had said was like a spreading stain. No amount of rubbing would remove it.

May God damn you and yours.

When Sally had been offered the curacy at Kensal Vale, it had seemed almost too good to be true, an answer to prayer. Although she was not personally acquainted with Derek Cutter, the vicar of St George's, his reputation was impressive:

he was said to be a gifted and dedicated parish priest who had breathed new life into a demoralized congregation and done much good in the parish as a whole.

The timing had seemed right, too. Sally's father had died the previous winter, bringing both sorrow and an unexpected sense of liberation. Lucy was ready to start school. Sally could at last take a full-time job with a clear conscience. And Kensal Vale was geographically convenient: she could walk from Hercules Road to St George's Vicarage in forty minutes and drive it in much less, traffic permitting. The only drawback had been Michael's lack of enthusiasm.

'What about Lucy?' he had asked in an elaborately casual voice when she mentioned the offer to him. 'She won't be at school all the time.'

'We'll find a child minder. It could actually do her good. She needs more stimulation than she gets at home.'

'Maybe you're right.'

'Darling, we've discussed all this.' Not once, Sally thought, but many times. 'I was never going to be the sort of mother that stays at home all day to iron the sheets.'

'Of course not. And I'm sure Lucy'll be fine. But are *you* sure Kensal Vale's a good idea?'

'It's just the sort of parish I want.'

'Why?'

'It's a challenge, I suppose. More rewarding in the end. Besides, I want to show I can do it, that a woman can do it.' She glared at him. 'And I need the stimulation, too. I've been freewheeling for far too long.'

'But have you thought it through? I wouldn't have said that Kensal Vale's particularly safe these days.' He hesitated. 'Especially for a woman.'

'I'll cope,' Sally snapped. 'I'm not a fool.' She watched his mouth tightening and went on in a gentler voice, 'In any case, jobs like this don't grow on trees. If I turn this down, I may not be offered another for years. And I need to have experience before I can be priested.'

He shrugged, failing to concede the point, and turned the discussion to the practical details of the move. He was unwilling to endorse it but at least he had not opposed it.

As summer slipped into autumn, Sally began to wonder if Michael might have been right. She was sleeping badly and her dreams were going through a patch of being uncomfortably vivid. The work wasn't easy, and to make matters worse she seemed to have lost her resilience. In the first week, she was rejected by a dying parishioner because she was a woman, a smartly dressed middle-aged man spat on her in the street, and her handbag was stolen by a gang of small boys armed with knives. Similar episodes had happened before, but previously she had been able to digest them with relative ease and consign them to the past. Now they gave her spiritual indigestion. The images stayed with her: the white face on the pillow turning aside from the comfort she brought; the viscous spittle gleaming on her handkerchief; and, hardest of all to forget, the children, some no more than five years older than Lucy, circling her in their monstrous game with knives in their hands and excitement in their faces.

Nothing went right at home, either. Michael had retreated further into himself since the squabble on the way back from church and the subsequent discovery that Sunday lunch had turned into a burnt offering. There were no open quarrels but the silences between them grew longer. It was possible, Sally thought, that the problem had nothing to do with her – he might be having a difficult time at work.

'Everything's fine,' he replied when she asked him directly, and she could almost hear the sound of the drawbridge rising and the portcullis descending.

Sally persevered. 'Have you seen Oliver lately?'

'No. Not since his promotion.'

'That's great. When did it happen?'

'A few weeks back.'

Why hadn't Michael told her before? Oliver Rickford had been his best man. Like Michael, he had been a high-flier at Hendon police college. They had not worked together since they had been constables, but they still kept in touch.

'Why's he been made up to inspector and not you?'

'He says the right things in committee meetings.' Michael looked at her. 'Also he's a good cop.'

'We must have him and Sharon over for supper. To celebrate.' Sally disliked Sharon. 'Tuesdays are usually a good
evening for me.'

Michael grunted, his eyes drifting back to the newspaper
in front of him.

'I suppose we should ask the Cutters sometime, too.'

'Oh God.' This time he looked up. 'Must we?'

Their eyes met and for an instant they were united by
their shared dislike of the Cutters. The dislike was another
of Sally's problems. As the weeks went by, she discovered
that Derek Cutter preferred to keep her on the sidelines of
parish work. He made her feel that wearing a deacon's stole
was the clerical equivalent of wearing L-plates. She suspected
that in his heart of hearts he was no more a supporter of
women clergy than Michael's Uncle David. At least David
Byfield made his opposition perfectly clear. Derek Cutter, on
the other hand, kept his carefully concealed. She attributed
her presence in his parish to expediency: the archdeacon was
an enthusiastic advocate of the ordination of women, and
Derek had everything to gain by keeping on the right side
of his immediate superior. He liked to keep on the right side
of almost everyone.

'Lovely to see you,' Derek said to people when he talked
to them after a service or at a meeting or on their doorsteps.
'You're looking blooming.' And if he could, he would pat
them, young or old, male or female. He liked physical
contact.

'It's not enough to love each other,' he wrote in the parish
magazine. 'We must *show* that we do. We must wear our
hearts on our sleeves, as children do.'

Derek was fond of children, though he preferred to look
resolutely on the sunny side of childhood. This meant in
effect that his benevolent interest was confined to children
under the age of seven. Children grew up quickly in Kensal
Vale and the area had an extensive population of little crimi-
nals. The picture of him in the Parish Room showed him
beaming fondly at a photogenic baby in his arms. In his
sermon on Sally's second Sunday at St George's he quoted
what was evidently a favourite text.

'Let the children come to me, Jesus told his disciples. Do not try to stop them. For the kingdom of God belongs to such as these. Mark ten, fourteen.'

There should be more to being a vicar, Sally thought, than a fondness for patting people, a sentimental attachment to young children and a range of secular skills that might have earned him a decent living in public relations or local government.

Sally knew that she was being unfair to Derek. As an administrator he was first class. The parish's finances were in good order. The church was well-respected in the area. There was a disciplined core congregation of over a hundred people. As a parish, St George's had a sense of community and purpose: Derek deserved much of the credit for this. And some of the credit must also be due to his wife. The Cutters, as Derek was fond of telling people, were a team.

Margaret Cutter was a plump woman who looked as if she had been strapped into her clothes. She had grey hair styled to resemble wire wool. Her kindness was the sort that finds its best expression in activity, preferably muscular. She invited Sally for coffee at the Vicarage on the Tuesday after Sally's first service at St George's. They sat in a small, overheated sitting room whose most noteworthy features were the bars on the window and the enormous photocopying machine behind the sofa. On top of the television set stood a toy rabbit with soft pink fur and a photograph of Derek and Margaret on their wedding day. Sally thought that she looked older than her husband.

'Just us two girls,' Margaret said, offering Sally a plate of digestive biscuits, which proved to be stale. 'I thought it would be nice to have a proper chat.' The chat rapidly turned into a monologue. 'It's the women who are the real problem. You just wouldn't believe the way they throw themselves at Derek.' The tone was confiding, but the dark eyes flickered over Sally as if measuring her for a shroud. 'Of course, he doesn't see it. But isn't that men all over? They're such fools where women are concerned. That's why they need us girls to look after them.' Here she inserted a pause which gave Sally ample time to realize that, astonishing as it might seem,

Margaret was warning her that Derek was off limits as a potential object of desire. 'I knew when I married him that he was going to be a full-time job. I used to be a lecturer, you know, catering was my subject; they begged me to stay but I said, "No, girls, I only wish I could but I have to think of Derek now." Well, that's marriage, isn't it, for better or for worse, you have to give it top priority or else you might as well not do it.' She stroked her own forearm affectionately. 'You must find it very hard, Sally, what with you both working and having the kiddie to think of as well. Still, I expect your Lucy's grown used to it, eh? Such a sweet kiddie. In some ways it's a blessing that Derek and I haven't had children. I honestly don't think we would have had time to give them the love and attention they need. But that reminds me, I promised to give you Carla Vaughan's phone number. I must admit she's not to everyone's taste, but Derek thinks very highly of her. He sees the best in everyone, Derek does. You do realize that Carla's a single parent? Two little kiddies, with different fathers and I don't think she was married to either. Still, as Derek says, who are we to cast the first stone? Did he mention she likes to be paid in cash?'

The following day, Wednesday, Sally took Lucy to meet Carla. She lived in a small terraced house which was almost exactly halfway between St George's and Hercules Road. Half West Indian and half Irish, she had an enormous mop of red curly hair which she wore in a style reminiscent of a seventeenth-century periwig. The house seethed with small children and the noise was formidable. Carla's feet were bare, and she was dressed in a green tanktop and tight trousers which revealed her sturdy legs and ample behind; she was not a woman who left much to the imagination.

Carla swept a bundle of magazines from one of the chairs. 'Do you want a Coke or something? And what about you, Lucy?'

Lucy shook her head violently. She kept close to her mother and stared round-eyed at the other children, who ignored her. Carla took two cans from the refrigerator and gave one to Sally.

'Saves washing up. You don't mind, do you?' She stared

with open curiosity at the dog collar. 'What should I call you, by the way? Reverend or something?'

'Sally, please. What a lovely big room.'

'One of my fellas did it for me. He was a builder. I told him to knock down all the walls he could without letting the house fall down. And when he'd finished I gave him his marching orders. I'm through with men. If you ask me, you're better off without them.' She leaned forward and lowered her voice slightly. 'Sex. You can keep it. Mind you, men have their uses when you need a bit of DIY.'

Sally glanced round the room, ostensibly admiring the decor. She noticed that most of the horizontal surfaces held piles of washing, disposable nappies, toys, books, empty sweet packets and video tapes. The back door was open and there was a sunlit yard beyond with a small swing and what looked like a sandpit. Sally thought that the place was fundamentally clean under the clutter and that the children seemed happy; she hoped this was not wishful thinking.

While she and Carla discussed the arrangements, Lucy feigned an interest in the twenty-four-inch television set, which was glowing and mumbling in a recess where there had once been a fireplace; she pretended to be absorbed in an episode from *Thomas the Tank Engine*, a programme she detested.

'Why don't you leave her for an hour or two? Trial run, like.'

Sally nodded, ignoring the sudden surge of panic. Lucy lunged at her arm.

'You just go, honey.' Carla detached Lucy with one hand and gave Sally a gentle push with the other. 'Have you ever made gingerbread robots with chocolate eyes?' she asked Lucy.

The crying stopped for long enough for Lucy to say, 'No.'

'Nor have I. And we won't be able to unless you can help me find the chocolate.'

Sally slipped out of the house. She hated trusting Lucy to a stranger. But whatever she did, she would feel guilty. If you had to list the top ten attributes of modern motherhood, then guilt would be high up there in the top three.

Sally Appleyard could not say when she first suspected that she was being watched. The fear came first, crawling slowly into her life when she was not looking, masquerading as a sense of unease. Her dreams filled with vertiginous falls, slowly opening doors and the sound of footsteps in empty city streets.

Rightly or wrongly she associated the change in the emotional weather with the appearance in mid-September of Frank Howell's feature in the *Evening Standard*. In his idiosyncratic way the balding cherub had done St George's proud. Here, Sally was interested to learn, was the real Church of England. Two photographs accompanied the piece: one of Derek equipped with dog collar, denim jacket and Afro-Caribbean toddler; the other of Sally. In the text Howell described the incident at Sally's first service.

'Pity he had to choose St George's,' Michael said when he saw the article.

'Why?'

'Because now all the nutters will know you're there.'

She laughed at him but his words lingered in her memory. There was no shortage of rational explanations for what she felt. She was tired and worried. It was not unnatural, particularly for a woman, to equate a sense of unease with being watched. She knew that a solitary and reasonably attractive woman was vulnerable in parts of the parish. To a certain type of male predator her profession might even add to her allure. Perhaps Michael had inadvertently planted the idea in her mind. Besides, to some extent she really was under observation: she was still a novelty in Kensal Vale: the woman with the dog collar was someone to stare at, to point out, sometimes to laugh at, and occasionally to abuse.

She-devil. Blasphemer against Christ. Apostate. Impious bitch. Whore of Babylon. Daughter of Satan.

One evening near the end of the month she was later home than expected. Michael was watching from the window.

'Where the hell were you?' he demanded as he opened the door to her. 'Do you know what time it is?'

'I'm sorry,' she snapped, her mind still full of the room she had left, with the bed, the people, the smells and the chattering television and the view from a high window of Willesden Junction beneath an apocalyptic western sky. 'Someone was dying and there wasn't a phone.'

'You should have sent someone out, then. I've phoned the Cutters, the hospitals, the police.'

His face crumpled. She put her arms around him. They clung together by the open door. Michael's hands stroked her back and her thighs. His mouth came down on hers.

She craned her head away. 'Michael –'

'Hush.'

He kissed her again and this time she found herself responding. She tried to blot out the memory of the room with the high window. One of his hands slipped round to the front of her jeans. She shifted back to allow his fingers room to reach the button of the waistband.

'Mummy,' Lucy called. 'I'm thirsty.'

'Oh God.' Michael drew back, grimacing at Sally. 'You go and see her, love. I'll get the drink.'

The following evening, he came home with a personal alarm and a mobile phone.

'Are you sure I need all these?'

'*I* need you to have them.'

'But the cost. We –'

'Bugger the cost, Sal.'

She smiled at him. 'I'm no good with gadgets.'

'You will be with these.'

She touched his hand. 'Thank you.'

The alarm and the phone helped at least for a time. The fact that Carla could now contact her at any time was also reassuring. But the fear returned, a familiar devil. Feeling watched was a part of it. So too was a sense of the watcher's steady, intelligent malevolence. Behind the watching was a fixed purpose.

But there was nothing, or very little, to pin it to. The evidence was skimpy, almost invisible, and capable of innocent interpretations: a small, pale van which one after-noon followed her car round three successive left turns; someone in a long raincoat walking down Hercules Road late at night and glancing up at the windows of the flat; warm breath on the back of her neck in a crowd swirling down the aisle of a supermarket; Lucy's claim that a man had winked at her in the library when she went there with Carla and the other children. As to the rest, what did it amount to but the occasional shiver at the back of the neck, the sense that someone might be watching her?

To complicate matters, Sally did not trust her instincts. She couldn't be sure whether the fear was a response to some-thing in the outside world or merely a symptom of an inner disturbance. This was nothing new: since her teens, she had trained herself to be wary of her intuitions partly because she did not understand them and partly because she knew they could be misleading. She lumped them together with the uncomfortably vivid dreams and the moments when time seemed to stand still. They were interesting and disturbing: but there was nothing to show that they were more than freak outbreaks of bioelectrical activity.

The scepticism was doubly necessary at present: she was under considerable strain, in a state which might well induce a certain paranoia. In the end it was a question of degree. Carrying a rape alarm was a sensible precaution against a genuine danger: acting as if she were a potential terrorist target was not.

7

In November, leaves blew along the pavements, dead fire-works lined the gutters, and mists smelling of exhaust fumes and decaying vegetables softened the outlines of buildings. In November, Uncle David came to lunch.

The 'Uncle' was a courtesy title. David Byfield was Michael's godfather. He had been a friend of his parents and his connection with Michael had survived their deaths and the cooling of his godson's religious faith. An Anglo-Catholic, he was often addressed as 'Father Byfield' by those of the same persuasion. The November lunch in London had become a regular event. In May the Appleyards went to Cambridge for a forbiddingly formal return fixture at the University Arms.

This Saturday was the worst yet. It began badly with an emergency call from Derek, who had gone down with tooth-ache and wanted Sally to take a wedding for him. Sally abandoned the cooking and Lucy to Michael. Neither the service nor the obligatory appearance at the reception did much for her self-esteem. The bride and groom were disgruntled to see her rather than Derek, and the groom's mother asked if the happy couple would have to have a proper wedding afterwards with a real clergyman.

When Sally returned to Hercules Road she found the meal over, the sink full of dirty plates, the atmosphere stinking of David's cigarettes and Lucy in tears. Averting his eyes from her dog collar, David stood up to shake hands. Lucy chose this moment to announce that Daddy was an asshole, an interesting new word she had recently picked up at Carla's. Michael slapped her leg and Lucy's tears became howls of anguish.

'You sit down,' Michael told Sally. 'I'll deal with her.' He towed Lucy away to her room.

David Byfield slowly subsided into his chair. He was a tall, spare man with prominent cheekbones and a limp due to an arthritic hip. As a young man, Sally thought, he must have been very good-looking. Now he was at least seventy, and a lifetime of self-discipline had given his features a harsh, almost predatory cast; his skin looked raw and somehow thinner than other people's.

'I'm so sorry not to have been here for lunch,' Sally said, trying to ignore the distant wails. 'An unexpected wedding.'

David inclined his head, acknowledging that he had heard.

'The vicar had to go to casualty. Turned out to be an abscess.' Why did she have to sound so bright and cheery? 'Has Lucy been rather a handful?'

'She's a lively child. It's natural.'

37

'It's a difficult age,' Sally said wildly; all ages were difficult. 'She's inclined to play up when I'm not around.'

That earned another stately nod, and also a twitch of the lips which possibly expressed disapproval of working mothers.

'I hope Michael has fed you well?'

'Yes, thank you. Have you had time to eat yourself?'

'Not yet. There's no hurry. Do smoke, by the way.'

He stared at her as if nothing had been further from his mind.

'How's St Thomas coming along?'

'The book?' The tone reproved her flippancy. 'Slowly.'

'Aquinas must be a very interesting subject.'

'Indeed.'

'I read somewhere that his fellow students called him the dumb ox of Sicily,' Sally said with a touch of desperation. 'Do you have a title yet?'

'*The Angelic Doctor.*'

Sally quietly lost her temper. One moment she had it under firm control, the next it was gone. 'Tell me, do you think that a man who was fascinated by the nature of angels has anything useful to say to us?'

'I think St Thomas will always have something useful to say to those of us who want to listen.'

Not trusting herself to speak, Sally poured herself a glass of claret from the open bottle on the table. She gestured to David with the bottle.

'No, thank you.'

For a moment they listened to the traffic in Hercules Road and Lucy's crying, now diminishing in volume.

The phone rang. Sally seized it with relief.

'Sally? It's Oliver. Is Michael there?'

'I'll fetch him.'

She opened the living-room door. Michael was sitting on Lucy's bed, rocking her to and fro on his lap. She had her eyes closed and her fingers in her mouth; they both looked very peaceful. He looked at Sally over Lucy's face.

'Oliver.'

For an instant his face seemed to freeze, as though trapped

38

by the click of a camera shutter. 'I'll take it in the bedroom.'

Lucy whimpered as Michael passed her to Sally. In the sitting room, Lucy curled up on one end of the sofa and stared longingly at the blank screen of the television. Sally picked up the handset of the phone. Oliver was speaking: '. . . complaining. You know what that . . .' She dropped the handset on the rest.

'It's a colleague of Michael's. I'm afraid it may be work.'

'I should be going.' David began to manoeuvre himself forward on the seat of the chair.

'There's no hurry, really. Stay for some tea. Anyway, perhaps Michael won't have to go out.' Desperate for a neutral subject of conversation, she went on, 'It's Oliver Rickford, actually. Do you remember him? He was Michael's best man.'

'I remember.'

There was another silence. The subject wasn't neutral after all: it reminded them both that David had refused to conduct their wedding. According to Michael, he had felt it would be inappropriate because for theological reasons he did not acknowledge the validity of Sally's orders. He had come to the service, however, and hovered, austere and unfestive, at the reception. He had presented them with a small silver clock which had belonged to his wife's parents. The clock did not work but Michael insisted in having it on the mantelpiece. Sally stared at it now, the hands eternally at ten to three and not a sign of bloody honey.

Michael came in. She knew from his face that he was going out, and knew too that something was wrong. Lucy began to cry and David said he really should leave before the light went.

The last Friday in November began with a squabble over the breakfast table about who should take Lucy to Carla's. As the school was closed for In-Service Training, Lucy was to stay with the child minder all day.

'Can't you take her this once, Michael? I promised I'd give Stella a lift to hospital this morning.'

'Why didn't you mention it before?'

'I did – last night.'

'I don't remember. Stella's not ill, is she?'

'They're trying to induce her daughter. It's her first. She's a couple of weeks overdue.'

'It's not going to make that much difference if Stella gets there half an hour later, is it?'

'It'll be longer than that because I'll hit the traffic.'

'I'm sorry. It's out of the question.'

'Why? Usually you can –'

Michael pushed his muesli bowl aside with such force that he spilled his tea. 'This isn't a usual day.' His voice was loud and harsh. 'I've got a meeting at nine-fifteen. I can't get out of it.'

Sally opened her mouth to reply but happened to catch Lucy's eye. Their daughter was watching them avidly.

'Very well. I'd better tell Stella.'

She left the room. After she made the phone call she made the beds because she couldn't trust herself to go back into the kitchen. She heard Michael leaving the flat. He didn't call goodbye. Usually he would have kissed her. She was miserably aware that too many of their conversations ended in arguments. Not that there seemed to be much time at present even to argue.

On the way to Carla's, Sally worried about Michael and tried to concentrate on driving. Meanwhile, Lucy talked incessantly. She had a two-pronged strategy. On the one hand she emphasized how much she didn't want to go to Carla's today, and how she really wanted to stay at home with Mummy; on the other she made it clear that her future happiness depended on whether or not Sally bought her a conjuring set that Lucy had seen advertised on television. The performance lacked subtlety but it was relentless and in its primitive way highly skilled. What Lucy had not taken into account, however, was the timing.

'Do be quiet, Lucy,' Sally snarled over her shoulder. 'I'm not going to take you to Woolworth's. And no, we're not spending all that money on a conjuring set. Not today, and not for Christmas. It's just not worth it. Overpriced rubbish.'

Lucy tried tears of grief and, when these failed, tears of rage. For once it was a relief to leave her at Carla's.

The day moved swiftly from bad to worse. Driving Stella to hospital took much longer than Sally had anticipated because of roadworks. Stella was worried about her daughter and inclined to be grumpy with Sally because of the delay; but once at the hospital she was reluctant to let Sally go.

The hospital trip made Sally late for the monthly committee meeting dealing with the parish finances which began at eleven. She arrived to find that Derek had taken advantage of her absence and rushed through a proposal to buy new disco equipment for the Parish Room, a scheme which Sally thought unnecessarily expensive. Despite his victory, Derek was in a bad mood because during the night someone had spray-painted a question on the front door of the Vicarage: IS THERE LIFE BEFORE DEATH?

'Infuriating,' he said to Sally after the meeting. 'So childish.'

'At least it's not obscene.'

'If only they had come and talked to me instead.'

'There are theological implications,' she pointed out. 'You could use it in a sermon.'

'Very funny, I'm sure.'

He scowled at her. For a moment she almost liked him. Only for a moment. She walked back to her car in the Vicarage car park. It was then that she discovered that she had left her cheque book and a bundle of bills at home. The bills were badly overdue and in any case she wanted to draw cash for the weekend. Skipping lunch, she drove back to Hercules Road where to her surprise she found Michael. He was sitting at his desk in the living room going through one of the drawers. There was a can of lager on top of the desk.

'What are you doing?'

He glanced at her and she knew at once that their quarrel at breakfast time had not been forgotten or forgiven. 'I have to check something. All right?'

Sally nodded as curtly as he had spoken. In silence she collected her cheque book and the bills. On her way out, she forced herself to call goodbye. Once she reached the car she discovered that she had managed to leave her phone behind. She didn't want to go back for it because that would mean seeing Michael again.

She drove miserably back to Kensal Vale. It wasn't just that she knew that Michael was capable of nursing a grudge for days. She worried that this grudge was merely a symptom of something worse. Perhaps he wanted to leave her and was summoning up the strength to make the announcement. Not that there was much to keep him. Their existence had been reduced to routine drudgeries coordinated by a complicated timetable of draconian ferocity. At the thought of life without him her stomach turned over.

She was down to visit a nursing home for the first part of the afternoon, but when she reached the Vicarage (IS THERE LIFE BEFORE DEATH?) she found a message in Derek's neat, italic hand.

> *Tried to reach you on your mobile. Off to see Archdeacon. Margaret at Brownies p.m. Please ring police at KV – Sergeant Hatherly – re attempted suicide. Paint apparently indelible.*

She picked up the telephone and dialled the number of the Kensal Vale police station. She was put through to Hatherly immediately.

'We had this old woman tried to kill herself last night. She's in hospital now. Still in a coma, I understand. I think she's one of your lot so I thought we'd better let you know.'

'What's her name?'

'Audrey Oliphant.'

'I don't know her.'

42

'She probably knows you, Reverend.' Hatherly used the title awkwardly: like many people inside and outside the Church he wasn't entirely sure how he should address a woman in holy orders. 'She's got a bedsit at twenty-nine Belmont Road. You know it? She's one of the DSS ones, according to the woman who runs the place. Very religious. Her room's full of bibles and crucifixes.'

'What makes you think she's one of ours?'

'She had one of your leaflets. Anyway, I've checked with the RCs. They don't know her from Adam.'

Sally pulled a pad towards her and jotted down the details.

'Took an overdose, it seems. Probably sleeping tablets. According to the landlady, she's a few bricks short of a load. Used to be in some sort of home, I understand. Now they've pushed her out into the community, poor old duck. Poor old community, too.'

'I'll ring the hospital and ask if I can see her. I could go via Belmont Road and see if there's anything she might need.'

'The landlady's a Mrs Gunter. I'll give her a ring if you like. Tell her to expect you. I think she'll be glad if someone else will take the responsibility.'

That makes two of you, thought Sally.

9

'I knew that one was trouble,' Mrs Gunter said over her shoulder. 'People like Audrey can't cope with real life.' She paused, panting, on the half-landing and stared at Sally with pale, bloodshot eyes. 'When all's said and done, a loony's a loony. You don't want them roaming round the streets. They need looking after.'

They moved slowly up the last flight of stairs. They were on the top floor of the house. Someone was playing rock music in a room below them. The house smelled of cooking and cigarettes. Mrs Gunter stopped outside one of the three doors on the top landing and fiddled with her keyring.

'I phoned that woman at Social Services this morning. I'm

sorry, I said, I can't have her back here. It's not on, is it? They pay me to give her a room and her breakfast. I'm not a miracle-worker.' Mrs Gunter darted a hostile glance at Sally. 'I leave the miracles to you.'

She unlocked the door and pushed it open. The room was small and narrow with a sloping ceiling. The first thing Sally noticed was the makeshift altar. The top of the chest of drawers was covered with a white cloth on which stood a wooden crucifix flanked by two brass candlesticks. The crucifix stood on a stepped base and was about eight inches high. The figure of Christ was made of bone or ivory.

'If you met her on the stairs she was always muttering to herself,' Mrs Gunter said. 'For all I know she was praying.'

The sash window was six inches open at the top and overlooked the back of the house. The air was fresh, damp and very cold. The single bed was unmade. Sally stared at the surprisingly small indentation where Audrey Oliphant had lain. There were no pictures on the walls. A portable television stood on the floor beside the wardrobe; it had been unplugged, and the screen was turned to the wall. In front of the window was a table and chair. Against the wall on the other side of the wardrobe was a spotlessly clean washbasin.

'She left a note.' Mrs Gunter twisted her lips into an expression of disgust. 'Said she was sorry to be such a trouble, and she hoped God would forgive her.'

'How did you find her?'

'She didn't come down to breakfast. I knew she hadn't gone out. Besides, it was time for her to change her sheets. And I wanted to talk to her about the state she leaves the bathroom.'

They found a leather-and-canvas bag with a broken lock in the wardrobe. As they packed it, Mrs Gunter kept up a steady flow of complaint. Meanwhile her hands deftly folded faded nightdresses and smoothed away the wrinkles from a tweed skirt.

'She's run out of toothpaste, the silly woman. I've got a bit left in a tube downstairs. She can have that. I was going to throw it away.'

'Do you know where she went to church?'

'I don't know if she did. Or nowhere regular. If you ask me, this was her church.'

Sally picked up the three books on the bedside table. There was no other reading material in the room. All of them were small and well-used. Sally glanced at them as she dropped them in the bag. First there was a holy bible, in the Authorized Version. Next came a book of common prayer, inscribed 'To Audrey, on the occasion of her First Communion, 20th March 1937, with love from Mother'.

The third book was Sir Thomas Browne's *Religio Medici*, a pocket edition with a faded blue cloth cover. Sally opened the book at the page where there was a marker. She found a faint pencil line in the margin against one sentence. 'The heart of man is the place the Devils dwell in: I feel sometimes a Hell within my self; Lucifer keeps his Court in my breast, Legion is revived in me.'

As Sally read the words her mood altered. The transition was abrupt and jerky, like the effect of a mismanaged gear change on a car's engine. Previously she had felt solitary and depressed. Now she was on the edge of despair. What was the use of this poor woman living her sad life? What was the use of Sally's attempt to help?

The despair was a familiar enemy, though today it was more powerful than usual. Its habit of descending on her was one of those inconvenient facts which she had to live with, like the bad dreams and the absurd moments when time seemed to stop; just another outbreak of freak weather in the mind. While she was driving to the hospital she tried to pray but she could not shift the mood. Her mind was in darkness. She felt the first nibbles of panic. This time the state might be permanent.

On one level Sally continued to function normally. She parked the car and went into the hospital. In the reception area she exchanged a few words with a physiotherapist who sometimes came to St George's. She took the lift up to the seventh floor. A staff nurse was slumped over a desk in the ward office with a pile of files before her. Sally tapped on the glass partition. The nurse looked at the dog collar and rubbed her eyes. Sally asked for Audrey Oliphant.

'You're too late. Died about forty minutes ago.'

'What happened?'

The nurse shrugged – not callous so much as weary. 'The odds are that her heart just gave way under the strain. Do you want to see her?'

They had given Audrey Oliphant a room to herself at the end of the corridor. The sheet had been pulled up to the top of the bed. The staff nurse folded it back.

'Did you know her?'

Sally stared at the dead face: skin and bone, stripped of personality; no longer capable of expressing anger or unhappiness. 'I saw her once in church. I didn't know her name.'

On the bed lay the woman who had cursed her.

10

Sally found it difficult not to feel that she was in one respect responsible for Audrey Oliphant's death. It made it worse that the old woman now had a name. Perhaps if Sally had tried to trace her, Audrey Oliphant might still be alive. The pressure must have been enormous for a woman of that age and background to kill herself.

She phoned Mrs Gunter from the hospital concourse and gave her the news.

'Best thing for all concerned, really.'

Sally said nothing.

'No point in pretending otherwise, is there?' Mrs Gunter sniffed. 'And now I suppose I'll have to sort out her things. You'd think she'd be more considerate, wouldn't you, being a churchgoer.'

Sally said she would return Audrey Oliphant's bag.

'Hardly seems worth bothering. Audrey said she hadn't got no relations. Not that they'd want her stuff. Nothing worth having, is there? Simplest just to put it out with the rubbish. Except Social Services would go crazy. Crazy? We're all crazy.'

During the afternoon the despair retreated a little. It was biding its time. Sally visited the nursing home. She let herself into St George's and tried to pray for Audrey Oliphant. The church felt cold and alien. The thoughts and words would not come. She found herself reciting the Lord's Prayer in the outmoded version which she had not used since she was a child. The dead woman had probably prayed in this way: 'Our Father, which art in heaven.' The words lay in her mind, heavy and indigestible as badly cooked suet.

Halfway through, she glanced at her watch and realized that if she wasn't careful she would be late picking up Lucy. She gabbled the rest and left the church. The Vicarage was empty but she left a note for Derek, who was still enjoying himself with the archdeacon.

It was raining, sending slivers of gold through the halos of the streetlamps. As Sally drove, she wondered whether Lucy had forgotten the conjuring set. It was unlikely. For one so young she could be inconveniently tenacious.

Sally left the car double-parked outside Carla's house and ran through the rain to the front door. The door opened before she reached it.

Carla was on the threshold, her hands outstretched, her face crumpled, her eyes squeezed into slits and the tears slithering down her dark cheeks. The big living room behind her was in turmoil: it seethed with adults and children; and the television shimmered in the fireplace. A uniformed policewoman put her hand on Carla's arm. She said something but Sally didn't listen.

Michael was there too, talking angrily into the phone, slashing his free hand against his leg to emphasize what he was saying. He stared in Sally's direction but seemed not to register her presence: he was looking past her at something unimaginable.

Two

'I am naturally bashful; nor hath conversation, age,
or travel, been able to effront or enharden me . . .'

Religio Medici, I, 40

1

Eddie called her Angel and so had the children. He knew
the name pleased her but not why. Lucy Appleyard refused
to call Angel anything at all. In that, as in so much else, Lucy
was different.

Lucy Philippa Appleyard was unlike the others even in the
way Angel chose her. It was only afterwards, of course, that
Eddie began to suspect that Angel had a particular reason
for wanting Lucy. Yet again he had been manipulated. The
questions were: how much, how far back did it go – and
why?

At the time everything seemed to happen by chance. Eddie
often bought the *Evening Standard,* though he did not always
read it. (Angel rarely read newspapers, partly because she
had little interest in news for its own sake, and partly because
they made her hands dirty.) Frank Howell's feature on
St George's, Kensal Vale, appeared on a Friday. Angel
chanced – if that was the appropriate word – to see it the
following Tuesday. They had eaten their supper and Eddie
was clearing up. Angel wanted to clean her shoes, a job which
like anything to do with her appearance was too important to
be delegated to Eddie.

She spread the newspaper over the kitchen table and
fetched the shoes and the cleaning materials. There were two
pairs of court shoes, one navy and the other black, and a

48

pair of tan leather sandals. She smeared the first shoe with polish. Then she stopped. Eddie, always aware of her movements, watched as she pushed the shoes off the newspaper and sat down at the table. He put the cutlery away, a manoeuvre which allowed him to glance at the paper. He glimpsed a photograph of a fair-haired man in dog collar and denim jacket, holding a black baby in the crook of his left arm.

'Wouldn't like to meet him on a dark night,' Eddie said. 'Looks like a ferret.' Imagine having *him* running up your trousers, he thought; but he did not say this aloud for fear of offending Angel.

She looked up. 'A curate and a policeman.'

'He's a policeman, too?'

'Not him. There's a woman deacon in the parish. And she's married to a policeman.'

Angel bent her shining head over the newspaper. Eddie pottered about the kitchen, wiping the cooker and the work surfaces. Angel's stillness made him uneasy.

To break the silence, he said, 'They're not really like vicars any more, are they? I mean – that jacket. It's pathetic.'

Angel stared at him. 'It says they have a little girl.'

His attention sharpened. 'The ferret?'

'Not him. The curate and the policeman. Look, there's a picture of the woman.'

Her name was Sally Appleyard, and she had short dark hair and a thin face with large eyes.

'These women priests. If you ask me, it's not natural.' Eddie hesitated. 'If Jesus had wanted women to be priests, he'd have chosen women apostles. Well, wouldn't he? It makes sense.'

'Do you think she's pretty?'

'No.' He frowned, wanting to find words which Angel might want to hear. 'She looks drab, doesn't she? Mousy.'

'You're right. She's let herself go, too. One of those people who just won't make the effort.'

'The little girl. How old is she? Does it say?'

'Four. Her name's Lucy.'

Angel went back to her shoes. Later that evening, Eddie

49

heard her moving around the basement as he watched television in the sitting room above. It was over a year since he had been down there. The memories made him feel restless. He returned to the kitchen to make some tea. While he was there he reread the article about St George's, Kensal Vale. He was not surprised when Angel announced her decision the following morning over breakfast.

'Won't it be dangerous?' Eddie stabbed his spoon at the photograph of Sally Appleyard. 'If her husband's in the CID, they'll pull out all the stops.'

'It won't be more dangerous if we plan it carefully. You've never really understood that, have you? That's why you came a cropper before you met me. A plan's like a clock. If it's properly made it has to work. All you should need to do is wind it up and off it goes. Tick tock, tick tock.'

'Are we all right for money?'

She smiled, a teacher rewarding an apt pupil. 'I shall have to do a certain amount extra to build up the contingency fund. But it's important not to break the routine in any way. I think I might warn Mrs Hawley-Minton that I may have some time off around Christmas.'

During the next two months, from mid-September to mid-November, Angel worked on average four days a week. Sometimes these included evenings and nights. Mrs Hawley-Minton's agency was small and expensive. Word of mouth was all the advertising it needed. Most of the clients were either foreign business people or expatriates paying brief visits home. They were prepared to pay good money for reliable and fully qualified freelance nannies with excellent references and the knack of controlling spoiled children. The tips were good, in some cases extravagantly generous.

'It's a sort of blood money,' Angel explained to Eddie. 'It's not that the parents feel grateful. They feel guilty. That's because they're not doing their duty – they're leaving their children to be brought up by strangers. It's not right, is it? Money can't buy love.'

They were very busy. On the agency days, Angel took the tube down from Belsize Park and made her way to Westminster, Belgravia, Knightsbridge and Kensington. She looked very smart in her navy-blue outfit, her blonde hair tied back, the hem of her skirt swinging just below the knee. Mrs Hawley-Minton's girls did not have a uniform – after all, they were ladies, not servants – but they were encouraged to conform to a discreetly professional house style. Meanwhile, Eddie saw to the cooking, the cleaning and most of the shopping.

In their spare time they made their preparations. For one thing, Angel insisted on repainting the basement, a refinement which Eddie thought unnecessary.

'What's the point? We only did it eighteen months ago.'

'I want everything to be nice and fresh.'

They shared the outside research. Angel liked to say there was no such thing as useless knowledge. If you gathered all the information that could possibly be relevant, and tried to predict every contingency, then your plan could not fail. Working separately, they quartered the broad crescent of north London between Kentish Town in the east and Willesden Junction in the west. They went in the van, on foot and by public transport. Afterwards Angel would set little tests.

'Suppose you're travelling from Kensal Vale: it's rush hour, and there are roadworks on Kilburn High Road, and you want to cut down to Maida Vale: what's your best route?'

The riskier part of the research involved the surveillance of Lucy and her parents. Angel insisted that they be even more cautious than they had been on other occasions because of Michael Appleyard's job. It was easier once they had worked out the geography of the Appleyards' routine. Like the majority of Londoners, the Appleyards spent most of their lives at a handful of locations or travelling to and from them; their city was really an invisible village.

Angel spread out the map on the kitchen table. 'Four main possibilities. St George's, the flat in Hercules Road, the child minder's house, Kensal Vale library.'

'What about shops?' Eddie put in. 'She and her mother often go down West End Lane. And they've driven up to Brent Cross at least twice since we started.'

Angel shook her head. 'I don't like it. Too many video

cameras around, especially at Brent Cross. Remember that boy Jamie. Jamie Bulger.'

That year a dank autumn slid imperceptibly into a winter characterized by cutting winds and relentless rain; pedestrians wrapped up warmly and hurried half-disguised along the pavements. On research trips Angel usually wore her long, hooded raincoat, often with the black wig and glasses.

'It makes you look like a monk,' Eddie said with a chuckle as she checked her appearance in the hall mirror one evening. 'Or rather, a nun.'

She slapped him. 'Don't ever say that again, Eddie.'

He rubbed his tingling cheek and apologized, desperate as always for her forgiveness. However hard he tried, he sometimes managed to upset her. He hated himself for his clumsiness. It made everything so uncomfortable when Angel was upset.

Eddie worried about Angel going out alone in the evening. These days no one was safe on the streets of London, and beautiful women were more vulnerable than anyone. One night in October she returned home towards midnight with a torn coat, her colour high and the glasses missing. She told Eddie that a drunk had pawed her in Quex Road.

'It was disgusting. It's made me feel physically sick.'

'But what happened?' Eddie drew her towards the sitting room. For once the roles were reversed. He felt fiercely protective towards her. 'How did you get away?'

'Oh, that wasn't a problem.' She drew her right hand out of her pocket. Silver flashed before his eyes.

'What is it?' He looked more closely and frowned. 'A *scalpel*?'

'I cut open his hand and then his face. Then I ran. If people behave like animals, they have to be treated like animals.'

On another occasion they went together to St George's and stared at the grubby redbrick church with its sturdy spire and rainwashed slate roofs. Angel tried the door but it was locked. Eddie was surprised how angry this made her.

'It's terrible. They never used to lock churches when I was young. Not in the daytime.'

'Did you go to church?' Eddie asked, suddenly curious. 'We didn't.'

'Didn't you?' Angel raised her eyebrows. 'Shall we go?'

By the middle of November, Angel had decided that it would be best to take Lucy while she was in the care of the child minder. According to the Voters' List, her name was Carla Vaughan. Angel summed up the woman with three adjectives: fat and vulgar and black.

'You think it'll be easier if we take her from there?' Eddie asked.

'Of course. The Vaughan woman takes far too many children. There's no way she can keep track of them all the time.'

'She was giving them sweets when they were at the library. I bet *she* doesn't make them clean their teeth afterwards. And they were making a dreadful racket in there. She was almost encouraging it.'

'She's a disgrace,' Angel said. 'When she's at home with them, she probably sits them in front of the television and feeds them chocolate to keep them quiet. I'm sure she hasn't any professional qualifications.'

'Lucy'll be better off with us,' Eddie said.

'There's no question of that. She's just not a fit person to have charge of children.'

By the afternoon of Friday the twenty-ninth of November their preparations were almost complete. That was when Eddie acted on the spur of the moment; as so often, it seemed to him that he had no choice in the matter. The sense of his own helplessness outweighed even his fear of what Angel might say and do when she discovered what had happened.

Circumstances played into his hands – forced him to act. Rain, a cold dense blanket like animated fog, had been falling from a dark sky for most of the afternoon, persuading people to stay inside if they had any choice in the matter. At Angel's suggestion, Eddie set out to explore the geography of Carla Vaughan's neighbourhood.

The prospect of plodding through a dreary network of back streets between Kilburn and Kensal Vale would have been boring if it had not scared him so much. In his imagination, this part of London was populated almost exclusively by drug addicts, dark-skinned muggers, gangs of uncontrollable teenagers and drunken Irishmen with violent Republican sympathies.

Shivering at his own daring, he parked the van in the forecourt of a pub called the Rose of Connemara. With the help of a map he navigated his way through the streets around Carla's house. Much of the housing consisted of late-Victorian terraces, with windows on or near the pavement. Lights were on in many of the windows. He glimpsed snug interiors, a series of vignettes illustrating lives which had nothing to do with him: a woman ironing, children watching television, an old man asleep in an armchair, a black couple dancing together, pelvis to pelvis, oblivious of spectators. He met few other pedestrians and none of them tried to mug him.

The way he found Lucy – no, the way Lucy came to him – seemed in retrospect little short of miraculous; if he believed in God he could have taken it as evidence of a divine providence hovering benignly over his affairs. He had been exploring an alley which ran between the back gardens of two terraces. One of the houses on his right was Carla's, and he had carefully counted the gardens in order to establish which belonged to her. He saw no one, though at one point an Alsatian flung itself snarling against a gate as he passed.

He identified Carla's house without trouble. The windows were of the same type as those at the front – UPVC frames with the glass patterned to imitate diamond panes; wholly out of period with the house but typical of the area and the sort of person who lived in it.

The little miracle, his present from Father Christmas, was waiting for him, her dark hair gleaming with pearl-like drops of rainwater.

'It was Lucy's fault,' Eddie told Angel later. 'She's such a tease. She was asking for it.'

Angel was furious when they reached Rosington Road. She didn't say much, not with Lucy there, but she suggested in an icy voice that Eddie might like to go to his room and wait there until she called him. Angel took Lucy to the basement. By that time Lucy had started to cry, which increased Eddie's misery. It made him so sad when children were unhappy.

'I'm too soft for my own good,' he murmured to himself. 'That's my trouble.'

Eddie sat on his bed, hands clasped over his plump stomach, as though trying to restrain the sour ache inside from bursting out. On the wall opposite him was a picture, a brightly coloured reproduction in a yellowing plastic frame. It showed a small girl in a frothy pink dress; she had a pink bow in her dark hair, a mouth like a puckered cherry and huge eyes fringed with dark lashes. The picture had been a Christmas present to Eddie's mother in 1969.

The girl, now seen through water, blurred and buckled. *Oh God. Why don't you help me? Stop this.* There was no God, Eddie knew: and therefore no chance of help. He thought briefly of Lucy's parents, the policeman and the deacon. Let the woman's God console them. That was his job. In any case, Eddie was not responsible for the Appleyards' pain. It had been Angel's decision to take Lucy. So it was her fault, really, her fault and Lucy's. Eddie had been no more than the agent, the dupe, the victim.

Time passed. Eddie would have liked to go down to the kitchen and make himself a drink. Better not – there was no point in upsetting Angel any further. He heard cars passing up and down Rosington Road and snatches of conversation from the pavement. The house itself was silent. The basement was soundproofed and Angel had not switched on the intercom.

'Lucy,' he said softly. 'Lucy Philippa Appleyard.'

Eddie stared at the picture of the girl and stroked his soft little beard. He had been five that Christmas. Had the artist been lucky enough to have a real model, someone like Lucy? He remembered how his mother slowly unwrapped the picture and stared at it; how she picked a shred of tobacco from her lips and flicked it into the ashtray; how she stared across the hearthrug at his father, who had given her the picture.

What he could not remember was whether she had spoken her verdict aloud, or whether he had merely imagined it.

'Very nice, Stanley. If you like that sort of thing.'

2

What had Eddie's father liked? If you asked different people you received different answers: for example, making dolls' houses, taking artistic photographs and helping others less fortunate than himself. All these answers were true.

Stanley Grace spent most of his life working at the head office of Paladin Assurance. The company no longer existed – it had been gobbled up by a larger rival in one of the hostile takeovers of the late 1980s. In the days of its independence, the Paladin had been a womb-like organization which catered for all aspects of its employees' lives. Eddie remembered Paladin holidays, Paladin Christmas cards, Paladin pencils, Paladin competitions and the Paladin Annual Ball. Stanley Grace bought 29 Rosington Road in 1961 with a mortgage arranged through the Paladin, and promptly insured the house, its contents, himself and his wife with Paladin insurance policies.

Eddie never discovered what his father actually did at Paladin. The relationship between his parents was equally mysterious. 'Relationship' was in fact a misleading word since it implied give and take, a movement from one to the other, a way of being together. Stanley and Thelma did not live together: they coexisted in the wary manner of animals from different species obliged by circumstances beyond their control to use the same watering hole.

Eddie remembered asking his mother when he was very young whether he was human.

'Of course you are.'

'And are you human, too?'

'Yes.'

And Daddy?'

'Oh, for heaven's sake. Of course he is. I wish you'd stop pestering me.'

Stanley was a large, lumbering man built like a bear. He towered over his wife. Thelma was skinny and small, less than five feet high, and she moved like a startled bird. She had a long and cylindrical skull to which features seemed to have been added as an afterthought. Her clothes were usually drab and a size or so too large for her; her cardigans and skirts were dappled with smudges of cigarette ash. (Until the last year of her life she smoked as heavily as her husband.) When, later in life, Eddie came across references to people wearing sackcloth, he thought of his mother.

She was nearly forty when Eddie was born, and Stanley was forty-seven. They seemed more like grandparents than parents. The boundaries of their lives were precisely defined and jealously guarded. Thelma had her headquarters in the kitchen, and her writ ran in the sitting room, the dining room and all the rooms upstairs. The basement was Stanley's alone; he installed a five-lever lock on the door from the hall because, as he would say jocularly, if he left the basement door unlocked, the Little Woman would start dusting and tidying, and he wouldn't be able to find anything. Stanley also had a controlling interest in the tiny paved area which separated the front of the house from the pavement, and in the wilderness at the back.

Gardening was not among Stanley's hobbies and in his lifetime the back garden remained a rank and overgrown place, particularly at the far end, where an accidental plantation of elder, ash and buddleia had seeded itself many years before. Over the tops of the trees could be seen the upper storeys of a block of council flats, which Thelma said lowered the tone of the neighbourhood. At night the lighted windows of the flats reminded Eddie of the superstructure of a liner. He liked to imagine it forging its way across a dark ocean while the passengers ate, drank and danced.

As a child, Eddie had associated the tangle of trees with the sound of distant trains, changing in direction as the wind veered from Gospel Oak and Primrose Hill to Kentish Town and Camden Road. He heard their strange, half-animal noises more clearly than in the house or even in the street – the throbbing of metal on metal, the rush of air and sometimes a scream. When he was very young indeed, he half-convinced himself that the noises were made not by trains, but by dinosaurs who lay in wait for him among the trees or in the patch of wasteland on the other side of the fence.

Though Stanley had no time for gardening, he liked to stand outside on a summer evening while he smoked a cigarette. His head cocked, as if listening carefully to the rumble of the trains, he would gaze in the direction of the trees and sometimes his pale, sad face would look almost happy.

3

In those days, the late 1960s and early 1970s, Rosington Road was full of children. Most of the houses had been occupied by families, whereas nowadays many of them had been cut up into flats for single people and couples. There had been fewer cars, children played in the street as well as in the gardens, and everyone had known one another. Some of the houses had belonged to the same families since the street was built in the 1890s.

According to Thelma, the house had been Stanley's choice. She would have preferred somewhere more modern in a nice leafy suburb with no blacks or council housing. But her husband felt that his leisure was too important to be frittered away on unnecessary travel and wanted to live closer to the City and the head office of the Paladin. The house was semi-detached, built of smoke-stained London brick, two storeys above a basement. The ground sloped down at the back, so the rear elevation was higher than the front. The other older houses in the road were also semi-detached, though the gaps between each pair and its neighbours were tiny. During the war the area had suffered from bomb damage. One bomb had fallen on the far end of the road and afterwards the council had cleared the ruins to make way for garages and an access road for blocks of flats, newly built homes for heroes, between Rosington Road and the railway line.

Adult visitors rarely came to the house. 'I can't abide having people here,' said Thelma. 'They make too much mess.'

When his mother went out, she would hurry along Rosington Road with her head averted from the windows, and her eyes trained on the kerb. When Eddie was young she would drag him along in her wake, her fingers digging into his arm. 'We must get on,' she would say with an edge of panic to her voice when he complained of a stitch. 'There's so much to do.'

Stanley was very different. As he was leaving home he picked up another persona along with his umbrella, hat and briefcase. He became sociable, even gregarious, as he strolled along Rosington Road on his way to the station. Given a choice, he walked slowly, his chest thrust out, his feet at right angles to each other, which gave his gait more than a suspicion of a waddle. As he progressed down the street, his white, round face turned from side to side, searching for people – for anyone, neighbour or stranger, adult or child.

''Morning. Lovely day. Looks like it's going to last.' He would beam even if it was raining, when his opening gambit was usually, 'Well, at least this weather will be good for the garden.'

At the office Stanley had a reputation for philanthropy. For many years he was secretary to the Paladin Dependants Committee, an organization which provided small luxuries for the widows and children of former employees of the company. It was he who organized the annual outing to Clacton-on-Sea, and the week's camping holiday, also once a year, which involved him taking a party of children for what he called 'a spot of fresh air under canvas'.

Eddie never went on these outings. 'You wouldn't enjoy it,' Thelma told him when he asked to go. 'Some of the children come from very unfortunate backgrounds. Last year there was a case of nits. Do you know what they are? Head lice. Quite disgusting.' As for his mother, Eddie found it impossible to imagine her in a tent. The very idea was essentially surreal, a yoking of incongruities like a goat in a sundress – or indeed like the marriage of Stanley and Thelma Grace.

His parents shared a bedroom but to all intents and purposes there might have been a glass wall between them. Then why had they stayed together at night? There was a perfectly good spare bedroom. Thelma and Stanley must have impinged on each other in a dozen different ways: her snoring, his trips to the lavatory; her habit of reading into the early hours, his rising at six o'clock and treading ponderously across the room in search of his clothes and the contents of his pockets.

Loneliness? Was that the reason? It seemed such an inadequate answer to such a complicated question.

4

As it happened, Stanley enjoyed his own company. He spent much of his time in the basement.

The stairs from the hall came down to a large room, originally the kitchen, at the back of the house. Two doors opened from it – one to the former coal cellar, and the other to a dank scullery with a quarry-tiled floor. Because of the lie of the land, the scullery and coal cellar were below ground level at the front of the house. A third door had once given access to the back garden, but Stanley screwed this to its frame in the interests of security.

The basement smelled of enamel paint, turpentine, sawdust, photographic chemicals, cigarettes and damp. Always good with his hands, Stanley built a workbench across the rear wall under the window overlooking the garden. He glued cork tiles to the wall to make a notice board on which he pinned an ever-changing selection of photographs and also a plan of the dolls' house he was working on. He kept free-standing furniture to a minimum – a stool for use at the workbench; a two-seater sofa where he relaxed; and a low Victorian armchair with a button back and ornately carved legs. (The latter appeared and reappeared in many of Stanley's photographs, usually with one or more occupants.)

Finally, there was the tall cupboard built into the alcove on the left of the chimney breast. It had deep, wide shelves and was probably as old as the house. Stanley secured it with an enormous padlock.

In the early days, the basement was forbidden territory to Eddie (and even later he entered it only by invitation). Usually the door was closed but once, as he passed through the hall, Eddie noticed that it was half-open. He crouched and peered down the stairs. Stanley was standing at the workbench examining a photograph with a magnifying glass.

His father turned and saw him. 'Hello, Eddie. I think Mummy's in the kitchen.' With the magnifying glass still in his hand he came towards the stairs, smiling widely in a way that made his cheeks bunch up like a cat's. 'Run along, now. There's a good boy.'

Eddie must have been five or six. He was not usually a bold boy – quite the reverse – but this glimpse of the unknown room had stimulated his curiosity. In his mind he cast about for a delaying tactic. 'That door, Daddy. What's the padlock for?'

The smile remained fixed in place. 'I keep dangerous things in the cupboard. Poisonous photographic chemicals. Very sharp tools.' Stanley bent down and brought his cat's smile very close to Eddie. 'Think how dreadful it would be if there were an accident.'

5

Eddie must have been about the same age when he overheard an episode which disturbed him, though at the time he did not understand it. Even as an adult he understood it only partly.

It happened during a warm night in the middle of a warm summer. In summer Eddie dreaded going upstairs because he knew it would take him longer than usual to go to sleep. Pink and sweating, he lay in bed, holding a soft toy, vaguely humanoid but unisex, whom he called Mrs Wump. As so often happens in childhood, time stretched and stretched until it seemed to reach the borders of eternity. Eddie stroked himself, trying to imagine that he was stroking someone else – a cat, perhaps, or a dog; at that age he would have liked either. His palms glided over the curve of his thighs and slipped between his legs. He slid into a waking dream involving Mrs Wump and a soft, cuddly dog.

The noises from the street diminished. His parents came upstairs. As usual his door was ajar; as usual neither of them looked in. He was aware of them following their usual routine – undressing, using the bathroom, returning to their bedroom. Some time later – it might have been minutes or even hours – he woke abruptly.

'Ah – ah –'

His father groaned: a long, creaking gasp unlike any other noise Eddie had heard him make; an inhuman, composite sound not unlike those he associated with the distant trains. Silence fell. This was worse than the noise had been. Something was very wrong, and he wondered if it could somehow be his fault.

A bed creaked. Footsteps shuffled across the bedroom floor. The landing light came on. Then his mother spoke, her voice soft and vicious, carrying easily through the darkness.

'You bloody animal.'

6

One reason why Eddie liked Lucy Appleyard was because she reminded him of Alison. The resemblance struck him during the October half-term, when Carla took Lucy and the other children to the park. Eddie followed at a distance and was lucky enough to see Lucy on one of the swings.

Alison was only a few months younger than Eddie. But when he had known her she could not have been much older than Lucy was now. The girls' colouring and features were very different. The resemblance lay in how they moved, and how they smiled.

Eddie did not even know Alison's surname. When he was still at the infants' school at the end of Rosington Road, she and her family had taken the house next door on a six-month lease. She had lived with her parents and older brother, a rough boy named Simon.

The father made Alison a swing, which he hung from one of the trees at the bottom of their garden. One day, when Eddie was playing in the thicket at the bottom of the Graces' garden, he discovered that there was a hole in the fence. One of the boards had come adrift from the two horizontal rails which supported them. The hole gave Eddie a good view of the swing, while the trees sheltered him from the rear windows of the houses.

Alison had a mass of curly golden hair, neat little features and very blue eyes. In memory at least, she usually wore a short, pink dress with a flared skirt and puffed sleeves. When she swung to and fro, faster and faster, the air caught the skirt and lifted it. Sometimes the dress billowed so high that Eddie glimpsed smooth thighs and white knickers. She was smaller than Eddie, petite and alluringly feminine. If she had been a doll, he remembered thinking, he would have liked to play with her. In private, of course, because boys were not supposed to play with dolls.

Eddie enjoyed watching Alison. Gradually he came to suspect that Alison enjoyed being watched. Sometimes she shifted her position on the swing so that she was facing the hole in the fence. She would sing to herself, making an elaborate pretence of feeling unobserved; at the time even Eddie knew that the pretence was not only a fake but designed to be accepted as such. She made great play with her skirt, allowing it to ride up and then smoothing it fussily over her legs.

Memory elided the past. The sequence of events had been streamlined; inessential scenes had been edited out, and perhaps some essential ones as well. He remembered the smell of the fence – of rotting wood warmed by summer sunshine, of old creosote, of abandoned compost heaps and distant bonfires. Somehow he and Alison had become friends. He remembered the smooth, silky feel of her skin. It had amazed him that anything could be so soft. Such softness was miraculous.

Left to himself, Eddie would never have broken through the back fence. There were two places behind the Graces' garden, both of which were simultaneously interesting and frightening, though for different reasons: to the right was the corner of the plot on which the council flats had been built; and to the left was the area known to adults and children alike as Carver's, after the company which had owned it before World War II.

The council estate was too dangerous to be worth investigating. The scrubby grass around the blocks of flats was the territory of large dogs and rough children. Carver's contained different dangers. The site was an irregular quadrilateral bounded to the north by the railway and to the south by the gardens of Rosington Road. To the east were the council flats, separated from Carver's by a high brick wall topped with broken glass and barbed wire. To the west it backed on to the yards behind a terrace of shops at right angles to the railway. The place was a labyrinth of weeds, crumbling brick walls and rusting corrugated iron.

According to Eddie's father, Carver's had been an engineering works serving the railway, and during a wartime bombing raid it had received a direct hit. In the playground at Eddie's school, it was widely believed that Carver's was haunted by the ghost of a boy who had died there in terrible, though ill-defined, circumstances.

One morning Eddie arrived at the bottom of the Graces' garden to find Alison examining the fence. On the ground at her feet was a rusting hatchet which Eddie had previously seen in the toolshed next door; it had a tall blade with a rounded projection at the top. She looked up at him.

'Help me. The hole's nearly large enough.'

'But someone might see us.'

'They won't. Come *on*.'

He obeyed, pushing with his hands while she levered with the hatchet. He tried not to think of ghosts, parents, policemen and rough boys from the council flats. The plank, rotting from the ground up, cracked in two. Eddie gasped.

'Ssh.' Alison snapped off a long splinter. 'I'll go first.'

'Do you think we should?'

'Don't be such a baby. We're explorers.'

She wriggled head first into the hole. Eddie followed reluctantly. A few yards from the fence was a small brick shed with most of its roof intact. Alison went straight towards it and pushed open the door, which had parted company with one of its hinges.

'This can be our place. Our special place.'

She led the way inside. The shed was full of rubbish and smelled damp. On the right was a long window which had lost most of its glass. You could see the sky through a hole in the roof. A spider scuttled across the cracked concrete floor.

'It's perfect.'

'But what do you want it for?' Eddie asked.

She spun round, her skirt swirling and lifting, and smiled at him. 'For playing in, of course.'

Alison liked to play games. She taught Eddie how to do Chinese burns, a technique learned from her brother. They also had tickling matches, all the more exciting because they had to be conducted in near silence, in case anyone heard. The loser, usually Eddie, was the one who surrendered or who was the first to make a noise louder than a whisper.

There were other games. Alison, though younger than Eddie, knew many more than he did. It was she who usually took the lead. It was she who suggested the Peeing Game.

'You don't know it?' Her lips formed an O of surprise, behind which gleamed her milk-white teeth and tip of her tongue. 'I thought *everyone* knew the Peeing Game.'

'I've heard about it. It's just that I've never played it.'

'My brother and I've been playing it for years.'

Eddie nodded, hoping she would not expose his ignorance still further.

'We need something to pee into.' Alison took his assent for granted. 'Come on. There must be something in here.'

Eddie glanced round the shed. He was embarrassed even

by the word 'pee'. In the Grace household the activity of urination was referred to, when it was mentioned at all, by the euphemism 'spending a penny'. His eye fell on an empty jam jar on a shelf at the back of the shed. The glass was covered on both sides with a film of grime. 'How about that?'

Alison shook her head, and the pink ribbons danced in her hair. 'It's far too small. I can do tons more than that. Anyway, it wouldn't do. The hole's too small.' Something of Eddie's lack of understanding must have shown in his face. 'It's all right for you. You can just poke your willy inside. But with girls it goes everywhere.'

Curiosity stirred in Eddie's mind, temporarily elbowing aside the awkwardness. He picked up a tin. 'What about this?'

Alison examined it, her face serious. The tin was about six inches in diameter and had once contained paint. 'It'll do.' She added with the air of one conferring a favour, 'You can go first.'

His muscles clenched themselves, as they did when he was about to step into cold water.

'Boys always go first,' Alison announced. 'My brother Simon does.'

There seemed no help for it. Eddie turned away from her and began to unbutton the flies of his khaki shorts. Without warning she appeared in front of him. She was carrying the paint tin.

'You have to take your trousers and pants down. Simon does.'

He hesitated. His lower lip trembled.

'It's only a game, stupid. Don't be such a baby. Here – I'll do it.'

She dropped the tin with a clatter on the concrete floor. Brisk as a nurse, she undid the snakeskin buckle of his elasticated belt, striped with the colours of his school, green and purple. Before he could protest, she yanked down both the shorts and his Aertex pants in one swift movement. She stared down at him. He was ashamed of his body, the slabs of pink babyish fat that clung to his belly and his thighs. A boy at the swimming baths had once said that Eddie wobbled like a jelly.

Still staring, Alison said, 'It's smaller than Simon's. And he's a roundhead.'

To his relief, Eddie understood the reference: Simon was circumcised. 'I'm a cavalier.'

'I think I like cavaliers better. They're prettier.' She scooped up the tin. 'Go on – pee.'

She held out the tin. Eddie gripped his penis between the forefinger and thumb of his right hand, shut his eyes and prayed. Nothing happened. In normal circumstances he would have had no trouble in going because his bladder was full.

'If you're going to take all day, I might as well go first.' Alison glared at him. 'Honestly. Simon never has any trouble.'

She placed the tin on the floor, pulled down her knickers and squatted. A steady stream of urine squirted into the can. She raised the hem of her dress and examined it, as though inspecting the quality of the stitching. So that was what girls looked like down there, Eddie thought, still holding his penis; he had often wondered. He craned his neck, hoping for a better view, but Alison smiled demurely and rearranged her dress.

'If you keep on rubbing your willy, it goes all funny. Did you know?' Alison raised herself from the tin and pulled up her knickers. 'At least, Simon's does. Look – I've done gallons.'

Eddie looked. The tin was about a quarter full of liquid the colour of pale gold. Until now he had assumed that he was shamefully unique in having a penis which sometimes altered shape, size and consistency when he touched it; he had hoped that he might grow out of it.

'It's nearly half-full. I bet you can't do as much.'

As Eddie glanced towards Alison, he thought he caught a movement at the window. When he looked there was no one there, just a branch waving in the breeze.

'What did I tell you? It's going stiff.'

Eddie was still holding his penis – indeed, his fingers had been absent-mindedly massaging it.

'Empty my pee outside the shed,' Alison commanded. 'Then you can try again.'

Eddie realized suddenly how absurd he must seem with his shorts and pants around his knees. He pulled them up quickly, buttoned his flies and fastened his belt.

'I don't know why you're bothering to do yourself up. You'll only have to undo it all again.'

He went outside the shed and emptied the can under a bush. The tin was warm. The liquid ran away into the parched earth. It didn't look or smell like urine. He wondered what it would taste like. He pushed the thought away – *disgusting* – and straightened up to return to the shed, his mind full of the ordeal before him. For an instant he thought he smelled freshly burned tobacco in the air.

7

Eddie and Alison played the Peeing Game on many occasions, and each time they explored a little further.

Fear of discovery heightened the pleasure. When they went into Carver's, there was often a woman on the balcony of one of the council flats. The balcony overlooked both Carver's and the garden of 29 Rosington Road. Sometimes the woman was occupied – hanging washing, watering plants; but on other occasions she simply stood there, very still, and watched the sky. Alison said the woman was mad. Eddie worried that she might see them and tell their parents that they were trespassing in Carver's. But she never did.

Eddie's memories of the period were patchy. (He did not like to think too hard about the possibility that he had willed this to be so.) He must have been six, almost seven, which meant that the year was 1971. It had been summertime, the long school holidays. He remembered the smell of a faded green short-sleeved shirt he often wore, and the touch of Alison's hand, plump and dimpled, on his bare forearm.

The end came in September, and with shocking suddenness. One day Alison and her family were living at number 27, the next day they were gone. On the afternoon before they left, she told Eddie that they were moving to Ealing.

'But where's Ealing?' he wailed.

'How do I know? Somewhere in London. You can write me letters.'

Eddie cried when they parted. Alison forgot to leave her address. She slipped away from him like a handful of sand trickling through the fingers.

Three

1

Sleep caught Sally in mid-sentence, as sudden as a drawn
curtain or nightfall in the Tropics. One moment she was lying
in bed, holding the hand of a policewoman she had never
met before; the policewoman's lips were moving but Sally
wasn't listening because she was too busy wondering why
she was holding the hand of a total stranger. Then the sleeping tablets cut in, blending with whatever the hypodermic
had contained, probably a tranquillizer.

Michael had not been there. She hadn't seen him for
hours.

Her mind went down and down into a black fog. Smothered by chemicals, she slept for hours, so deeply asleep that
she was hardly a person any more. In the early hours of
Saturday morning, the fog began gradually to clear. She slept
on but now there were dreams, at first wispy and insubstantial – a suspicion of raised voices, a hint of bright lights, a
sense of overwhelming sadness.

Later still, the images coalesced into a whole that was
neither a picture nor a story. Afterwards, when Sally woke
bathed in sweat on a cold morning, she remembered a bell
tolling, its sound dulled by the winter air. She saw dirty snow
on cobbles, mixed with fragments of straw and what looked
like urine and human excrement. A spire built of raw, yellow

stone and surmounted by a distant cross rose towards the grey sky.

In the dream a man was speaking, or rather declaiming slowly in a harsh, deep voice which Sally instinctively disliked. She could not make out the words, or even the language they were spoken in, partly because she was too far away and partly because they were distorted by hissing and cracking and popping in the background. Still in the dream, Sally was reminded of the 78-r.p.m. records she played as a child on the wind-up gramophone in her grandparents' attic; the scratches had overwhelmed the ghostly frivolities of the Savoy Orpheans and Fats Waller.

When Sally woke up, her mouth was dry and her mind clouded. The dream receded as she neared consciousness, details slipping away, drifting downwards beyond retrieval.

'Come back,' she called silently. Her eyes, still closed, were wet with tears. Something terrible was happening in the dream, which at all costs had to be put right. But at least it was only a dream. For a split second relief touched her: only a dream, thank God, only a dream. Then she opened her eyes and saw a woman she had never seen before sitting by her bed. Simultaneously the truth hit her. *No, it's not true, NOT true, NOT TRUE.*

'You all right, love?' the woman asked, bending forward.

Sally levered herself up on one elbow. *Not true, please God, NOT TRUE.* 'Have they found Lucy?'

The woman shook her head. 'They'll be in touch as soon as there's any news.'

Sally stared at her. It didn't matter who the woman was. Who cared? She was younger than Sally, her face carefully made up, her brown eyes wary, the teeth projecting slightly, pushing out the lips and giving the impression that the mouth was the most important feature in this face. The *Daily Telegraph* was open on her lap, folded to one of the inside pages. She did not wear a wedding ring. Sally clung to these details as though they formed a rope strung across an abyss; and if she let go, she would fall.

'It's true, isn't it?' she heard a voice saying, *her* voice. 'All true?'

71

'Yes. I'm so sorry.'

Sally let her head fall back on the pillow. She closed her eyes. Her mind filled with a procession of images that made her want to scream and scream until everything was all right again: Lucy crying for her mother and no one answering; Lucy naked and bleeding in a narrow bedroom smelling of male sweat; Lucy lying dead on a railway embankment with her clothes strewn around her. How could anyone be so cruel, so cruel, so cruel?

'She might have just wandered off,' Sally said, trying to reassure herself. 'Got tired out – fallen asleep in a shed or something. She'll wake up soon and knock on someone's door.'

'It's possible.'

Possible, Sally thought, but highly improbable.

The woman stirred. 'They say no news is good news.'

Sally opened her eyes again. '*Has* there been no news? Truly?'

'If there had been news, any news at all, they'd have told you and your husband straightaway. I promise. I'm D C Yvonne Saunders, by the way. I took over from Judith.' The woman hesitated. 'You remember Judith? Last night?'

Sally's head twitched on the pillow. More memories flooded back. A plain-clothes policewoman, Judith, holding her arm while a doctor with ginger curls pushed a hypodermic into the skin. Herself saying – shouting – that she wasn't going to stay with friends or go to hospital: she was going to stay *here*, at home in Hercules Road because that was where Lucy would expect to find her; she and Michael had made Lucy memorize both the address and the phone number.

'They'll find her, Sally. We're pulling out all the stops.' Again a hesitation, a hint of calculation. 'Doctor left some medicine. Something to help you not to worry. Shall I give you some?'

'No.' The refusal was instinctive, but the reasons rushed after it: if they tranquillized her she would be no use to Lucy when – *if* – they found her; if they turned her into a zombie, she wouldn't be able to find out what was happening, they wouldn't tell her anything; she needed to be as clear-headed as possible, for Lucy's sake. Sally leant back against her pillows. 'Where's Michael? My husband?'

The eyes wavered. 'He's out. He'll be back soon, I should think. I expect you'd like to freshen up, wouldn't you? Shall I make some tea?'

Sally nodded, largely in order to get the woman out of her bedroom. Michael – she needed to think about him but she couldn't concentrate.

Yvonne stood up, her face creasing into an unconvincing smile. 'I'll leave you to it, then.' She added slowly, as if talking to a person of low intelligence, 'I shall be in the kitchen, if you need me. All right, love?'

No, Sally wanted to say, it's not all right; it may never be all right again; and I'm not your love, either. Instead, she returned the smile and said thank you.

When she was alone, she pushed the duvet away from her and got out of bed. The sweat cooled rapidly on her skin and she began to shiver. They had given her clean pyjamas, she realized, clinging to the security of domestic details. She was ashamed to see that the pyjamas were an old pair: the material was faded, a button was missing from the jacket, and there were undesirable stains on the trousers. The shivering worsened and once more the impact of what had happened hit her. Her knees gave way. She sat down suddenly on the bed. *My baby. Where are you?* The tears streamed down her cheeks.

She dared not make a noise in case Yvonne came back. *This is all my fault. I should have kept her with me.* She fell sideways and curled up on the bed. Her body shook with silent sobs.

Water rustled through the pipes. Sally, familiar with the vocabulary of the plumbing, knew that Yvonne was filling the kettle. The thought galvanized her into changing her position. At any moment the policewoman might return. With her hand over her mouth, trying to prevent the terror from spurting out like vomit, Sally scrambled off the bed and pulled open the wardrobe. She avoided looking at the accusing faces in the photographs on the chest of drawers.

She selected clothes at random and, with a bundle in her arms, sneaked into the bathroom and bolted the door.

Boats, ducks and teddies had colonized the side of the bath. One of Lucy's socks was lying under the basin. Automatically Sally picked it up, intending to drop it in the basket for dirty clothes. Instead she sat on the lavatory. She held the sock to her face, breathing its essence, hoping to smell Lucy, to recreate her by sheer force of will. Did Lucy at least have Jimmy, her little cloth doll? Or was she entirely without comfort?

Tears spilled down Sally's cheeks. When the fit of crying passed, she sat motionless, her fingers clenched round the sock, and sank into depths she had not known existed.

There was a tap on the door. 'How are you doing, love? Tea's ready.'

'I'm fine. I'll be out in a moment. I might have a shower.'

Sally brushed her teeth, trying to scour the taste of that long, drugged sleep from her mouth. She dropped the pyjamas on the floor, stepped into the bath and stood under the shower. Making no move to wash herself, she let the water stream down her body for several minutes. Last night, she remembered dimly, she had given way. She remembered shouting and crying in Carla's house and later at the flat. She remembered Michael's face, white and accusing, and police officers whom she did not know, their expressions concerned but somehow detached from what was happening to her and to Lucy. The ginger-haired doctor had been tiny, so small that he came to below her shoulder. She must not let them give her drugs again.

She turned off the shower and began to dry herself. There was another tap on the door.

'How about a nice slice of toast, love?'

Seeing if I'm still alive. 'Yes, please. There's a loaf in the fridge.'

The thought of food disgusted her but she would be no use to anyone if she starved herself. She dressed quickly in jeans, T-shirt and jersey. In her haste, she had provided herself with two odd socks, one with a hole in the heel. She ran a comb through her hair. As an afterthought she pushed

74

Lucy's sock into the pocket of the jeans. The routine of showering and dressing had had a calming effect. But as she unbolted the door the fact of Lucy's disappearance hit her like a flail, making her gasp for air.

She could not face Yvonne. She staggered back to the bedroom. Directly opposite the doorway was the crucifix on the wall above the mantelpiece. She looked at the little brass figure on the cross and realized as if for the first time how terribly pain had contorted the miniature face and twisted the muscles of the legs, the arms and the stomach. How could you forgive God for inflicting such suffering? But God hadn't forgiven God. He had crucified him. And if he had done that to his own child, what would he do to Lucy?

The unmade bed distracted her. She pulled up the duvet and plumped the pillows. After making the bed, she reminded herself, she normally tidied the room. But it looked tidy already. Usually there would have been Michael's dirty clothes flung over the chair, a magazine or a book on the floor by his side of the bed, a glass of water and his personal stereo on the table: he was a man who left a trail of domestic chaos behind him.

A pile of books on the chest of drawers caught her eye. They were small, shabby and unfamiliar. She picked up the first of them, a prayer book, and as she did so she remembered where they had come from. She turned to the flyleaf. 'To Audrey, on the occasion of her First Communion, 20th March 1937, with love from Mother.'

Audrey Oliphant's suicide seemed no more real than a story read long ago and half-forgotten. Sally could hardly believe that she had seen the woman dead on a hospital bed less than twenty-four hours earlier. She remembered the cheerless bedsitter, a shrine to lost beliefs. Most of all she remembered the woman standing up in St George's as Sally began to preach her first sermon.

She-devil. Blasphemer against Christ. Apostate. Impious bitch. Whore of Babylon. Daughter of Satan. May God damn you and yours.

She dropped the Prayer Book as if it were contaminated. *May God damn you and yours.* She almost ran from the room, shutting the door behind her. Yvonne was no longer some-one to be avoided but a potential refuge.

This feeling vanished as soon as Sally reached the living room. Yvonne had laid the table in the window; usually Sally and Michael ate breakfast in the kitchen, often on the move. She had managed to find the wrong plates, the wrong mugs and the wrong teapot. There were paper napkins, a choice of both jam and marmalade, and a tablecloth which the Appleyards had last used on Christmas Day. Sally thought of little girls playing house and tried to suppress her exasper-ation. She also wished that she had remembered to wash the cloth.

'Perhaps you prefer honey?' Yvonne was poised to dash into the kitchen. 'And is there any butter? I can only find margarine. That's what I have, but perhaps – '

'That's fine,' Sally lied. 'Margarine's fine. Everything's fine.'

She drank a glass of fruit juice and then sipped a mug of sweetened tea. The first mouthful of toast almost made her gag. She allowed Yvonne to pour her a second mug of tea and used it to moisten her throat between mouthfuls. Yvonne made her feel a guest in her own home, confronted by an overanxious hostess.

Parish reflexes came to Sally's rescue: automatically she asked questions. Yvonne told her that she worked at Pad-dington, that her boyfriend, also a policeman, was a sergeant in traffic control, and that they had a small flat in Wembley, but were hoping to move to somewhere larger soon. The illusion of intimacy lasted until Yvonne used the phrase 'liv-ing in sin' to describe what she and her boyfriend did.

'Sorry.' A blush crept up underneath her make-up. 'Per-haps I shouldn't be talking like this. What with you being a vicar and all.'

'Before I decided to become ordained, I lived with two men.' Sally inserted a practised pause and then slipped in her usual punchline: 'Not at the same time, of course.'

Yvonne tittered, and the mask slipped, revealing the youth and vulnerability behind. Usually, Sally thought, she would not have talked so readily to a stranger. But Michael was a police officer, which made Sally an honorary insider, at least on a temporary basis. And Yvonne was nervous – perhaps she had not done this job before. The flail of memory slapped her again: *baby-sitting*, they might call it, or *child minding*. For the next few seconds Sally fought the urge to bring up her breakfast over Great Aunt Mary's linen tablecloth.

The telephone rang.

'I'll get it.' Yvonne was already on her feet. She picked up the phone. She listened, then said, 'I'm a police officer, sir . . . Yes, Mrs Appleyard is awake . . . I'll ask her.' She covered the mouthpiece of the handset. 'Someone called Derek Cutter. Says he's your boss. Do you want to talk to him? Or he says he'd be pleased to come over.'

Sally opened her mouth to say that she didn't want to see Derek, or talk to him; and if she never did either again, she for one would not waste any tears. Instantly she restrained herself. This wasn't Derek's fault. She had a duty both to him and to the parish. And, more selfishly, it was important to create the illusion that she was in control; otherwise they might starve her of information.

'Ask him to come over if he can spare the time.' Sally decided to kill two birds with one stone: Derek could take Miss Oliphant's belongings.

Yvonne relayed the message and put down the phone. 'He won't be long. He's over at the community centre in Brondesbury Park.'

'What's that phone doing? It's not ours.'

'No. We're taping and tracing all calls.' Yvonne stiffened. 'It's standard procedure. Nothing to get worried –'

Sally pushed back her chair and stood up. She was shaking so much that she had to support herself on the table. 'You're sure Lucy's been kidnapped. Aren't you? *Aren't you?*'

Derek took both Sally's hands in his and said how very, very sorry he was. He had ridden over from Kensal Vale on the Yamaha. Sally thought he fancied himself in motorcycle leathers. As she introduced him to Yvonne, he loosened the white silk scarf around his neck, revealing the dog collar beneath.

With unnecessary tact, Yvonne retreated to the kitchen, leaving Sally unwillingly alone to savour the experience of Derek in full pastoral mode.

'We are all praying for you, my dear.'

'Thank you.' Sally didn't want prayers, she wanted Lucy.

Still holding her hands, Derek went on to say that there must be no question of her coming into work until Lucy was safe and sound. She need not worry, they could manage perfectly well.

'Would you and Michael like to come to stay with us? Margaret and I would love to have you. The bed's made up in the spare room.'

Sally's mind filled with an unwanted picture of Derek in his pyjamas. Would the hair of his chest be as white-blond as the hair on his head? Had he any hair on his chest at all, or just pink skin stretched over his bony ribcage, with the two nipples as the only points of interest to break the monotony? She wanted to giggle and she felt sick. She heard herself thanking Derek for his (and Margaret's) kind offer, and promising to discuss it with Michael. Certainly, she said, they would bear it in mind.

'Lots of people send their love. Stella in particular.'

'Stella.' It was little more than twenty-four hours since Sally had driven her to the hospital. 'Has her daughter had her baby?'

There was a pause. 'Yes. Last night. It's a girl. Mother and baby are doing fine, I gather.'

Sally concentrated very hard on Stella's joy. 'Lovely. Tell Stella how pleased I am.' She made an intense effort to blot out the rising hysteria and the knowledge that Lucy needed her. 'Audrey Oliphant?'

'Eh?' Derek released her hands. 'Who?'

'The woman who tried to kill herself. You remember? You asked me to see her yesterday.'

'I remember.'

'She died before I reached the hospital.'

'Was she one of ours?'

'Yes. In a sense.' Sally sat down. 'She was the woman who made a disturbance when I preached my first sermon.'

'Oh, yes. Poor woman. Where did she worship?'

'I don't know if she went anywhere. Her landlady thought not. But I think we should see she gets a proper burial.'

'Better make sure it's a man who conducts the service.' Derek began to smile, then stopped, remembering why he was here.

'Anglo-Catholic for choice. Her room was like an oratory. I've got a bag of her clothes.' She looked wildly round the room, wondering where the bag was. 'And also some books.' Had she taken the books out last night? If so, why?

'It doesn't matter now. We'll sort it out.'

Derek's voice was so soothing that Sally realized she must be sounding overwrought. She made an effort to turn the conversation back to the parish and the arrangements which needed to be made.

Derek slipped from the pastoral mode to the managerial. Here he was in his element; his efficiency was a virtue. He had already arranged cover for her services. Margaret would see to the Mothers and Toddlers and the Single Mums for as long as needed. As he went through her responsibilities, Sally had a depressing vision of Derek rising unstoppably, committee by committee, preferment by preferment, up the promotional ladder of the Church. It wasn't the meek that inherited the earth but people like Derek. She told herself that the Church needed the Dereks of this world, and that she had no reason to feel superior in any respect.

'And if there's anything that you or Michael need,' he was saying when she pulled her mind back on course, 'just phone us. Any time, Sally – you know that. Day or night.'

He stood up, tied the silk scarf round his thin neck and slipped the strap of his helmet over his arm. In its way, it had been a polished performance, and part of Sally was able to admire its professionalism. It made her squirm. Yvonne had almost certainly been eavesdropping through the open door of the kitchen.

'Look after yourself, my dear.' He seized her hands again and pressed them between his. 'And once more, if there's anything I can do.' Another, firmer squeeze, even the suggestion of a stroke. 'You have only to ask. You know that.'

Good God, Sally thought, as her skin crawled: I think he fancies me. With a wave of his hand, Derek called goodbye to Yvonne and left the flat. Too late, Sally remembered Miss Oliphant's bag but could not bear to call him back.

Yvonne came into the living room. 'Quite a charmer.'

'He does his best.' Sally forgot about Derek. 'Who's in charge of the case?'

'Mr Maxham. Do you know him?'

Sally shook her head.

'He's very experienced. One of the old school.'

'Shouldn't he be asking me questions? Shouldn't someone ask me something?' She heard her voice growing louder, and was powerless to stop it. 'Damn it, I'm Lucy's *mother*.'

'Don't worry, love, they'll send someone round soon. Maybe Mr Maxham will come himself. They're doing everything that can be done. Why don't you sit down for a bit? I'll make us a nice hot drink, shall I?'

'I don't want a drink.'

Sally sat down and started to cry. Yvonne dispensed paper handkerchiefs and impersonal sympathy. In a while the tears stopped. Sally went to the bathroom to wash her face. The reflection in the mirror showed a stranger with moist, red-rimmed eyes, pinched cheeks and lank hair. She went back to the living room. Being with Yvonne, with anyone, was better than being alone. Solitude was full of dangers.

The minute hand crawled round the clock, each minute an hour, each hour a week. Everywhere Sally looked there were reminders of Lucy – photographs, paintings, toys, clothes and books.

The worst reminders were those which were coupled with regrets. Lucy had wanted her to play Matching Pairs on Thursday evening; and Sally had said no, she needed to cook supper. Lucy had demanded another chapter of the book they were reading at bedtime, an enormously dull chronicle of life among woodland folk, and had thrown a theatrical tantrum when Sally declined. Lucy had also wanted Michael to kiss her good night, but he had not been at home; she had not cried on that occasion but her silence had been worse than her tears and screams. Lucy had wanted to bake gingerbread men the other day, Lucy had wanted the conjuring set from Woolworth's, Lucy this and Lucy that. Sally sat placidly at her desk and pretended to read a magazine while, all around her, the flat hummed with lost opportunities and reminders of her failure to be the mother that Lucy needed and deserved.

Suffering had a monotonous quality; Sally had never known that before. Only the phone broke into the tedium. Each time it rang, Sally willed it to herald news of Lucy; or, failing that, that it should be Michael. Yvonne answered all the calls. Sally held her breath, digging her fingernails into the palms of her hands, until it became clear that the caller was just a time-waster – or rather, worse than that, someone who might be preventing news of Lucy from reaching Sally.

'Mr and Mrs Appleyard aren't available for comment . . .'

Sally's fingernails left raw, red half-moons on her palms. Some of the calls were from friends but more were from journalists.

'I'm afraid they'll soon be camping on the doorstep.' Yvonne went to the window and looked down at the road below. 'Not a lot we can do about that except move you somewhere else.'

'Why are they so interested?' Sally made an enormous effort to be objective about what had happened. 'Thousands of children must vanish every year. They aren't news.'

'They are if their dad's in the CID and their mum's a vicar. Let's face it, love, that makes it a news story whether we like it or not.'

Michael did not ring. She wanted him very badly. What

the hell was keeping him? Sally tried to prise information out of Yvonne but had no success: either the policewoman knew no more than Sally or had been forbidden to discuss the case.

By ten-thirty, there were three journalists outside the front of the block. Sally felt sorry for them: though they were well wrapped up against the weather, they looked pinched and cold. One of them tried to sneak into the service entrance at the rear and was indignantly shooed out of the communal garden by the owner of a ground-floor flat.

Sally tried to phone Carla but there was no reply. Sally wondered how the child minder was feeling. Did she blame herself? Sally perversely wanted to monopolize the blame.

At eleven o'clock Sally made some coffee. By then she and Yvonne had stopped trying to talk to each other. Sally sat at her desk in front of the window, nursing the steaming mug between her hands, and waited for something to happen. In her mind, the pictures unfolded: she saw a pool of blood sinking into bare earth under trees; Lucy's broken body half-concealed under a pile of dead leaves; a man running. She heard laughter. Fire crackled; a bell tolled; there was snow, straw and excrement on the cobbles. Briefly she glimpsed the dream that had filled her mind just before waking. Had there been a woman screaming? In the dream or in reality? Another or herself?

'Do you do crosswords?' Yvonne asked.

Sally hauled herself out of the confusion. 'No – well, I used to, but I haven't had much time recently.'

Yvonne was working on the crossword in the *Daily Telegraph* and had already completed a respectable number of clues. 'It passes the time. Do you want a clue?'

Sally shook her head. She tried to read but it was impossible to concentrate. Her mind fluttered like a butterfly. She pushed her hand into her pocket and touched Lucy's sock, her talisman, her Jimmy.

Please God, may Lucy have her Jimmy. Please God, bring my darling back to me.

It was important to act normally, otherwise they might sedate her heavily or even put her in hospital. But what was normal now? Reality had lurched into unreality. The substantial was insubstantial, and vice versa. Sally felt that if she poked her forefinger at the surface of the pine table in front of her, the finger might pass straight through the wood and into the vacancy beyond. It was unreal to be sitting at home doing nothing; unreal not to be helping at the Brownies' jumble sale in St George's church hall; and most of all unreal not to know where Lucy was. Like a small hungry animal, Lucy's absence gnawed at Sally's stomach.

'Are you sure you wouldn't like a tablet?' Yvonne's voice was elaborately casual.

'No. No, thanks.'

There was shouting in the street outside. Sally looked down, and a second later Yvonne joined her at the window. A man was shouting at the journalists, waving his arms at them.

'Who's that?' Yvonne asked. 'Anyone you know?'

'It's Michael. My husband.'

3

Michael was very tired. When Sally hugged him, he leaned against her but otherwise he barely responded. His face was unshaven, his eyes bloodshot; he wore yesterday's clothes and smelled of sweat.

'The bastards won't tell me anything,' he muttered fiercely into her hair. 'And they won't let me do anything.'

Sally heard footsteps in the hallway. And the sound of voices, Yvonne's and a man's.

Michael raised his head. 'Oliver brought me home. Maxham phoned him up, someone told him we were friends. I want to do something, and all they can think of is give me a fucking nanny.'

Oliver Rickford hesitated in the doorway. He was wearing a battered wax jacket over a guernsey and paint-stained jeans. Yvonne bobbed up and down behind him. Yvonne was short, and in thirty years would be stout, whereas Oliver was tall and thin. Sally saw them both with the eyes of a stranger: they might have belonged to different species.

'I'm so sorry.' Oliver spread out his hands as if intending to examine his nails. 'Maxham really is doing everything he can.'

'And those bloody vultures outside,' Michael went on. 'I could kill them.'

'You need to rest,' Sally said.

Michael ignored her. 'If they're still there when I go down, I'm going to hit one of them. Tell them, Oliver. It's a fair warning.'

Sally stepped back and shook his arm. 'Why don't you have a bath and get into bed?'

Michael's eyes focused on hers. 'Don't be ridiculous. Sleep? Now? You must be out of your mind.' The hostility ebbed from his face. 'Sal, I'm sorry.' He put his hand on her arm. 'I don't know what I'm saying.'

'Sally's right.' Oliver had a hard face and a soft voice. 'You're practically asleep on your feet. You're no use to anyone like that.'

'Don't tell me what to do. I'm not one of your bloody minions.' Michael looked wildly from Oliver to Sally. His face crumpled. 'Oh shit.'

He stumbled out of the room and into the bathroom.

Oliver peeled off his jacket and dropped it on a chair. 'Can I help?'

She didn't answer, but he followed her into the bathroom. Michael was sitting on the side of the bath with his head resting on the rim of the basin. Sally turned on the taps. Between them, she and Oliver persuaded him through the bath, into pyjamas and into bed. Yvonne dispensed two sleeping pills from the supply the doctor had left behind. Sally sat with him until he went to sleep.

'When they get the man I'm going to kill him. I could kill Maxham, too. Devious little shit.' As time slipped by, Michael's words grew less distinct. Once he opened his eyes and looked straight at Sally. 'It shouldn't be like this, should it, Sal? It's all our fault.'

She bowed her head to hide the tears. Michael was being

unreasonable and part of her feared that he was right.

He wasn't looking at her now but talking to himself. 'For Christ's sake. Lucy.'

He drifted into silence. His eyes closed, and after a while his breathing became slow and regular. Sally stood up. She tiptoed towards the door. As she touched the handle, the figure on the bed stirred.

'It's always happening,' Michael mumbled, or that was what it sounded like to her. 'It's not fair.'

She closed the bedroom door softly behind her. The living room was empty. She found Oliver Rickford stooping over the sink in the kitchen, scouring a saucepan.

'Where's Yvonne?'

'She went out to buy sandwiches.'

Sally automatically picked up a tea towel and began to dry a mug. 'You shouldn't be doing this.'

'Why not?'

'Shouldn't you be at work?'

'I'm on leave. How's Michael?'

'Sleeping.'

'This is very hard for him.' Oliver hesitated, perhaps guessing Sally wanted to yell, *And don't you think it's hard for me too*? 'I mean, even worse than it would be for many other fathers in the same position. As you know, he's worked on similar cases.'

Jealousy twisted through her. Sally busied herself with the drying up. Michael rarely talked about his work to her. It had been different for a few months around the time of their marriage. Then the barriers had gone up. Michael was made that way, she told herself fiercely; it wasn't her fault.

Not for the first time she had a depressing vision of her husband's life as a series of watertight compartments: herself, Lucy and the flat; his job and the friendships he shared with men like Oliver; and the past he shared with his godfather, David Byfield. Cutting like a sword across this line of thought came the fact of Lucy's absence. Sally turned away, pretending to put the mug in its cupboard. Her shoulders shook.

A moment later she heard Oliver say, 'I'm sorry. I shouldn't have said that.'

She turned round to him. The kitchen was so small that they were very close. 'It's not your fault. What's Michael been doing?'

'Getting in the way. Mounting his own private investigation. At one point he was hanging round the house where the child minder lives and trying to question neighbours.'

Sally wished he had come home instead. 'He had to do something.' It was a statement of fact, not an argument for the defence.

'Maxham was not amused.'

'What are we going to do?'

'There's not much we can do except wait. Maxham's said to be good. He gets results.'

Alert to nuances, Sally said, 'You don't like him, do you?'

'I don't know him. He's one of the old school. Must be coming up for retirement quite soon. The important thing is that he's good at his job.' Oliver hesitated, and she sensed that he was holding something back. 'They'll probably ask if you'd like psychological counselling,' Oliver went on. 'Might be sensible to say yes. Good idea to take all the help you're offered. No point in making life harder for yourselves.'

'You mean Michael needs help?'

'Anyone in your position needs help.'

They finished the washing and drying in silence. Oliver went to check on Michael. Meanwhile, desperate for the activity, Sally emptied the contents of the dirty-clothes basket into the washing machine. When she had switched it on, she realized that she hadn't bothered to sort the clothes, and that the machine was still set for the fast-coloured programme.

'He's asleep.' Oliver leaned against the jamb of the kitchen door. 'Sally?'

'What?'

'This isn't my case. I've got no jurisdiction.'

'What are you trying to say?'

'That I can't do much to help.'

'You're not doing badly so far.'

'I mean I can't tell you any more about what's in Maxham's head than Michael can.'

'Of course.'

Sally's voice sounded low and reasonable, which was all the more remarkable because simultaneously she was screaming to herself, *I don't give a fuck about Maxham: I just want Lucy.* Oliver stood aside to let her pass into the living room. *I am ordained. I must not use language like that even in my own mind.* As she passed him, she was aware of his height and of the way he held himself back to minimize the possibility of accidental contact between their bodies. In the living room she crossed to the window and looked down to the street.

Oliver picked up his jacket from the back of the armchair. 'Still there, are they?'

'I can see six of them, I think. Two of them are talking to the neighbours.' She moved back from the window. 'We're besieged.'

'You could go and stay with relations or friends.'

'But this is where Lucy would come. She knows the phone number and the address.'

'We could transfer the calls and leave someone here just in case Lucy turns up on the doorstep.' Oliver stared down at Sally, making her feel like a specimen on a dish. 'Think about it. This is just the beginning. If it goes on, there'll be more of them. Maybe radio and TV as well. The whole circus.'

She shrugged, accepting that he might have a point but unwilling to think about it.

'I'll phone this evening if that's OK.' He rubbed his nose, which was long and thin and with a slight kink to the right near the end. 'Shall I leave my number?'

As she passed him a pen and a pad, their eyes met. She wondered whether he was being diplomatic; whether he realized that Michael had erected an invisible barrier between his family and his friends. Sally knew that the Rickfords had bought a flat in Hornsey, but she had no idea of the address or the phone number.

'I'm on leave till the new year,' he said.

'You and Sharon aren't going away, then?'

'Sharon's already gone, actually.' Oliver rubbed a speck of paint on his jeans. 'Permanently. She moved out a couple of months ago. We decided it just wasn't working out.'

'I'm sorry.' She had stumbled on another of Michael's failures in communication. She was past feeling humiliated.

'She got a chance of a job with our old force – Somerset.' Perhaps Oliver sensed a need for a diversion, any diversion. 'It came up at just the right time.'

'It gave you a positive reason to separate as well as all the negative ones?'

He nodded. He was very easy to talk to, Sally thought – quick on the uptake, unthreatening. She was not surprised that Oliver and Sharon had separated. They had made an ill-assorted couple. Sharon had struck her as a tough, sharp-witted woman, very clear about what she wanted from life.

'We're still good friends.' Oliver's fingers twitched, enclosing the last two words with invisible inverted commas. 'But you don't want to hear about all this now. Is there anything I can do before I go?'

Sally shook her head. 'Thank you for bringing Michael back.'

The words sounded absurdly formal. Sally felt like a mother thanking a comparative stranger for bringing her child home after a party. A silence ambushed them as each waited for the other to speak. The sound of a key turning in the lock was a welcome distraction. They both turned as Yvonne came into the flat. She looked pale beneath her make-up.

'You haven't watched the news, have you?' she blurted out. 'Or had the radio on?'

Sally took a step towards her, swayed and clung to the back of a chair. 'What's happened?' she whispered.

Yvonne opened her mouth, revealing the prominent and expensively regular teeth. No sound came out.

'Come on,' Oliver snapped.

'It was those journalists, sir.' Yvonne blinked rapidly. 'They asked me if I'd heard.' She turned to Sally. 'Look, I'm sorry about this. They said someone found a child's hand this morning. Just a hand. It was lying on a gravestone in Kilburn Cemetery.'

Four

'. . . we carry private and domestick enemies
within, publick and more hostile adversaries
without.'

Religio Medici, II, 7

1

On the morning of Saturday the thirtieth of November, Angel
opened Eddie's bedroom door and stood framed like a picture
in the doorway.

'Are you awake?'

He sat up in bed, reaching for his glasses. Angel was wearing the cotton robe, long, white and in appearance vaguely
hieratic, which she used as a dressing gown. As usual at this
time of day, her shining hair was confined to a snood. Eddie
liked seeing Angel without make-up. She was still beautiful,
but in a different way: her face had a softness which cos-
metics masked; he glimpsed the child within the adult.

'Just the two of us for breakfast today. We'll let Lucy sleep
in.'

'OK. Have you been down yet?' He had heard the stairs
creaking.

'You know I have. And yes, Lucy's fine. Sleeping like a
baby.'

He felt relief, a lifting of guilt. 'I'll put the kettle on.'

A few moments later, Eddie trotted downstairs to the
kitchen. He filled the kettle and set the table while waiting
for the water to boil. The washing machine was already on,
and through the porthole he glimpsed something small and
white, perhaps Lucy's vest or tights. In the quieter phases of

its cycle, he heard Angel moving about in the bathroom. He had hardly slept during the night and now felt light-headed. He did not know whether Angel had really forgiven him for acting on impulse the previous afternoon. But he could tell she was pleased to have Lucy safely in the basement. The latter, he hoped, would outweigh the former.

At length Angel came downstairs, carrying the receiving end of the intercom to the basement. She plugged it into one of the sockets over the worktop. The tiny loudspeaker emitted an electronic hum.

'I thought I'd do a load while Lucy's asleep,' Angel said. 'Lucy's things, mainly. That toy of hers stinks.'

'Jimmy?'

Angel stared at him. 'Who?'

'The doll thing.'

'Is that what she calls it? It's not what I call a doll.'

Eddie shrugged, disclaiming responsibility.

'It had to be washed sooner or later,' Angel went on, 'so it might as well be washed now. It's most unhygienic, you know, as well as being offensive.'

Eddie nodded and held his peace. Jimmy was a small cloth doll, no more than four or five inches high. Yesterday Lucy had told Eddie that her mother had made it for her. It was predominantly blue, though the head was made of faded pink material, and Sally Appleyard had stitched rudimentary features on the face and indicated the existence of hair. Eddie guessed that Jimmy was special, like his own Mrs Wump had been. (Mrs Wump was still in his chest of drawers upstairs, lying in state in a shoe box and kept snug with sheets made of handkerchiefs and blankets made of scraps of towelling.) The previous evening, Lucy had kept Jimmy in her hands the whole time, occasionally sniffing the doll while she sucked her fingers. She had not relaxed her grip even in sleep.

'Lucy looks rather like how I used to look at that age,' Angel told Eddie over breakfast. 'Much darker colouring, of course. But apart from that we're really surprisingly similar.'

'Can I see her this morning?'

'Perhaps.' Angel sipped her lemon verbena tea. 'It depends

how she is. I expect she'll feel a little strange at first. We must give her a chance to get used to us.'

But it's me she knows, Eddie wanted to say: it was I who brought her home. 'She wants a conjuring set,' he said. 'You can get them at Woolworth's; they cost twelve ninety-nine, apparently. I thought I might try and buy it for her this morning. I have to go out for the shopping in any case.'

'I think she's like me in other ways.' Angel's voice was dreamy. 'In personality, I mean. Much more so than the others. She's our fourth, of course. I knew the fourth would be significant.'

'How do you mean?'

'Because –' Angel broke off. 'What was that about a conjuring set?'

'Lucy wants one. Perhaps I could buy it and give it to her this afternoon.'

Angel stared at him, her spoon poised halfway between the bowl and her mouth. 'Lucy isn't like the others. Do you understand me?'

'Yes.' He dropped his eyes: facing that blue glare was like looking at the sun. 'I think so.'

Eddie didn't understand: why wasn't Lucy like the others? She was no more attractive than Chantal or Katy, for example, and probably less intelligent, certainly less articulate, than Suki. And why should the fact that Lucy was their fourth visitor be significant?

As he spread a thin layer of low-fat sunflower margarine on his wholemeal toast, he thought that Angel resembled one of those rich archaeological sites which humans have occupied for thousands of years. You laboriously scraped away a layer only to find that there was another beneath, and another below that, and so the process went on. How could you expect to understand later developments if you did not also know the developments which had preceded them and shaped them?

Angel dabbed her mouth with her napkin. 'If you want to give Lucy a present, why don't you buy her a doll?'

'But she wants the conjuring set.'

'A doll might distract her from that little bundle of rags.
What does she call it?'

'Jimmy.'

The intercom crackled softly.

Angel cocked her head. 'Hush.'

A cat-like wail drifted into the kitchen.

2

Jenny Wren had liked dolls, especially the sort which could
be equipped with the glamorous accessories of a pseudo-
adult lifestyle. Her real name was Jenny Reynolds but Eddie's
father always called her Jenny Wren. She had been overweight, with dark hair, small features and a permanent look
of surprise on her face.

Her father was a builder in a small way. He and his wife
still lived in one of the council flats on the estate behind
Rosington Road. The Reynoldses' balcony was visible above
the trees from the garden of number 29. When Eddie discovered which flat was theirs, he realized that the woman
on the balcony whom he and Alison had seen, the woman
who stared at the sky over Carver's, must have been Mrs
Reynolds.

Jenny Wren was their only child, about two years older
than Eddie. She started to come to the Graces' house in the
summer of 1971, the Alison summer, always bringing her
favourite doll, who was called Sandy. Alison used to laugh
at Jenny Wren and Eddie had joined in, to show solidarity.

Eddie did not know how Jenny Wren had come to his
father's attention. Stanley did house-to-house collections for
several charities and this helped to give him a wide acquaintance. Or Mr Reynolds might have done some work on the
house, or his father might have advised the Reynoldses on
financial matters. Stanley might even have stopped Jenny
Wren on the street. Eddie had witnessed his father's technique at first hand.

'You've got a dolly, haven't you?' Stanley would say to

the girl. 'What's her name?' Eventually the girl would tell him. 'That's a pretty name,' he would say. 'Did you know I make dolls' houses? Do you think your dolly would like to come and see them? We'd have to ask Mummy and Daddy, of course.'

If there were concerned parents in the picture, as with the Reynoldses, he took care to reassure them. 'Yes, Eddie likes a bit of company. He's our only one, you know, and it can get a bit lonely, eh? Tell you what, I'll get my wife to give you a ring and confirm a time, shall I? Around tea time, perhaps? I know Thelma likes an excuse to bake a cake.'

Thelma lent her authority to the invitations, though they sometimes made it necessary for her to talk to neighbours, an activity she detested. But she had as little as possible to do with the girls as soon as they had crossed the threshold of 29 Rosington Road. Among themselves, Stanley and Thelma referred to the girls as 'LVs', which stood for 'Little Visitors'.

The proceedings usually opened with tea around the kitchen table. This would be much more lavish than usual. There would be lemonade or Coca-Cola, chocolate biscuits and cake.

'Ah, tea.' Stanley would bunch up his pale cheeks in a smile. 'Splendid. I'm as hungry as a hunter.'

During the meal Thelma spoke only when necessary, though as usual she would eat greedily and rapidly. Afterwards Thelma and Eddie cleared away while Stanley took the LV down to the basement, closing the door behind them. Eddie and Thelma carried on with their lives as normal, as though Stanley and a little girl were not in the basement looking at a dolls' house. When it was time for the LV to go home, Thelma and Eddie often walked her back to her parents, usually in silence, leaving Stanley behind.

If all had gone well, there would be other visits. Then Stanley would introduce the subject of his second hobby, photography. As ever, he was meticulously careful in his handling of the parents. Would they mind if he took a few photographs of their daughter? She was very photogenic. There was a national competition coming up, and Stanley would like – with the parents' agreement, of course – to submit a photograph of her. Perhaps the parents would like copies of the photograph for themselves?

It was after Alison moved away that Stanley Grace first asked Eddie into the basement when one of the little visitors was there.

'I'd like a two-headed shot in the big chair,' he explained to the space between Thelma and Eddie. 'Could be rather effective, with one fair head and one dark.'

Eddie was excited; he was also pleased because he interpreted the invitation as a sign that he had somehow earned his father's approval. The LV in question was Jenny Wren.

He remembered that first afternoon with great clarity, though as so often with memories it was difficult to know whether the clarity was real or apparent. He and Jenny Wren had been too shy to talk much to each other, and in any case, the two-year age gap between them was at that time a significant barrier. His father posed them in the low Victorian armchair, which was large enough to hold both children, their bodies squeezed together from knee to shoulder. He arranged their limbs, deftly tweaking a leg here, draping an arm there. The camera was already mounted on its tripod.

'Now try and relax,' Stanley told them. 'Pretend you're brother and sister. Or *very* special friends. Lean your head on Jenny's shoulder, Eddie. That's it, Jenny Wren: give Eddie a nice big smile. Watch the birdie now.' His father squinted through the viewfinder. 'Smile.'

The shutter clicked. Jenny Wren's breath smelled sweetly of chocolate. Her dress had ridden up almost to the top of her thighs. The rough fabric of the upholstery rubbed against Eddie's bare skin and made him want to scratch. He remembered the musty smell of the chair, the essence of a long and weary life.

'And again, children.' *Click.* 'Very good. Now hitch your legs up a bit, Jenny Wren: lovely.' *Click.* 'Now, Eddie, let's pretend you're kissing Jenny Wren's cheek. No, not like that: look up at her, into her eyes.' *Click.* 'Now let's have some with just you, Jenny Wren. How about a chocolate first?'

It wasn't all photographs. Stanley encouraged them to examine the dolls' house. He allowed Jenny Wren to push her doll Sandy about the rooms and sit her in the chairs and lie her on the beds, even though Sandy was far too large for the house and Jenny Wren's movements were so poorly coordinated that the fragile furniture was constantly in danger. The children helped themselves from the large box of chocolates. Eddie ate so many that he felt sick. At last it was time for Jenny Wren to go home.

'You can come again next weekend, if you like.'

Jenny Wren nodded, with her mouth stuffed with chocolate and her eyes on the dolls' house.

'By that time I'll have developed the films. Tell Mummy and Daddy I'll give you some photos to take home for them.'

Next weekend the photographs were ready. There were more chocolates, more posing, more games with the dolls' house. Stanley took some of his special artistic photographs, which involved the children taking off some of their clothes. Next weekend it was very warm, one of those early autumn days which until the evening mimic the heat of summer. At Stanley's suggestion the children took off all their clothes.

'All artists' models pose without their clothes. I expect you already knew that. And I dare say neither of you would say no to a little extra pocket money, eh? Well, famous artists always pay their models. So I suppose I shall have to pay you. But this is our secret, all right? That's very important. Our secret.'

After taking the photographs he suggested that they played a game until it was time to go home. It was so hot that he decided to take off his clothes himself.

'You won't mind, will you, Jenny Wren? I know Eddie won't. He's seen me in the buff enough times. All part of our secret, eh?'

So it continued, first with Jenny Wren and later with others. The children who excited Stanley's artistic sensibilities were always girls. Even as a child, Eddie was aware that he was of secondary importance. In the photographs and in the games his role was not much more significant than that of the Victorian armchair. His father's attention was always on the girl, never on him. As time went by, the invitations to the basement became rarer and rarer.

Once Eddie had reached puberty, his father did not want him there at all. On one occasion he plucked up his courage and knocked on the basement door. He was fourteen, and his father was about to photograph the latest L V, a girl called Rachel with light-brown hair, wary eyes and a freckled face. His father's feet clumped slowly up the stairs. The key turned in the lock and the door opened.

'Yes?'

'I wondered if I could –' Eddie looked past his father into the basement: the camera was on its tripod; Rachel was fiddling with the dolls' house. 'You know – like I used to.'

Stanley stared down at him, his face moon-like. 'Better not. Nothing personal. But for child photography you have to get the atmosphere just right.'

'Yes.' Eddie backed away, hot and ashamed. 'I see that.'

'Young children are more artistic.' Stanley rarely missed an opportunity to stress that his photography was driven by a high, aesthetic purpose. 'Ask any sculptor from the Classical world.' At this point he glanced behind him, down into the basement, as if expecting to see Phidias nodding approval from the Victorian armchair, or Praxiteles leaning on the workbench by the window and smiling encouragement. Instead, Stanley looked at Rachel, who was pretending to be absorbed in the dolls' house. 'Children are so *plastic*.'

3

As a very young child Eddie had admired Stanley and wanted to please him. Then his father had become a fact of life like the weather – neither good nor bad in itself, but liable to vary in its effects on Eddie. Then, with Stanley's lecture on the aesthetics of his hobby, came the moment of revelation: that Eddie hated his father, and had in fact done so for some time.

The strength of Eddie's hatred took him unawares and had a number of consequences. Some of these were trivial: he used to spit discreetly in his father's tea, for example, and once he took one of his father's shoes and pressed the heel into a dog turd on the pavement. Other consequences were more far-reaching, and affected Eddie rather than his father. It was Stanley's fault, in a manner of speaking, that Eddie became a teacher, and Eddie never forgave him for that.

In his final year at school, Eddie told his father that he thought he might like to be an archaeologist. This was a few months before Stanley retired from the Paladin.

'Don't be absurd,' said his father. 'There's no money in archaeology. I bet there aren't many jobs, either. Not real jobs.'

'But it interests me.'

'That's no good if it won't pay the mortgage, is it? Can't you do it as a hobby?'

'There *are* jobs for archaeologists.'

'For the favoured few, maybe. Top scholars. One in a million. You've got to be realistic. Why don't I arrange for you to have an interview at the Paladin? There's a chap I know in Personnel.'

The upshot of this conversation was that Eddie attempted to lay the foundations for a career in archaeology by studying for a degree in history at a polytechnic on the outskirts of London. It was not a happy time. As a student he floundered: it was not so much that the work was too demanding; it was more that there seemed such a lot to do, and it was difficult to know what was important and what wasn't, and besides, his mind had a tendency to drift into daydreams. He lived at home, which distanced him from the other students. In the first summer vacation he spent a fortnight on an archaeological dig in Essex, where he began to grow a beard. It rained all the time and the work was hard and tedious. Eddie's interest in the subject never recovered.

He kept the beard, however, wispy and unsatisfactory though it was, primarily because it annoyed his father. ('Makes you look a scruffy little wretch. You'll have to shave it off if you want to find a proper job.') As a token of rebellion, the beard made a poor substitute for a career in archaeology, but it was better than nothing.

Stanley continued to badger Eddie about the Paladin,

showering him with information about vacancies for graduates.

'I've already dropped a word in the right ear,' he said towards the end of Eddie's final year. 'Or rather ears. It's never a bad thing to have a few friends at court, is it? And naturally, anyone who's the son of a former employee is bound to have a head start. But you'd better get rid of that beard.'

With hindsight, Eddie agreed that a job at the Paladin might have suited both his talents and his needs. At the time, however, the source of the suggestion automatically tainted it. Desperate to find an alternative, he glanced round the room. His father had draped the *Evening Standard* over the arm of his chair, and one of the headlines caught Eddie's eye: TEACHERS IN NEW PAY TALKS. Beside it was a photograph of a group of teachers armed with placards. Several of the men had beards. That was the deciding factor.

'If my results are good enough, I'm going to be a teacher.'

His father's attention sharpened. 'Really? I hope you've got the sense to teach younger children. If what you hear nowadays is anything to go by, older children are becoming quite unmanageable.'

'Secondary education's much more interesting. Intellectually, I mean.' Eddie hoped this last remark would remind his father that he had left school at sixteen, and therefore lacked his son's qualifications.

'It's your life,' Stanley replied, apparently oblivious of his intellectual inferiority. 'People don't look up to teachers as much as they used to in my day. There's the long holidays, I suppose.'

'Teachers have to work in the holidays. It's not a cushy job.'

His father took his time over lighting a cigarette. 'Yes.' He blew out a cloud of smoke. 'Well – as I say, it's your life. I doubt if you'll be able to cope, but that's your affair.'

His mother had been in the room but contributed nothing to the conversation. Eddie still felt that if his parents had handled the situation more diplomatically, they could have helped him avoid the disasters which followed. Thanks to them, he forced himself to spend another year at college doing a postgraduate certificate of education. He was lucky – or perhaps unlucky – in his teaching practice: they sent him to a quiet, middle-class school where class sizes were small and his stumbling attempts to teach were carefully and even kindly supervised. At that stage, he had realized that he was not a natural teacher, but he had hoped that with luck and perseverance he might grow used to it.

Nothing had prepared Eddie for Dale Grove Comprehensive. It was a school in north-west London, not far from Kensal Vale, in an area which even then seemed to be slipping away from the control of the authorities. He applied for the job because the school was an easy tube journey from Rosington Road, and without discussing the matter both he and his parents assumed that for the time being it would be best if he continued to live at home.

Keeping order was by far the worst aspect of the job. His failure in this department affected his relationships with other teachers, who regarded him with a mixture of irritation and scorn. It was not unusual for Eddie to find himself trying to teach three or four children at the front, while in the rest of the room the remainder of the class split up into small noisy groups engaged in disruptive activities.

He was scared of the children: and they knew it. He thought them outlandish and disgusting, too, with their croaking voices, their shrill laughter, their burps, their farts, their blackheads, their acne, their strange clothes and stranger customs. The girls were worse than the boys: strapping, big-boned brutes; delighting in mockery and subtler in their methods; scenting weakness as sharks scent blood in the water. He had fallen among savages.

Matters came to a crisis towards the end of the summer term. There was no one he could talk to about it. There were problems at home, too: his father's health was worsening, and his mother was never easy to live with. In the circumstances was it any wonder that things went wrong?

Two girls orchestrated what amounted to a campaign of sexual harassment against him. Their names were Mandy and Sian. Both were taller than he was. Mandy was thin, with spots and lank red hair. Sian was overweight and unusually well-developed. They began with innuendo, with whispers at the back of the class. 'Do you think sir's sexy?' Gradually the campaign picked up momentum. 'Please, sir, there's a word in this book I don't understand. What does S-P-E-R-M mean?'

After each of Eddie's failures to control them, his torturers would take one small step further.

'I can't go to sleep without my teddy in my bed,' Mandy confided to the class.

'Me, too,' Sian remarked. 'Mine's called Eddy-Teddy. He's so warm and cuddly.'

Eddie found repellent drawings on his table when he returned from the staff room. Mandy, something of a raconteur in her primitive way, told dirty jokes to anyone in the class who would listen, which was most of them.

As the weeks passed, Sian hitched her skirt higher and higher. She and Mandy fell into the habit of sitting at a table near the front of the class. They would pull their chairs out and sit facing the front with their legs apart, forcing Eddie to glimpse their underwear, some of which was most unsuitable for schoolgirls, or indeed for any woman who wasn't the next best thing to a prostitute. One day, early in July, Mandy sat in a pose which revealed beyond any possible doubt that she was wearing no knickers at all.

The crisis arrived late on a Friday afternoon. Eddie's guard was down because he thought the children had gone; he was alone in his classroom, sitting at his table, trying to plan the next week's lessons and feeling relieved that the teaching week was over.

Mandy, Sian and three other girls strolled nonchalantly into the room. Mandy and Sian came to stand beside him, one on each side. A third girl lingered by the door, keeping watch; the other two constituted an audience.

'Wouldn't you like to fuck me, sir?' whispered Mandy on the left. She put a hand on the back of his chair and leaned over him.

'No – me.' Sian undid the top two buttons of her shirt. 'I

can give you a much better time. Honest, sir. Why don't I suck your cock?'

Eddie tried to push back his chair, but it wouldn't move because Mandy now had her foot behind one of the rear legs as well as her hand on the back.

The other girls were sniggering, and one of them said in a loud whisper: 'Look – he's getting a hard-on.'

Mandy was now unbuttoning her shirt too. 'Go on, sir. Lick my titties. They taste nicer than hers.'

Eddie found his voice at last. 'Stop this.' His voice rose. 'Stop this at once. Stop it. Stop it.'

'You don't mean that, sir. You like it. Go on, admit it.'

'Stop it. Stop it. I shall report you to –'

'If you report us we'll say you were interfering with us.'

'Mr Grace is a bloody pervert,' said Sian. 'We got witnesses to prove it.'

The latter's shirt was now entirely unbuttoned. She pushed up her breasts, encased in a formidable black bra, and poked them hard into his face. The lace was rough against his nose. There was a smell of stale sweat.

'Fuck me, darling,' she murmured.

Eddie leapt up, knocking over his chair. Mandy shrieked and groped at his crotch. Abandoning his briefcase, he ran for the door. Their hands clutched at him. He collided with the sentry in the doorway, pushing her against the wall. The girls' laughter pursued him down the corridor. As he ran across the school car park, scattering a knot of teenagers, the laughter drifted after him through the open windows. In a way it was a relief that the final humiliation had come at last. Failure had its compensations.

4

The following Monday morning Eddie phoned the school secretary and, having pleaded illness too often in the past, desperately invented a dying grandmother. The same day, he saw his GP, who listened to him for five minutes and gave him a prescription for tranquillizers. On Tuesday he wrote a letter of resignation to the head teacher.

'I'm not surprised,' Stanley said when Eddie told him the news. 'I saw that coming from the start. I told you, didn't I?'

'You don't understand. I've decided that I don't approve of the philosophy behind modern education.'

His father raised his eyebrows, miming the disbelief he did not need openly to express. 'What now? You've probably missed the boat with the Paladin, but if you like, I –'

'No.' *Stuff the Paladin.* 'I don't want to work there.'

'So what *are* you going to do?'

At the time Eddie could not answer the question, but over the years an answer had evolved as if by its own volition. First he had made a half-hearted attempt to see whether he could retrain as a primary-school teacher. But he could not whip up much enthusiasm even for teaching younger children. In any case, he guessed that the head teacher at Dale Grove would give him an unsatisfactory reference. Quite apart from the discipline problem, there was also the possibility that Mandy and Sian had circulated rumours of sexual harassment, with Eddie in the role of predator rather than victim.

Worse was to come that summer – the unpleasant business at Charleston Street swimming baths. As a schoolboy, Eddie had learned to swim there, though not very well. It was an old building, full of echoes, with an ineradicable smell of chlorine and unwashed feet. In the first few months after he left Dale Grove, Eddie paid several visits to Charleston Street, partly to give himself a reason to get out of the house and away from his father, now a semi-invalid.

He disliked the male changing room, where youths who reminded him of the pupils at Dale Grove indulged in loud horseplay. The pool, too, was often too crowded for his taste. Nor did he like taking off his clothes in front of strangers. He was very conscious of the soft flab which clung to his waist and the top of his thighs, of his lack of bodily hair, and of his small stature. But he enjoyed cooling down in the water and watching the younger children.

He clung to the side and watched girls swimming races and mothers teaching their children to swim. Some young children appeared to have no adults watching over them, even from the balcony overlooking the swimming pool. Latchkey children, Eddie supposed, abandoned by mothers going out to work. He felt sorry for them – his own mother had always been at home when he came back from school and during the holidays – and tried to keep a friendly eye on them.

Sometimes he became quite friendly with those deserted children and would play games with them. His favourite was throwing them up in the air above the water, catching them as they descended, and then tickling them until they squealed with laughter.

On one occasion Eddie was playing this game with a little girl called Josie. She was in the care of her older brother, a ten-year-old who for most of the time horsed about with his friends in the deep end. Eddie felt quite indignant on Josie's behalf: the little girl was so vulnerable – what could the mother be thinking of?

'You funny man,' she said. 'Your name's Mr Funny.'

He came back the following day to find Josie there.

'Hello, Mr Funny,' she called out.

They played together for a few minutes. As Eddie was preparing to throw Josie into the air for the fourth time, he noticed surprise spreading over her face. An instant later he felt a tap on his shoulder. He turned. Beside him, standing on the edge of the pool, was one of the lifeguards, accompanied by a thickset, older man in a tracksuit.

The latter said, 'All right. You're getting out now. Put the kid down.'

Eddie looked from one hostile face to the other. Another lifeguard was walking towards them with Josie's brother. It was unfair but Eddie did not argue, partly because he knew there was no point and partly because he was scared of the man in the tracksuit.

He climbed up the ladder. Eddie was conscious that other people were looking at him – the other two lifeguards on duty, and also some of the adults who were swimming. It seemed to him that everyone had stopped talking. The only sounds were the slapping of the water against the sides of the swimming pool and the rhythmic thudding of the distorted rock music coming over the public-address system. The two men escorted him back to the changing room.

'Get dressed,' ordered the older man.

One on either side, they waited while he struggled into his clothes. He did not dry himself. It was very embarrassing. Eddie hated people watching him while he was getting dressed. Gradually the other people in the changing room realized something was up. The volume of their conversations diminished until, by the time Eddie was strapping on his sandals, no one was talking at all.

'This way.' The older man opened the door. Eddie followed him down the corridor towards the reception area. The young lifeguard fell in step behind. Instead of leading him outside, the thickset man swung to the left, stopped and unlocked the door labelled MANAGER. He stood to one side and waved Eddie to precede him into the room. It was a small office, overcrowded with furniture, and with three people inside it was claustrophobic. The lifeguard, a burly youth with tight blond curls, shut the door and leant against it.

'Identification.' The manager held out his hand. 'Come on.'

Eddie found his wallet, extracted his driving licence and handed it over. The manager made a note of the details, breathing heavily and writing slowly, as if using a pen was not an activity that came naturally to him. Eddie trembled while he waited. Their silence unnerved him. He thought perhaps they were planning to beat him up.

At last the man tossed the driving licence back to Eddie, who missed it and had to kneel down to pick it up from the floor. The manager threw down his pen on the desk and came to stand very close to Eddie. The lifeguard gave a small, anticipatory sigh.

'We've been watching you. And we don't like what we see. There've been complaints, too. I'm not surprised.'

Eddie's voice stumbled into life. 'I've done nothing. Really.'

'Shut up. Stand against that wall.'

Eddie backed towards the wall. The man opened a drawer in the desk and took out a camera. He pointed it at Eddie, adjusted the focus and pressed the shutter. There was a flash.

'You're banned,' the manager said. 'And I'll be circulating your details around other pools. You want to keep away from children, mate. You're lucky we didn't call the police. If I had my way I'd castrate the fucking lot of you.'

5

It was so unfair. Eddie had been only playing with the children. He couldn't help touching them. They touched him, too. But only in play, only in play.

It frightened him that the people at the swimming pool had seen past what was happening and through into his mind, to what might have happened, what he wanted to happen. He had given himself away. In future he would have to be very careful. The conclusion was obvious: if he wanted to play games it would be far better to do it in private, where there were no grown-ups around to spoil the fun.

Summer slid into autumn. Goaded by his parents, Eddie applied for two clerical jobs but was offered neither. He also told them he was on the books of a tutorial agency, which was a lie. He looked into the future, and all he foresaw was boredom and desolation. He felt the weight of his parents' society pressing down on him like cold, dead earth. Yet he was afraid of going out in case he met people who knew him from Dale Grove or the Charleston Street swimming baths.

While the weather was warm, he would often leave Stanley and Thelma, encased in their old and evil-smelling carcasses, in front of the television and escape to the long, wild garden. He listened to the trains screaming and rattling on the line beyond Carver's. Sometimes he glimpsed Mrs Reynolds among the geraniums on the balcony of the Reynoldses' flat. Once he saw her talking earnestly with a large, fat woman who he guessed was Jenny Wren. The ugly duckling, Eddie told himself, had become an even uglier duck.

Over the years the tangle of trees and bushes at the far end of the Graces' garden had expanded both vertically and horizontally. The fence separating the back gardens of 27 and 29 Rosington Road had been repaired long before. But there was still a hole in the fence at the back: too small for Eddie's plump adult body, but obviously used by small animals – cats, perhaps, or even foxes.

Thelma said that Carver's was an eyesore. According to Stanley, the site of the bombed engineering works had not been redeveloped because its ownership was in dispute – a case of Dickensian complexity involving a family trust, missing heirs and a protracted court case.

'Someone's sitting on a gold mine there,' Stanley remarked on many occasions, for the older he became the more he repeated himself. 'You mark my words. A bloody gold mine. But probably the lawyers will get the lot.'

Time had on the whole been kind to Carver's, for creepers had softened the jagged brick walls and rusting corrugated iron; saplings had burst through the cracked concrete and grown into trees. Cow parsley, buddleia and rosebay willowherb brought splashes of white and purple and pink. It was a wonder, Eddie thought, that the ruins had not become a haven for crack-smoking delinquents from the council flats or Social Security parasites in search of somewhere to drink and sleep. Perhaps the ghosts kept them away. Not that it was easy to get into Carver's, except from the back gardens of Rosington Road. To the north was the railway, to the east and west were high walls built when bricks and labour were cheap. Access by road was down a narrow lane beside the infants' school which ended in high gates festooned with barbed wire and warning notices.

Eddie was safe from prying eyes at the bottom of the garden. He liked to kneel and stare through the hole into Carver's. The shed was still there, smaller and nearer than in memory, with two saplings of ash poking through its roof. One evening in September, he levered out the plank beside the hole and, his heart thudding, wriggled through the enlarged opening. Once inside he stood up and looked around. Birds sang in the distance.

Eddie picked his way towards the shed, skirting a large clump of nettles and a bald tyre. The shed's door had parted company with its hinges and fallen outwards. He edged inside. Much more of the roof had gone. Over half of the interior was now filled with the saplings and other vegetation. There were rags, two empty sherry bottles and a scattering of old cigarette ends on the floor; occasionally, it seemed, other people found their way into Carver's. He looked slowly around, hoping to see the paint tin that he and Alison had used for the Peeing Game, hoping for some correspondence between past and present.

Everything had changed. A sob wrenched its way out of his throat. He squeezed his eyes tightly shut. A tear rolled slowly down his left cheek. Here he was, he thought, a twenty-five-year-old failure. What had he been expecting to find? Alison with the pink ribbon in her hair, Alison twirling like a ballerina and smiling up at him?

Eddie stumbled outside. On his way back to the fence he looked up. To his horror, he saw through the branches of trees, high above the top of the wall, Mrs Reynolds on the balcony of her flat. Something flashed in her hands, a golden dazzle reflecting the setting sun. Eddie ran through the nettles to the fence and flung himself at the hole. A moment later he was back in the garden of 29 Rosington Road. His glasses had fallen off and he had torn a hole in his trousers.

When his breathing was calmer, Eddie forced himself to stroll to the house. At the door he glanced back. Mrs Reynolds was still on her balcony. She was staring over Carver's through what looked like a pair of field glasses. At least she wasn't looking at him. Not now. He shivered, and went inside.

Autumn became winter. After Christmas, Stanley caught a cold and the cold, as often happened with him, turned to bronchitis. No one noticed until it was too late that this time the bronchitis was pneumonia. He died early in February, aged seventy-two.

In recent years the trickle of LVs had died away. But until a few days before his death Stanley continued to visit the basement to work on the latest dolls' house.

Since his retirement he had slowed down, and the quality of his work had also deteriorated. But the last model was nearly complete, a tall Victorian terraced house looking foolish without its fellows on either side. He had been sewing the curtains at the time of his death.

Stanley died in hospital in the early hours of the morning. The following afternoon Eddie found the miniature curtains bundled into the sitting-room wastepaper basket, together with Stanley's needles and cottons. The discovery brought home to him the reality of his father's death more than anything else before or later, even the funeral.

This was a secular event. The Graces had never been churchgoers. Eddie's experience of religion had been limited to the services at school, flat and meaningless affairs.

'He was an atheist,' Thelma said firmly when the funeral director tentatively raised the subject of the deceased's religious preferences. 'You can keep the vicars out of it, all right? And we don't want any of those humanists, either.'

His mother's reaction to Stanley's death took Eddie by surprise. She showed no outward sign of grief. She gave the impression that death was an irritation and an imposition because of the extra work it entailed. In many ways widowhood seemed to act as a tonic: she was brisker than she had been for years, both physically and mentally.

'If we can clear out some of your father's stuff,' Thelma said as they ate fish and chips in the kitchen on the evening after the funeral, 'perhaps we can find a lodger.'

Eddie put down his fork. 'But you wouldn't want a stranger in the house, would you?'

'If we want to stay here, we've no choice.'

'But the house is paid for. And haven't you got a pension from the Paladin?'

'Call it a pension? Don't make me laugh. I've already talked to them about it. I'll get a third of what your father got, and that wasn't much to begin with. It makes me sick. He worked there for over forty years, and you'd think by the way they used to go on that they couldn't do enough for their staff. They're sharks. Just like everyone else.'

'But surely we could manage?'

'We can't live on air.' She stared at him, pursing her lips. 'When you get another job, perhaps we can think again.'

When. The word hung between them. Eddie knew that his mother meant not *when* but *if.* Like his father, she had a low opinion of his capabilities. He thought that she could not have made the point more clearly if she had spoken the word *if* aloud.

'So we're agreed, then,' Thelma announced.

'I suppose so.'

She nodded at his plate, at half a portion of cod in greasy batter and a mound of pale, cold chips. 'Have you finished, then?'

'Yes.'

'Well, pass it here.' Thelma's appetite, always formidable for such a small person, had increased since she had stopped smoking the previous summer. 'Waste not, want not.'

'So we'll need to clear the back bedroom?'

'It won't clear itself, will it?' said Thelma through a mouthful of Eddie's supper. 'And while we're at it, we might as well sort out the basement. If we have a lodger we'll need the extra storage space.'

The next few days were very busy. His mother's haste seemed indecent. The back bedroom had been used as a boxroom for as long as Eddie could remember. Thelma wanted him to throw out most of the contents. She also packed up her husband's clothes and sent them to a charity shop. One morning she told Eddie to start clearing the basement. Most of the tools and photographic equipment could be sold, she said.

'It's not as if you're that way inclined, after all. You'd better get rid of the photos, too.'

'What about the dolls' house?'

'Leave that for now. But mind you change your trousers.

Wear the old jeans, the ones with the hole in the knee.'

Eddie went through the photographs first – the artistic ones in the cupboard, not the ones on the open shelves. The padlock key had vanished. In the end Eddie levered off the hasp with a crowbar.

The photographs had been carefully mounted in albums. The negatives were there too, encased in transparent envelopes and filed in date order in a ring binder. Against each print his father had written a name and a date in his clear, upright hand. Usually he had added a title. 'Saucy!' 'Blowing Bubbles!' 'Having the Time of Her Life!'

Eddie leafed slowly through the albums, working backwards. Some of the photographs he thought were quite appealing, and he decided that he would put them to one side to look at more carefully in his bedroom. Most of the girls he recognized. He came across his younger self, too, but did not linger over those photographs. He found the Reynoldses' daughter, Jenny Wren, and was astonished to see how ugly she had been as a child; memory had been relatively kind to her. Then he found another face he knew, smiling up at him from a photograph with the caption 'What a Little Tease!' He stared at the face, his excitement ebbing, leaving a dull sadness behind.

It was Alison. There was no possible room for doubt. Stanley must have taken the photograph at some point during the same summer as the Peeing Game. When else could it have been? Children grew quickly at that age. In the photograph Alison was naked, and just as Eddie remembered her from their games in Carver's. He even remembered, or thought he did, the ribbon that she wore in her hair.

They had both betrayed him, his father and Alison. Why hadn't Alison told him? She had been his friend.

After lunch that day his mother sent him out to do some shopping. Eddie was glad of the excuse to escape from the house. He could not stop thinking of Alison. He had not seen her for nearly twenty years, yet her face seen in a photograph still had the power to haunt him.

On his way home, Eddie met Mr and Mrs Reynolds in Rosington Road. He turned the corner and there they were. He had no chance to avoid them. The Graces and the Reynoldses had been on speaking terms since Jenny Wren's visits to the dolls' house. Eddie glanced at Mrs Reynolds's sour, unsympathetic face, wondering whether she had seen him trespassing in Carver's the previous autumn.

'Sorry to hear about your dad,' Mr Reynolds said, his face creasing with concern. 'Still, at least it was quick: that must have been a blessing for all of you.'

'Yes. It was very sudden.'

'Always a good neighbour. Couldn't have asked for a nicer one.'

The words were intended to comfort, but made Eddie smile, an expression he concealed by turning away and blowing his nose vigorously, as though overwhelmed by the sorrow of the occasion. As he did so he noticed that Mrs Reynolds was staring at him. He dropped his eyes to her chest. He noticed on the lapel of her coat a small enamel badge from the Royal Society for the Protection of Birds.

Perhaps that was why she spent so much time staring over Carver's, why she had the field glasses. Mrs Reynolds was a bird-watcher, a *twitcher*. The word brought him dangerously close to a giggle.

'Let us know if we can help, won't you?' Mr Reynolds patted Eddie's arm. 'You know where to find us.'

The Reynolds turned into the access road to the council estate, passing a line of garage doors daubed with swastikas and football slogans. Eddie scowled at their backs. A moment later, he let himself into number 29.

'Where have you been?' his mother called down from her

room. 'There's tea in the pot, but don't blame me if it's stewed.'

The hall felt different from usual. There was more light. An unexpected draught brushed his face. Almost instantaneously Eddie realized that the door to the basement was standing wide open; Stanley's death was so recent an event that this in itself was remarkable. Eddie paused and looked through the doorway, down the uncarpeted stairs.

The dolls' house was still on the workbench. But it was no longer four storeys high. It had been reduced to a mound of splintered wood, torn fabric and flecks of paint. Beside it on the bench was the rusty hatchet which Alison had used to break through the fence between the Graces' garden and Carver's, and which Stanley had found lying under the trees at the end of the garden.

Eddie closed the basement door and went into the kitchen. When she came downstairs, his mother did not mention the dolls' house and nor did he. That evening he piled what was left of it into a large cardboard box, carried it outside and left it beside the dustbin. He and his mother did not speak about it later because there was nothing they wanted to say.

Five

1

Oliver Rickford put down the phone. 'It's all right,' he said
again. 'It's not Lucy's.'

Sally was sitting in the armchair. Her body was trembling.
Yvonne hovered behind the chair, her eyes on Oliver. He
knelt beside Sally, gripped her arm and shook it gently.

'Not Lucy's,' he repeated. 'Not Lucy's hand. I promise.'

Sally lifted her head. On the third try, she succeeded in
saying, 'They can't be sure. They can't *know* it's not Lucy's.'

'They can in this case. The skin is black. Probably from a
child of about the same age.'

'Thank God.' Sally dabbed at her eyes with a paper handkerchief. 'What am I saying? It's someone else's child.' Still
the shameful Te Deum repeated itself in her mind: *Thank
God it's not Lucy, thank God, thank God.* 'Did they tell you
anything else?'

Oliver hesitated. 'They haven't had time to look at the
hand properly. But it looks as if it was cut off with something
like an axe. It was very cold.' He paused again. 'In fact,
they think it may have been kept in a freezer. It was still
defrosting.'

Yvonne sucked in her breath. 'Jesus.' She glanced at Sally.
'Sorry.'

Sally was still looking at Oliver. 'No link with Lucy? You're
sure?'

'Why should there be? The only possible connection was in the minds of those hacks downstairs.'

Sally clenched her hands, watching without interest as the knuckles turned white.

'Would it be a good idea to try to rest for a while?' Oliver suggested. 'There's nothing you can do at present.'

Sally was too tired to argue. Her strength had mysteriously evaporated. Clutching the box of paper handkerchiefs, she smiled mechanically at the two police officers and left the room. The door of the room she shared with Michael was closed. She did not want to disturb him, and if he woke up she would not know what to say. Instead she took a deep breath and went into Lucy's bedroom.

It was like a cell – small, and with a window placed high in the wall. They had intended to decorate before Lucy was born but had failed to find the time. After Lucy's birth there had been even less time. The wallpaper showed a trellis with a stylized clematis growing up it. In places the wallpaper was coming adrift from the wall, a process which Lucy had actively encouraged, revealing another wallpaper beneath, psychedelic swirls of orange and turquoise from the 1960s.

Sally had dreaded coming here. She had known that the room would smell of Lucy, that everywhere there would be reminders. But it had to be done, sooner or later; in the long run avoiding the room would be worse. She sat down heavily on the bed, which was covered with a duvet whose design showed teddy bears gorging themselves on honey and apparently oblivious of a squadron of enormous bees patrolling the air around their heads. The duvet had been Lucy's choice, the bribe which had persuaded her to move from her cot to a proper bed.

Automatically, Sally began to tidy the books and toys which were scattered on and around the bedside table. Were all four-year-olds like this? Was chaos their natural environment? Or was Lucy exceptional in this as in so much else?

The book they had been reading on Thursday evening was lying between the bed and the wall. Sally rescued it and marked the place they had reached with a scrap of paper. She ran out of energy and let herself fall back on the bed.

She buried her face in the pillow. Why did children smell sweet?

She supposed that she should pray for Lucy. It was then that she realized that she had not read the Morning Office today, or indeed the Evening Office last night. Discipline and regular exercise were as necessary in prayer as in athletics. She closed her eyes and tried to bring her mind into focus.

Nothing happened. No one was there. It was dark and cold and God was absent. It was not that he no longer existed, Sally discovered: it was simply that it no longer mattered to her whether he existed or not. He had become an irrelevancy, something pushed beyond the margins of her life. She tried to say the Lord's Prayer, but the words dried up long before she had finished. Instead she thought of the severed hand. What sort of person would leave it on a gravestone? Was there a significance in the choice of grave? Perhaps it belonged to a relative of the owner of the hand.

She hoped the child had been dead when they cut off the hand. The idea that he or she had been chopped up, perhaps parcelled in clingfilm and deep-frozen, made it worse for two reasons: it added an illusion of domesticity to what had been done, and it suggested premeditation and a terrible patience. What could have been the motive for such an action? A desire to hurt the child's mother? Punishment for a theft, a perversion of the Islamic penal code? Sally tried to imagine a need grown so egocentric and powerful that it would stop at nothing, even the carefully calculated destruction of children.

She dug her hand into the pocket of her jeans and wrapped her fingers round Lucy's sock. She thought of herself and Michael, Lucy and the unknown child, the child's parents, the old woman gobbling pills in the bedsitter in Belmont Road, the diseased and the abused, the tortured and the dying. The human race never learned by its mistakes: it merely plunged deeper and deeper into a mire of its own making.

At that moment, lying on Lucy's bed, it became clear to Sally that a loving God would not permit such things. At theological college she had learned the arguments why he might allow suffering. She had even parroted them out for parishioners. Now the arguments were suddenly revealed as specious: at last God was unmasked and revealed as the shit he really was.

She heard voices in the sitting room, one of them a man's but neither Oliver's nor Michael's. She sat up on the bed and wiped away her tears and blew her nose. There was a tap on the door and Yvonne put her head into the room.

'Mr Maxham's here. He wondered if you'd be up to having a word with him.'

Sally nodded, and dragged herself to her feet. 'Has Oliver gone?'

'About ten minutes ago. He didn't want to disturb you. He left a note.'

Sally's body felt hot and heavy. In the bathroom she washed her face and dragged a comb through her hair. In the mirror her face confronted her: a haggard stranger, pale and puffy-eyed, no make-up, hair in a mess.

In the living room, Yvonne was standing by the window, her head bowed, an anxious smile on her face.

'This is Chief Inspector Maxham. Mrs Appleyard.'

A small, thin man was examining the photographs on the mantelpiece. He turned round, a fraction of a second later than one would have expected.

'Mrs Appleyard.' Maxham ambled towards her, hand outstretched. 'I hope we haven't disturbed you.'

'I wasn't asleep.' His handshake was dry, hard and cold. She noticed that the hands were a blue-purple colour; he probably suffered from poor circulation. 'Is there any news?'

'I'm afraid not. Not yet.' He gestured to a tall man standing by the door to the kitchen. 'This is Detective Sergeant Carlow.'

The sergeant nodded to her. He wore a chain-store suit, a dark grey pinstripe whose sleeves and trouser legs were a little too short for him. His skin, his hair and even his eyes looked etiolated, as if he spent too much of his waking life staring at a computer screen under artificial light. His jaw was so prominent that the lower part of his face was broader than the upper.

Maxham nodded to one of her chairs. 'Do sit down, Mrs Appleyard.'

She remained standing. 'Have you found anything, anything at all?'

'It's early days.' Maxham had a plump face, the skin crisscrossed with red veins. Behind black-rimmed glasses the eyes were pale islands, neither grey nor blue but somewhere between. The accent was Thames Estuary, very similar to Derek Cutter's. 'As far as we can tell, Lucy just walked out of the back door. She –'

'But she wouldn't do that. She's not a fool. She's been told time and time again –'

'It seems that she and Ms Vaughan had had a bit of a disagreement. Lucy wanted Ms Vaughan to buy her something, a Christmas present, and Ms Vaughan said no. Then Ms Vaughan went upstairs to the bathroom. She left Lucy sulking behind the sofa. Five minutes later, maybe ten, Ms Vaughan comes down again, hoping Lucy had calmed down. But she was gone. The other little girl and boy hadn't noticed her going – one was watching TV, the other was upstairs with Ms Vaughan. Lucy's coat's missing. And so's Ms Vaughan's purse. Big green thing – it was in her handbag on the kitchen table.'

The little madam, Sally thought: she's not getting away with that sort of behaviour; just wait till I get my hands on her. In an instant she lurched back to the reality of the situation. Her legs began to shake. She sat down suddenly. Maxham sat down, too. He looked expectantly at her. She found a tissue in her sleeve and blew her nose.

At length she said, 'I thought Carla always locked the doors, put the chain on.'

'So she says,' he agreed. 'But on the back door she's only got a couple of bolts and a Yale. We think Lucy may have pulled over a stool and climbed up. The bolts had been recently oiled and the catch might have been up on the Yale – Ms Vaughan said she went out in the yard to put something in the dustbin earlier that afternoon, and she wasn't sure she'd put the catch down when she came in.'

Sally clung to past certainties, hoping to use them to prove that this could not be happening. 'She couldn't have got out of the yard. The fence is far too high for her. And there's a drop on the other side – she doesn't like jumping down from a height. There's a gate, isn't there, into some alley? It's always locked. I remember Carla telling me.'

'The gate was unbolted when we got there, Mrs Appleyard.'

'It's a high bolt, isn't it?' Sally closed her eyes, trying to visualize the yard which she'd seen on a sunny afternoon in the autumn. Dead leaves, brown, yellow and orange, danced over the concrete and gathered in a drift between the two dustbins and the sandpit. 'Was the bolt stiff?'

'As it happens, yes. Would you say that Lucy is a physically strong child for her age?'

'Look at me, Mum.' Lucy was standing on the edge of her bed in her pyjamas, holding Jimmy up to the ceiling. 'I'm King Kong.'

'Not particularly. She's a little smaller than average for her age.'

Sergeant Carlow was sitting at the table and writing in his notebook. The cuffs of the trousers had risen halfway up his calves, exposing bands of pale and almost hairless skin above the drooping black socks.

A soft hiss filled the silence: Maxham had a habit of sucking in breath every moment or so as if trying to clear obstructions lodged between his teeth; and as he did so he pulled back his lips in the mockery of a smile. 'We've talked to the neighbours all along the street. We've talked to the people whose gardens back on to the alley. No one saw her. It was a filthy evening, yesterday. No one was out unless they had to be.'

Sally shouted, 'Are you saying that someone opened that gate from the outside?'

Maxham shrugged his wiry little body. The plump face looked all wrong on such a scraggy neck. 'I'm afraid we're not in a position to draw any conclusions yet, Mrs Appleyard. We're just investigating the possibilities, you understand. Gathering evidence. I'm sure you know what these things are like from your husband.'

The condescension in his voice made Sally yearn to slap him. He sat there smiling at her. He was going bald at the crown and the grey hair needed cutting. He wore an elderly tweed suit, baggy at the knees and shiny at the elbows, which gave him the incongruous appearance of a none-too-successful farmer on market day. She did not like what she saw, but that did not mean he was bad at his job. Once more he hissed. Now that she had noticed the habit, it irritated and distracted her. She thought of protective geese and hostile serpents.

'What about dogs?' she asked, her voice astonishingly calm.

'We tried that. No joy. Doesn't prove anything one way or the other. All that rain didn't help.'

'And how can I help you?'

Maxham's head nodded, perhaps as a sign of approval. He took off his glasses and began to polish them with a handkerchief from the top pocket of his jacket. 'There's a number of things, Mrs Appleyard. Most of them obvious. We'll need a good up-to-date photograph of Lucy. We'll need to talk to you about what she's like – not just her appearance, what she's like inside. We'd like to find out exactly what she's wearing. Everything.' He inserted a delicate little pause in the conversation. 'Also, any toys she may have had with her, that sort of thing. Ms Vaughan said she wanted them to go to Woolworth's and buy a conjuring set. Can you confirm that?'

'Yes. Lucy and I had an argument about it on the way to Carla's yesterday morning. My daughter can be very persistent. If she wants something, she's inclined to go on and on about it until she gets it. And if she doesn't get it, which is what often happens, she sometimes throws a tantrum.'

'So you'd agree that her going off all by herself in a huff like that wouldn't be untypical?'

'Of course it would be untypical. She's never done anything like that before.' Yes, she had, Sally thought: Lucy had tried to run off in shops several times: but surely this was different in kind as well as in degree? 'But she's very self-willed. Her trying to run off like that shocks me but it doesn't altogether surprise me.'

'Ah.' Maxham breathed on his glasses one last time, gave

them another polish and settled them on the bridge of his nose. 'I have to say your husband sees Lucy a little differently. He insisted that she wouldn't run off of her own accord, that she's far too sensible.'

'Lucy likes being with her father.' Sally chose her words carefully, unwilling to point out that she saw about five times more of Lucy than Michael did, and that Michael spoiled her terribly. 'Perhaps she tends to be better behaved with him than she is with me. But I don't think that there's any doubt about the determination she can show. You can ask Carla. Or Margaret Cutter.' She rushed on, answering the question before Maxham had time to ask it. 'She's our vicar's wife. She runs a crèche at St George's.'

'Would you have any objection if we had a look round?'

'A look where?'

'All over the flat, if you don't mind. Lucy's room, especially, of course. It can help us get a feeling of the missing child, you understand. And if you'd come with us, perhaps you'll notice if there's anything missing.'

What did they expect to find, Sally wondered? Lucy's body under her bed? 'All right. But my husband's asleep at present.'

'Yes, your husband.' Maxham drew out the words until he was speaking almost in a drawl. He sucked in air. 'We wouldn't want to disturb him.'

'He needs to sleep.'

'He was up all night.' Maxham's voice was neutral, uninflected. 'I had to ask his friend Mr Rickford to come and collect him this morning. So he got home safely?'

'Yes.' Before she could stop herself, Sally added a plea on Michael's behalf: 'He was very upset, yesterday. Still is. He's not himself.'

'That's understandable.' The voice was still neutral, and the want of sympathy was in itself an accusation. 'I gather he's had a lot on his plate lately.'

'Obviously.' A doubt niggled in Sally's mind: had Michael had something else to worry about, something that had happened *before* Lucy's disappearance? But there was no time for that now. 'What do you think might have happened?'

She was suddenly furious with Maxham. 'Come on – you must have some ideas. What are the main possibilities?'

'Three main scenarios,' he said briskly. 'One, she wandered off by herself, and hopefully found shelter. Two, a man or maybe some kids were passing by and thought they'd take her with them. It happens, Mrs Appleyard, I won't conceal it from you; but it happens less often than you'd believe, so try not to think too much about it.' His tone was still neutral, and she wondered whether kindness or insensitivity lay behind it. 'Three: a woman took her. That counts as a separate option because usually the motives are different. You know, mothers who've lost their babies and need a replacement. Girls who want a young child to play with, a sort of doll. If that's what's happened, we'll probably get her back safe and sound.'

'Safe and sound?' Sally whispered, so angry and so scared that her teeth wanted to chatter together.

'These things are relative, Mrs Appleyard. You must understand that.'

'Why do these women do it?' Sally was reluctant to consider the other options; she knew they would haunt her later.

'Sometimes it's someone who thinks her relationship's breaking up. It's a way to keep a man with her. Usually that's a baby, though. Or then you get a young girl with a history of parental neglect. Broken home – Dad's in jail, Mum's got a new man. You could say they need someone to love. Don't we all, eh? And then you get the mentally ill. Usually no previous history of delinquency. Generally a one-off case, committed while the woman's in an acute psychotic state.' Maxham glanced at her, assessing the effect his words were having. 'We'll just have to see what –'

Without warning, Michael shambled into the room and leant on the back of the sofa. He stared at them as if at a roomful of strangers. Sergeant Carlow stood up, snapping shut his notebook. Yvonne looked at Maxham, asking mutely for guidance. Maxham simply sat there, his hands clasped loosely on his lap.

Sally had left the door open when she came into the room.

121

Had Michael been standing in the hallway and listening for long? He was in his pyjamas, and he looked terrible: the jacket unbuttoned, his hair tousled, his face unshaven, his body dazed by the sleeping pill.

'Find her, Maxham,' Michael whispered. 'Just find her. Stop talking and find her.'

2

Sally did not like Maxham but she had to admit that he handled the situation shrewdly. He asked Sally to show himself and Carlow round the flat. He left Yvonne sitting at the table with Michael. Michael might have picked a quarrel if he had been left alone with either of the men. But he would not quarrel with a woman. He treated women he did not know well as if they were delicate beings, easily damaged by rough handling.

Sally heard Michael and Yvonne talking as she showed the two police officers round the flat. She could not hear what they were saying, but their voices rose and fell, stopped and started, in a reassuringly normal pattern.

When they returned to the living room, however, Michael looked up at Maxham and Sally knew from Michael's face that nothing had changed.

'The odds are a man took her,' he said. 'You know that. Women tend to take babies.'

Maxham drew back his lips and hissed. 'We'll have to see.' He turned to Sally. 'Thank you for your help, Mrs Appleyard. We'll be in touch. And don't worry – we're doing everything we can.'

'Bastard,' Michael muttered audibly in the living room as Sally was showing the police officers out.

Michael shaved and showered. By now it was mid-afternoon. Sally made a pot of tea which only Yvonne wanted. The policewoman was doing her best, Sally thought, but it was like having a nanny on the premises. She sat by the phone, apparently engrossed in the last few clues of the *Daily Telegraph* crossword.

Michael pushed aside his mug. 'I'm sorry, Sal. I can't stay here. I feel like the walls are pressing in. I'm going to get some fresh air.'

She wanted to seize his hand. *Don't leave me alone.* Instead she said, 'Will you be long?'

He didn't answer the question. He found his jacket and dropped his wallet in one pocket and his keys in the other. It was a waxed jacket, which reminded her of Oliver.

'Should you phone Oliver at some point?' she asked.

'When I get back.' He bent down and kissed the top of her head. 'I love you,' he murmured, too low for Yvonne to hear. He straightened up. 'I won't be long.'

His hand touched Sally's shoulder for an instant. He nodded to Yvonne and left the room. The two women sat in silence. The front door opened and closed. They heard his footsteps moving steadily down the stairs. Sally hoped that he wouldn't get into a fight with the journalists. In a moment or two she relaxed because no one was shouting in the street.

That was the last she saw of Michael on Saturday. She spent most of the next five hours near the phone. When the phone rang, Yvonne would answer it, shaking her head at Sally when it became clear that Michael wasn't the caller.

Sally thought of Michael getting himself arrested; of him wandering in tears through the streets of London in search of Lucy; of accident, madness and suicide. Even in her misery she knew that Lucy's absence was far more worrying than Michael's; the greater fear did not cast out the lesser, but it made it easier to bear. This did not stop her feeling angry with him.

'The bloody man!' she burst out after yet another phone call from someone she did not want to talk to.

'That's right, dear,' Yvonne said helpfully. 'Get it out of your system.'

'Does Maxham know that Michael's gone?'

Yvonne nodded. 'I had to tell him. I'm sorry.'

'It's not your fault.'

On the mantelpiece, Sally found the note from Oliver propped against the broken silver clock, the wedding present from David Byfield. *Michael and Sally: Please phone me if I can do anything. Oliver.* Underneath his name he had had the sense to put his phone number. A polite man, too. When Yvonne was making tea in the kitchen, Sally picked up the phone. Oliver answered at the second ring.

'It's me. Sally.'

'Any news?'

'No. Not really.' She told him about Michael. 'I – I wondered if he might be with you.'

'I wish he was. Actually, Maxham's already phoned. Shall I come over?'

'No.' She heard a clatter from the kitchen. 'I've got to go.'

'Phone me, Sally. Any time. All right?'

'All right.' She broke the connection as Yvonne came in with mugs of tea. 'Just checking with Oliver Rickford. Michael's not there, either.'

Sally sat down with the tea. What hurt, then and later, was the way Michael had locked her out. *For better or for worse*: didn't it mean anything to him? If it didn't mean anything, why did he bother getting married? He could have found someone else to screw. Maybe that's where he was now: with a prostitute, paying for what his wife was too tired to give him.

Yvonne went to the lavatory. The phone began to ring. Sally flung herself at it, spilling uncomfortably hot tea over her leg.

'*Shit.* Hello.'

'Is that the Reverend Appleyard speaking?' A man's voice; unfamiliar. 'Sally? This is Frank Howell. Remember me? I did that piece on St George's for the *Standard*.'

'I'm sorry. I've nothing to say.'

'I understand, Sally.' The voice was unctuous. 'I don't want to ask you anything. Truly.'

She remembered the man's face now: the balding cherub with red-rimmed eyes; Derek's friend. 'I'm going to put the phone down, Mr Howell.'

He began to gabble: 'Sooner or later you and Michael are going to have to deal with the press. Maybe I can help. You need someone who knows the ropes, someone on your side, someone who – '

'Goodbye.' She broke the connection.

'Who was that?' Yvonne asked, a moment later.

'A journalist named Frank Howell.'

'He's already rung twice before. Leave the phone to me.'

'I thought it might be Michael.' *Or Lucy.* Sally started to cry again.

Yvonne gave her a handful of paper handkerchiefs. 'Try not to worry, love. I'm sure there's some perfectly simple explanation. He'll be back. You'll see.'

Through her tears Sally snarled, 'I'm not sure I want him back.' *I want Lucy.*

4

Afterwards, Sally learned that Michael turned right into the main road, walking towards the tube station. He went into the saloon bar of the King of Prussia and ordered a pint of beer and a double whisky. He sat by himself at a table in the corner of the room. According to the barman he gave no trouble. He drank two more double whiskies and repelled an attempt to draw him into conversation.

He took the underground to King's Cross Station, where he bought a standard single to Cambridge. He had time to kill before catching the train so he killed it in a bar. From Cambridge railway station he walked slowly into the centre of the town and out the other side, stopping at two pubs on the way. He staggered up the Huntingdon Road. Just before eight-thirty he reached a small but ugly block of modern flats near Fitzwilliam College. He rang one of the bells and lay down on the wet grass to rest. Soon he was asleep.

A little later, the telephone rang in the Appleyards' living room in Hercules Road. Yvonne answered. She listened for a moment, pressed the mute button and looked across the room at Sally.

'It's someone called Father Byfield. Do you want to speak to him? He says your husband's with him.'

Sally was furious and relieved when she heard Uncle David's voice. Jealousy was there, too, and also a sense of failure. She should have realized that in times of trouble Michael would turn not to her but to his godfather.

Six

'Therefore for Spirits, I am so far from denying their existence, that I could easily believe, that no onely whole Countries, but particular persons, have their Tutelary and Guardian Angels.'

Religio Medici, I, 33

1

'Mummy. Mummy, where are you?'

Over the intercom, Lucy's voice sounded mechanical, like a juvenile robot's. Without the intercom and with the doors closed, they would not have heard her because the basement was now so well soundproofed.

'Mummy.' The voice sharpened and rose to a wail. 'Where are you?'

Angel dropped her napkin on the table and stood up, stretching her long white arm towards the keys on the worktop. At the door she glanced back at Eddie.

'You sort things out in here. I'll deal with her.'

Lucy was crying now. Eddie imagined her standing by the door or curled up in bed. She was wearing the pyjamas he had bought especially for her at Selfridges; they had red stars against a deep yellow background and in normal circumstances would suit her colouring. Last night, however, Lucy had not been looking her best: by the low-wattage light of the bedside lamp, her face had been white, almost green, mouth a black, ragged hole, the puffy eyes squeezed into slits.

'Daddy. Mummy.'

The intercom emitted a series of crackles: Angel was unlocking and opening the door to the basement.

'*Mummy*. I want –'

'You'll see Mummy very soon.' Angel's voice was tinny and precise. There was a click as she closed the door behind her. 'Now, what are you doing out of bed without your slippers?'

'Where's Mummy? Where am I? Where's Daddy?'

'Mummy and Daddy had to go away for a night or two. Don't you remember? Eddie and I are looking after you.' There was a pause, but Lucy did not respond. 'I'm Angel.'

Lucy began to cry again. The intercom twisted and distorted her sorrow.

'That's enough, dear. I don't want to have to get cross. Think how sad Mummy would be if she heard you've been naughty.'

The crying grew louder.

'Lucy. You won't like it if I have to get cross. Naughty children have to be punished.'

The wails continued. There was a sharp report like the crack of a whip. The crying stopped abruptly.

'We don't allow cry babies here, dear. You're going to have to pull your socks up, aren't you?'

Eddie could bear it no longer. He switched off the intercom and listened to the silence seeping into the kitchen like water flowing into a pool.

2

Here we all were on this overcrowded planet, Eddie thought, all members of the same species and yet each of us a mystery to everyone else. Especially Angel, who, like Churchill's Russia, was a riddle wrapped in a mystery inside an enigma. For example, where did she come from? How old was she? Who was she? If she did not particularly like little girls, why did she spend so much time with them? Last but not least, why had Angel said that Lucy was special? What made Lucy different from the other three?

Nothing about Angel was straightforward. To all intents

128

and purposes she might have been born adult less than six years before, on the March evening when Eddie met her. She came to the house in Rosington Road in answer to an advertisement which Eddie's mother had put in the *Evening Standard*. The advertisement gave the name of the road but not the Graces' name or the number of the house. Eddie's mother said that you couldn't be too careful, what with all the strange people roaming round the streets today.

From the start, Thelma refused to consider male applicants. 'They're dirty beasts. Women are tidier and cleaner.' Eddie himself was excepted from this general view of the male sex, which confirmed his suspicion that his mother did not think him entirely masculine.

When Angel phoned, Eddie's mother gave her the number of the house almost immediately. She liked Angel's voice.

'At least she speaks the Queen's English. More than you can say for the rest of them. And she says she's got a job. I don't want one of those Social Security scroungers under my feet all day.'

There had been nine other calls before Angel's, but none of them had led to an invitation to see the room. Thelma disliked the Irish, West Indians, Asians and anyone with what she termed a 'lower class' accent.

When the doorbell rang, Eddie and his mother were watching television in the front room.

'She's on time,' Thelma commented, looking at her watch. 'I'll say that for her.'

Eddie went into the hall and peeped through the fish-eye lens at the person on the doorstep. He could see very little of her, because she had turned to stare at the traffic on the road; and in any case, she was wearing a long, pale mackintosh with a hood. As he opened the door she turned to face him.

She was beautiful. For an instant her perfection paralysed him. He had never seen anyone so beautiful in real life, only on television, in pictures and in films. She stared at him as though she were assessing his suitability rather than the other way round.

'Ah,' he said. 'Ah, Miss – ah – come in.'

There was an infinitesimal pause. Then, to his relief, she smiled and came out of the rain. Angel was about his own height, which was five feet six. She had a long, fine-boned face, the skin flawless as a child's. Thelma, pop-eyed with suspicion, escorted her upstairs to see the spare room. Eddie lurked in the hall, listening.

'How lovely,' he heard Angel say. 'And, if I may say so, how tastefully decorated.' Her voice was self-assured, the crisp enunciation hinting at a corresponding clarity of thought.

By the time they came downstairs again the two women were chatting almost like friends. To Eddie's amazement, he heard his mother offering hospitality.

'We generally have a glass of sherry at this time, Miss Wharton. Perhaps you'd care to join us?'

'That would be lovely.'

Thelma stared at Eddie, who after an awkward hiatus leapt to his feet and went to the kitchen to search for the bottle of sweet sherry which his father had opened the Christmas before last. When he returned with three assorted glasses on a tray, the women were discussing how soon Angel could move in.

'Subject to a month's deposit and suitable references, of course.'

'Naturally.' Angel opened her handbag. 'I have a reference here from Mrs Hawley-Minton. She's the lady who runs the agency I work for.'

'A nursing agency?'

'Nursery nursing, actually. Essentially it's an agency for nannies with nursing training.'

'Eddie,' Thelma prompted. 'The sherry.'

He handed round the glasses. Angel passed an envelope to Thelma, who extracted a sheet of headed paper and settled her reading glasses on her nose. Eddie and Angel sipped their sherry.

'I see that Mrs Hawley-Minton knew your parents,' Thelma said, her stately manner firmly to the fore.

'Oh, yes. That's why she took me on. She's very careful about that sort of thing.'

Thelma peered interrogatively over her reading glasses.

'An agency like hers is a great responsibility,' Angel explained. 'Particularly as children are concerned. She believes one can't be too careful.'

'Quite,' said Thelma; and after a pause she added, 'I do so agree.' She folded the letter and handed it back to Angel. 'Well, Miss Wharton, that seems quite satisfactory. When would you like to move in?'

3

In those days, Angel was always Miss Wharton. Thelma took refuge in obsolete formality. Eddie avoided calling Angel anything to her face, but sometimes at night he whispered her Christian name, Angela, trying it for size in his mouth, where it felt awkward and alien.

By and large, Angel kept to her room. She was allowed the use of the bathroom, of course, and she had her own latchkey. For a time she had all the virtues, even negative ones.

'I'm so glad she doesn't smoke,' said Thelma, who had converted her former pleasure into a vice. 'It would make the whole house smell, not just her room. But I suppose she wouldn't, being a nurse.'

Before Angel moved in, Thelma had worried a great deal about the telephone. She had visions of Angel making unauthorized calls to Australia, of the phone ringing endlessly (a woman who looked like that was bound to have an active social life), of long conversations with girlfriends and, even worse, boyfriends.

Angel soon calmed Thelma's fears. She rarely used the phone herself, and when she did she kept a meticulous record of the cost. Nor did she receive many incoming phone calls. Most of them were to do with her work – usually from Mrs Hawley-Minton's agency. As the weeks went by, Thelma developed a telephonic acquaintance with Mrs Hawley-Minton.

'They value Miss Wharton very highly,' she reported to Eddie. 'Mrs Hawley-Minton tells me that her clients are always asking to have her back. One of them was a real prince. His father was a king. Bulgaria, was it? He was deposed a long time ago, of course, but even so.'

Eddie envied Angel her job. He thought a good deal about her children and what she might do with them. Sometimes he tried to imagine that he was she, that he was in her clothes, in her skin, behind her eyes.

'She's working in Belgrave Square this week,' Thelma would say, telling Eddie for want of anyone better to talk to. 'He's a Peruvian millionaire, and she's something to do with the embassy.' And Eddie would see dark-haired children with solemn faces and huge eyes in an attic nursery with barred windows; he would see himself looking after them and playing with them, just as Angel did.

Thelma was curious about Angel's antecedents, and about her apparently non-existent social life. 'If you ask me, she's been unlucky in love. Don't tell me a girl like that hasn't had plenty of opportunities. I bet she has men chasing after her with their tongues hanging out every time she walks down the street.'

Thelma's coarseness surprised Eddie, even shocked him. She had never shown that side of herself when Stanley had been alive. He noticed that the hypothetical fiancé appealed greatly to her.

'I wonder if she was engaged, and then he was killed, and since then she's never looked at another man.' Thelma also had a strong sentimental streak, buried deep but liable to surface unexpectedly. 'Perhaps he was in the army. Miss Wharton's father was, you know.' It transpired that Mrs Hawley-Minton's late husband had been a brigadier, and he and Angel's father had served together in India during the war. 'I think both parents must be dead,' Thelma confided. 'She seems quite alone in the world.'

Thelma's curiosity about Angel extended to her possessions. Angel kept her room clean and made her own bed. But Thelma retained a key, and every now and then, when Angel was out, she would unlock the door of the back bedroom and cautiously investigate her lodger's private life.

'I'm not being nosy. But she's my responsibility in a way. And I have to make sure she's not burning holes in the bedspread or leaving the fire on when she goes out.'

Eddie watched his mother on one of these incursions. He stood in the doorway of the back bedroom – a landlady's dream: clean, tidy, smelling faintly of polish and Angel's perfume. Thelma moved slowly round the room in a clockwise direction. She opened doors and pulled out drawers. On top of the wardrobe was a large modern suitcase.

'Locked,' Thelma commented, curious but not annoyed.

In the cupboard by the bed was a japanned box, and that was locked too. 'Probably keeps family papers in there, mementoes of her parents and her fiancé. Funny she doesn't have any photographs of them. There's plenty of room on the dressing table.'

'You haven't got any pictures of Dad,' Eddie pointed out.

'That's quite different.' Thelma wheezed, her attention elsewhere. 'She's got an awful lot of books, hasn't she? I wonder if she's actually read them.' She peered at the spines. 'You wouldn't have thought she was *religious*, would you?' His mother spoke the word 'religious' in a tone in which incredulity, pity and curiosity were finely balanced. 'You'd never have guessed.'

Eddie noticed a bible, a prayer book and a hymnal. He ran his eyes along the row of spines and other titles leapt out at him: G. K. Chesterton's biography of Thomas Aquinas; the *Religio Medici* of Sir Thomas Browne; *The Christian Faith*; *The Four Last Things*; *A Dictionary of Christian Theology*; *The Shield of Faith*; *Man, God and Prayer*.

'She doesn't go to church,' Thelma said, her voice doubtful. 'I'm sure we would have noticed.' She drifted over to the dressing table, picked up a small bottle of perfume and sniffed it. 'Very nice.' She put down the perfume. 'Mind you, it should be. That stuff isn't cheap. You could feed a family of four on the amount she spends on dolling herself up.'

Insignificant though it was, the remark lodged in Eddie's memory. It was the first sign of a rift developing between Thelma and Angel. His mother was by nature a critical person, always willing to find fault and never satisfied with anyone or anything for long. She pursued perfection all her life and would not have known what to do if she had caught up with it.

As a mild grey spring slipped into a mild grey summer, the carping gathered strength. Thelma fired criticisms like arrows – at first one or two, every now and then, but steadily increasing in number.

As with Stanley, so with Angel: Thelma did not try to get rid of her lodger any more than she had tried to get rid of her husband. Angel's unwillingness to take remarks in the spirit they'd been uttered infuriated Thelma. But there was nothing she could do about it – Angel wore her placidity like a suit of armour.

On a sunny morning in the middle of summer, Eddie took a cup of coffee into the garden. His mother was out of the house for once – every four weeks she went by taxi to the health centre where she had her blood pressure checked and collected her monthly ration of pills and sprays – and he felt unusually relaxed. He wandered towards the trees at the far end.

The peaceful mood was shattered when he heard the back door opening behind him. He turned. Angel came towards him, picking her way between a weed-infested flowerbed and the long grass of the lawn. Her hair was loose, and she wore a short green dress and sandals. The sun was to her right and a little behind her, casting a golden glow over her hair and throwing her face into shadow.

'I'm not disturbing you?'

'No.' He shrank back towards the fence.

'It's such a lovely day. I couldn't resist coming outside.'

He sipped his coffee, scalding his tongue.

'Do you know, I saw a fox the other day.' Angel pointed down the garden towards Carver's. 'It went down there. Probably into the wasteland at the back.'

'There's a lot of wildlife there.'

'Shame it's such a mess.' She stopped beside him, and he caught a suggestion of her perfume. Her eyes swung towards the council flats. 'Still, better a jungle than something like that.'

Eddie nodded.

After a pause, Angel went on, 'Have you noticed the woman with the binoculars? She's often on the balcony with the geraniums.'

Only one balcony had geraniums. It stood out starkly from its neighbours partly because of this, and partly because of its tidiness, the fresh paint on the railing and the absence of a satellite dish. No one was standing there now.

'I think she watches birds,' Eddie said. 'Her name's Mrs Reynolds.'

'She was there just now. I was looking out of my bedroom window, and for a moment I thought she was watching you.'

'Are you sure? Why?'

'She was probably looking at the house. Or at next door. Perhaps there's a bird on the roof.' She smiled at him. 'In any case, even if she was looking at you, I wouldn't take it personally.'

'Oh no. Of course not.'

'Old women do strange things.' Angel glanced back at the house, and Eddie knew that Mrs Reynolds was not the only old woman she had in mind. 'But it's their problem, not ours.'

4

Over the summer, as Thelma's criticisms multiplied, Eddie found himself warming towards Angel. The process was gradual and subtle. She would smile at him as they passed in the hall, or ask him what he thought the weather was going to do this morning and listen to his answer as if his opinion really counted. When Thelma was being more than usually absurd, Angel would occasionally glance at Eddie; and when their eyes met there was the delicious sense of a shared secret, of shared amusement.

Eddie was flattered and alarmed by these hints. Women

135

had never shown any interest in him before, especially not beautiful women like Angel. Not that he liked her specifically as a woman, he told himself, but as a person. And there was no doubt that her beauty affected the way he responded to her: it added significance to everything she said and did.

Then came the first Sunday in September. It was a fine late summer day, and after breakfast Eddie decided to walk up to the Heath. (Since his father's death he had lost his fear of going out.) He happened to glance back as he was walking up Haverstock Hill and noticed, some way behind him, Angel walking slowly in the same direction. Her presence irritated him. On his walks he liked to be among strangers. He quickened his pace and cut down the next side road. He looked back more than once but there was no sign of her. He thought that she had probably continued up Rosslyn Hill to Hampstead Village.

He spent a pleasant hour on the Heath. It was a place he avoided in the evenings because parts of it were rough and dangerous and, they said, haunted by men doing horrible things to each other. But in daytime at weekends and during the holidays the Heath was full of children, some with grown-ups, some without. Eventually he found a bench on Parliament Hill and watched irritable fathers flying kites for bored children. Below him stretched the city, brick and stone, glass and tarmac, blues and greys and greens, trembling like a live thing in the haze.

To Eddie's delight, two girls of about eight began to do gymnastics near his bench. They were of an age when they were still unselfconscious about their bodies, when competition came naturally to them. One was wearing jeans, but the other – a girl with a pale, serious face spotted with freckles – wore a sweatshirt over a skimpy dress. Eddie watched her covertly. He tried to decide whether she was consciously teasing him, as Alison used to do in that far-off summer when she swung higher and higher, revealing more and more, and pretending that she didn't know he was watching her. He stared at her, wondering how soft the skin would be above the bony knees.

136

Then, with an abruptness which made him gasp, this pleasant reverie was shattered.

'Aren't they sweet?' Angel sat down beside him. 'All that energy. Where do they get it from?'

Eddie stared wildly at her. Her sudden appearance would have shocked him in normal circumstances and brought about another attack of shyness. But this was worse. Had his face revealed something of his thoughts? Angel was a nanny. She would be alert for strange men who watched children.

'It's a lovely day for the Heath. The best part of summer.'

'Yes,' he managed to say. 'Very sunny.'

The breeze blew a strand of her hair towards him. She smoothed it back into place. For an instant her sleeve brushed his and he smelt her perfume. She was wearing a blue sweatshirt and jeans. Her left hand was now lying on her leg, long-fingered, smooth-skinned, the nails not quite oval but egg-shaped, with the narrow ends embedded in the fingers; she wore no rings.

He looked away, worried that she might think he was staring at her. To his relief the two girls were running down the hill, shrieking to someone below. He no longer had to worry about betraying his interest in them.

'Would you like one?' Bewildered, Eddie turned towards her, for a moment thinking she was referring to the girls. But Angel was holding out a packet of Polos to him, the foil at the end of the tube peeled back. He took one because a refusal might offend her. For a moment they sat in silence. The mint seemed unnaturally strong, and he coughed.

'I like coming here,' Angel said. 'So nice to see the children playing.'

Eddie bit hard on the Polo, and it disintegrated. Two boys on the fringe of puberty raced by on their bikes. One of them dropped a crisp packet as he passed.

'When they're older, they're not nearly so appealing. Don't you agree?' She seemed not to expect an answer. 'But I wouldn't like to have children around all the time. They can be very tiring. What about you?'

Hastily he swallowed the fragments of Polo, the sharp edges snagging against his throat. 'I'm sorry?'

She smiled at him. 'I wondered if you'd like children of your own. I know I wouldn't.'

'No.' The word came out much more vehemently than Eddie had intended. He thought of the boys on the bicycles, of Mandy and Sian at Dale Grove Comprehensive, and of all the children who grew up. He was frightened that he might have revealed too much, so he took refuge in a generality. 'I think there're far too many people in the world as it is. Five and a half billion, isn't it, and more being born every day.'

Angel nodded, her face serious. 'That's a very good point.' Her tone implied that she'd never considered the question from that angle before. 'Still, they are sweet when they're young, aren't they? That's what I like about my job. I get most of the fun, but none of the long-term responsibility.'

'That must be nice.'

They sat there for another five minutes, talking in spurts about the city below them and its history. Slowly Eddie relaxed. He was surprised to find that he was enjoying the conversation, or rather the novelty of having someone to talk to.

'By the way, how did our road get its name?' Angel asked. 'I asked your mother but she didn't know.'

'It's because back in the Middle Ages the land round there used to belong to the Bishop of Rosington.'

A cloud slid across the sun.

'I thought it might be that. It's getting cold.' Angel hugged herself, dramatizing the words. 'Shall we find a cup of coffee? There's a café on South End Green.'

Before Eddie knew what was happening, they were walking down the hill together. He felt lighter than usual, floating like a spaceman. *This can't be happening to me.* Part of him would have liked to run away, but this was swamped by other feelings: running away would be a very rude thing to do; he was flattered to be in Angel's company, and even hoped that someone he knew would see them; and he also liked the sense, obscure but powerful, that by being together he and Angel were somehow fooling his mother. For once, Eddie was not alone; he was part of a couple, and two was company. Soon they were sitting at a table by themselves, with coffee sending up twin pillars of steam between them.

'This is nice.' Angel smiled at him. 'It's good to get out. I worry about your mother sometimes. She spends so much time in the house.'

'Oh, she likes being at home. She's always been like that, even when my father was alive.'

'As long as it makes her happy.'

'She's getting old,' Eddie said, meaning that he couldn't imagine how old people could be happy.

Angel answered the thought, not the words: 'Old age is very sad. I'd hate to be old.' For an instant, her face changed: she pressed her lips and frowned; wrinkles gouged their way across her skin, a glimpse of what might be to come. Then she smiled, and the years retreated. 'That's one of the things I like about children. It's impossible to imagine them ever being old.'

Eddie nodded. He thought of Alison again – at present she was in his mind a good deal – and wished with all his heart that she could have stayed for ever young in the summer when they'd played the Peeing Game, and that he could have been young with her. He smiled across the years at Alison.

'What's funny, Eddie?' Angel asked.

'What? Nothing.' He bent his head to hide his embarrassment. Steam from the coffee misted his glasses.

'You don't mind if I call you Eddie?'

He felt himself blushing. 'Of course not.'

'But don't call me Angela. Horrible name.'

He looked up. She was leaning towards him, her face blurred by the steam like the city by its smog. It seemed to him that her features were dissolving in the vapour. She said something he didn't catch.

'What was that?'

'My friends always call me Angel.'

Over the next four months it seemed natural to keep Thelma in the dark about what was happening, though there was no reason to be secretive about their growing friendship. Eddie derived great pleasure from pretending at home in front of his mother that he and Angel were still on the old footing of lodger and landlady's son. It amused Angel, too.

'Children enjoy make-believe,' she told him on one of their outings. 'I think I still do.'

They met in a succession of public places – cinemas, Primrose Hill, the National Portrait Gallery, a coffee shop attached to an Oxford Street store, a pub near the Heath where children played while their parents drank.

Being with Angel allowed Eddie to watch children without worrying about what adults might be thinking. After all, he and Angel were roughly the same age: they might be taken for a married couple; in any case, a man and a woman together were much less threatening than a single man.

Once, in the garden outside the Hampstead pub, a little girl fell off a swing and scraped her knee. Angel picked her up and calmed her down. Eventually the child managed to tell them that her mother was inside the pub.

'Then we shall go and find your mummy.' Angel picked up the child, who was no more than three, and handed her to Eddie. 'This nice man will give you a ride.'

The girl nestled in Eddie's arms. He could not help wondering whether Angel had known that carrying her would give him pleasure. The three of them went into the pub.

'Where's Mummy?' Angel asked the girl.

The mother found them first. She rushed in front of Angel and snatched her child from Eddie. She clung so tightly to the little girl that the latter, until then perfectly happy, began to cry.

The woman stared at Eddie, her face reddening. 'What happened? What – ?'

Angel cut in with an explanation which was an implicit accusation, delivered in her clear, confident voice. The mother reacted with an unlovely mixture of gratitude, guilt and surliness. She was a squat little woman in a long, dusty skirt; she wore no make-up and her arms were tattooed; piggy eyes glinted behind gold-rimmed glasses. She was also quite young, Eddie realized, perhaps not much older than the girls he had taught at school.

'You can't be too careful. Not these days,' she said in an unconscious echo of Thelma. She backed away from them, swallowed the rest of her drink and towed the child outside.

Eddie and Angel queued at the bar.

'If I hadn't been with you,' Angel said casually, 'that wretched woman would probably have thought you were trying to steal her child.'

6

As autumn turned to winter, Thelma seemed to sense that the atmosphere in the house had changed, that the emotional balance had tilted away from her. She grumbled more about Angel to Eddie. She became suspicious, wanting to know exactly where he'd been. There was not an open quarrel between her and Angel, but the old cordiality was no more than a memory.

Eddie was cautious by nature. (It was this which had kept him away from the networks of people who shared his special interests; he knew they existed because he read about them in the newspapers.) He did not want a rift with his mother. Sometimes he tried to imagine what life would be like if he and Angel could afford a flat or even a small house together. But financially this was out of the question. He had nothing to live on except what the state and his mother doled out to him.

It was wiser to keep a foot in both camps, at least for the time being. This was why Eddie did not tell Angel about his mother's snooping. He did not want to run the risk of provoking a quarrel between them.

The policy worked well until midway through January.

One evening Eddie ran downstairs. He was due to meet Angel in Liberty's in Regent Street: they planned to see a film and then have a pizza before coming home.

'Eddie,' Thelma called from the kitchen. 'Come in here a moment.'

He glanced at his watch, irritated because he was already a little on the late side and he didn't like to keep Angel waiting. He hesitated in the kitchen doorway. His mother was sitting at the table, breathing heavily. Her colour was high and there were patches of sweat under her arms.

'I'm in a bit of a hurry.'

'Where are you off to?'

'Just out.'

'You're always going out these days.'

'Just a film.'

Thelma's face darkened still further. 'You're seeing that woman. Go on, admit it.'

Surprised by the sudden venom, Eddie took a step backwards into the hall. 'Of course not.' Even to himself, his voice lacked conviction.

'I can smell her on you. That perfume she wears.'

Powerless to move, he stared at her.

'I tell you one thing,' Thelma went on, 'she's paid up till the end of the week, but after that she's out on her ear.'

'No!' The word burst out of Eddie before he could stop himself. 'You can't do that. There's no reason to do that.'

'She fooled me at the start, I admit that. But I'm not alone in that. She's fooled everyone.' Thelma tapped a sturdy manila envelope which lay on the table before her. 'Wait till Mrs Hawley-Minton hears about this. Unless she's in it, too. It's fraud, I tell you, bare-faced fraud. It's a matter for the police, I shouldn't wonder.'

Eddie stared at her. 'What do you mean? Are you all right?'

His mother opened the envelope and took out a British passport. She flicked over the pages until she found the photograph. She pushed the passport across the table towards Eddie, pinning it open with grubby fingers.

Reluctantly he came into the room and peered at the

photograph, which showed a thin-faced, short-haired woman he had never seen before.

'So? Who is it?'

'Are you blind?' his mother shouted. 'Look at the name, you fool.'

Eddie stooped, holding the glasses on the bridge of his nose. The name swam into focus.

Angela Mary Wharton.

7

Eddie's memories of the next few hours were vivid but patchy. This was, he supposed later, a symptom of shock. He remembered slamming the front door of 29 Rosington Road, a thing he'd never done before, but after that there were missing links in the chain of events.

He must have walked to Chalk Farm underground station and taken the Northern Line to Tottenham Court Road. He could not remember whether he had changed on to the Central Line for Oxford Circus or simply walked the rest of the way. But he had a clear picture of himself standing just inside the main entrance of Liberty's: the place was full of people and brightly coloured merchandise; a security guard stared curiously at him; he tried to find Angel, but she wasn't there, and he felt despair creeping over him, a sense that everything worthwhile was over.

Suddenly she touched his shoulder. 'Let's go outside. I've got you a present.'

Taking his arm, which was something she had never done before, she urged him outside. There, standing on the pavement in Great Marlborough Street, she gave him a small Liberty's bag.

'Go on, open it.' Angel was like a child, incapable of deferring pleasure. 'I knew I had to get it for you as soon as I saw it.'

People flowed steadily past them like a stream around a rock. Inside the bag was a silk tie, blue with thin green stripes running diagonally across it. Eddie stroked the soft material, his eyes filling with tears as he tried to find the right words.

'See,' she said. 'It picks out the blue in your eyes. It's perfect.'

Everything except himself and Angel receded, as though rushing away – the black-and-white frontage of Liberty's, the people eddying along the pavement, the snarling engines and the smell of fast food.

'Put it on.' Angel did not wait for him to respond but buttoned the collar of his shirt, which he was wearing without a tie. 'That shirt will do perfectly.' She turned up his collar, took the tie from his hand and put it round his neck. Deftly she tied the knot, making him feel like a child or even a doll. She stood back and looked assessingly at him. 'Yes, perfect.'

'Thank you. It's wonderful.'

Angel looked at her watch. 'We're going to miss the film if we're not careful.'

'I'm sorry I'm late. My mother . . .'

'What is it? Something's happened.'

'My mother's been in your room.'

'That's nothing new.'

Eddie snatched at the diversion, a temporary refuge. 'You knew?'

'She pokes her nose in there most days. I leave things so I can tell. Now, what is it?'

He felt hot and embarrassed: he hoped she did not know that he too had sometimes been in there. 'She found something in a tin box.'

Angel wrapped her hand around his arm and squeezed so hard that he yelped. She was pale under the make-up, and she pulled her lips back and the wrinkles appeared, just as they had done on Parliament Hill. 'It was locked.'

'She must have found the key. Or found one of her own that fitted. Or maybe for once it wasn't locked. I don't know.' He stared miserably up at her. 'She's got the passport. She's going to show it to your boss at the agency. And maybe the police.'

At this point there was another broken link in the memories. The next thing he knew they were deep in Soho, in Frith Street, and he was following Angel's shining head down a flight of stairs to a basement restaurant whose sounds and smells rose up around him like a tide. They sat at a table in an alcove, an island of stillness. A single candle stood between them in a wax-coated bottle. Eddie could not recall what they ate, but he remembered that Angel bought first one bottle of red wine and then another.

'Drink up,' she told him. 'Come along, you need it. You've had a shock.'

The wine tasted harsh and at first he found it hard to swallow. As glass succeeded glass, however, it became easier and easier.

'Can you keep a secret?' Angel asked when they had finished the starter. 'No one else knows the truth, but I want to tell you. Can I trust you?'

'Yes.' *Angel, you can always trust me.*

She stared into the candle flame. 'If my mother had lived, everything would have been different.'

Her mother, she told Eddie, had died when she was young, and her father had married again, to a wife who hated Angel.

'She was jealous, of course. Before she came along, my father and I had been very close. But she soon changed that. She made him hate me. Not just him, either – she worked on everyone we knew. In the end they all turned against me.'

Desperate to get away, Angel found work as an au pair, at first in Saudi Arabia and later in South America, mainly in Argentina. Then she became a nanny. Her employers had been delighted with her: she had stayed with one family for over five years. Finally, she had been overcome by a desire to come back to England.

'It gets to you sometimes: wanting to go back to your roots, to your past. Then I met Angie Wharton. She was English but she had been born in Argentina. Her parents emigrated there after the war. Angie wanted to come home, too. Not that she'd ever been here before.'

'How could this be her home?' asked Eddie owlishly. 'If she hadn't been here, I mean?'

'Home is where the heart is, Eddie. Anyway, Angie was a nursery nurse – she'd trained in the States before her parents died. We thought we'd travel home together, share a flat and so on. It's thanks to Angie that I know Mrs Hawley-Minton. Poor darling Angie.'

'What happened to her?'

'It was terribly sad.' Angel's eyes shone, and an orange candle flame flickered in each pupil. 'It hurts to talk about it.' She turned away and dabbed her eyes with a napkin.

'I'm sorry,' Eddie said, drunk enough to feel that he was somehow responsible for her sorrow. 'Let's talk about something else.'

'No. One can't hide away from things. It was one of those awful, stupid tragedies. Our first night in London. We'd only been here a few hours. Oh, it was my fault. I shall always blame myself. You see, I knew that Angie was – well, to be blunt, she was a lovely person but she had a weakness for alcohol.' Angel topped up Eddie's glass. 'Not like this – a glass or two over a meal. She'd go on binges and wake up the next day not knowing what had happened, where she'd been. It was terrible.'

Eddie pushed away his plate. 'What was?'

'It was on our first evening here,' Angel said, her eyes huge over the rim of the wine glass. 'Life can be so unfair sometimes. She'd been drinking on the plane. One after the other. When we got here, we found a hotel in Earl's Court and then we had a meal. Wine with the meal, of course. And then she wanted to carry on. "I want to celebrate," she kept saying. "I've come home." Poor Angie. I just couldn't cope. I was fagged out. So I went back to our room and went to bed. Next thing I knew it was morning and the manager was knocking on the door.'

The waiter brought their main course and showed a disposition to linger and chat.

'That'll be all, thank you,' said Angel haughtily. When she and Eddie were alone again she went on, 'I hate men like that. So pushy. Where was I?'

'The manager knocking on the door.'

The irritation faded from Angel's face. 'He had a

146

policewoman with him. Apparently Angie had gone up to the West End. Drinking steadily, of course. Somehow she managed to fall under a bus in Shaftesbury Avenue. There was a whole crowd coming out of a theatre, and people coming out of a pub, and a lot of pushing and shoving.' Angel sighed. 'She was killed outright.'

'How awful.' Eddie hesitated and then, feeling more was required, added, 'For you as much as her.'

'It's always harder for those who are left behind. No one else grieved for her. And then – well, I must admit I was tempted. I mean, who would it harm if I pretended to be Angie? Without a qualification I couldn't hope to get a decent job. It was so unfair – I knew more about the practical side of nursery nursing than she ever did, and I could easily read up the theory. And then she had this ready-made contact in Mrs Hawley-Minton, who'd never met her. So I told the police that Angie was me, and I pretended to be her.'

'But didn't they know her name? From her handbag, or something?' Sensing Angel's irritation at the interruption, he added weakly, 'I mean, they knew the hotel where she was staying.'

'She didn't have any identification on her – just cash, and a card with the name of the hotel.' Angel smiled sadly. 'She'd left her passport and so on with me, in case they got stolen.'

'Oh yes. I see now. But surely the passport photo –?'

'I had an old one in mine. And physically we weren't dissimilar.'

'There must have been an inquest.'

'Of course. I didn't tell any lies. I didn't want to. There was no need to.'

'Didn't they ask your father to identify the body?'

'He'd gone to work in America years before this happened. We'd lost touch completely. He simply couldn't be bothered with me.' Angel leant closer. 'The point is, Eddie, I know Angie would have wanted me to do what I did. Just as I would have wanted her to do the same if the positions had been reversed.'

'I think you were right.' Eddie's voice was thick and his

tongue felt a little too large for his mouth. 'I mean, it didn't hurt anyone.'

Briefly she patted his hand. 'Exactly. In a way, quite the reverse: I like to think I take my job very seriously, that I've made a difference for a lot of children.'

'What was your real name, then?'

'It doesn't matter. I gave it to Angie, and it's buried with her. Look forward, that's my motto. Don't look back. After the funeral I just waited until the dust had settled, and then I wrote to Mrs Hawley-Minton. And from there everything's gone like a dream.' She broke off and rested her head in her hands. 'Until now.' Her voice was almost inaudible. 'It's such a shame – just as everything was going so well.'

'I'll talk to my mother. I'll make her see sense.'

'You're a darling. But I don't think you'll succeed.'

'Why not?' He was almost shouting now and heads turned towards him.

'Hush, keep your voice down.'

'She wouldn't like us both to go away. She'd be lonely.'

'She's jealous of us. Don't you see? I wish I were richer – then we could get somewhere together, just you and me. As friends, I mean, just good friends. Would you like that?'

'Yes. Oh God, yes.'

There was a long pause, filled with the noise from the rest of the restaurant.

Angel picked up the bottle. 'Let's talk about something else.'

Eddie said, elaborately casual, 'What sort of children do you look after? You could always bring them to the house if you wanted. For tea, I mean. Make a sort of treat for them.'

'They often want to see where I live. But I don't think the idea would go down very well with your mother.'

Another silence stretched between them, heavy with silent suggestions and questions. Angel refilled their glasses.

'Drink up.' She held up her glass and clinked it against his. 'This may be our last chance of a celebration, so we'd better make the most of it.'

They finished that bottle before they left. By now Eddie was very drunk. Angel had to support him up the stairs. In

Frith Street the fresh air made his head spin and the light seemed very bright. He vomited partly into the gutter and partly on the bonnet of a parked car.

'There, there,' Angel said, patting his arm. 'Better out than in.' Later he heard her calling out in her patrician voice: 'Taxi! Taxi!'

Eddie remembered little more of the evening. Angel took him home. He could not remember seeing his mother – it was very late, so perhaps she was asleep.

'Come on,' she said when they got home. 'Up the wooden stairs to Bedfordshire.'

In his mind there was a picture of the palm of Angel's right hand extended towards him with three white tablets in the middle of it.

'Take these. Otherwise you're going to feel terrible in the morning.'

He must have managed to swallow them. After that he fell into a dark, silent pit. The first thing that made an impression on him, hours later, was the pain in his head. This was followed, after an immeasurable period of time, by the discovery that his bladder was extremely full. Later still, he realized that if anything the headache was worse. He dozed on, reluctant to leave the peace of the pit and physically unable to cope with the complicated business of getting out of bed.

The next time he woke the light on the other side of the curtains was much brighter, and the sight of it made his headache worse. Someone was shaking him.

'Eddie. Eddie.'

Shocked, he turned over. As far as he knew Angel had never been in his room before. What would his mother say when she found out?

Daylight poured through the open door. Angel shimmered so brightly that he could not look at her. She was wearing her long white robe and, though her face was immaculately made up, her hair was still confined to its snood. His eyelids began to droop.

'Eddie,' Angel called. 'Eddie, wake up.'

Seven

'. . . we are somewhat more than our selves in our sleeps, and the slumber of the body seems to be but the waking of the soul.'

Religio Medici, II, 11

1

Sally had not expected to sleep on Saturday night, the second since Lucy's disappearance. Part of her was determined to stay awake in case Lucy needed her. When David Byfield rang with the news that Michael was safe, however, tiredness dropped over her like a blanket.

Judith, the policewoman who had been on duty on Friday, and who had relieved Yvonne in the early evening, took advantage of this weakness. She persuaded Sally to go to bed, brought her a cup of cocoa and cajoled her into taking another sleeping tablet.

'It'll just send you to sleep,' Judith said, her Welsh voice rising and falling like a boat on a gentle swell. 'It's not one of these long-term ones that knock you out for ages. There's no point in you flogging yourself to keep awake.'

'But what if –?'

'If there's any news, I promise I'll fetch you straightaway.'

Sally took the tablet and drank her cocoa. Judith lingered for a moment, her eyes moving round the room.

'Do you want something to read? A magazine?'

'Could you pass me the books over there? The ones on the chest of drawers.'

Judith brought them to her. 'I'll look in a little later. See how you're doing.'

Sally nodded. The door closed behind Judith and she was at last alone. *Lucy.* Her eyes smarted with tears. She wanted to bang her head against the wall and scream and scream.

Miss Oliphant's books lay before her on the duvet: unfinished business that would normally have nagged Sally until she had dealt with it. She touched their covers one by one with the fingertips of her right hand. The Bible. The Prayer Book. The *Religio Medici.* The first two were bound in worn black leather, dry with age, their spines cracking and in places breaking away from the covers. Sally knew without looking that the paper would be so thin that it was almost invisible, and that the type would be so small that even someone with 20:20 vision would have an effort to read it. The *Religio Medici* had a larger typeface but the book was as battered as the others. All three smelled musty: tired, repulsive and unwashed. Sally shivered, reluctant to open any of them. Each book might be a miniature Pandora's Box full of unexpected evils.

'You mustn't blame yourself,' David Byfield had told her on the telephone.

'Then who else do you suggest? God?'

There was a silence at the other end. Then David said dryly, 'The person who took Lucy, perhaps.' He had overridden her attempt to interrupt. 'Concentrate on this: you mustn't worry about Michael. He'll sleep it off tonight and be with you tomorrow. You mustn't blame him, either, or yourself. Do you understand, Sally? It's most important. Nor must you stop hoping and praying.'

'I can't pray.'

'Of course you can.'

'Listen,' Sally began, 'I don't like –'

'Don't argue. Pray, go to bed and try to sleep. That is the best thing you can do.'

David Byfield's voice had sounded unexpectedly youthful over the phone. Like Derek Cutter, the old man had been in full pastoral mode, but his technique differed completely from Derek's: the former's had made her squirm; David's infuriated her. Talk about arrogant, Sally thought. What did he know about losing a child? The autocratic, patronizing bastard: who had given him the right to give her orders? She glowed with anger at the memory. Only then did it occur to her that David might have intended to achieve just that effect. He was a clever man, she conceded: an old fool, but still clever.

Her eyelids drooped, she slid down the bed. Endowed with a life of their own, her fingertips continued to stroke the binding of the three books. Audrey Oliphant, she thought sleepily: that's a strange name. Oliphant sounded like elephant. Had there once been a saint called Audrey? Then, as sudden and as violent as a flash of lightning, the knowledge that Lucy was not there slashed across Sally's mind. She sat up in bed and screamed. But the sound which came out of her mouth was no more than a whimper. She sank back against the pillows.

The movement had dislodged the books. The corner of a piece of card protruded from the *Religio Medici*. Sally pulled it out. It was a postcard of the west front of a great church, an old-fashioned colour photograph bleached with age. The building was familiar, but for the moment her mind refused to produce the name. She flipped the card over: Rosington Cathedral. There was writing, too. She squinted at the postmark. April 1963? 1968? It was addressed to 'Miss A. Oliphant, Tudor Cottage, The Green, Roth, Middlesex'. The name Roth was faintly familiar. Somewhere west of London? Near Heathrow Airport? She tried to decipher the message.

Too many tourists and more like Feb. than April but choral evensong was super. Our mutual friend still remembered. Small world! See you on Tuesday. Love, Amy.

A glimpse of other lives, Sally thought, of a time when Audrey Oliphant had perhaps been happy. Why do we even bother to try?

The card slipped from Sally's hand, and she sank into sleep. Thanks to the tablets she lay there for what she afterwards discovered was almost seven hours. For much of the time she moved restlessly through the dark phantasmagoria of her dreams, searching for Lucy. *This must be hell.* When she awoke, she swam up from a great depth, painfully conscious of changing pressure and a desperate need to reach the surface.

Lucy.

Still with her eyes closed, she made an enormous effort and gathered together the pain, the fear and the anger. She made a ball of it in her mind and kneaded it like dough. The ball was streaked with colours: red, brown, green and black, the colours of the emotions. She picked it up and threw it over her shoulder. Then she found the strength to open her eyes.

The bedroom was in darkness, apart from a band of light from the streetlamp slipping between the curtains and the red digits glowing on the clock display. Her pulse was racing, her mouth was dry and her eyelids were swollen and sore.

No Lucy, she thought, and no news of her either: they would have woken me.

Something had driven her awake. She had fled to consciousness as if to a refuge. Had something *down there* been even worse than this waking knowledge of Lucy's absence?

It was six-fifteen. She switched on the bedside light. Judith must have come in to turn it off last night. Miss Oliphant's books were in a neat pile on the bedside table. Sally lay back on the pillows, fighting the despair that threatened to overwhelm her. She tried to pray: it was no use – the lines were down, the airwaves jammed, or perhaps no one was bothering to answer at the other end. Pray, David Byfield had told her; pray and hope. She could do neither.

Gradually, fragments of her dreams slipped into her conscious mind. She glimpsed Miss Oliphant, attired in episcopal robes, standing in front of the high altar of a great church, which Sally knew must be Rosington Cathedral. Miss Oliphant was reading the Service of Commination from the office for Ash Wednesday in the Book of Common Prayer. *Is that why they've taken Lucy, because we were cursed?* But there are no woman bishops, Sally remembered thinking in her dream, not in this country. Have they changed the rules and not told me? In the dream world this possibility had been far more unsettling than the sight of Miss Oliphant, last seen dead in a hospital bed, apparently alive and well.

Another fragment of another dream had concerned David Byfield. He had seen an angel flying low over Magdalene Bridge in Cambridge.

'Real feathers,' he insisted to Sally and Michael, 'rather like a buzzard's.'

'But Lucy's *missing*!' Sally shouted.

'This is far more important.'

In a different part of the same dream, she and Uncle David were in a police station that smelled like a public lavatory. Chief Inspector Maxham leaned across the counter towards them, sucking in his breath, the air hissing between his tongue and his teeth.

'Couldn't have been an angel, sir. Angels don't exist.'

Sally was embarrassed. Grown men did not believe in angels. David became very angry with Maxham.

'Don't be naive, Officer. You're not competent to make wild assertions like that.'

The chief inspector smiled, revealing Yvonne's perfect teeth. 'You were dreaming.'

'I was not.'

Uncle David raised his arms and spread them wide. To her horror, Sally saw that his dark clerical suit was sprouting two rows of silvery-white feathers, one for each arm, running down the sleeves from shoulder to cuff. Uncle David was growing wings.

2

By eight o'clock, Sally had showered, dressed and had breakfast, which in her case consisted of three cups of coffee. She and Judith sat at the table in the living room. Judith tried to entice Sally's appetite from its hiding place by filling the flat with the smell of toasting bread and boiling herself an egg.

'No news is good news.' Judith's face creased with anxiety, and Sally felt guilty for spurning all those good intentions.

'Why don't you have a spoonful of cereal – something light like cornflakes?'

Sally reached for the coffee pot. 'Perhaps I'll have something later.'

'I expect you'll want to go to church this morning. I'm sure Yvonne will drive you.'

Bugger church. 'I don't want to, thanks.' Sally glimpsed, or imagined, hurt surprise in Judith's eyes. *Bugger Judith.* But it wasn't that easy to slough off the habit of being considerate. She heard herself saying soothingly, as if Judith, not herself, were the victim: 'It's kind of you to think of it, but I want to be here when my husband comes home.' *With his slippers warming by the fire, the newspaper on the arm of his chair and fresh tea in the pot?* 'And of course there might be some news.'

'I do understand.' Some of Judith's creases vanished. 'Won't be long now, will it? It will be easier with the two of you.'

Sally nodded and sipped her coffee. She doubted if it would be easier when Michael came. Nothing could be easy without Lucy. In the second place, there wouldn't be just the two of them because David Byfield was coming up to London too. In the third place, Michael, much as she loved him, was likely to create more problems than he solved. He habitually repressed his emotions, which meant when they did come to the surface they tended to be under great pressure and boiling hot.

'I wonder if the newspaper's come,' Sally said, her eyes meeting Judith's.

'I'll see, shall I?'

Before Sally could protest, Judith was on her feet and moving towards the door. A moment later she returned with the *Observer*.

'Would you like me to . . . ?'

Sally held out her hand for the newspaper. 'I'd rather find out myself.'

The story was confined to a few paragraphs on one of the inside pages. Lucy Appleyard, four, had disappeared from her child minder's; the police had not ruled out the possibility of foul play. Chief Inspector Maxham provided a guarded comment, which in effect said no more than that the police were investigating.

'The whole parish is praying for Lucy, Sally and Michael,' Derek Cutter had told the *Observer*'s reporter. 'Sally's a marvellous curate. She's already made her mark at St George's.'

Sally pushed the newspaper, open at the story, across the table. Judith read it quickly.

'Fair enough, I suppose,' she said brightly.

'I wonder what the tabloids are saying.' Sally winced. 'Perhaps it's better not to know.'

A key scraped in the lock of the door to the landing.

'That'll be Yvonne.' Judith gathered up her handbag, and risked a small joke. 'Just in time for the washing-up.'

The living-room door opened and Maxham came in. Yvonne's blonde head bobbed above his shoulder in the hallway behind him. Judith glanced at Sally and stiffened, ready to take action. Sally put her hand to her mouth and stared at Maxham.

'There's been a development, Mrs Appleyard.' Air hissed into his mouth. 'It may not be connected with Lucy, so don't get upset.'

Maxham came to a halt a few paces inside the room. Yvonne moved round Maxham and came to stand beside Sally. Judith edged closer. *My God, what are they? Wardresses?*

'Do you know a church called St Michael's?' he asked.

'Which one?' she snapped. 'There must be dozens.'

'In Beauclerk Place – west of Tottenham Court Road, near Charlotte Street.'

She shook her head, unable to speak.

'When the caretaker – churchwarden, would it be? – came to unlock this morning, he found a black bin-liner in the porch. I gather there are wrought-iron gates on the outer arch of the porch and a proper door inside. Someone must have slipped the bin-liner through the railings or maybe over the top.'

Get on with it. Sally watched Maxham's face, saw the pale eyes blinking behind the black-rimmed glasses and the muscles twitching at the corners of the mouth. With a shock she realized that he was stalling because he found this no easier to say than she did to hear.

Air hissed. 'The fact of the matter is, Mrs Appleyard, there were some clothes inside that bag. A pair of child's tights and a pair of boots. They seem to resemble the ones you described Lucy as wearing.'

'For Christ's sake – what about Lucy? Is she there, too?'

Maxham hesitated, greedily sucking in breath. 'Well,' he said slowly. 'Yes and no.'

3

St Michael's, Beauclerk Place, stood at the end of a cul-de-sac squeezed between higher, younger buildings to either side and behind it. It was a scruffy little building built of red brick, rectangular in design, with pinnacles at the corners and debased perpendicular windows. The visible windows were protected with iron grilles and decades of grime. The church was like a child who has never had quite enough love or money devoted to it.

The uniformed policeman pulled aside the barrier to allow Maxham's unmarked Rover to drive into the cul-de-sac. The buildings on either side were post-war, with plate-glass windows and Venetian blinds: probably offices, empty on a Sunday. As yet, there were no sightseers, but the police were ready. The car slid to a halt near the church. Two police cars were parked nearby.

The porch had been tacked on to the south-west corner of the church. The police had screened off the entrance. On the left of the porch was a row of iron railings which ended in a matching gate.

Sergeant Carlow switched off the engine. He looked over his shoulder at Maxham, sitting in the back of the car with Sally. Maxham nodded. Carlow extracted his long body from the car and walked towards the screened-off porch. His hips were unusually wide for a man's, Sally registered automatically, and as he walked his bottom swayed like a woman's.

Maxham folded his hands in his lap. 'Just going to see what's what.'

For a few seconds, silence spread through the car. In the front passenger seat Yvonne stared fixedly through the windscreen. The inspector rubbed his fingers on his thigh. Carlow reappeared. He looked paler than ever.

Maxham turned his head towards Sally. 'You sure you're up to it? Still time to change your mind.'

'I'm quite sure.'

'We can wait till your husband –'

'No.' *My baby.* 'Can we get it over with?'

Maxham nodded. The three of them got out of the car. It was suddenly cold: the wind funnelled through the cul-de-sac and escaped into the dull, grey sky. Sally forced herself to look away from the porch. She noticed that the gap between the railings and the church had silted up with a thick mulch of empty lager cans and fast-food wrappings, and that the gate at the north-west corner guarded the entrance to a narrow alleyway between the north side of the church and the adjacent building.

According to a notice on the wall, the Anglicans now shared St Michael's with a Russian Orthodox congregation and a Methodist one. Otherwise it would probably have been made redundant long ago. Perhaps that would have been better than this unloved half-life.

Half a life, half a person?

Sally found herself staring at the porch. From what she could see above the screens, it was about six feet wide and nine feet deep; it was covered with a pitched roof of cracked pantiles streaked with lichen and moss.

Maxham put a hand under Sally's elbow. They walked towards the screen. Yvonne and Sergeant Carlow fell in behind. A one-legged pigeon with frayed feathers hopped across their path. *An amputee.* To those in fear, creation was nothing but a mass of portents. Sally pulled away from Maxham and thrust her hands deep into the pockets of her long navy-blue coat. They rounded the corner of the screen.

The light dazzled her. For a moment she stopped to blink and stare. Two floodlights gave the interior of the porch a hallucinogenic clarity. The outer gates were open. On either side were benches, with notice boards above. It should have been sheltered in there, but the notices fluttered and rustled in the wind. A photographer was shooting away seemingly at random, the shutter falling in a stammering rhythm like irregular rifle fire.

The little space was crowded. Beside the photographer, another scene-of-the-crime officer was dictating into a hand-held machine. A third was measuring the dimensions of the porch. A fourth man, with a bag next to him, was kneeling in the far left-hand corner. Sally glimpsed shiny black plastic.

'This is Dr Ferguson,' Maxham said. 'Mrs Appleyard.'

The kneeling man half-turned and nodded, acknowledging the introduction.

Sally swallowed. 'Where – ?'

'Here, Mrs Appleyard.' The doctor rose to his feet in one supple movement. He was younger than Sally, fresh-faced, with a healthy tan and a Liverpool accent. His eyes slid to Maxham, then back to Sally. 'Are you sure you want to see this?'

'Yes.' With an effort she kept her voice low, concealing the scream inside her head.

Ferguson nodded. 'Over here.'

He gestured not as Sally had expected towards the black plastic on the floor behind him, but to a plastic sheet on the bench on the left. Two L-shaped ridges showed underneath in relief, each about twenty inches long. Automatically Sally looked up, unable to keep her eyes on the two ridges. She examined the notice immediately above, noted with furious concentration the yellowing paper, the nearly illegible typed letters and the circular rust stains left by vanished drawing pins.

She was aware that Maxham and Yvonne had moved a step nearer and were now standing directly behind her. The other police officers had stopped what they had been doing. The doctor was watching her, too. All of them were in position, she realized, ready to catch her when she fainted. Ironically, the thought braced her.

'You're ready?'

Ferguson drew back the plastic sheet. Beneath was a transparent plastic bag with a neatly written tag. The bag contained a pair of small, white, woollen tights with ribbing on the legs. For an instant they looked as if they had been stuffed with kapok like cuddly toys. The tights were lying in a reddish-brown puddle of blood. Sally compressed her lips and swallowed. She thought of meat from a supermarket defrosting on its plastic tray. Blood need only be blood: nothing more, nothing less: largely composed of water, a means of supplying living tissues with nutrients and oxygen and of removing waste products. Once separated from the pumping heart, it was nothing but a reddish-brown liquid.

Drink ye all of this; for this is my blood.

'Mrs Appleyard?' Ferguson murmured. 'Steady, now.'

'I'm fine.'

The waist of the tights lay flat against the plastic. There was no kapok in there. The blood was thickest from the top of the thighs to the waist of the tights. You could no longer see the whiteness of the wool.

O Lamb of God –

Sally's eyes travelled down the length of the legs to the feet. The feet were wearing miniature red cowboy boots. They were dainty things, the leather supple, a delicate pattern stitched in black thread at the ankles. In the toe of the nearer one was a shallow cut about half an inch in length.

You naughty girl. Have you any idea how much those cost?

'The ankle boots are Italian.' As Sally paused, she heard a faint, collective sigh behind her. 'They're made by someone with a name like Rassi. I bought them at a shop in Covent Garden about two months ago.' The boots had been an extravagance that Sally had been unable to resist. She had put towards the cost the money that David Byfield had sent for Lucy's last birthday. Michael had been furious. 'I wrote Lucy's name on the back of the maker's label.' Not the sort of boots you could afford to lose, she had thought. 'As for the tights, I'm pretty sure she was wearing ones like that on Friday. It's hard to be absolutely certain because of the blood.'

Lucy's blood. Oh Christ – can't you stop this?

They had known what Lucy was wearing, down to the maker's name in the boots. But they needed to be sure. *Sure?* Gingerly, Sally stretched out her hand towards the two legs.

'Mrs Appleyard –' the doctor began.

Sally ignored him. She touched the leg very gently with the tip of the index finger of her right hand. 'It's *icy.*'

'It may have been deep-frozen until recently.' Maxham's voice was harsher than usual.

'Like the hand they found in Kilburn Cemetery?'

'Yes.'

What struck Sally now was the silence. Here they were in one of the world's great cities, in the middle of a pool of silence. There must have been at least a dozen police officers within thirty yards and they all seemed to be holding their breath.

Dear God, the pain. Had they had the decency to kill her first, and kill her swiftly?

Sally ran her fingertip delicately down the leg, following the curve of the knee, on down the shin to the top of the boot. She bowed her head.

'Mrs Appleyard?' Maxham sounded anxious, with just a hint of exasperation. 'That's all we need, thank you. You've been very helpful. Very brave.'

Sally slipped the thumb and forefinger of her hand right round the ankle and squeezed it, through the plastic bag and the leather. She felt the hardness of the bone underneath.

'Mrs Appleyard,' said Ferguson, 'there's a possibility of postmortem damage. That could give us problems at the autopsy.'

Yvonne put her hand on Sally's arm. Sally shook her off. Someone snarled like a dog deprived of a bone. *Me.* Puzzled, she ran her hand round the bend of the L and on to the foot itself. Maxham grabbed her other arm. She felt the toes. It wasn't possible. Yvonne and Maxham pulled her gently back.

'I'm sorry, Mrs Appleyard.' Maxham allowed his exasperation to show plainly. 'Now we'll get you home. Your husband will be back soon.'

I don't want my husband: I want Lucy.

Then Sally saw how the impossible might have happened. *Must* have happened.

'The legs are too long,' she said slowly. 'So they aren't Lucy's.'

4

Maxham allowed Sally to sit inside the church because he could not think of a valid reason to prevent her. Besides, she knew, he had assumed that she wanted to pray, a possibility which embarrassed him. His embarrassment was a weapon she could use against him.

It was very cold. The gratings set into the cheap red tiles suggested underfloor heating, but either the system didn't work or the people using the church could not afford to run it. The silence pressed down on her. The air smelt faintly of incense. The brass of the lectern was smudged and dull. She glanced up at the roof, plain pitch pine, full of darkness, shadows and spiders' webs.

Her eyes drifted along the line of the roof to the east wall. A large picture in a gilt frame hung above the altar. The light was poor and the paint was dingy. Maybe the Last Judgement, Sally thought, a cheap and nasty Victorian copy if the rest of the church was anything to go by. Christ in Glory in the centre of the picture, a river of fire spewing forth at his feet; flanked by angels and apostles; and below them the souls of the righteous queuing for admission to paradise; and the archangel with the scales – Michael or Gabriel? – weighing the souls of the risen dead. A picture story for children afraid of the dark.

And Lucy? Was she afraid? Or already dead?

Sally let out her breath in a long, ragged sigh. *Don't think about that. Think about the good news.* The legs were not Lucy's, any more than the hand had been. They were the wrong shape, wrong size, wrong everything. Lucy's were thinner and less muscular, and her feet were much smaller than the feet which had been stuffed into Lucy's red Italian cowboy boots.

At first Maxham had not believed Sally. Even Yvonne and Dr Ferguson had been sceptical. They had all been suspicious of her certainty, willing to attribute it to wishful thinking.

I'm her mother, damn you. Of course I know.

Sally bowed her head. Once again she tried to pray, to thank God that the legs were not Lucy's, and that therefore Lucy might still be alive. But her mind swerved away from prayer like a horse refusing a jump. An invisible barrier hemmed her in, enclosing her in her private misery. It was as if the church itself had surrounded her with a wall of glass which cut off the lines of communication. For an instant she thought she glimpsed the building's personality: sour, malevolent, unhappy – a bricks-and-mortar equivalent of Audrey Oliphant, the woman who had cursed her.

What's happening to me? Churches don't have personalities.

Gratitude was in any case misplaced. The legs had belonged to another child. Should she thank God for the other child's death and mutilation? Beside that terrible fact, the goodness of God receded to invisibility.

Sally opened her eyes, desperate to find a distraction. On the wall nearest to her hung a board with the names of the incumbents inscribed in flaking gold letters, beginning with a Reverend Francis Youlgreave MA in 1891 and ending, seven names later, with the Reverend George Bagnall, who had left the parish in 1970. It was a big board and three-quarters of it was blank. No doubt Youlgreave and his immediate successors had imagined that the list of incumbents would stretch on and on, and that the building would always be a place of worship.

Things could never get better, she thought bitterly, only worse. How those long-gone priests would have hated the thought of her, a woman in orders. And what was the purpose of it anyway? It now seemed absurd that she had fought so hard to be ordained, and that she should devote her life to playing a minor part in the affairs of a dying cult. So far the effect had been wholly evil: she had ruined her own life, damaged Michael's and abandoned Lucy. She was to blame.

She was too angry with herself even to share the blame with God. Oh yes, he was still there. But he didn't matter any more. If the truth were told, he never had. He didn't care.

You mustn't blame yourself. David Byfield's words twisted in her memory and took on a bitter and no doubt intended irony. *He* blamed her. He always had blamed her, the woman who had committed the double sin of wanting to be a priest and taking away his Michael. She wondered yet again what bound the two men so tightly together. Whatever the reason, now she had her reward for breaking into their charmed relationship, and no doubt David was rejoicing.

Sally stared at the list of priests. The church's dedication was written in gothic capitals at the head of the board: ST MICHAEL AND ALL ANGELS. Her mind filled with a thrumming sound, as though a thousand birds had risen into the air and were flying across the mud flats of an estuary. Her husband's name was Michael, and the church was dedicated to Michael. Just a coincidence, surely. It was a common name. Only a paranoiac would think otherwise.

And yet –

This evil was beginning to take shape. It had been planned and executed over a long period. The brown-skinned hand in Kilburn Cemetery and the bleeding legs in the porch must be connected with each other because there were so many correspondences: both had been deep-frozen; both were parts of a child's anatomy; both had been left in places which were sacred; and they had been found within twenty-four hours of each other. It was theoretically possible that the two were separate incidents – that the story of the severed hand had inspired a copycat crime – but this seemed less likely. The boots and the tights left no doubt at all that Lucy was at the mercy of the same person. Had there been a message there?

Lucy's dismembered, too.

Whoever had taken her had not done so merely for sexual gratification or from emotional inadequacy; or if he had, that was only a part of it. What lay in the porch had been designed to shock. And the urge to shock had been so great that it had outweighed the risk of being seen.

The wings rustled and whirred. *Not just to shock: also to tease.*

Had Lucy been chosen not for herself but because she was a policeman's child? Sally remembered Frank Howell's feature on St George's in the *Evening Standard*. Perhaps someone had read it who had a grudge against the police in general or Michael in particular.

Then why not leave the remains outside a police station? Why the church today and the cemetery yesterday? Perhaps the hatred was aimed at God rather than the police. A further possibility struck her: that this might be a more extreme form of the loathing which had gripped Audrey Oliphant; and in that case it followed that Sally herself, by wanting to become a priest, could have been directly responsible for bringing down on Lucy's head the attention of whoever had taken her.

'I'm getting paranoid,' she told herself, her voice thin and childlike in the empty spaces of the cold church; she shocked herself, for she had not realized that she had spoken aloud. 'Stop it, stop it.'

The thoughts spurted through her mind – fragmented and disjointed. The noise of the wings grew louder until it obliterated all other sounds and swamped her ability to think. The thrumming was so loud that Sally hardly felt like Sally: she was merely the sound of the wings. She drowned in the sound, as if in the black mud of the estuary.

'No. No. Leave me alone.'

The thrumming grew even louder. It was dark. She could no longer breathe. She heard a great crack, so loud that for a moment it dominated the thrumming of the wings. Cold air swirled around her.

'That's quite enough.' The voice was furious and male. 'This must stop at once.'

Sally opened her eyes and turned her head. Through her tears she saw Michael's godfather, David Byfield, stalking down the aisle towards her.

Eight

1

'Lucy's as good as gold with me.' Angel rinsed the soap from
the back of Lucy's neck. 'Aren't you, poppet?'

Lucy did not reply. She looked very young and small in
the bath, her body partly obscured by a shifting mound of
foam. She was staring at a blue plastic boat containing two
yellow ducks; the boat bobbed up and down in the triangular
harbour created by her legs. Her wet hair, plastered to her
skull, was as black as polished ebony.

'It's the first of December today,' Angel went on, briskly
sponging Lucy's back. 'Did you know, if you say "White rabbits" on the first of the month and make a silent wish, then
the wish will come true? Well, that's what some people say.'

Eddie thought that Lucy's lips might have trembled, and
that perhaps she was saying 'White Rabbits' to herself and
making a wish. *I want Mummy.* She had had very little to eat
for over thirty-six hours and this was beginning to show in
her appearance. Children, Eddie had noticed, reacted very
quickly to such changes. Now it was Sunday morning, and
Lucy's shoulders looked bonier than they had done on Friday
evening, and her stomach was flat. She was still listless from
the medication, and perhaps from the shock, too, otherwise
Angel would not have risked taking her out of the soundproofed basement to give her a bath.

166

(This had been Angel's rule since the incident with Suki, a sly girl who acted as if butter wouldn't melt in her mouth until Angel went out to fetch a towel, leaving her alone with Eddie: as soon as the door closed, Suki had bitten Eddie's hand and screamed like a train. After that, Angel gave their little visitors regular doses of Phenergan syrup, which kept them nicely drowsy. If a visitor became seriously upset, Angel quietened her with a dose of diazepam, originally prescribed for Eddie's mother.)

'There's a good girl. Stand up now and Angel will dry you.' With Angel's help, Lucy struggled to her feet. Water and foam dripped down her body. Eddie stared at the pink, glistening skin and the cleft between her legs.

'Uncle Eddie will pass the towel.'

He hurried to obey. There had been an unmistakable note of irritation in Angel's voice, perhaps brought on by tiredness. He noticed dark smudges under her eyes. He knew she had gone out the previous evening and had not returned until well after midnight. Eddie had tried the door to the basement while she was out, only to find that it was locked.

Angel wrapped the large pink towel, warm from the radiator, around Lucy's body, lifted her out of the bath and sat her on her knee. Eddie thought they made a beautiful picture, a Pre-Raphaelite Virgin and child: Angel in her long white robe, her shining hair flowing free; and Lucy small, thin and sexless, swaddled in the towel, sitting on Angel's lap and enclosed by her arms. He turned away. His head hurt this morning, and his throat was dry.

The clothes they had bought for Lucy were waiting on the chair. Among them was a dark-green dress from Laura Ashley, with a white lace collar, a smocked front and ties at each side designed to form a bow at the back. Angel liked her girls to look properly feminine. Boys were boys, she once told Eddie, girls were girls, and it was both stupid and unnatural to pretend otherwise.

'Perhaps Lucy would like to play a game with me when she's dressed,' Eddie suggested.

The girl glanced at him, and a frown wrinkled her forehead.

'She might like to see the you-know-what.'

'The *what*?' Angel said.

Eddie shielded his mouth with his hand, leaned towards her and whispered, 'The conjuring set.'

He had bought it yesterday morning and he was longing to see Lucy's reaction: all children liked presents, and often they showed their gratitude in delightful ways.

Angel rubbed Lucy's hair gently. 'Another day, I think. Lucy's tired. Aren't you, my pet?'

Lucy looked up at her, blinking rapidly as her eyes slid in and out of focus. 'I want to go home. I want Mummy. I –'

'Mummy and Daddy had to go away. Not for long. I told you, they asked me to look after you.'

The frown deepened. For Lucy, Eddie guessed, Angel's certainty was the only fixed point among the confusion and the anxiety.

'Now, now, poppet. Let's see a nice big smile. We don't like children who live on Sulky Street, do we?'

'Perhaps if we played a game, it would take Lucy's mind off things.' Eddie removed his glasses and polished the lenses with the corner of a towel. 'It would be a distraction.'

'No.' Angel picked up the little vest. 'Lucy's not well enough for that at present. When we've finished in here, I'm going to make her a nice drink and sit her on my knee and read a nice book to her.'

To his horror, Eddie felt tears filling his eyes. It was so unfair. 'But with the others, we always –'

Angel coughed, stopping him in mid-sentence. It was one of her rules that they should never let a girl know that there had been others. But when Eddie looked at her he was surprised to see that she was smiling.

'Lucy isn't like the others,' she said, her eyes meeting Eddie's. 'We understand each other, she and I.' Her lips brushed the top of Lucy's head. 'Don't we, my poppet?'

What about me?

Eddie held his tongue. A moment later, Angel asked him to go down and warm some milk and turn up the heating. He went downstairs, the jealousy churning angrily and impotently inside him as pointlessly as an engine in neutral revving into the red. The two of them made such a beautiful picture, he accepted that, the Virgin and child, beautiful and hurtful.

He altered the thermostat for the central heating and put the milk on the stove. His headache was worsening. He stared into the pan, at the shifting disc of white, and felt his eyes slipping out of focus.

Virgin and child: two was company in the Holy Family. Poor old Joseph, permanently on the sidelines, denied even the privilege of making the customary biological contribution to family life. The mother and child made a whole, self-contained and exclusive, Mary and the infant Jesus, the Madonna and new-born king, the Handmaiden of the Lord with the Christ Child.

Where did that leave number three? Somewhere in the crowd scene at the stable. Or leading the donkey. Negotiating with the innkeeper. No doubt paying the bills. Acting as a combination of courier and transport manager and meal ticket. No one ever said what happened to old Joseph. No one cared. Why should they? He didn't count.

What about me?

It seemed to Eddie that almost all his life he had been condemned to third place. Look at his parents, for example. They might not have liked each other, but their needs interlocked and they excluded Eddie. Even when his father allowed Eddie to join in the photographs, Stanley's interest was always focused on the little girl, and the little girl always paid more attention to Stanley than to Eddie; they treated him as part of the furniture, no more important than the smelly old armchair.

When Stanley died, the pattern continued. His mother hadn't wasted much time before deciding to find a lodger. But why? There had been enough money for them to continue living at Rosington Road by themselves. They could have managed on Thelma's widow's pension from the Paladin, her state pension, and what Eddie received from the DSS. They would have had to live frugally, but it would have been perfectly possible with just the two of them. But no. His mother had wanted someone else, not him. She found

169

Angel and there was the irony: because Angel preferred Eddie, at least for a time.

Only Alison and Angel had ever taken him seriously. But Alison had gone away and now Angel no longer needed him because she had Lucy instead. But what made Lucy so special?

Eddie's eyes widened. The milk was swelling. Its surface was pocked and pimpled like a lunar landscape. A white balloon pushed itself over the rim of the saucepan. The boiling milk spat and bubbled. He lunged at the handle of the saucepan and a smell of burning filled the air.

2

I blame you.

Mummy, Mum, Ma, Mother, Thelma. Eddie could not remember calling his mother by name, not to her face.

Angel had taken charge when Thelma died. Eddie had to admit that she had worked miracles. When he finally managed to drag himself downstairs on the morning of his mother's death, he had sat down at the kitchen table, in the heart of Thelma's domain, and laid his head on his arms. Still in the grip of an immense hangover, he hadn't wanted to think because thinking hurt too much.

He had heard Angel coming downstairs and into the room; he had smelled her perfume and heard water gushing from the tap.

'Eddie. Sit up, please.'

Wearily he obeyed.

She placed a glass of water in front of him. 'Lots of fluids.' She handed him a sachet of Alka-Seltzers which she had already opened to save him the trouble. 'Don't worry if you're sick. It usually helps to vomit.'

He dropped the tablets one by one into the water and watched the bubbles rising. 'What happened to her?'

'I suspect it was a heart attack. Just as she expected.'

'What?'

'You knew she had a heart condition, didn't you?'

A new pain penetrated Eddie's headache. 'She never told me.'

'Probably she didn't want to worry you. Either that or she thought you'd guessed.'

'But how could I?' Eddie wailed.

'Why do you think she gave up smoking? Doctor's orders, of course. And those tablets she took, not to mention her spray . . . Didn't you ever notice how breathless she got?'

'But she's been like that for years. Not so bad, perhaps, but –'

'And the colour she went sometimes? As soon as I saw that I knew there was a heart problem. Now drink up.'

He drank the mixture. At one point he thought he might have to make a run for the sink, but the moment passed.

'It's a pity she didn't change her diet and take more exercise,' Angel went on. 'But there. You can't teach an old dog new tricks, can you?'

'I wish – I wish I'd known.'

'Why? What could you have done? Given her a new set of coronary arteries?'

He tried to rid his mind of the figure on the bed in the front room upstairs. Never large, Thelma had shrunk still further in death. He glanced at Angel, who was making coffee. She was quite at home here, he thought, as if this were her own kitchen.

'What happened last night?'

She turned, spoon in hand. 'You don't remember? I'm not surprised. The wine had quite an effect on you, didn't it? I didn't realize you had such a weak head.'

He remembered the basement restaurant in Soho. Snatches of their conversation came back to him. The silk tie, blue with green stripes. Himself vomiting over the shiny bonnet of a parked car. Orange candle flames dancing in Angel's pupils. The three white tablets in the palm of her hand.

'Did you see my mother last night?'

'No.'

'So what happened when we got back?'

'Nothing. I imagine she must have been asleep. I took you upstairs and gave you some aspirin. You went out like a light. So I covered you up and went to bed myself.'

'You're sure?'

Angel stared at him. 'I'm not in the habit of lying, Eddie.'

He dropped his eyes. 'Sorry.'

'All right. I understand. It's never easy when a parent dies. One doesn't act rationally.'

She paused to pour water into a coffee pot which Eddie had never seen before. He sniffed. Real coffee, which meant that it was Angel's. His mother had liked only instant coffee.

A moment later, Angel said in a slow, deliberate voice: 'We had a pleasant meal out last night. Your mother was asleep when we got home. We went to bed. When I got up this morning I was surprised that your mother wasn't up before me. So I tapped on her door to see if she was all right. There was no answer so I went in. And there she was, poor soul. I made sure she was dead. Then I woke you and phoned the doctor.'

Eddie rubbed his beard, which felt matted. 'When did it happen?'

'Who knows? She might have been dead when we got home. She was certainly very cold this morning.'

'You don't think . . . ?'

'What?'

'That what happened yesterday might have had something to do with it?'

'Don't be silly, Eddie.' Angel rested her hands on the table and stared down at him, her face calm and beautiful. 'Put that right out of your mind.'

'If I'd stayed with her, talked with her –'

'It wouldn't have done any good. Probably she would have made herself even more upset.'

'But –'

'Her death could have happened at any time. And don't forget, it's psychologically typical for survivors to blame themselves for the death of a loved one.'

'Shouldn't we mention it to the doctor? The fact she was . . . upset, I mean.'

172

'Why should we? What on earth would be the point? It's a complete irrelevance.' Angel turned away to pour the coffee. 'In fact, it's probably better *not* to mention it. It would just confuse the issue.'

3

The dreams came later, after Thelma's funeral, and continued until the following summer. (Oddly enough, Eddie had the last one just before the episode with Chantal.) They bore a family resemblance to one another: different versions of different parts of the same story.

In the simplest form, Thelma was lying in the single bed, her small body almost invisible under the eiderdown and the blankets. Eddie was a disembodied presence near the ceiling just inside the doorway. He could not see his mother's face. The skull was heavy and the two pillows were soft and accommodating. The ends of the pillows rose like thick white horns on either side of the invisible face.

Sometimes it was dark, sometimes misty; sometimes Eddie had forgotten his glasses. Was another pillow taken from Stanley's bed and clamped on top of the others? Then what? The body twitching almost imperceptibly, hampered by the weight of the bedclothes and by its own weakness?

More questions followed, because the whole point of this series of dreams was that nothing could ever be known for certain. What chance would Thelma have had against the suffocating weight pressing down on her? Had she cried out? Almost certainly the words would have been smothered by the pillow. And if any sound seeped into the silent bedroom, who was there to hear it? Who, except Eddie?

There had not been an inquest. Thelma's doctor had no hesitation in signing the medical certificate of cause of death. His patient was an elderly widow with a history of heart problems. He had seen her less than a week before. According to her son and her lodger she had complained of chest pains during the day before her death. That night her heart had given up the unequal struggle. When he saw the body, she was still holding her glyceryl trinitrate spray, which suggested that she might have been awake when the attack began.

'Just popped off,' the doctor told Eddie. 'Could have happened any time. I doubt if she felt much and it was over very quickly. Not a bad way to go, all things considered – I wouldn't mind it myself.'

4

After Thelma had gone, 29 Rosington Road became a different house. On the morning after the funeral Angel and Eddie wandered through the rooms, taking stock and marvelling at the possibilities that had suddenly opened up. For Eddie, Thelma's departure had a magical effect: the rooms were larger; much of the furniture in the big front bedroom, robbed of the presence which had lent it significance, had become shabby and unnecessary; and his and Angel's footsteps on the stairs were brisk and resonant.

'I think I could do something with this,' Angel said as she examined the basement.

'Why?' Eddie glanced at the ceiling, at the rest of the house. 'We've got all that room upstairs.'

'It would be somewhere for me.' She laid her hand briefly on his arm. 'Don't misunderstand me, but I do like to be by myself sometimes. I'm a very solitary person.'

'You could have the back bedroom.'

'It's too small.' Angel stretched out her arms. 'I need space. It wouldn't be a problem, would it?'

'Oh no. Not at all. I just – I just wasn't quite clear what you wanted.'

There was a burst of muffled shouting. Eddie guessed that it emanated from the basement flat next door, which was occupied by a young married couple who conducted their relationship as if on the assumption that they were standing on either side of a large windy field, a situation for which each held the other to blame.

'Wouldn't this be too noisy for you?' he asked.

'Insulation: that's the answer. It would be a good idea to dry-line the walls in any case. Look at the damp over there.'

As they were speaking, she moved slowly around the basement, poking her head into the empty coal hole and the disused scullery, peering into cardboard boxes, rubbing a clear spot in the grime in the rear window, trying the handle of the sealed door to the garden. She paused by the old armchair and wiped away some of the dust with a tissue.

'That's nice. Late nineteenth century? It's been terribly mistreated, though. But look at the carving on the arms and legs. Beautiful, isn't it? I think it's rosewood.'

Eddie remembered the smell of the material and the feeling of a warm body pressed against his. 'I was thinking we should throw it out.'

'Definitely not. We'll have it reupholstered. Something plain – claret-coloured, perhaps.'

'Won't all this cost too much?'

'We'll manage.' Angel smiled at him. 'I've got a little money put by. It will be my way of contributing. We'll need to find a builder, of course. Do you know of anyone local?'

'There's Mr Reynolds.' Eddie thought of Jenny Wren. 'He lives in the council flats behind. The one with the geraniums.'

Angel wrinkled her nose. 'So his wife's the bird-watcher?'

'He's nicer than she is. But he may be retired by now.'

'I'd prefer an older man. Someone who would take a pride in the job.'

Angel decided that they should leave a decent interval – in this case a fortnight – between Thelma's death and contacting Mr Reynolds. She spent the time making detailed plans of what she wanted done. Eddie was surprised both by the depth of her knowledge and the extent of her plans.

'We'll put a freezer in the scullery. One of those big chest ones. It will pay for itself within a year or so. We can take advantage of all the bargains.'

She examined the little coal cellar next to the scullery with particular care, taking measurements and examining the floor, walls and ceiling. There was a hatch to the little forecourt in front of the house, but Stanley had sealed this by screwing two batons across the opening.

'This would make a lovely shower room. If we tile the floor and walls we needn't have a shower stall. We can have the shower fixed to the wall. I wonder if there's room for a lavatory, too.'

'Do we really need it?'

'It would be so much more convenient.'

At length Eddie phoned Mr Reynolds and asked if he would be interested in renovating the basement.

'I don't do much now,' Mr Reynolds said.

'Never mind. Is there anyone you'd recommend?'

'I didn't say I wouldn't do it. I like to keep my hand in, particularly when it's a question of obliging neighbours. Why don't I come round and have a shufti?'

Ten minutes later Mr Reynolds was on the doorstep. He seemed to have changed very little in all the years Eddie had known him. He found it hard to keep his eyes off Angel, whom he had not previously met. They took him down to the basement.

'We were thinking that we might let it as a self-contained flat,' Angel told him.

'Oh aye.'

'There's more that needs doing than meets the eye. That's the trouble with these older houses, isn't it?'

Mr Reynolds agreed. As time went by, Eddie realized that Mr Reynolds would have agreed to almost anything Angel said. Soon they were discussing insulation, dry-lining and replastering. Angel said that the tenants might be noisy so they decided to insulate the ceiling as well. They touched lightly on plumbing, wiring and decorating. Neither of them mentioned money. Within minutes of Mr Reynolds's arrival they both seemed to take it for granted that he would be doing the work.

'Don't you worry, Miss Wharton. This will be a Rolls-Royce job by the time we're done.'

'Please call me Angela.'

Mr Reynolds stared at his hands and changed the subject by suggesting that they start by hiring a skip. Neither then nor later would he call Angel anything but Miss Wharton. His was a form of love which took refuge in formality.

Mr Reynolds did most of the work himself, sub-contracting only the electrical and plumbing jobs. It took him over two months. During this time a friendship developed between the three of them, limited to the job which had brought them together but surprisingly intimate; narrow but deep. Mr Reynolds worked long hours and, when reminded, invoiced Eddie for small sums. Angel paid the balance with praise.

'I'm not sure I can bear to let this room, Mr Reynolds. You've made it such a little palace that I think I might use it as my study.'

Mr Reynolds grunted and turned away to search for something in his tool bag.

The weeks passed, and gradually the jobs were completed. First the new floor, then the ceiling, then the walls. A hardwood door was made to measure, as was the long, double-glazed window overlooking the back garden.

'Beginning to come together now, isn't it?' Mr Reynolds said, not once but many times, hungry for Angel's praise.

If Mr Reynolds was curious about the relationship between Angel and Eddie, he never allowed his curiosity to become obtrusive. Almost certainly he guessed that Eddie and Angel were not living together as man and wife. Nor did Angel behave like a lodger: she behaved like the mistress of the house. Eddie came to suspect that Mr Reynolds did not ask questions because he did not want to hear the answers. Mr Reynolds was never disloyal to his wife, but from hints dropped here and there it became clear that he did not enjoy being at home; he liked this job which kept him out of the wet, earned him money and allowed him to see Angel almost every day.

When he had finished, the basement was dry and as airless as a sealed tomb. The acoustics were strange: sounds had a deadened quality. It seemed to Eddie that the insulation absorbed and neutralized all the emotion in people's voices.

'It's perfect,' Angel told Mr Reynolds.

'Tell me if you need any more help.' The tips of his ears glowed. The three of them were sitting round the kitchen table with mugs of tea while Eddie wrote another cheque. 'By the way, what did happen to all those old dolls' houses?'

Eddie glanced up at him. 'My father used to raffle them at work for charity.'

'Which reminds me,' Angel said. 'Some of his tools are still in the cupboard downstairs. Would you have a use for any of them, Mr Reynolds?'

The flush spread to his face. 'Well – I'm not sure.'

'Do have a look. I know Eddie would like them to go to a good home.'

'I remember your dad making those dolls' houses,' Mr Reynolds said to Eddie. 'Your mum and dad used to ask our Jenny round to look at them. She loved it.' He chuckled, cracks appearing in the weathered skin around his eyes and mouth. 'Do you remember?'

'I remember. She used to bring her dolls to see the houses, too.'

'So she did. I'd forgotten that. And look at her now: three children and a place of her own to look after. It's a shame about Kevin. But there – it's the modern way, I'm afraid.'

'Kevin?' Angel said.

Mr Reynolds took a deep breath. Angel smiled at him.

'Kevin – Jen's husband. Well, sort of husband.' He hesitated. 'It's not general knowledge, but he's a bad lot, I'm afraid. Still, he's gone now. Least said, soonest mended.'

'I'm so sorry. Children are such a worry, aren't they?'

'He ran off with another woman when she was expecting her third. What can you do? My wife doesn't like it known, by the way. You'll understand, I'm sure.'

'Of course.' Angel glanced at Eddie. 'You and Jenny were friends when you were children, weren't you?'

Eddie nodded. He'd given Angel an edited version of his relationship with Jenny, such as it had been.

'Your mum and dad were very kind to her,' Mr Reynolds went on, apparently without irony. 'And she wasn't the only one, they say. Maybe they'd have liked a little sister for you, eh?'

'Very likely,' Eddie agreed.

'And he took some lovely photographs, too,' said the little

builder, still rambling down Memory Lane. 'He gave us one of Jenny: curled up in a big armchair, looking like butter wouldn't melt in her mouth. We had it framed. We've still got it in the display cabinet.'

'Photographs?' Angel said, turning to Eddie. 'I didn't know your father took photographs.'

Eddie pushed the cheque across the table to Mr Reynolds. 'Here you are.'

'Do you have some of them still?' Angel smiled impartially at the two men. 'I love looking at photographs.'

5

Angel questioned Eddie minutely about his past, which he found flattering because no one else had ever done so. The questions came by fits and starts and over a long period of time. Eddie discovered that telling Angel about the difficulties and unfairness he had suffered made the burden of them easier to bear. He mentioned this phenomenon.

'Nothing unusual about that, Eddie. That's why so many people find psychotherapy appealing. That's why confession has always been such a widespread practice among Catholics.'

Since his father's death, Eddie had kept the surviving photographs in a locked suitcase under his bed. Angel cajoled him into showing them to her. They sat at the kitchen table and he lifted them out, one by one. The photographs smelled of the past, tired and musty.

'How pretty,' Angel commented when she saw the first nude. 'Technically quite impressive.'

In the end she saw them all, even the ones with Eddie, even the one with Alison.

What a Little Tease!

'That one's Mr Reynolds's daughter,' Eddie said, pointing to another print, anxious to deflect Angel's attention from Alison.

Angel glanced at Jenny Wren. 'Not as photogenic as this

179

one.' She tapped the photograph of Alison with a long fingernail. 'What was her name?'

Eddie told her. Angel patted his hand and said that children were so sweet at that age.

'Some people don't like that sort of game.' Eddie paused. 'Not with children.'

'That's silly. Children need love and security, that's all. Children like playing games with grown-ups. That's what growing up is all about.'

Eddie felt warm with relief. Then and later, he was amazed by Angel's sympathy and understanding. He even told her about his humiliating experiences as a teacher at Dale Grove Comprehensive School. She coaxed him into describing exactly what Mandy and Sian had done. The violence of her reaction surprised him. Her lips curled back against her teeth and wrinkles bit into the skin.

'We don't need people like that. They're no better than animals.'

'But what can you do with them? You can't just kill them, can you?'

Angel arched her immaculate eyebrows. 'I think one should execute them if they break certain laws. There's nothing wrong with capital punishment if the system is sensible and fair. As for the others, why don't we put them in work camps? We could make the amount of food and other privileges they get depend on the amount of work they produce. Then at least they wouldn't be such a total liability for society. You have to admit, it would be a much fairer way of doing things.'

'I suppose so.'

'There's no suppose about it. You have to be realistic.' Angel's face was serene again. 'One has to use other people – except one's friends, of course; they're different. Otherwise they abuse you. Obviously one tries to be constructive about how one uses them. But it's no use being sentimental. They'll just take advantage, like Mandy and Sian did. In the long run it's kinder to be firm with them right from the start.'

Angel furnished her little palace as a bed-sitting room. She and Eddie brought down the bed which had belonged to Stanley and installed it on the wall opposite the long window. The reupholstered Victorian chair stood by the window. Beside it was a hexagonal table which Angel had found in an antique shop. She scattered small rugs, vivid geometrical patterns from Eastern Anatolia, over the floor. There were no pictures on the severe white walls.

Eddie went down to the basement only by invitation. By tacit consent, the new shower room was reserved for Angel's use. If they needed something from the big freezer in the former scullery, it was always Angel who fetched it.

'I know where things are,' she explained. 'I've got my little system. I don't want you confusing it.'

She bought a small microwave and installed it on a shelf over the freezer.

'Wouldn't it be more convenient in the kitchen?' Eddie asked.

'It would take up too much space. Besides, we'll use it mainly for defrosting. And having it down there will be handy if I want to heat up a snack.'

Despite the bed, Angel did not usually sleep in the basement, but in Thelma's old room upstairs. There was not enough space for her clothes in the wardrobes which had belonged to Eddie's parents, so she asked Mr Reynolds to fit new ones with mirrored doors along one wall of the front bedroom.

One morning in early May while Mr Reynolds was working upstairs, there was a ring on the doorbell. Eddie answered it. Mrs Reynolds was on the step, both hands gripping the strap of her handbag. For a second she stared at Eddie. She had bright brown eyes behind heavy glasses, a snub nose and small lips like the puckered skin round an anus.

'I'd like a word with my husband, if you please.'

Eddie called Mr Reynolds and went back into the kitchen, closing the door behind him with relief. Sometimes, when he was washing up in the winter months, he looked through the kitchen window, through the screen of leafless branches, and glimpsed Mrs Reynolds with her binoculars on the balcony of the flat. Mr Reynolds had told Angel at great length about how he had bought a new and more powerful pair of binoculars as a surprise birthday present for his wife.

There was a tap on the kitchen door. Mr Reynolds edged into the room.

'Sorry – something's come up. I'll have to go now. I'll give you a ring in the morning, if that's OK?' He looked perfectly normal. It wasn't what he said but how he said it. His voice trembled, and his breathing was irregular. He sounded ten years older than he really was.

Eddie stood up. 'Is everything all right?' He knew that Angel would want to know why Mr Reynolds had left early.

'It's our Jenny,' said Mr Reynolds, retreating backwards out of the room as if withdrawing from royalty. 'There's been an accident.'

7

Poor Jenny Wren. Who better than Eddie to know that patterns repeated themselves? Sometimes he thought of his father and wondered what had happened to him when he was young; and so on with his father's father and his father's father's father; and back the line went through the centuries, opening a vertiginous prospect stretching to the birth of mankind.

Even as a child, Jenny Wren had been marked out as a failure. Fat, clumsy and desperate for love, she carried her self-consciousness around with her like a heavy suitcase handcuffed to her wrist. Her children, Eddie learned later from Mr Reynolds, had been taken into care. And after the third one was born, Jenny Wren plunged into a post-natal depression from which she never really emerged.

She lived in Hackney, in a council flat on the fourth floor of a tower block. On that morning when her father was putting the finishing touches to Angel's fitted wardrobes, she took a basket of washing on to her balcony. Instead of hanging out the clothes, however, she leant over the waist-high wall and stared down at the ground. Then – according to a witness who was watching, powerless to intervene, from a window in the neighbouring block – she lifted first one leg and then the other off the ground and rolled clumsily over the wall.

Characteristically, the suicide attempt was a failure. Though she dived head first on top of her cerebral hemispheres, the fall was partly broken by a shrub. She did a good deal of damage to herself – a badly fractured skull and other broken bones – but unfortunately she survived. A week after the fall, Mr Reynolds returned to 29 Rosington Road to finish off the wardrobes.

'Jen's in a coma. May never wake up. If she does, there may be brain damage.'

Angel patted his hand and said how very, very sorry they were. She and Eddie had sent flowers to the hospital.

'How's Mrs Reynolds coping?'

'Not easy for her. The chaplain's been very kind.' The shock had made Mr Reynolds less talkative, and everything he said had a staccato delivery. 'Not that we're churchgoers, of course. Time and a place for everything.'

'Are you sure you want to carry on with the wardrobes?' Angel asked. 'I'm sure we could find someone else to finish off. You must have so much to do. We'd quite understand.'

'I'd rather keep busy, thanks all the same.'

8

Halfway through June, about six weeks after Jenny Wren's fall, the first little girl came to stay at 29 Rosington Road.

Chantal was the daughter of an English investment analyst and his French wife. The family lived in Knightsbridge, a long stone's throw from Harrods. Chantal was the third child and her parents did not pay her much attention, preferring to hire nannies and au pairs to provide it instead. Angel had first noticed her at a birthday party for one of Chantal's school friends; at the time, Angel had been acting as a relief nanny for the school friend's younger sister.

Despite frequent temptation, Angel never took one of her own charges. 'Only stupid people run unnecessary risks,' she told Eddie when they were preparing the basement for Chantal. 'And they're the ones who get caught.'

Chantal's father was black and she had inherited his pigmentation. (Angel despised people like Thelma who were racist.) They dressed her in white dresses, which set off her rich dark skin. She had a tendency to giggle when Eddie played games with her. Occasionally Angel acted – in Eddie's phrase – as Mistress of Ceremonies. But he did not think she enjoyed the games very much.

Human beings were such a mass of contradictions. Although Angel was wonderful at looking after children, and skilled at making them do as she wanted, she seemed not to like playing with them.

Eddie had a wonderful time for two weeks and three days. One morning he woke to find Angel beside his bed. She was carrying a cup of tea for him, a rare treat. He sat up and thanked her, his mind already running ahead to the treats planned for the day.

'Eddie.' Angel stood by the bed, adjusting the knot that secured her robe. 'Chantal's gone.'

'Where? What happened?'

'Nothing's wrong, don't worry. But I took her back home last night. Back to her mummy and daddy.'

He stared at her. 'Why didn't you tell me?'

'Because I knew you'd be upset. I knew you'd hate having to say goodbye to her.' She paused. 'And she wouldn't want to leave you.'

Eddie felt his eyes filling with tears. 'She could have stayed with us.'

'No, she couldn't. Not for ever and ever. There would have been all sorts of difficulties as she grew older.'

Eddie turned his face towards the wall and said nothing.

'Think about it.'

Eddie sniffed. Then a new problem occurred to him. 'What happens if she tells her parents about us, and they tell the police?'

'What can she say? All she's seen is our faces. She doesn't know where the house is, or what the outside looks like. She only saw the basement. Besides, the police aren't going to try too hard. Chantal's back home, safe and sound. No harm done, is there?'

'I still wish I could have said goodbye.'

'It made sense to do it this way. We didn't want tears before bedtime, did we?'

'Maybe she could come and stay with us again?'

Angel sat down on the edge of the bed. 'No. That wouldn't be a good idea. But perhaps we can find someone else to come and stay.'

'Who?'

'I don't know yet. But no one who lives in Knightsbridge. The police look for patterns, you see. They try to pinpoint the recurring features.'

For Katy they travelled up to Nottingham and rented a flat there for three months. Katy was an unwanted child who escaped from her foster parents at every opportunity and wandered the streets and in and out of shops.

'Looking for love,' Angel commented. 'It's so terribly sad.'

Suki, their third little girl, had a stud in her nose and a crucifix dangling from one ear; she belonged to some travellers camping in the Forest of Dean. Angel said that the mother was a drug addict; certainly Suki smelled terribly, and when they washed her for the first time the bath water turned almost black. (This was the occasion when Suki bit Eddie's hand and screamed like a train.)

'Some parents shouldn't be trusted with children,' Angel used to say. 'They need to be taught a lesson.'

She repeated this so often, in so many ways and with such force, that Eddie thought it might amount to part of a pattern, albeit one invisible to the police.

On Sunday the first of December, after Lucy's bath, Angel spent the rest of the morning reading to her in the basement. At least, that was what Angel said she was doing. Eddie was both hurt and angry. Angel had never been possessive with the others: she and Eddie had shared the fun.

To make matters worse, he wasn't sure what Angel was really doing down there. The soundproofing made eavesdropping impossible. After a while, Eddie unlocked the back door and went into the garden.

It was much colder today. The damp, raw air hurt his throat. He could not be bothered to fetch a coat. He walked warily down to the long, double-glazed window of the basement. As he had feared, the curtains were drawn. The disappointment brought tears into his eyes. His skin was burning hot. He leant his forehead against the cool glass.

The movement brought his head closer to the side of the window. There was a half-inch gap between the frame and the side of the curtains.

Scarcely daring to breathe, he knelt down on the concrete path and peered through the gap. At first he saw nothing but carpet and bare, white wall. He shifted his position. Part of the Victorian armchair slid into his range of vision. Lucy was sitting there. All he could see was her feet and ankles, Mickey Mouse slippers and pale-green tights, projecting from the seat. She was not moving. He wondered if she were sleeping. She had seemed very tired in the bath, perhaps because of the medication.

At that moment Angel came into view, still wearing her white robe. Round her neck was a long, purple scarf, like a broad, shiny ribbon with tassels on the end. Her eyes were closed and her lips were moving. As Eddie watched, she raised her arms towards the ceiling. Eddie licked dry lips. What he could see through the gap, the cross section of the basement, seemed only marginally connected with reality; it belonged in a dream.

Angel moved out of sight. Eddie panicked. She might have

seen him at the window. In a moment the back door would open and she would catch him peeping. *I just came out for a breath of fresh air.* He straightened up quickly and glanced around. There was enough wind to stir the trees at the bottom of the garden and in Carver's beyond. The leafless branches made a black tracery, through which he glimpsed Mrs Reynolds on her balcony. Eddie shivered as he walked back to the house.

Mrs Reynolds watches me, I watch Angel: who watches Mrs Reynolds? Must be God.

Eddie giggled, imagining God following Mrs Reynolds's movements through a pair of field glasses from some vantage point in the sky. According to Mr Reynolds, his wife had become a born-again Christian since Jenny Wren had sent herself into a coma.

'It's a comfort to her,' Mr Reynolds had said. 'Not really my cup of tea, but never mind.'

Eddie opened the back door and went inside. The warmth of the kitchen enveloped him but he could not stop shivering. He went into the hall. The basement door was still closed. He pressed his ear against one of the panels. All he heard was his own breathing, which seemed unnaturally loud.

Clinging to the banister, he climbed the stairs and rummaged in the bathroom cupboard until he found the thermometer. He perched uncomfortably on the side of the bath while he took his temperature. *It's not fair. Why won't she let me in the basement too?* He took the thermometer out of his mouth. His temperature was over 102 degrees. He felt strangely proud of this achievement: he must be really ill. He deserved special treatment.

He found some paracetamol in the cupboard, took two tablets out of the bottle and snapped them in half. He poured water into a green plastic beaker which he had had since he was a child. The flowing water so fascinated him that he let it flood over the rim of the beaker and trickle over his fingers. At last he swallowed the tablets and went into his bedroom to lie down.

Alternately hot and cold, he lay fully clothed under the duvet. He thought how nice it would be if Angel and Lucy brought him a hot-water bottle and a cooling drink. They could sit with him for a while, and perhaps Angel would read a story. *Nobody cares about me.* He stared at the picture of the little girl which his father had given his mother all those years ago. *Very nice, Stanley. If you like that sort of thing.* A little later he heard his parents talking: dead voices from the big front bedroom; perhaps they were not really dead after all – perhaps they were watching him now.

Eddie drifted in and out of sleep. Just before three in the afternoon he woke to find his mouth dry and his body wet with sweat. He dragged himself out of bed and stood swaying and shivering in the bedroom. *I need some tea, a nice cup of tea.*

He found his glasses and went slowly downstairs. To his surprise, he heard voices in the kitchen. He pushed open the door. Lucy was sitting at the table eating a boiled egg. Angel was now dressed in jeans and jersey; her hair was tied back in a ponytail. As Eddie staggered into the room, he heard Lucy saying, 'Mummy always cuts my toast into soldiers, but Daddy doesn't bother.'

She stopped talking as soon as she saw Eddie. Angel and Lucy stared at Eddie. *Two's company, three's none.*

'What are you doing in the kitchen?' Eddie said, his voice rising in pitch. 'It's against the rules.'

'The rules aren't written in stone. Circumstances alter cases.' Angel stroked Lucy's dark head. 'And this is a very special little circumstance.'

'But they never come in the kitchen.'

'That's enough, Eddie. How are you feeling?'

Thrown off balance, he stared at her.

'Cat got your tongue?'

'How did you know I'm ill?'

'You should try looking at yourself in the mirror,' Angel said, not unkindly.

'I think it's flu.'

'I doubt it: probably just a virus. You need paracetamol and lots of fluids.'

Eddie sat down at the table. Lucy looked at him, her spoon halfway to her mouth, and to his delight she smiled.

'Finish your egg, dear,' Angel said. 'It's getting cold.'

'I don't want any more.'

'Nonsense. You need some food in that little tummy. And don't forget your Ribena.'

Lucy dropped her spoon on the table. 'But I've had enough.'

'Come along: eat up.'

'I'm full.'

'You'll do as I say, Lucy. You must always finish what's on your plate.'

'Mummy doesn't make me when I'm full.' Lucy's eyes brimmed with tears but her voice was loud so she sounded more angry than afraid. 'I want Mummy.'

'We're not at home to Miss Crosspatch,' Angel announced.

Eddie laughed. He would not usually have dared to laugh, but now the boundaries were shifting. After all, he was not entirely sure that this was really happening. It might be a dream. At any moment he might wake up and see, hanging on the wall by the door, the picture of the little girl which his father had given his mother. The girl like Lucy.

'You're really not yourself, Eddie.' Angel walked into the hall. 'I'm going to take your temperature.' Her footsteps ran lightly up the stairs.

Lucy pushed the toast aside with a violent movement of her right arm. The far side of the plate caught the plastic cup, which slid to the edge of the table. Ribena flooded across the floor.

For an instant, Eddie and Lucy looked at each other. Then Lucy slithered off her seat and ran for the door – not the door to the hall but the door to the garden. Eddie knew he should do something, if this were not a dream, but he wasn't sure he would be able to stand up. In any case, it wouldn't matter: they kept the back door locked when they had a little girl staying with them.

He watched Lucy twisting the handle and pulling. He watched the door opening and felt cold air against his skin. Only then, as Lucy ran into the garden, did he realize that she really was outside. He was aware, too, that this was his fault – that he had unlocked the door when he went out to look through the basement window at Angel and Lucy. Seeing Mrs Reynolds on her balcony had made him forget to relock it when he came in. Angel would blame him, which was unfair: it was Mrs Reynolds's fault. He stood up, propping himself on the table.

Angel took him by surprise. She ran across the kitchen from the hall, the ponytail bouncing behind her, and out of the back door. Eddie heard a crack like an exploding firework. There was another crack, then a pregnant silence, the peace before the storm. He let himself sink back on to his chair.

It was almost a relief when Lucy began to cry: jagged sobs, not far from hysteria. Angel dragged her inside, kicked the door shut and turned the key in the lock. Angel was pale and tight-lipped.

'Very well, madam.' Angel was holding Lucy by the ear, her nails biting in to the pink skin. 'Do you know what happens to naughty children? They go to hell.'

Eddie cleared his throat. 'In a way, it's not her fault. She's –'

'Of course it's her fault.'

Lucy pressed her hand against her left cheek. The sobbing mutated into a thin, high wail.

'Perhaps she's tired,' Eddie muttered. 'Perhaps she needs a rest.'

Angel pushed Lucy away. The girl fell against a chair and slid to the floor. She stayed there, half-sitting, half-sprawling, with an arm hooked round a chair leg and her head resting against the side of the seat. Ribena soaked into the skirt of her dress.

The crying stopped. Lucy's mouth hung open, the lips moist and loose. Fear makes children ugly.

'It's all right, Lucy.' Eddie sat down on the chair beside hers and patted Lucy's dark head. She jerked it away. 'You're a bit overexcited. That's all it is.'

'That's not all it is.' Angel tugged open the drawer where they kept the kitchen cutlery. 'She needs a lesson. They all need a lesson.'

Eddie rubbed his aching forehead. '*Who* need a lesson? I don't understand.'

Angel whirled round. In her hand was a pair of long scissors with orange plastic handles. She pointed them at Eddie, and the blades flashed. 'You'll never understand. You're too stupid.'

He looked at the table and noticed the swirl of the grain around a knot shaped like a snail. He wished he were dead.

'If they do wrong,' Angel shouted, 'they have to pay for it. How else can they make things right?'

Eddie examined the snail. He wanted to say: *But she only spilled some Ribena.*

'And if they don't want to, then I shall *make* them.' Angel's face was ablaze. 'We all have to suffer. So why shouldn't they?'

But who are 'they'? The four girls or –

'Come here, Lucy,' Angel said softly.

Lucy didn't move.

Angel sprang across the kitchen, the scissors raised in her right hand.

'No,' Eddie said, trying to get up. 'You mustn't.'

With her left hand, Angel seized Lucy by the hair and dragged her to her feet. Lucy screamed. Oddly detached, Eddie noticed that there were toast crumbs and a long stain of yolk on the green Laura Ashley dress.

Angel pulled Lucy by the hair. Lucy wrapped one arm round a table leg and screamed. Angel pulled harder. The table juddered a few inches over the kitchen floor.

'Angel, let her go. Someone might hear.'

Lucy squealed. Angel yanked the little girl away from the table. She towered over Lucy, holding the scissors high above the girl's head.

'No, Angel, no!' Eddie cried. 'Please, Angel, no.'

Nine

1

If you wanted a model for the devil, you could find worse than David Byfield. Not one of the coarser manifestations: Uncle David would be a sophisticated devil, the sort who charms or terrifies according to his whim.

'You're being very foolish.' The old priest's voice was quiet but carrying; Uncle David had learned to fill the empty spaces of churches in the days before public-address systems.

Wide-eyed, Sally stared up at him. St Michael's filled with a blessed silence. Her mind had cleared as if a fever had receded, leaving her weak but in control. She concentrated on David Byfield, glorying in his ordinariness; he was real, safe and sane. He was wearing a dark, threadbare overcoat with a navy-blue scarf wound loosely round his neck, and between the woollen folds Sally glimpsed the white of his dog collar and old, sagging skin. He was neatly shaved. In the years since she had met him he had developed a stoop: his bony face curved over her like a gargoyle on a church roof.

'At times like this,' he went on, 'you need company. You do not sit alone in dank churches.' With a speed that took her by surprise, he placed his right palm lightly but firmly over the fingers of her left hand. 'You're freezing. You've probably had next to no breakfast. Is it any wonder that you're seeing devils waving toasting forks?'

'Don't be ridiculous.' The echo of her thoughts unnerved her. 'I was just thinking. And in my situation it's not surprising I'm a little depressed.'

'You're doing more than thinking. You're leaving yourself defenceless.' He sat down in the pew in front of her and turned slowly towards her. 'Devils – I should have known that word would embarrass you.'

'I'm not embarrassed.'

He ignored her. 'It's simply a metaphor. Why should that be so hard for your generation to grasp? All language is metaphor. When did you last talk to a priest?'

Sally stared at her lap. 'Yesterday morning.'

'Who?'

'My vicar.' She shied away from her reasons for not wanting to talk to Derek. 'He's being very supportive. So's his wife – and so's the whole parish.'

'Derek Cutter.'

She looked up, surprised. 'You know him?'

'Only by reputation.' David inserted a small, chilly pause. 'Did you pray together?'

'It's none of your business.' She paused but he said nothing, so after a while she muttered, 'As it happens, no. There wasn't the time. But I expect I'll be seeing him later today.' She knew she should at least phone Derek; she felt guilty about rejecting his offers of help, guilty about not liking him.

'Do you talk to any other priest on a regular basis? Do you have a confessor?'

'I'm sorry, but I really don't see that this is any of your business.'

'It's not just a question of what you think.'

'Where's Michael?' Sally was suddenly desperate to see him. 'And what are you doing here?'

'He's talking to the policemen outside. They met us at King's Cross and brought us straight here.'

'You know what they've found?'

He hesitated. 'They told us on the way. You're sure the – the remains aren't Lucy's?'

'Yes.'

'I don't understand how you can be so sure.'

'That's because you're not Lucy's mother.'

To her surprise he nodded. 'You know your own flesh and blood.'

She turned her face away from him, appalled by the images his words conjured up. A door creaked. David looked up.

'Here's Michael,' he went on. 'We must get you home.'

'I don't want to go home. I want to do something useful.'

Michael's quick footsteps clattered down the aisle. He was pale, but he had shaved and his hair was brushed. His jacket was open and Sally did not recognize the shirt and jersey underneath; he must have borrowed them from David. She gripped the back of the pew in front and pulled herself to her feet. David Byfield stepped away from her and tactfully feigned an interest in the list of the church's incumbents.

'Sally.' Michael hugged her. 'I'm sorry.'

She clung to him. 'It's all right. It's all right.' She found that she was patting his back. 'It doesn't matter, not now you're here.'

Over Michael's shoulder she watched David walking eastwards. He stopped at the step before the chancel and bowed towards the high altar. Bowed not genuflected: which in a priest of his type meant that the sacrament was not reserved here. He straightened up and stood there, apparently absorbed in contemplating the east window.

Michael pulled away from Sally. 'They're talking to someone, the landlord of the pub round the corner. He thinks he saw someone turning into Beauclerk Place last night when he was locking up.'

David turned round. 'Any description?'

'No – he wasn't paying much attention. Someone wearing a longish coat, he thought. Medium height, whatever that means.'

'Man or woman?'

'He couldn't tell.' Michael turned his back on his godfather and touched Sally's cheek. 'Shall we go?'

Sally allowed him to lead her into the little vestry, where there were mousetraps on the floor and dust on the table, and out by the side door into the alley beyond. Michael was saying something but she neither knew nor cared what. In her mind she was concentrating on the shapeless figure in the long coat: sexless, of medium height, and possibly completely unconnected with the package in the vestry. But even a possibility was better than nothing: it was something to focus on, something to hate. *May God damn you and yours.* The words set up echoes in her memory. Audrey Oliphant had used them when she cursed her, Sally, in St George's: only three months ago, and already so remote that it might have happened to someone else.

May God damn you and yours.

'Steady,' David said behind her.

Michael slipped his hand under her elbow. 'Are you all right?'

She stared blankly at him. Why did people keep asking if she was all right? She was all wrong.

Maxham was waiting for them at the end of the alley, leaning against the tall spiked gate that separated it from Beauclerk Place. 'There's a car here for you. You're going back to Hercules Road?'

'Yes.' When Michael was level with Maxham, he stopped. 'This person the landlord saw. Which way down the street was he coming?'

Maxham hesitated long enough to show that he was seriously considering refusing to answer. 'From the north.'

'Fitzroy Square? Euston Road?'

'Maybe.'

'When?'

'Between eleven-forty-five and midnight. That's all we know, Sergeant. OK? And there may not even be a connection.'

The two men stared at each other. Antagonism flickered between them. Sally tugged at Michael's arm. He allowed her to pull him away.

They were to travel back to the flat in the car which had brought Sally. Sergeant Carlow was leaning against the wing, smoking. Yvonne Saunders raised her hand a few inches, a token wave, and opened one of the back doors.

'You go on without me,' David said.

Michael glanced back. 'You're very welcome. We'd *like* you to come.'

'I know.' The old man stopped and folded his arms. 'And I shall, later, if Sally doesn't mind.'

'But where will you go?' In other circumstances Michael's surprise would have been comical.

'Oh, don't worry about me. I shall go to church.'

2

As soon as the car turned into Hercules Road, it was obvious that news of the discovery at St Michael's had gone before them. There were more cars, more reporters and men with cameras. A uniformed policeman stood at the entrance to the Appleyards' block of flats.

'Drive on,' Michael said to Carlow. 'Drive past the house and out the other end of the road.'

Carlow accelerated. 'Where do you want to go? A hotel?'

Sally touched Michael's sleeve. 'But what happens if Lucy tries to –'

'Maxham has someone in the flat round the clock, hasn't he?'

Carlow nodded. As they passed the house, a reporter recognized someone in the car, probably Sally. She saw him pointing, his mouth opening in a soundless shout. The group on the pavement fragmented into scurrying individuals. Two men started to run after the car but gave up after a few yards.

Sally said, 'But we'd need clothes and things.'

Yvonne glanced back from the front passenger seat. 'If you give me a list I can fetch what you need and bring it to the hotel.'

'Don't forget your mobile,' Michael said. 'Which hotel?'

Sally folded her arms. 'I don't want to go to a hotel.'

'As you like.' Michael twisted his lips. 'Well, where then?'

'I don't know.'

The car turned out of Hercules Road and nosed into a

stream of traffic. A horn sounded behind them. For a moment no one spoke.

Michael looked at Sally. 'What about David? We'll need to find somewhere for him.'

'I don't see why.'

'Because he asked if I'd like him to stay and I said yes. I thought we'd be at the flat –'

'At the flat? So where was he going to sleep?'

'He could have –' Michael stopped.

'No,' Sally said. 'We couldn't have put him in Lucy's room, could we?'

'Maybe not.'

'No.'

They were back in West End Lane now. Sergeant Carlow pulled over to the kerb.

'Where to, then? Have you decided?'

Michael glanced at Sally. 'Christ knows.'

3

In the end they went to stay with Oliver Rickford. It was Sally's idea. She thought it would be better for Michael and better for her. Besides, Oliver had invited them. Michael was not enthusiastic, but on this occasion she was prepared to be more obstinate than he was.

'If that's what you want,' he said a mild voice, 'that's what we'll do.'

Michael's habits were cracking and dissolving like ice in a thaw. Sally knew that he hated asking favours; he preferred to keep his family separate from his friendships; he hated betraying signs of personal weakness, and since Lucy had gone his behaviour had been one long confession of inadequacy.

Oliver lived in Hornsey, about half a mile south of Alexandra Park. There was little traffic and Sergeant Carlow drove fast, a man anxious to be rid of his awkward passengers. He took them south round the Heath and then north on Junction Road.

At first no one talked. Carlow and Yvonne, models of discretion, stared through the windscreen. Sally rested her hand on the back seat between her and Michael, but he appeared not to notice.

At last, as they were approaching Archway, she put her hand back on her knee and said: 'There's no real need for David to come to Oliver's too.'

'Why shouldn't he?' Michael turned and stared at her. 'He's expecting to stay with us.'

'Couldn't we find him a hotel or a bed-and-breakfast? I'm sure he'd be far more comfortable.'

Michael shook his head. 'Oliver says he's got two spare rooms, and it's no problem having David as well as us.'

Sally lowered her voice. 'But it's not as if David can do any good here. I'm not quite sure why he's come.'

'I told you: he came because he offered and I asked him to. All right?'

She glared at the necks of the two police officers in front of them. 'At present we've got enough to worry about. David's just one more problem.'

'David is not a problem.'

'He bloody well isn't a solution, either.'

Michael stared out of his window. Sally squeezed her fingers together on her lap and fought back tears. After Archway, they drove along Hornsey Lane, Crouch End Hill and Tottenham Lane.

Inkerman Street was a short road with a church at the far end. Two Victorian terraces, built of grey London brick, faced each other across a double file of parked cars. Most of the houses had been cut up into flats. Oliver's was one of the exceptions.

A FOR SALE sign stood in the little yard in front of the house. Oliver must have been watching for their arrival because his front door opened almost as soon as their car pulled up outside the gate.

Michael's fingers closed around Sally's hand. 'You go in. I'm going back into town.'

'Why?' Sally was conscious of the listening ears in the front of the car. 'There's nothing you can do.'

'At least I can try and make sure that Maxham does what he should be doing.'

'If you think it will help.'

'God knows if it will help. But I have to do something.'

4

Frowning with concentration, Oliver pushed down the plunger of the cafetière. 'Milk? Sugar?'

'No, thank you.' Then Sally changed her mind. 'I'd like some sugar.'

He nodded and went to fetch it. Sally huddled in the armchair, hugging herself. Sugar was good for shock, for the wounded, for invalids. The gas fire was on full but she felt freezing. They were in a room at the front of the house, narrow and high-ceilinged, with a bay window to the street. The three-piece suite was upholstered in synthetic green velvet, faded and much stained. The Anaglypta wallpaper was dingy, and, near the window, strips of it were beginning to peel away. You could see where a previous inhabitant had put pictures and furniture against the wall, including a large rectangular object which had probably been a piano. Only the television, the stereo and the video looked new. Even they were covered with a layer of dust. Stacked along one wall were a number of cardboard boxes fastened with parcel tape and neatly labelled. She wondered how long ago they had been packed.

Oliver returned with the sugar. He made a performance out of pouring the coffee, reminding Sally incongruously of an elderly housewife, a regular at St George's, who had invited Sally to tea. His neat, finicky movements contrasted with the chaos in what she'd seen of his home.

'Have you had the house on the market long?' she said brightly.

'Since Sharon left.' His voice was unemotional. 'We're dividing the spoils.'

Sally lost interest in Oliver's problems. She warmed her cold fingers on the steaming cup of coffee and stared into its black, gleaming surface. She wished she could see Lucy's image there, as in a crystal ball. The reality of her loss swamped her. It was all she could do not to howl.

'It's much too big for me,' Oliver was saying. 'We bought it when we thought we might have kids.' He paused, perhaps aware that children were not the best subject to mention. 'I suppose I could take lodgers, but I don't much fancy having strangers in the house.'

'I wouldn't, either.' Sally made an enormous effort to concentrate on what he was saying. 'So you'll look for a flat or something?'

'Got to sell this place first. It means there's lots of room for you and Michael, anyway. And for his uncle, or whoever he is.'

'Godfather.' She registered in passing another of Michael's failures in communication. 'His name's David Byfield.'

'As long as he doesn't mind roughing it. I can manage a bed and a sleeping bag for him, but sheets and curtains are a bit awkward.'

'I'm sure it will be fine. It's very kind of you.'

Oliver stirred his coffee, the spoon scraping and tapping against the inside of the mug. The lull in the conversation rapidly became awkward. Oliver said all the right things, but his house was unwelcoming and she hardly knew him; and no doubt the Appleyards' invasion had ruined his plans for Christmas. She regretted their decision to come here. The old irrational doubt – that Lucy might not be able to find them if they weren't at home – resurfaced. She would look a fool if she changed her mind, but she no longer cared about that.

'I'm sorry,' she burst out, 'I think I'd better go back to Hercules Road.'

'I'll drive you, if you like. But would you rather wait until

Michael comes back? He may be on his way already. And so may David.'

'I don't know what to do for the best.'

'It's not easy. But don't worry about Lucy coming back to Hercules Road and finding no one there. Maxham will make sure that won't happen. Why don't you have some more coffee before you decide?'

Automatically she passed her mug to him.

As he handed it back to her, he said, 'What exactly did they find at that church?'

She stared at him. 'No one told you?'

'Not in any detail. There wasn't time.' His lips twitched. 'Maybe everyone assumed that someone would do it. But perhaps it's too painful for you? I'm sorry – I shouldn't have asked.'

'It's all right.' In a brisk, unemotional voice she told him about the package in the porch of St Michael's. 'They're keeping the details to themselves at present. And there was something else: there's a pub round the corner, and the landlord thought he saw someone turning into Beauclerk Place just before midnight. Wearing a long coat – could have been a man or a woman.'

'Is he trustworthy?'

'How can you tell?'

'You can't. Or not easily. You get all sorts in an investigation like this: people so desperate to help that they invent things; people who want to feel important; even people who think it's all a bit of a joke to waste police time.' He smiled anxiously at her. 'You must think me very insensitive. But in the long run it's wise to be realistic, not pin your hopes on that sort of evidence.'

'What hopes?'

He ignored the question. 'There's also the point that even if there was someone there, he might have had nothing to do with the case.'

'Then who was it? Besides the church, I think there's only offices in Beauclerk Place. No one should have been there on a Saturday night.'

'As far as we know. People do work odd hours. Anyway,

it could have been someone looking for somewhere to doss down. A drunk, a drug addict. One of the homeless, and God knows there are plenty of those. Or just someone who took a wrong turning.'

To her surprise and embarrassment, she found herself smiling. 'You're a great help.'

There was a glimmer of an answering smile. 'The landlord's vagueness is a good sign. It suggests he's not making it up. And it was only last night, so he's not likely to have got confused about the day. But where does that leave you? A man or a woman turning into Beauclerk Place.'

'It has to be a man. A woman wouldn't do that sort of thing, not to children.'

Oliver shook his head. 'What about the Moors Murders? Myra Hindley was in it just as much as Ian Brady.'

The weight of the suffering, past and present, oppressed her. Sally stood up and walked to the window. She was aware that Oliver was watching from his armchair. She stared at the rows of parked cars and the blank windows of the houses opposite. No journalists here, not yet.

'I'm sorry. I shouldn't have said all that.'

'I wanted to hear.' Sally turned back to the room. 'How common is it?'

'That women offer violence to children? It's much more widespread than you might think. Some of it you can almost understand: it's the product of circumstance.'

'Mothers trapped with a small child in a bedsitter – that sort of thing?'

'Exactly. Or under the influence of a man. But some of it isn't like that. It's willed.'

Willed. Someone had decided to take Lucy, decided to cut off the hand of another child, decided to chop off the legs of a third, decided to leave them where they would be found. How did you explain that? You couldn't justify it, Sally thought, any more than you could pardon it.

'Evil,' she said quietly.

'Evil? What do you mean?' Oliver said sharply. 'I don't mean to be rude, but that's the trouble with clergy. Anything nasty they can't understand – no problem, they just label it evil. The work of the devil. All part of the divine plan, eh? Ours is not to reason why.'

'Maybe you're right. Maybe we don't try hard enough to understand. But right now I don't want to try. I just want Lucy.'

'Sally – I'm sorry. I didn't mean to – '

'It doesn't matter.'

She sat down again and sipped her coffee. It was cold here, in this unloved room in an unloved house. For an instant she thought she heard the thrumming of wings. She caught herself glancing up at the ceiling, as if expecting to see a giant bird hovering above her head. *I must not go mad. Lucy needs me.* Oliver was still watching her. His concern irritated her.

'You're having a hell of a time at present,' he told her in a low, sympathetic voice which brought her to the verge of screaming at him. 'All this on top of Michael's problems.'

'Yes.' Sally's mind made an unexpected connection: Oliver's phone call two weeks ago on that disastrous Saturday when Uncle David had come to lunch. She looked down, afraid her eyes would betray her. Suddenly cunning, she murmured, 'Poor Michael.'

'Don't worry too much. Maybe they'll drop the complaint.'

'And if not?'

'Hard to tell.' This time he avoided her eyes. 'Michael's record is in his favour. And most people feel a lot of sympathy. We're all tempted.'

'But Michael didn't resist.' It was not quite a question: more an intelligent guess.

'Obviously he acted on impulse and under great provocation.' Oliver sounded like counsel for the defence. 'It's not as if he makes a habit of hitting people. And in the circumstances . . .' His voice trailed into silence. Then: 'I assumed he'd have told you.'

'I'm sorry,' Sally said. 'I shouldn't have tricked you. But will you tell me the rest? Who did he hit, and why?'

'A man he'd just arrested.'

'But *why*?'

'Why the arrest? Handling stolen goods. Possession of a

firearm. But that wasn't why Michael hit him. This guy liked putting out cigarettes on a toddler's arm. His own daughter. And he was acting as if it made him some kind of hero. A hard man doing what hard men do. So Michael punched him in the mouth: to shut him up, Michael said.'

Sally sat there, her head bowed, and tried to pray.

'I'd have done the same.' Oliver leaned forward in his chair. 'It's possible that the man was trying to provoke Michael into taking a swing at him. The lawyers on both sides are hoping for a deal. That was what the meeting on Friday morning was about.'

She remembered finding Michael in the flat at lunch time on Friday when he should have been at work; he had been drinking lager, which he never did on duty. Those and other signs had been there. She should have asked questions.

'Don't blame him,' Oliver said. 'He probably didn't want to worry you.'

Sally shook her head. 'It's as much my fault as his.' *Now as then.* It was abruptly clear to her that the kidnapping did not release her from other responsibilities.

'It all seems irrelevant now,' he went on.

She did not want to talk about it with Oliver. 'Do you mind if I make a phone call? I ought to get in touch with my boss.'

Oliver took her to a room at the back of the house. The only furniture was a dark, ugly dining table and a set of matching chairs. On the table was a phone, a computer, files and books. She tapped in the number for St George's. With luck, Derek and Margaret would still be in church. In her mind she composed a warmly impersonal message for the answering machine.

'St George's Vicarage. Derek Cutter speaking.'

'Derek – it's Sally.'

'My dear, how are you? I tried ringing the flat before church, but –'

'I – we had to go out.'

'Any news?'

Sally hesitated. 'Not really.'

'We prayed for you today.'

Then it didn't do much good. 'Thank you. It's a great comfort.'

'Now, is there anything we can do in other respects? Margaret was saying only at breakfast that you shouldn't be left to cope with all this by yourselves. Why don't you come and stay with us? At times like this friendship can be a very real blessing. Besides, on a purely practical level –'

'In fact, we've decided to stay with a friend of Michael's.' Knowing that she was accepting another's offer while rejecting Derek's made her feel even guiltier.

'Ah. Well, the offer's still open.'

'It's so kind of you.' Sally heard the insincerity in her voice and tried to banish it. 'Do thank Margaret. And – and give her my love.'

'Would you like a word with her? She's here.'

'I'd better not. I'm in rather a hurry. And we want to leave the line free.'

'Of course. But shall I take your phone number? Just in case something comes up at this end.'

Fortunately the number was on the base unit of the phone. Sally read it out to Derek.

'Shall I phone you this evening?' he suggested. 'Unless you'd rather phone me. Just for a chat.'

'I'm not sure.' Sally's good resolutions dissolved. 'We may be out. I'm afraid I have to go now.'

She said goodbye and put down the phone. It was much easier to think charitably about Derek when you weren't dealing directly with him. At least she hadn't actually lied. Her conscience prodded her: there are silent lies as well as spoken ones.

Thanks to Derek, Sally realized, or rather thanks to her dislike of Derek, she hadn't thought about Lucy for at least a moment. But now her mind was making up for lost time. Sally stumbled into the hall and followed the sound of rushing water into the kitchen.

The room was clean and tidy, the real heart of the house.

It had been recently redecorated. Oliver was washing up the coffee mugs.

'Would you mind if I went out for a walk?' she heard herself saying. 'I've been cooped up ever since this happened. I feel I need some air.'

That wasn't the entire truth, either: she also needed to find a church, to try to put right what had gone wrong inside St Michael's.

Oliver fussed over her, establishing first that she wanted to go by herself, second that her coat was warm enough and third that she did not need a street map.

'What happens if you need to phone? You've got a mobile, haven't you?'

'Yes, but I left it at home. Besides, I'm only going out for a few minutes.'

Oliver was treating her like a child, she thought crossly: nanny knows best. Couldn't he understand that she wouldn't be long because there might be some news of Lucy?

At last he let her go. Outside the air was raw, the wind cutting at her exposed skin. She turned left without a backward glance, walking briskly down the street in the direction of the church, hands deep in the pocket of her jacket. The road was seedier than she had first thought: the cars were older, the gutters lined with litter; satellite dishes projected from crumbling brickwork, pointing in the same directions like flying saucers on parade; and the curtains in many of the windows were ragged and unmatching, always a giveaway.

A line of railings sealed the far end of the road. A gate, standing open, pierced the railings and on the other side was the churchyard. It was lunch time, so the morning's services would have finished. The door might well be locked, but with luck the key holder would live nearby.

The church itself was partly masked by a screen of yews and hawthorns which ran parallel to the railings just inside them. The nave and choir were a single, brick-built oblong with an apse projecting from the east end. Early nineteenth century, Sally thought automatically, perhaps a little older.

The base of the tower, a mass of weathered masonry at the west end, must have belonged to a previous church on the site; the upper storeys were Victorian gothic.

She slipped through the gateway and into the churchyard. Almost immediately she realized that she had made a mistake. She would find no consolation here. Most of the gravestones had been removed, though a few remained propped up against the wall of the church. Tiles were missing from the roof. Two of the windows near the east end were broken, despite the grilles which covered them. A network of tarmac paths criss-crossed the muddy grass, with black litter bins standing like sentinels at the junctions. Under the drab sky the only signs of vitality and warmth came from the brightly coloured crisp packets and chocolate wrappings that drifted among the dog turds.

Sally followed one of the paths round the east end of the church. On this side of the churchyard there were benches, more trees, more railings, beyond which was the main road, heavily used by traffic even on Sunday. She slowly walked the length of the church, deciding to make a circuit of it before returning to Oliver's.

The gates of the south porch had been boarded up and secured with two padlocks. In the angle between porch and nave she noticed a pile of what looked like human excrement. Adolescents had been active with their aerosol sprays, displaying their limited grasp of literacy with the usual obscenities and tribal slogans.

Were such people human like herself? And if they were, what about child molesters and child murderers? Or the nurse who killed the children in her charge, or the father who stubbed out cigarettes on his baby's arm? Or, worst of all, the person who had stolen Lucy to practise unknown obscenities on her mind and body. 'Christ knows,' Sally muttered aloud, knowing that old certainties had grown misty and insubstantial.

The path narrowed as it turned into the dark, urine-smelling ravine between the tower and the blank gable wall of the terrace of shops on the western boundary of the churchyard. *The shadow of death.* Sally accelerated. Just as she was about to emerge into the wider spaces of the churchyard beyond, a man stepped round the corner of the tower and blocked her path. She stopped, her heart thudding.

He was almost six feet tall, with dark hair, a broken nose set in the middle of a pale, lined face, and a long, thin body. Despite the cold, he was wearing a T-shirt, a pair of thin trousers, and muddy trainers. The T-shirt had once been white, but was now stained and torn at the neck. He dug his hand in his pocket.

Sally took a step backwards, nearer the dangerously enclosed space between the tower and the wall. With a speed that caught her unawares, the man moved to her right and then drew closer to her, forcing her back against the wall of the tower. She put her hand in her jacket pocket and felt for the money which Oliver had given her in case she needed to phone: two or three pounds in change.

He was very close to her now. His mouth hung open, revealing the rotting teeth within. For an instant she smelled his breath and thought of open graves. He stretched out his arm towards her. Suddenly she realized that the lips were pulled back into a smile.

'Do you believe in Jesus? Do you?'

'Yes.'

'You've got to really believe.' He looked in his forties but was probably younger than she was. He had a Midlands accent and spoke in a near whisper, breathless as if he had been running. 'Listen, just saying you believe isn't enough.'

'No.'

'Are you sure? Remember, Jesus can see into your inner-most soul.'

'Yes. Do *you* believe?'

'He chose me. Look, he put his sign on me.'

The man pointed to the inner edge of his left forearm. Among the scars and goose pimples was a red cross in faded felt-tip, surrounded by a wavering wreath of letters which made up the words JESUS SAVES.

'He pulled me up from the gutter. He sent an angel to

wash away my sins in the water of life.' The man stretched his arms wide. 'Look – I'm clean. Like driven snow.'

'I can see that.'

'You must be clean, too. Otherwise you'll never enter the Kingdom of Heaven.'

Sally took a step to her left, trying to outflank him.

'You must pray with me. Now.'

'I must go. My husband –'

He came even closer. 'You haven't much time. The Kingdom of God is at hand. We must kneel.'

He touched her shoulder, trying to force her to her knees. Revulsion welled inside her and she reacted instinctively: she slapped his face with all the strength she could muster. His skin was rough with stubble, like flabby sandpaper.

The man gasped, his face a parody of dismay, and stepped backwards. Sally flung herself through the gap between his arm and the wall of the tower. His hand gripped her wrist. She screamed, a long howl of fear and anger, and dragged her arm free.

'Piss off, you shithead!' Sally heard herself shrieking.

She broke into a run, crouching low, and escaped. The churchyard stretched before her. She glimpsed the railings through the branches of the trees. The panic affected her vision: nothing was fixed any more; the path, the trees, the grass – everything pulsed with a dull, menacing life, as if visible reality were nothing more than the skin of an enormous, dozing monster.

At the gateway she glanced back. The man was not pursuing her. The churchyard was empty. She clung to a railing and tried to get her breathing back to normal. The monster slipped away. Her body felt limp, as if each muscle had been individually drained of energy. Now the crisis was past, she could hardly walk, let alone run.

'Sally –?'

She turned. Oliver was jogging down Inkerman Street towards her. She stared blankly at him. Her legs could barely support her weight. A moment later he was beside her, his face dark and angry.

'What happened?'

'There was a man . . .'

'Easy, now. It's all right.' He put his hand under her arm. 'A mugger?'

She shook her head and began to laugh with the irony of it. Once she started laughing, it was hard to stop.

'OK, Sally. Calm down. It's OK.'

Oliver had his arm round her now. He half-carried, half-dragged her towards a bench a few yards away. They sat down. Trembling, she hugged him.

'What happened?'

'This man – he tried to *convert* me.'

'Are you hurt?'

'No. Oliver, I swore at him. I hit him.' She started to cry.

His arm tightened around her. 'Listen. Your reactions are out of kilter at present. It's hardly surprising.'

For a moment she thought Oliver's lips were nuzzling her hair. She said angrily, 'He shouldn't have been on the streets. If we had a halfway decent society someone would be looking after him properly.'

'A mental patient? Pushed back into the community?'

'It's possible. There were knife scars on his arms. I should go and find him. He can't have got far. I – '

'No. You're in no fit state to go after anyone. In any case, we don't want to go too far from the house.'

'I failed him.' As she spoke the words, she realized that she did not believe what she was saying: what did that shambling apology for a human being matter beside the fact that Lucy was missing? But old habits took a long time to die. She heard herself mouthing words which were no longer true. 'People like him are part of my job.'

'If you like I'll phone the local nick, see what they can do.'

She allowed this to satisfy her. A moment passed. She looked up at Oliver. His face was very close to hers.

'What were you doing? Did you come after me?'

'I was worried. I don't know why.'

She tried to smile. 'My guardian angel?'

He kissed her decorously on the forehead. 'We should go home. You're cold.'

For an instant Sally did not want to move. For an instant she wanted to stay on that bench for ever with Oliver's arms, warm and strong, wrapped around her. For an instant she felt, faint but unmistakable, a stirring of desire.

Ten

'... we are what we all abhor, *Anthropophagi* and Cannibals, devourers not onely of men, but of our selves ... for all this mass of flesh which we behold, came in at our mouths; ... in brief, we have devour'd our selves.'

Religio Medici, I, 37

1

Eddie pulled the front door closed behind him and walked swiftly down Rosington Road, his fingers scrabbling through his pockets for the keys. He stopped by the van, which was parked a few doors down, and hammered the windscreen with his clenched fist. The keys were still in his bedroom, in the pocket of the jeans he had worn yesterday. All the keys – the keys of the house as well as the van's. He had also left his wallet behind, though he had a pound or two in loose change.

He thought he heard a door opening. Without looking back, he broke into a run. His coat flapped behind him. The cold air attacked his face, his neck and his hands, its sharpness making him gasp; in his mind he saw a curved, flexible knife with an icy blade.

The word *blade* reminded him of the scissors. Had the screaming stopped? He was not sure. He thought he could hear screams but they might have no basis in reality now; they might simply be echoes trapped within his mind. But he was certain of one thing: he could not go back to the house.

While he was running, he risked a glance behind him. No

one was there. Angel wasn't following him. He wasn't worth following.

Panting, he slowed to a walk and buttoned his coat with clumsy fingers. Even if she did come after him, it wouldn't matter. He would just walk on and on and on. It was a free country. She couldn't stop him. He crossed the access road leading to the council flats.

'You all right, then?'

Eddie stopped and stared. Mr Reynolds waved at him. The little builder was about to open his garage door, on which someone had recently sprayed an ornate obscenity.

Mr Reynolds hugged himself with exaggerated force, as if miming winter in a game of charades. 'It's bitter, isn't it?'

Eddie opened his mouth but could think of nothing to say. Panic rose in his throat.

'The odds are shortening for a white Christmas,' Mr Reynolds remarked. 'Heard it on the radio.'

The silence lengthened. Mr Reynolds's face grew puzzled. Eddie's limbs might be temporarily paralysed but his mind was working. First, Mr Reynolds would do anything for Angel. Second, why was he spending the coldest Sunday afternoon since last winter standing outside his garage? Conclusion: he was keeping his eyes open at Angel's request. He was spying on Eddie.

The paralysis dissolved. Eddie broke into a run again.

'Hey!' he heard Mr Reynolds calling behind him. 'Eddie, you OK?'

Eddie ran to the end of the road and turned right. He had no clear plan where he was going. The important thing was to get away. He did not want to be a part of what was happening behind that door. He did not want even to think about it. He wanted to walk and walk until tiredness overcame him.

He crossed a road. Two cars hooted at him, and one of the drivers rolled down his window and swore at him. He walked steadily on. Why was there so much traffic? It was Sunday, the day of rest. There hadn't been all those cars when he was a child. Even ten or fifteen years ago the roads would have been far quieter. Everything changed, nothing stood still. Soon the machines would outnumber the people.

'It doesn't matter,' he told himself. 'It really doesn't matter.'

The world was becoming less substantial, less well-defined. A bus rumbled down the road, overtaking him. The red colour spilled out of its outline. The bus's shape was no longer fixed but swayed to and fro like water in a slowly swinging bucket. You could rely on nothing in this world, and what other world was there?

Eddie remembered that he had a temperature. He might be very ill. He might die. A great sadness washed over him. He had so much to give the world, if the world would only let him. If Angel would let him. His mind shied away from the thought of her.

He was surprised that he was managing to walk so far and so well. It was not that he felt weak, exactly. His legs were as strong as usual but they did not seem quite so firmly attached to the rest of his body as they normally were.

'It's just the flu,' he said aloud, and the words – in blue, lower-case letters, sans serif – seemed to hang in mid-air beside him; he watched the wind muddling up the letters and whipping them away. 'I'll feel better in the morning.'

What if he felt worse? What if there was never any getting better?

Eddie forced himself to walk faster, as though the faster he walked the further he left these unanswerable questions behind.

The important thing was to get away. It was some time before he noticed where he was going. He crossed Haverstock Hill and zigzagged his way up to Eton Avenue. On either side were large, prosperous houses occupied by large, prosperous people. At Swiss Cottage, he hesitated, wondering whether to take the tube into town. It was too much of a decision: instead he kept walking, impelled by the fear that Angel might, after all, pursue him and by the need to keep warm. He drifted up the Finchley Road to the overground station for the North London Line. He went into the station because his legs were becoming weary and because it was starting to rain – thin, cold drops, not far removed from sleet. A westbound train clattered into the station. Eddie ran down the steps to the platform. The train was almost empty. He got on, grateful for the warmth and the seat.

At first, all went well. He closed his eyes and tried to rest. But the memory of what he had left behind in Rosington Road shouldered its way into his mind. Eddie tried to distract himself with the usual techniques – making his mind go blank; remembering Alison on the swing and in the shed at Carver's; imagining himself as Father Christmas in a big store, with a stream of little girls queuing for the honour of sitting on his knee, a long line of pretty faces, sugar and spice and all things nice.

Today, nothing worked. As the train drew into Brondes-bury Station, Eddie opened his eyes. He fancied that some of the other passengers were staring at him. Had he been talking aloud?

He stared out of the window at rows of back gardens. He was almost sure that someone was whispering about him. The words hissed above the sound of the train. He thought the whispers were coming from behind him, but he couldn't be sure without turning his head, which would betray to the watchers that he was aware that they were watching him and that someone was talking about him.

They reached another station. The whispering stopped with the train. A handful of passengers left and another handful boarded. As soon as the train began to move, the whispering started. It was a female voice, he was sure; probably a teenage girl's. Now he knew what to look for, he quickly found evidence to support this theory: the smell of perfume masking, but not quite concealing, the smell of sweat; and a sound which might have been a high-pitched giggle. Mandy or Sian? Of course not. They were no longer teenagers at Dale Grove Comprehensive.

Eddie could bear it no longer. At the next station he tensed himself. A man boarded the train but no one left. At the last moment, Eddie leapt to his feet, opened the door and jumped on to the platform.

No one followed him. The train moved away. Eddie stared into the windows as they slipped past him. There were no teenage girls behind where he had been sitting: only an old man, his eyes closed. Of course it proved nothing. The girls – he was now convinced that there had been at least two – could have ducked down beneath the sills of the windows just to confuse him. It would not do to underestimate their cunning; that was a lesson he had learned from Mandy and Sian.

It was only then that he realized where he was: Kensal Vale. He did not find this surprising. His feet had guided him along a familiar path while his mind was otherwise engaged. He knew the station and the area around it well because of the research he had done in the months before Lucy came to stay with them at Rosington Road. He had often taken the train here.

Eddie went out of the station. It was still raining. Usually Kensal Vale made him uneasy. Its reputation for violence was enough to make anyone wary. Today, however, Eddie felt almost relaxed. Because of the weather, and because it was Sunday, there were fewer people on the streets than usual. The buildings were innocent: only their inhabitants were evil.

Automatically, he made his way towards the squat broach spire of St George's, walking quickly because of the cold. The church, the Vicarage and the church car park occupied a compact site surrounded on all sides by roads, a moat of wet tarmac. The car park, once the Vicarage garden, filled most of the space between the church and the Vicarage. High brick walls and iron railings gave St George's the air of a place under siege.

By now it was early afternoon and services were over, at least until the evening. Eddie read the notice board outside the west door of the church. Sally Appleyard's name leapt out at him. Rainwater streamed down from a leaking gutter. The church was crying.

A bus passed, travelling further west. Eddie was growing colder now that he was neither in the warmth of the train nor generating his own warmth by walking. He looked up at the church, whose details were fading against the darkening sky. He would have to make a decision soon. He couldn't stay here for ever. He walked slowly onwards. As he drew level with the door of the Vicarage, he noticed that it, like Mr Reynolds's garage, had been defaced by a graffito. He stared at the capitals marching across the gleaming paint of the door. The letters huddled in a dyslexic tangle. For a few seconds his mind was unable to decode them.

IS THERE LIFE BEFORE DEATH?

Eddie stared at the question, uncertain whether to laugh or to shiver. Well, he thought, is there? At that moment the door opened. Eddie walked quickly away.

He was unable to resist the temptation to glance back at the doorway. There were two men on the doorstep. The one on the left, Eddie recognized immediately from the photograph in the *Standard*: the vicar, Derek Cutter, so pale he was almost an albino; the man who looked like a ferret in a dog collar. The second man was older, smaller and plumper. He had rosy cheeks, regular features and wispy hair. He was laughing at something Cutter had said. Eddie felt an unexpected and unsettling kinship with the unknown man: it was as if he, Eddie, were looking not in a mirror, but at the reflection of himself in twenty years' time.

The man glanced towards Eddie, who walked hurriedly away. It had been stupid to come to St George's, and worse than stupid to run the risk of being noticed. The rain brushed against the skin of his face, a cruel reminder of the dry heat in his throat. He was very thirsty. Had he not known he had a temperature, he would have been convinced he was going mad. No one could blame him for going mad. Not with all he had to put up with. Of course, a temperature and madness were not incompatible with each other: there was no reason why a lunatic should not have flu.

He looked over his shoulder, desperate for a bus, desperate for anything that would carry him away from St George's, away from the man who looked like an elderly Eddie. There were patterns and correspondences everywhere; why did people so rarely notice them?

Three black men spilled out of a doorway as Eddie passed it, and his insides clenched with terror. But the men ignored him, climbed into a car and drove noisily away. *Perhaps I am invisible.* He walked a little further down the road. Every step took him nearer to the centre of London. He did not want to go there. He wanted peace and quiet.

A bus shelter loomed up ahead, of a type that in fact offered very little shelter, because the main purpose of the design was not to protect people from the elements but to discourage muggers and vandals. He leant against it. Now he had a headache, too. The wind and the rain lashed him. Would anyone notice if he collapsed here? Would anyone notice if he died?

On the other side of the road was the long, high wall of Kensal Green Cemetery, a city of the dead. He noticed a black cab drawing up at one of the entrances and a tall, thin woman emerging from it. She turned back to the cab, her bright red lips moving. The noise of the traffic masked what she was saying, but Eddie knew from her movements that she was angry with the taxi driver. Abruptly she left him, stalking towards the entrance of the cemetery. The taxi swung across both carriageways of the road. Its yellow For Hire light came on. Eddie raised his hand and the taxi pulled over beside the bus shelter. Eddie opened the door, climbed inside and sat down heavily on the seat. The cab smelled strongly of a perfume similar to Angel's, which was no doubt all part of the pattern. The driver looked expectantly at him. Eddie looked back.

'Where to, then?' the man demanded.

Eddie stared blankly at him, remembering suddenly that he had only a handful of change in his pocket, hardly enough for a cup of coffee.

The driver was frowning now. 'Well?'

'Rosington Road,' Eddie blurted out, because he had no other answer to give.

'Where's that?'

'NW5. Off Bishop's Road.'

The taxi pulled away. Eddie sat back on the seat.

'That bloody woman wanted me to wait for her while she visited the dear departed,' the man said through the open partition, tossing the words like grenades over his shoulder. 'Didn't want to pay for it, though. Oh no. "Look, lady," I said, "I'm not a fucking charity, all right?" Jesus *Christ*.'

The man continued to complain for the whole journey, the angry words running as a counterpoint to Eddie's thoughts. Questions without answers flowed through his mind. Everything would depend on how angry Angel was when he reached the house. He wondered whether to ask the driver to wait while he went inside to collect his wallet. But then where would he go?

All too soon the taxi turned into Rosington Road. Eddie pointed out number 29. They drew up outside the house. Eddie stared at its blank windows.

'You getting out, mate? Or are you going to stay there all afternoon?'

The front door opened. Angel ran out to the taxi and opened the rear door. He smelled her perfume and it was identical to the perfume in the back of the taxi. Her hands stretched towards him.

'Eddie. Eddie, dearest. Are you all right?'

2

No one could be kind like Angel. She had the power to make you feel as if you were the centre of the universe. What she did was quite ordinary: she paid off the taxi and drew Eddie into the house; she made him sit on the sofa in the sitting room and covered him with a blanket; she brought him a cup of sweet, milky tea and a digestive biscuit; she felt his hands and told him that he had been foolish to go out with such a high temperature. She endowed all these trivial actions with enormous significance. Eddie knew he was honoured. He was very happy, all the more so because he realized that in the nature of things such happiness would not last.

'Ah – Lucy?' he asked, when he was safely tucked up on the sofa.

'What about her? She's fast asleep.'

'She's all right?'

'Why shouldn't she be?'

'She – she –'

'Her tantrum? That soon passed. She was as right as rain five minutes afterwards. Children are like that, Eddie.'

'But she was so upset.'

Angel smiled. 'If you'd dealt with as many overwrought children as I have, you'd know that sometimes you have to be firm. It's the only way. Believe me, if you give in to them, they turn into little monsters.'

'What's she doing now?'

'She's asleep. It was time for her medication. But what about you?' She paused for a moment, waiting for an answer which did not come, and then went on: 'I've been terribly worried. What did you think you were doing?'

Eddie turned his face towards the back of the sofa and smelled the ghost of his father's hair oil. 'I needed to get out,' he mumbled. 'I needed fresh air.'

There was a short silence. Then Angel sighed. 'Least said, soonest mended. I think the best thing is we draw a veil over the whole unfortunate business.'

'She really is OK?'

'Of course she is.' A hint of irritation had entered Angel's voice. 'Don't be silly.'

Eddie closed his eyes. 'I think I might rest. I'm very tired.'

'I'm not surprised. Anyway, what were you doing in Kensal Vale?'

'I didn't mean to go there. It was an accident. I didn't know what I was doing.'

'There's no such thing as accident,' Angel said.

'I saw the vicar. I don't think he saw me. In any case, he wouldn't have recognized me, would he?'

'No. Now go to sleep.' She smiled at him and slipped out of the room, closing the door behind her with a soft click.

Eddie fell into a doze. He slipped in and out of an inconclusive dream in which he was playing hide and seek with Lucy in a darkened church which he knew was St George's. In the dream, he never caught her. Once, however, he came close to it when she ran round a pillar and found him unexpectedly blocking her path. In the past, he had only seen her back view. Now she was facing him. Except that she had no face: the dark hair had swung in front of it, covering it completely, so that the back of her head was identical to the front of her head.

While this was going on, Eddie was aware of sounds around him in the house – not from below, of course, because the soundproofing prevented that. He heard Angel's footsteps in the hall and on the stairs. He heard her putting out the rubbish for the dustmen, who came on Mondays. He heard water rushing into the bath and Angel's footsteps moving to and fro in her bedroom, and the sounds of drawers being opened and cupboards closed.

He dozed again. When he woke, the room was dark, apart from light from the streetlamps filtering through the gap between the curtains. Now the house was silent. He lay on the sofa, his muscles aching, and tried to summon up the energy to go to the lavatory. Then the doorbell rang.

Automatically, he got up to answer it. The sudden movement made him dizzy and he swayed like a drunk as he crossed the room. At the doorway, he switched on the light and immediately regretted it. He didn't want to see anyone. If it was urgent they could telephone or come back later. But now it was too late: by switching on the light he had revealed his presence. Not answering the door would seem strange. It was one of Angel's rules that when they had a little visitor in the house they should be especially careful not to act in any way abnormally.

He went into the hall and, supporting himself with one hand on the wall, reached the front door. He peered through the spyhole. There was a small woman outside, staring towards the road, presenting her back to him; she was wearing a dark coat and a hat like a squashed cake. A memory stirred. Eddie had first seen Angel through this lens, and she too had been staring at the road. He opened the door.

The woman turned towards him and he saw the sour, shrivelled face of Mrs Reynolds. She was carrying a pile of magazines in the crook of her left arm.

'Hello, Eddie. I wondered if you'd like a copy of the parish magazine.' She edged towards him, and automatically he took a step backwards into the hall; now she was standing on the threshold, her sharp eyes sending darting glances over his shoulder. 'It's only twenty-five pence.'

'Yes, of course.'

It seemed a small price to pay for getting rid of Mrs Reynolds. Eddie turned back into the hall, wondering where to find some money. Almost immediately he realized his mistake. Mrs Reynolds advanced another step. Now she was actually in the house.

'Perhaps you'd like to take it regularly. It's once a month. I know you're not a churchgoer, but there's always something interesting in the magazine.'

'All right. Yes, thanks.'

Mrs Reynolds looked around, openly curious. 'You've changed the place quite a lot since your mum and dad were alive.'

'How much did you say?' Eddie rummaged desperately through the pockets of his coat, which was hanging in the hall. His wallet wasn't there.

'Twenty-five pence.'

The landing light was on. The door to the basement was shut. Perhaps Angel was still in the bath.

'Is Miss Wharton in?'

'I think so. I've been having a nap.'

'My husband saw you today. He wondered if you were all right.'

'I was in a bit of a hurry.' Eddie cast about in his mind for a diversion. 'How's Jenny?'

'No better, no worse.'

Eddie found some change in the pocket of his jeans. 'While there's life there's hope.'

'It's not life, Eddie. It's a living death. She's in a sort of limbo. And because of that we're all in limbo. Why did she do it? That's what I want to know. No one else seems to care.'

He thrust fifty pence towards her. 'I'm sorry.'

'So am I.' She took the money.

'Keep the change.'

222

She had shown no sign of wanting to give him any. 'Will you have children? You and Miss Wharton?'

'Oh no. It's not that sort of – she's a tenant, that's all.'

Mrs Reynolds stared up at him. 'It's your business, I suppose.' She wheeled round and marched outside. On the step, she turned, her head nodding towards him. 'Sometimes I wish she was dead. My own daughter. You know what, Eddie? I wish she'd died when she was a kiddie. When she was three or four. When she was a baby, even.'

Mrs Reynolds squeezed her lips together and glared at him. Without another word, she walked away.

3

That evening Lucy was drowsy. When she woke up from her long afternoon nap, she was thirsty and her eyes kept drifting out of focus.

Angel was very kind to both Lucy and Eddie. She invited Eddie down to the basement. Though he knew what to expect, he could not help being shocked by the sight of Lucy. Angel had cut off most of her hair. For an instant he thought that Lucy was a boy.

'It was getting in her way,' Angel explained. 'And she hated having it brushed, didn't you, pet?'

Eddie sat in the Victorian armchair and Angel put the little girl on his lap. She warmed a red beaker of milk in the microwave and allowed Eddie to feed Lucy.

Afterwards, Eddie read Lucy a story about a lion who had lost his roar, while Angel sat cross-legged on the bed and shortened a pair of trousers for him. They made a family. This was how life should have been, how it was, how it would be.

It was very warm in the basement. As Lucy became sleepier, her body seemed to become heavier. Eddie wondered whether she too had flu. He thought she had fallen asleep. Then she stirred.

'Jimmy,' she murmured. She smelled stale and sweet,

what Eddie thought of as the perfume of innocence. 'Where's Jimmy?'

'Here.' Angel picked up the little rag doll, which had been on the pillow of the bed, and passed it to Eddie. He gave it to Lucy. She stuffed the first two fingers of her right hand into her mouth and with her left hand pressed Jimmy against the side of her nose. Eddie smiled down at the dark head.

Suddenly Lucy squirmed on his lap. She threw Jimmy on to the carpet.

'What are you doing?' Angel asked sharply. 'He'll only get dirty again.'

Lucy began to cry.

Eddie patted her thin shoulder. 'What's wrong?'

The sobbing stopped for an instant. 'Doesn't smell right.'

'I told you so,' Eddie hissed across the room to Angel. 'He smells wrong when he's clean. And she's probably not used to the smell of our soap powder.'

'I can't help that. He was absolutely filthy. It's a question of basic hygiene.'

Angel's voice was calm but firm. Hampered by Lucy's weight, Eddie wriggled forward on the seat of the chair and stood up.

'What are you doing?' Angel said.

'I just want to get something.'

He carried Lucy towards the bed, towards Angel, who held out her arms. Lucy struggled and pointed at the chair.

'You want to stay there?' Eddie was secretly delighted, interpreting Lucy's choice as a sign of favour. He lowered her back into the Victorian armchair. 'I won't be long.'

He was aware of Angel looking strangely at him, but he ignored her. He went upstairs to his bedroom, slowly because any form of movement made his headache worse. Mrs Wump was in her – his? its? – bed in the shoe box in the bottom drawer of his chest. He took her out and sniffed her. She smelt of cardboard, clean clothes and old newspapers. There was a hint of Angel's washing powder, but not too much. Mrs Wump had never been through the washing machine.

He carried her down the stairs, knelt by the chair and said to Lucy, 'Would you like to meet Mrs Wump?'

Lucy, curled into a foetal ball, was still sucking the fingers of her right hand with furious concentration. She stared suspiciously at Eddie and then held out her left hand. Eddie laid Mrs Wump carefully on Lucy's palm. She sniffed it.

'It's not the same,' she said.

'Of course she doesn't smell the same. She wouldn't smell like Jimmy – she's Mrs Wump.'

Still holding Mrs Wump, Lucy rested her head wearily against the back of the chair.

'Time for beddy-byes,' Angel said. 'And perhaps Lucy should have some more medication before she does her teeth.'

Lucy was so tired that Eddie had to carry her into the shower room. Her head flopped against Eddie while he brushed her small white teeth. Afterwards, Angel pushed Lucy's limbs into pyjamas, settled her into bed and turned off the overhead light.

The only light was now from a lamp with a low-wattage bulb on the table by the window. Angel gathered up the discarded clothes. She washed out the red beaker and filled it with water in case Lucy wanted a drink in the night. Meanwhile, Eddie sat down in the armchair, which was very near the head of the bed, and passed Mrs Wump and Jimmy to Lucy. She laid Jimmy on the pillow and held Mrs Wump against her face.

'Are you all right?' Eddie whispered.

'I'm scared.'

'What of?'

Lucy didn't answer. Now that her head was shorn, she looked even smaller than before. Her eyes seemed larger, and shadows thrown by the lighting created the illusion that her cheeks were sunken. She reminded Eddie of photographs he had seen of concentration-camp victims.

'I'm going to make some supper.' Angel climbed the stairs. 'Are you coming?'

'I might stay here a little. Just till Lucy drops off.'

He dug his nails into the palms of his hands, waiting for

Angel to veto the proposal. But her footsteps continued to climb the stairs. He heard her opening the door to the hall.

'All right,' she called down. 'But don't be too long. I think we could all do with an early night.'

The door closed, and Eddie was alone with Lucy. She stared at him with dark, wary eyes. The duvet had fallen forwards over the lower part of her face. He was suddenly terrified that she would suffocate in the night. Slowly, so as not to frighten her, he reached out his hand and tucked the edge of the duvet under her chin. The movement dislodged Jimmy, who fell to the floor. Eddie picked up the little cloth doll and returned him to his place on the pillow.

As he did so, Lucy's eyes closed. Eddie froze, his hand still resting on Jimmy, unwilling to move in case he jarred her back into full consciousness. He felt her breath, warm against his skin, ruffling the hairs on the back of his hand. He had trapped himself in an uncomfortable position. Soon the muscles of his right arm and lower back were complaining. Just a little longer, he told himself, until she's properly asleep.

He watched, fascinated, as Lucy's hand emerged like a small, shy animal from the shelter of the duvet. It moved slowly over the pillow, the fingers working like miniature legs, and touched Eddie's hand. Her eyes were still closed. She gripped his forefinger.

The minutes passed. His finger grew sticky with sweat. He remained there, craning over the bed, his eyes fixed on Lucy's small, white face, until her breathing became slow and regular, until her grip relaxed.

4

When Eddie woke up in the morning, it was still dark. He knew at once that the fever was back in full force. It had receded during the previous evening but he had slept badly during the night, aware of a headache, feeling hot, and needing a drink.

He felt his forehead and the skin seemed to burn his hand.

He was more than ever certain that what he had was flu. He felt aggrieved that Angel was not looking after him properly. People could die from flu. He flung his feet out of the bed and felt for his slippers. The house was very warm. Since Lucy's arrival, Angel had taken to leaving the central heating on at night.

Movement made his head hurt. He struggled into his dressing gown, opened his door and padded on to the landing. Angel's door was closed. He tiptoed into the bathroom and had a long drink of water. The paracetamol seemed to have vanished from the bathroom cupboard. He tried to remember what had happened last night after leaving Lucy. He had gone to bed without any supper; he hadn't been able to face the idea of food. He rather thought that Angel had given him some paracetamol in the kitchen, in which case they were probably still down there.

Despite the warmth of the house, he shivered. But it was not the fever that made him shiver. He stared at himself in the bathroom mirror and silently mouthed the words that Lucy had used: 'I'm scared.'

There was no telling what would happen now. During the night, fragments of memory had mixed with his dreams, and the boundary between them was no longer clear. He had heard Lucy's screams again. He had seen the flashing blades of the scissors hacking into the dark hair. The points of the scissors had danced perilously close to Lucy's eyes. Lucy, struggling so violently in Angel's grip, could have half-blinded herself with one rash movement. He heard again what Angel had said to him when Lucy had been locked, sobbing, into the basement.

'Next time it won't be the hair.'

The face in the mirror was looking at him with Lucy's eyes. Eddie groaned, and backed away.

He went slowly down the stairs, clinging to the banister, and automatically trying to make as little noise as possible. Angel slept lightly, and she hated being disturbed. In the hall he paused, leaning on the newel post and listening.

There was a line of light underneath the kitchen door. All his efforts to be quiet had been in vain: Angel must be already up. Eddie padded along the hall, opened the kitchen door and poked his head into the room. It was empty. Frowning, he drifted over to the worktop where the paracetamol were. He swallowed two of them, washed down with a glass of water from the tap.

His parched throat cried out for a cup of tea. He wondered whether Angel would like some. Either she had returned upstairs to her room or she was in the basement, probably the latter. Somewhere inside him, excitement turned and twisted like a rope being uncoiled. It would be nice to see Lucy again. She was almost certainly asleep, but she might wake up. Offering Angel a cup of tea gave him a good excuse for going to the basement.

He put the kettle on and went back to the hall. As he had hoped, the basement door was unlocked. It opened silently; Angel had asked Eddie to oil all the hinges in the house.

A faint pink radiance filled the room, slightly brighter on the side nearer Lucy's bed. Angel had plugged in the night light and it was still burning. Eddie could just make out the tiny mound which was Lucy in the middle of the bed. There was no sign of Angel, but an oblong of light outlined one of the doors to the right, the door to the freezer room. He hesitated, wondering what to do. A soft, clear ping filled the basement. The sound was not loud but very clear and silvery, as if someone had tapped a small bell with a hammer. An instant later he recognized it for what it was: the microwave's announcement that it had reached the end of its programmed cycle. Angel must be defrosting something for lunch or supper.

He tiptoed down the stairs and crossed the carpet to the door of the freezer room. Unlike the door to the hall, this was not soundproofed. As Eddie drew closer, he heard Angel speaking, her voice muffled by the thickness of the wood. It was difficult to make out individual words. What she was saying had a rhythm, though, like footsteps in an empty street.

He drew nearer the door, stretching out his hand towards the handle. As he touched the knob, Angel's voice rose slightly in volume. He heard her say quite distinctly, 'My body.'

He had never heard her talking to herself before. But, as he knew only too well, you could do the most absurd things when you thought you were by yourself. His hand dropped to his side. Indecision gnawed at him. Should he disturb her, thereby running the risk of making her feel foolish, or slip silently back to the kitchen?

'Memory of me,' said Angel, her voice rising once again and then dropping back to an indistinct mumble.

Eddie backed away from the door. Better not to interrupt, he thought. The door was shut, after all. Angel liked to be alone sometimes. She had always made that clear.

As he backed away, his attention on the door to the freezer room, Eddie stumbled against the arm of the Victorian chair. He stopped, listening. The murmur behind the door continued. Lucy stirred in the bed. In the faint light he made out her dark head moving on the pillow.

'Mummy,' she whispered in a thin voice.

Eddie bent down. 'Hush now. It's not time to get up. Go back to sleep now.'

Lucy did not reply. Eddie counted to a hundred. Then he tiptoed up the stairs, slipped into the hall, and closed the basement door quietly behind him.

Memory of me. The words wriggled uneasily in his memory, defying his attempts to pin them down. What had Angel been talking about?

The kettle had boiled. Eddie made a pot of tea. While he waited for it to brew, he parted the kitchen curtains and stared into the absence of darkness beyond. London was never truly dark. When he pushed his face against the glass, he saw the trees at the bottom of the garden outlined against the yellow glow of the sodium lamps far to the north. The three blocks of council flats rose like black monoliths on the right of Carver's. There were plenty of lights in the flats, on the walkways and landings; over the front doors; at ground level. He wondered if one of the lights belonged to the Reynoldses' flat.

On impulse, he opened the window and let the cool air

flow on to his face. He felt it blowing away the wisps of his fever and leaving clarity behind. He thought of his mind like an empty desert beneath a starlit sky. Happiness caught him unawares. In the distance a goods train rattled over points and a whistle blew.

'What on earth are you doing?' asked Angel.

He swung round, in his agitation knocking the dishcloth on to the floor. Angel was standing in the kitchen doorway, her face unsmiling, her eyebrows raised. She wore jeans and a jersey and had her hair scraped back from her face.

'I'd shut the window if I were you. The gas bill's going to be bad enough as it is.'

He turned away and wrestled with the catch of the window. He heard her coming into the room.

'You're early,' she said.

'I couldn't sleep properly. I've still got a temperature.'

'Have you taken some paracetamol?'

'Yes.'

'Oh good – you've made some tea.'

He looked away from the window to find her opening the refrigerator. She glanced up at him as she slipped a package wrapped in foil and cardboard on to the top shelf.

'I thought we'd have moussaka this evening. In this weather you need something warming.'

He poured them both some tea. They sat at the table to drink it.

'I need to go out for a while,' Angel said.

'Now? It's not even six.'

'I've got one or two things to see to.' She gave him no chance to ask further questions. 'I think you should go back to bed. This fever's really knocked you out, hasn't it? You're not yourself.'

As ever, her concern warmed him. 'I am quite tired still,' he admitted. 'I spent a lot of the night tossing and turning. It wasn't very restful.'

'You go back to bed with another cup of tea. Lucy will be fine – she'll sleep until nine, at least. I'll look in on you when I get back.'

His body was reluctant to move, so Eddie sat at the kitchen

table, sipping tea, and wondering when the paracetamol would begin to work. He heard Angel moving about in the hall and upstairs. A moment later, she returned to the kitchen. She was wearing her long, pale raincoat. On her head she wore a black beret, into which she had piled her hair. The collar of her coat was turned up. She lifted her keys from the hook behind the door. In her other hand she carried a buff-coloured padded envelope.

'You'll be all right by yourself?'

'Fine. I'll just get some more tea and I'll go upstairs.'

'Plenty of fluids.' Angel touched his arm on her way into the hall. 'Try to get some rest.'

He listened to her footsteps in the hall and heard the click of the front door closing behind her. He was alone. This won't do, he told himself. Must get moving. Move where? If he looked inwards, he seemed to be enclosed by infinite space. As space was infinite, movement of any kind seemed pointless. But Angel would be cross if she found him here when she returned.

Supporting himself on the table, Eddie struggled to his feet. Angel had told him to have some tea. The teapot and the milk were on the worktop near the kettle. He crossed the room with enormous caution, like a man walking on ice which might be too thin to bear his weight. Not bothering to boil the kettle again, he filled up his mug with lukewarm tea.

Angel was a stickler for tidiness, just as Thelma had been. Eddie closed the carton of milk and opened the refrigerator to put it away. In order to put the milk inside, he had to move the moussaka which Angel had brought up from the basement. It was a supermarket meal for two, in a flat foil container enclosed by a cardboard sleeve. Eddie noticed a red dot no bigger than a squashed ant on the side of the sleeve. He touched it with a fingertip. The red smeared against the pale-blue background of the cardboard. A speck of blood from the moussaka? Poor dead lamb. Or perhaps Angel had pricked her finger like the princess in the fairy story.

As he staggered upstairs, Eddie wondered why Angel had

gone out so early. The Jiffy bag suggested she was going to the post office, a packet that size would need weighing. Wasn't there a twenty-four-hour post office in central London, somewhere near Leicester Square? But why the urgency? Why not wait until their local post office opened? Perhaps it was something to do with one of her clients. Eddie knew that Angel sometimes did extra jobs for them, little tasks that were paid in cash, that did not attract the commission from Mrs Hawley-Minton.

At six o'clock on a Monday morning?

Eddie shook his head, trying to clear simultaneously his headache and his confusion. It didn't matter. Angel was a very private person, who liked to keep the different compartments of her life separate from one another.

He reached the landing. His bed looked very inviting through the open door of his room. But he hesitated on the threshold. What would he do if Lucy woke up? It was all very well for Angel to say that Lucy would sleep through, but what if she didn't? Children were notoriously unpredictable. He should have thought of the possibility before Angel left. Angel should have thought of it.

Eddie crossed the landing and pushed open the door of Angel's room. Although he was doing it for the best of motives, going into her room seemed almost sacrilegious. He remembered Thelma, who had so much liked to pry among Angel's things: he wasn't like that.

The room smelled of Angel. As he had expected, everything was very tidy. The bed had been made. The horizontal surfaces were empty of clutter. The doors of Mr Reynolds's fitted wardrobes were closed.

The receiving unit of the intercom was plugged into the socket nearest to the single bed. Eddie pulled it out. He was sure that Angel would understand. Angel was scathing about adults who did not look after the children in their care.

Eddie turned to leave. At that instant it occurred to him that the intercom was useless. True, if Lucy woke up, he would hear her cries but he would not be able to get into the basement to comfort her. Angel had the key. It was on the same ring as her keys to the van and the front door.

Eddie leant against the wall, grateful for its coolness against the warmth of his cheek. It was very worrying. If Lucy woke up, he could go downstairs and try to talk to her through the door. But the door was soundproofed, so communication would not be easy. Besides, what good would talking through a door do to a frightened child?

A possible solution occurred to him. Mr Reynolds had given Angel two keys when he fitted the five-lever lock on the basement door. As far as Eddie knew, she had taken only one of them with her.

He looked around the room, wondering where Angel would keep spare keys. She was the sort of person for whom everything has its place. It should be possible to work out the key's location from first principles.

At that moment he heard a vehicle drawing up outside the house. The engine sounded like the van's. He scuttled to the window and peered down to the street below. To his relief, it was the red Ford Escort belonging to the quarrelsome young couple next door. But the incident had shaken him, physically as well as emotionally. Angel might come back at any time. Her movements were unpredictable. It would be terrible if she caught him poking around in her room. His legs felt weak, partly because of the fever and partly at the thought of her reaction.

Eddie abandoned the search and went into his own room and plugged the intercom into one of the sockets. He wasn't well. He needed to sleep. It wasn't fair that when he was ill he should have so much to worry about. He half-lay and half-sat on the bed and sipped the tea, which by now was tepid. Angel had been kind to him this morning, which was such a relief after yesterday. He shied away from the memory of her lunging at Lucy with the scissors. He had never seen Angel like that before, even with naughty little Suki. *Lucy's special.*

He tried to distract himself by thinking of Christmas. It was not much more than three weeks away now. He hoped Lucy would still be with them for Christmas. It would be

233

wonderful to share such an exciting day with her. He would make a list in his mind of the presents he might buy her.

It was true that none of the other children had stayed as long as that – a fortnight was the norm. *But Lucy's special.*

He lay back and closed his eyes. The intercom hissed and crackled, a comforting background noise, like the creaks and murmurs of a gas fire. Eddie drifted towards sleep. He was almost there when a wail emerged from the intercom.

'Mummy . . .'

Eddie swung his legs from under the duvet and stood up. He waited, holding his breath as though there were a danger of Lucy hearing him. Perhaps she would slip back asleep.

'Mummy . . . I'm thirsty.'

Eddie waited, hoping. But Lucy did not go back to sleep. Soon she began to cry. It was a little after seven-thirty.

The crying continued as Eddie pulled on his dressing gown and pushed his feet into his slippers. His breathing was fast and shallow. He went back to Angel's bedroom. In desperation, he pulled out drawers and opened wardrobe doors. Lucy's crying continued, more faintly because further away, and this made it worse. Distance lent a malign enchantment: it left more room for the imagination to play.

In the end it was not so very difficult to find the key. Angel hadn't hidden it at all. Why should she? This was her home. He found it, along with other duplicates, in the top left-hand drawer of the chest. The black japanned box was there too, the one that had contained Angela Wharton's passport. The keys had been wedged between it and a bundle of letters.

Eddie lifted out the ring. It held a complete set of their keys – house, car, back bedroom, basement and a smaller one which he assumed belonged to the chest freezer.

The crying changed gear – it became louder, sharper, higher in pitch; the sobs increased in frequency, too, as if fuelled by panic. *Nobody wants me, nobody loves me, they'll leave me here all alone until I die.*

With the crying filling his head, Eddie stumbled down the stairs, at one point almost falling. His hand was shaking so much that he found it difficult to push the key into the lock.

'It's all right,' he called, fearing that Lucy would not be able to hear him. 'I'm coming.'

At last the door opened. The bed was empty. His heart seemed to lurch. The night light was so faint that he could hardly see a thing. He brushed his hand against the switch and the overhead light came on. Lucy was curled up in the Victorian armchair with Jimmy in one hand and Mrs Wump in the other. She wasn't crying now. His appearance had shocked her into silence. She stared up at him with huge eyes, which in this light and from this angle looked black.

'Now what's all this, Lucy?' Eddie clattered down the stairs, knelt by her chair and put his arms round the tiny body. 'It's all right now. I'm here.'

She burrowed into him. 'I want to go home. I want Mummy. I want –'

'Hush. Do you want a drink?'

'No,' Lucy wailed. 'I want to go home. I want –'

'Soon,' Eddie heard himself saying. 'You'll go home to Mummy soon. But you have to be a good girl.'

Lucy's breath smelt stale. Her eyes were partly gummed up with sleep. She yawned.

'Angel won't be pleased if she finds you out of bed.' Angel would be even less pleased, Eddie suspected, if she found him down here. 'Why don't you snuggle under your duvet again?'

'I don't want to. I'm not tired.'

Eddie lifted her up and laid her down in the bed. She did not resist and her body was still heavy and uncoordinated.

'Don't go. Don't leave me alone.'

'I won't.' Eddie sat down in the Victorian armchair and passed Mrs Wump and Jimmy to Lucy. 'Now, you go to sleep.'

To his surprise, she did. Within five minutes she was fast asleep again. The medication was still affecting her. Eddie waited for a moment, just to make sure, before standing up.

The chair creaked when he moved, and Lucy opened her eyes.

'I want a drink.'

It was a delaying tactic, Eddie thought. The red beaker was

still beside the bed. He picked it up and discovered that it was empty.

'I'll fetch you some more water.'

'I want Ribena.'

'We'll see,' Eddie said weakly.

He opened the door of the freezer room. It smelled faintly of cooking. He found Ribena in the cupboard over the sink and refilled the mug. He took it back to Lucy, only to find that she had fallen asleep again.

He left the drink by the bed and returned to the freezer room to put back the Ribena bottle in the cupboard. Angel need never know that he had come down here. He noticed that there was a bowl on the draining board and a knife, fork and spoon in the rack. They had special cutlery for the children, but these were the normal adult size. For some reason, Angel must have eaten breakfast down here.

On the other hand, there was nothing for her to eat. Usually she had muesli for breakfast, or sometimes bread or toast. In any case, why had she needed a fork? The problem niggled at him. On impulse, he unlocked the freezer and opened the lid.

He hadn't seen inside the freezer since it was new and empty. There were three compartments, two of them filled with shop-bought frozen meals in bright packaging. The third compartment was full of uncooked meat, which surprised Eddie because Angel did not believe in wasting time in cooking and preferred convenience foods. The meat was packed in polythene freezer bags, some transparent, others white and opaque. The cuts varied considerably in size and shape. Some were large enough for a substantial Sunday joint. It was not easy to see exactly what the packages contained, because they were frosted with ice. Some of the cuts looked rather bony. Angel had labelled the packages. Eddie took out one of the smaller ones.

The label said, in Angel's small, neat writing, 'S – July '95'. The meat was in one of the transparent bags. Eddie held it in his hands and felt the cold seeping into his fingers. Sausages? Spare ribs?

I'm feverish. I'm dreaming.

The whiteness of bone gleamed at one end of the package. The ends looked sharp and jagged. S, Eddie thought: S for Suki. A shudder ran through his body. His fingers went limp. His hands fell to his sides. The other, smaller pair of hands fell back into the freezer.

Eleven

'For there are certain tempers of body, which, matcht with an humorous depravity of mind, do hatch and produce vitiosities, whose newness and monstrosity of nature admits no name . . .'

Religio Medici, II, 7

1

Sally thought that Michael was going to hit the man. He accosted them early on Monday morning as they left Oliver's house on their way to Paradise Gardens.

'Now look,' said Frank Howell, smiling his battered-cherub smile. 'It's not like I'm a stranger, is it? You and Mrs Appleyard know me. And these things work both ways.'

Sally moved forward, inserting her body as a barrier between the journalist and Michael. 'We're in a hurry, Mr Howell. Perhaps we can talk later.'

'How did you know where to find us?' Michael demanded as he unlocked the driver's door of the Rover.

'Ways and means.' Howell tried the effect of a smile. 'Just doing my job.'

'It must have been Derek Cutter,' Sally said, her voice suddenly bitter. Howell's eyelashes flickered. 'I gave him the phone number when I talked to him yesterday.'

Michael threw himself into the car and started the engine. Sally climbed into the front passenger seat. Howell, the perfect gentleman, held the door for her.

'Remember, Mrs Appleyard, it's a two-way process. Maybe there's things I know that you don't.'

Michael let out the clutch and Howell hurriedly slammed the door.

'I'm sorry.' Sally sensed the blood rushing to her face.

'It's not your fault,' Michael said. 'Bloody ghoul.'

After that they drove in silence. Damn Michael for mentioning ghouls. Sally tried to persuade herself that she was being unreasonable. How could he be expected to know that in Muslim legend a ghoul was an evil demon that ate human bodies, particularly stolen corpses or children?

There had been an accident in Fortis Green Road and the traffic slowed to a standstill. As they waited in the queue, Michael fidgeted in his seat, his eyes darting from side to side, looking for non-existent side streets, searching for ways of escape.

'I'll call Maxham. Can I have the mobile?'

'I left it at Oliver's,' Sally lied, her muscles tensing at the thought of yet another confrontation between Michael and Maxham.

Michael glowered at her. Sally felt sick with guilt. She opened her mouth to confess the lie, but at that moment the traffic began to move. Neither of them spoke again until they reached the North Circular.

'We've had a purple Peugeot 205 on our tail since Muswell Hill.'

'It's following us?' asked Sally. 'You sure?'

'Of course I'm not sure. All I know is, it's been two or three cars behind us since then.'

Sally turned round and tried without success to see the driver's face. 'Do you think Maxham's got someone keeping an eye on us?'

'I doubt it. He must be stretched enough as it is.' Michael overtook a lorry and, fifty yards behind them, the Peugeot pulled out to overtake as well. 'Unless he still suspects that we did it. That I did it.'

'Michael. Please don't.'

'Get the number.'

Sally opened her handbag and took out an old envelope and a pen. Michael became increasingly irritable as she struggled to read the licence plate of the Peugeot, which promptly ducked, perhaps intentionally, behind the cover afforded by the vehicles between them. She managed it in the end and then wished that there was something else she could do other than listen to her thoughts. Any job was better than none.

To distract herself from the ghoul within, Sally took out the A-Z road atlas. She turned to the index. There were three Paradise Roads and one each of Paradise Gardens, Paradise Passage, Paradise Place, Paradise Street and Paradise Walk. Paradise Gardens was the only scrap of heaven in north-west London. She wondered who had chosen the names and why. Probably nothing more significant than someone's sales technique: buy one of these houses and have an earthly foretaste of the joys to come. Tears filled her eyes. It was a cruel place to choose, a typical refinement, all of a piece with yesterday's discovery at St Michael's, Beauclerk Place.

'What was the message exactly?' she asked Michael.

'That Lucy Appleyard was in forty-three Paradise Gardens. The message was repeated once. It was received just before eight o'clock. They recorded it automatically. Maxham said they traced the call to a public telephone in Golders Green.'

'It wasn't much more than eight-forty-five when he phoned us.'

Michael changed gear unnecessarily. A moment later he said, 'The caller said one other thing: *Not just her tights this time.*'

'So?'

'So the call wasn't a hoax. They've not released the fact that Lucy's tights were found.'

Paradise Gardens was a little over a mile west of Kensal Vale, a long, curving road of redbrick terraced houses, perhaps ninety years old. Many of the houses were boarded up. Two police cars and an unmarked van were parked at the far end of the road.

'It's not Lucy,' Michael said. 'Just remember that. While there's life, there's hope.'

Sally stared through her window at two children, perhaps ten, who should have been at school and who were instead sitting on the wing of a car and sharing a companionable cigarette. 'If there's life.'

'God help me, I sometimes find myself hoping that there isn't.'

'Just so it could be all over?'

He nodded. 'For her. For us, too.'

'It's awful. Everything's changing because of this. You. Me. Everything.'

She was about to tell him of her lie about the phone. But he gave her no chance.

'We have to face it,' he said. 'Nothing will ever be the same again. Whatever happens. You can never go back. I found that out a long time ago.'

'What do you mean?' Sally asked.

'When I was a kid I was mixed up in a murder case.'

'What?' The word emerged as a gasp, as though someone had punched her in the stomach. 'Why did you never tell me?'

Michael drew up behind a police car. One of the two uniformed policemen on the pavement moved towards them.

'Because of Uncle David,' Michael said. 'At the time I promised him ... He and his family were involved much more than I was. And in the early days I wasn't sure how you'd react. Then I thought, least said, soonest mended. All this – what's happening to Lucy – it's like a punishment.'

'*Darling.*'

He looked at her, and she saw the tears in his eyes. He opened his mouth to speak but it was too late – the constable had come round the car and was bending down to Michael's window. Michael turned away to speak to him, leaving Sally to grapple with unanswered questions. *David's family?*

''Morning, Sarge.' The policeman was young and very nervous; he stared at Sally and quickly looked away, as if he had done something naughty. 'Mr Maxham is in the house. You're to go right in. If you leave the key in the car, we'll take care of it.'

As Sally crossed the pavement, she was aware of twitching curtains and watching eyes in the neighbouring houses. Apart from the boys further down the street, nonchalantly smoking their cigarette, there were no bystanders; it was not that sort of area. In Paradise Gardens, as in Kensal Vale, the police brought trouble, not reassurance: they were not the protectors of society but its agents of retribution.

The ground-floor window of number 43 had been boarded up. One of the windows above was broken, and none of them had curtains. As they approached, the second constable tapped on the front door and it opened from within.

Inside was a narrow hallway, its ceiling and walls covered with a yellow, flaking plaster and its floor carpeted with circulars and old newspapers; it smelled strongly of damp and excrement. The plain-clothes man who had let them in gestured towards the stairs. Maxham was coming down, talking to someone invisible on the landing above. 'Get her to make a statement. Don't take no for an answer. I want to see it in black and white by lunch time if not before.' He turned to Sally and Michael and, without changing his tone, went on, 'You took your time. Come and have a look at what we've got. I'd take you outside, where the smell isn't so bad, but then there's the problem of spectators. One of the bastards has got a pair of binoculars. And the next-door neighbour's playing with his video camera.'

He led them into a room at the back of the house. There were two mattresses on the floor and fading posters of footballers on the walls. The window was boarded up, but someone had rigged up a powerful lamp. Maxham looked ghostly by its light, his plump face bleached of colour. He had not shaved yet this morning and his face looked as tired as his tweed suit. It occurred to Sally that even Maxham might have feelings, that even he might find this case harrowing.

The only person in the room was a uniformed policewoman. Beside her, a kitchen chair without a back did duty as a table. Its top had been covered with a sheet of paper, and on this rested a padded envelope which was almost as large as the seat of the chair.

'You can buy them in any stationer's or newsagent's.' Maxham hissed, sucking air between his teeth. 'It's brand new. No address, no nothing.'

'Too big to get through the letterbox,' Michael said.

'It was folded. You can see the line.' Maxham's finger bisected the envelope. 'It wasn't even sealed.'

He pulled on a pair of gloves and, holding the envelope near its opening, gingerly lifted it so that the closed end was resting on the seat of the chair.

'Look. Not you, Sergeant. Mrs Appleyard.'

The policewoman altered the angle of the light. Sally peered into the open mouth of the envelope. There was a mass of dark hair inside.

'Don't touch,' Maxham ordered. 'Strictly speaking, I shouldn't be doing this. But I need to know if that hair's Lucy's. The sooner the better.'

'How can I tell? Especially if you won't let me touch.'

'Smell it.'

Sally bent down. The unwashed smell of the house fought with the plastic and paper of the envelope. Beyond those smells was another, a hint of the sort of perfume which is meant to remind you of Scandinavian forests.

'Some sort of pine-scented bath essence? Shampoo?'

'Do you use something like that? Could Lucy's hair smell of it?'

'No, we don't.' She looked more closely, longing to touch the dark cloud that might have been part of Lucy. 'It could be hers.'

'Then whoever's got her has given her a bath, maybe washed her hair.' Michael sounded very weary all of a sudden. 'I suppose we should be thankful for that.'

Sally turned to Maxham. 'Could it be a good sign? That they're looking after her?'

The black-rimmed glasses flashed, catching the light. 'Yes. It could be.'

'We can't tell,' Michael said. 'And nor can you.'

Maxham ignored him. 'We'll know for certain in an hour or two, Mrs Appleyard. We picked up samples of Lucy's hair from your flat. It's a simple matter of comparison.'

'And then what?' Michael demanded.

Maxham hissed but didn't answer.

'Thank you for showing us,' Sally said to Maxham. 'And thank you for showing us here.'

'I thought it would be better all round.' Maxham's voice was harsh, but for an instant there might have been a gleam of kindness in his face.

'Any witnesses?' Michael said. 'Surely someone must have seen something?'

'Nothing to speak of.' Maxham moved into the hall. 'A woman over the road thought she saw a light-coloured van pulling up outside around six-thirty. No idea of the make, or who was driving. We're taking a statement but it's the next best thing to worthless.'

The Appleyards followed him into the hall.

'You've not got someone watching us, have you?' Michael asked.

Maxham swung round. 'No. Why?'

'We had a purple Peugeot 205 behind us most of the way from Inkerman Street.'

'You got the number?'

'Here.' Sally opened her handbag and produced the envelope.

Maxham reached out a hand for it. 'I'll have it checked out and get back to you. You sure it was following you?'

'Probable,' Michael said. 'Not absolutely certain.'

The constable at the far end of the hall opened the door as they approached.

'I'll be in touch if there's anything more,' Maxham told them. 'And I'll let you know the results of the test as soon as I hear myself.'

Michael stared at him and said nothing.

Sally said, 'Thank you. Goodbye.'

The door closed behind them. The Rover was still where they had left it. The young constable gave them an embarrassed wave.

Michael drove slowly down Paradise Gardens.

'It's aimed at me, isn't it?' Sally said.

'Why do you think that?'

'All the religion.'

'You're assuming the three incidents are connected.'

'They must be.' Sally paused, but Michael did not disagree. 'First the hand in a cemetery,' she went on. 'Then the legs in Lucy's tights in a church porch. And now the hair in Paradise Gardens.' A bubble of laughter rose in her throat. She choked it back. 'He's playing with us, whoever he is. Don't you think so?'

'I don't know what to think.'

Michael joined the stream of traffic moving south-east down the Harrow Road. For a few moments neither of them spoke. Somewhere over to the left was the stumpy spire of St George's, Kensal Vale.

'There's another kind of pattern,' Michael said abruptly. 'Geographical. Apart from Beauclerk Place, everywhere else is in north-west London. Within a few square miles.'

'But there's only two other places. Paradise Gardens and Kilburn Cemetery.'

'And St George's. It's roughly equidistant between Harlesden and Kilburn. Like Carla's house. And Hercules Road is just east of Kilburn.'

Sally wriggled in her seat. 'Would it make a shape on the map?'

'A symbol or something? I doubt it. But maybe it means that the person we want is living or working between the two – somewhere between Beauclerk Place and the cluster of other locations. I wonder if – '

'Where are we going?' Sally interrupted, suddenly realizing that Michael was not taking them back to Inkerman Street but towards the centre of the city.

'I want to see Uncle David.' Michael glanced at her, his face half-angry, half-sheepish. 'It won't take long. In some ways it's a faster route.'

Sally stared at him. 'But what about Oliver? And have you told Maxham where we'll be? And what happens if there's some news?'

'If you'd remembered your phone, there'd be no problem.' His voice rose. 'All right, I'll call them.'

Without warning, Michael swerved into the kerb and parked the car on a double yellow line; Michael, who was so meticulous about obeying the smaller rules and regulations in life. For a few seconds, Sally was too surprised to speak. There was a pair of phone boxes outside a parade of shops.

She fumbled at the catch of her handbag. 'Michael, there's no need, I've –'

Before she could finish he was out of the car. He slammed the door and strode to the phone box without looking back. To Sally's relief, it was neither occupied nor out of order. She watched him through the glass, noting with a mixture of irritation and compassion that he chose to stand with his back to her. The knowledge that she had lied to him worked inside her like corrosive acid.

She was aware of a car drawing up behind theirs, and of a door closing, but paid no attention. Then there were footsteps on the pavement and she glanced over her shoulder. The purple Peugeot 205 was parked immediately behind them. Sally lunged for the door lock and pushed it down. Frank Howell's face bobbed down until it was level with hers. Reluctantly, she lowered the window.

'Mrs Appleyard? I don't want to bother you –'

'Then don't.'

'Look, I don't mean to pester you, but maybe I can help.'

'How?'

'I hear things.' The little eyes were bloodshot. 'I've got a contact who's on Maxham's team.'

'Good for you.'

'Maxham doesn't tell you everything, you know. He plays his cards very close to his chest.'

'Give me an example.'

'And in return –'

'That depends.' Somewhere Sally found the strength to haggle. 'Eventually, maybe a personal interview. But not yet. And not until you've shown what you can do.'

'It's not what you think,' Howell said awkwardly. 'All right, an interview would be nice but I really want to help. We all do. Derek was saying –'

'I've not got much time.' Sally wanted to trust him, but it was safer to take refuge in cynicism. 'So what can you tell me?'

'There's some good news. You know the disciplinary pro-ceedings against your husband, for hitting a suspect?'

Sally nodded. That part of the story had not been released to the public so it supported Howell's claim that he had a source within the police.

'The solicitors are meeting today. The word is, it's just for show. They've already met informally and done a deal. Your husband's in the clear.'

Sally concealed the relief she felt, which might in any case be premature. 'Is that all?'

Howell's mouth tightened. 'What about the first atrocity? Do you know where the hand was found?'

'In Kilburn Cemetery. There's no secret about that.'

'Exactly where the hand was found? On which grave? The police haven't released that detail. But I know. I've got a photograph.'

He pulled out a print about six by four inches from an inner pocket of his waxed jacket. He slid it through the open window.

'Keep it if you like. When can we talk? Maybe you'd like to make an appeal to the kidnapper.'

'What the hell are you doing?' Michael loomed up outside the window.

The journalist moved away. Sally rolled the window further down and put her head out. Howell was retreating towards his car and Michael was glaring down at him.

'It's all right, Michael. Come on – we've got to get going. Mr Howell won't be following us.'

'I'll phone you later then,' Howell said, keeping an eye on Michael. 'Good luck.'

He scuttled round to the driver's door of his car. By the time Michael had settled himself behind the wheel, the Peu-geot was receding rapidly on the Harrow Road.

Michael started the engine. 'What does Howell think he's up to?'

'He says he'll be our man in the media in return for an exclusive interview.'

'If I see him again – '

'It's OK. I can handle him.'

Michael took his eyes off the road and glared at her. *'You* can?'

'Don't be so bloody patronizing.'

The line of traffic in front of them slowed and stopped for a red light.

Michael turned to look at her. 'So did Howell tell you anything interesting?'

'It looks like the solicitors are going to sort out your little disciplinary problems.'

The Rover stalled, jerking as if stung by a wasp. Michael restarted the engine. 'What do you know about that?'

'Oliver told me, yesterday. He assumed I'd already heard about it from you. And it's just as well he did tell me, or else I wouldn't have had the slightest idea what Howell was talking about.'

The light changed to green. Sally wondered whether the hurt in her voice had been as obvious to Michael as it was to her.

'I was going to tell you on Friday evening,' he said, which was as near to an apology as he was likely to get.

'It doesn't matter.' Of course it mattered, as did whatever horrors he had shared as a child with David Byfield and now guarded so jealously. In both cases what mattered most was the fact that he had not told her.

Michael cleared his throat. 'How did Howell know?'

'He's got a source in the police. I don't know who or where. He also gave me a photo of the gravestone in Kilburn Cemetery, the one where they found the hand. There's a sort of medallion at the top of it, all rather cod Jacobean, a skull and so on.'

'It was probably chosen at random. Or because it wasn't overlooked – something like that.'

'Not necessarily.' The longer the nightmare continued, the more certain Sally became that everything was potentially significant.

After a while, Michael said, 'I phoned David while I was in the call box. They're expecting us.'

'I lied to you,' Sally blurted out. 'I have got the mobile. It's in my bag.'

'Why? I don't understand.'

'I thought you'd just shout at Maxham.'

'You were probably right.'

She shook her head and said flatly, 'I was wrong.'

For the rest of the journey, she closed her eyes and tried to pray. In the darkness of her mind she recited the Lord's Prayer. The words fell like stones into the cool, green silence. The silence was still there but God was absent, his attention elsewhere. *Oh my God, why do you leave me when I need you most?*

Time slowed and stopped. It was very quiet. Miss Oliphant was dead, dead, dead: among the angels. Sally reached out her hands in the darkness, trying to find Lucy. Her fingers closed on emptiness and she sank down and down into the dark. Is this what hell means, she wondered, this slow drowning in the black waters of your own mind? But if you are drowning, you seize anything which may help you float and breathe. So then, as before, Sally made herself say over and over again the words that no longer meant anything.

'Your will be done,' she said, or thought she said. 'Not mine.'

2

'It's the next left, I think,' Michael said. 'Or the one after that.'

Sally opened her eyes. They were in the northern half of Ladbroke Grove, travelling south towards the raised section of Westway. Michael had driven his godfather here yesterday evening; to Sally's relief, the old man had declined the offer of a bed at Oliver's.

'Who's David staying with?' Sally asked.

'Someone called Peter Hudson. He's a retired bishop. An old friend.'

'There was a Hudson who was Bishop of Rosington in the seventies.' Once a senior diocesan bishop, he had been one

249

of the more articulate opponents of the ordination of women, just the sort of friend for David Byfield.

'Could be him. David was there for a while himself. But that was much earlier.'

Sally remembered the Rosington postcard she had found in Miss Oliphant's books. *Our mutual friend still remembered. Small world!* Not so small you couldn't have secrets.

She said, 'So David had a family? A wife? Children?'

'A wife and child.'

'What happened to them?'

'They died.' Michael pulled over to the side of the road. 'I'll tell you about it later, Sal, OK?'

Neither Hudson nor his home were quite as Sally expected. The bishop lived in a small flat at the top of a nondescript modern block set back from the road. There was nothing overtly episcopal, or even clerical, about him: he wore slippers, baggy corduroy trousers and a tweed jacket with frayed cuffs; he had a pipe in his mouth when he opened the door to the Appleyards, and the pipe was never far away from him until they left. He was pink, plump and small – in appearance the opposite to his guest; Uncle David looked far more like a bishop than his host.

Hudson showed them into the living room, with its view of the bleak little garden at the back of the flats and the endless muddle of the city beyond. The walls and the ceiling were painted white. There was little furniture, few books and no pictures. The only ornament was a large wooden crucifix on the shelf over the gas fire. A pile of blankets and pillows on the floor suggested that the small sofa had spent the night as Uncle David's bed.

Within a couple of moments of their arrival, Hudson produced a tray of weak, instant coffee, with the milk already added, and a plate of sweet, slightly stale biscuits. He handed round the mugs and then sat down beside Sally.

'This is very terrible, my dear,' he said conversationally, a gambit which took her entirely by surprise. 'How on earth are you managing?'

'I'm not,' Sally muttered, and started to cry quietly.

Hudson produced a large, freshly ironed white handkerchief from his trouser pocket. Sally mentally gave him full marks for preparation. 'Carry on,' he said. 'I doubt if you've found much time to cry. And sometimes one can't, of course.'

Michael and David were talking by the window with their backs to the room. Neither of them appeared to have noticed that Sally was crying. The tears flowed in near silence for over a minute. Hudson sat with half-closed eyes; he did not attempt to touch her or to say anything else. Gradually Sally's tears subsided. She blew her nose and wiped her eyes.

Hudson put his pipe back in his mouth and reached for a box of matches. 'I don't know if you'd like to wash? It's the door at the end of the hall, if you want it. The one on the left.'

Sally went into an ascetic little bathroom and rinsed her face with cold water. Her face, red-eyed and ugly, stared accusingly at her from the mirror. She returned to the living room to find that nothing had changed in her absence: Michael and David were still talking by the window and Hudson was puffing his pipe in the armchair next to hers.

'Have Michael and David told you what's happening?' she asked.

Hudson nodded. 'As much as they can.'

'I feel it's my fault, all of it. What I've done, what I am, has attracted someone's hatred. And Lucy's paying the price.'

'My wife once told me that I had a terrible tendency to blame myself.' A match scraped, and Hudson held the flame dancing over the bowl of the pipe. '"Don't be so self-centred," she used to say. She was quite right.'

'But the longer this goes on, the more it seems that who-ever is doing it is trying to get back at me.'

'At you, or his parents, or himself, or God – what does it matter? The point is this: that person is responsible for his actions, not you. You mustn't blame yourself. I know it's tempting, but you must resist.'

'Tempting?'

'Because in general feeling guilty when it's patently not your fault is a soft option.' He beamed at her. 'Let's have a biscuit.'

Sally was so confused that she took one. 'I hope they're

all right,' Hudson went on. 'I keep them for visitors and I think the packet has been open for rather a long time.'

For an instant, the smaller problem elbowed aside the infinitely greater one. Should she be rude but honest, or dishonest and polite? Should she eat this horrible biscuit or not? How on earth could she avoid either distressing her host or lying to him?

'Have you got that photograph?' Michael said from the window. 'David would like to see it.'

Sally jettisoned the biscuit and delved into her handbag. All four of them looked at the photograph, passing it from hand to hand. It was a black-and-white shot of a small gravestone – a simple slab, originally upright, which over the years had listed a few degrees to the left. Two people, almost certainly male, were standing near it, one on each side. The camera had cut them off at waist level, and only parts of their legs were visible: pinstripe trousers, a little too short, to the right, and something indeterminate on the left. Only the legs, the stone and the grass immediately in front of it were in focus. Everything else was a grey blur.

'It's a very short depth of field,' Michael commented. 'Probably taken from one of the houses overlooking the cemetery with a long-distance lens.'

What caught the eye was the medallion at the top, raised in bas relief. It showed a cowled death's head with the blade of a scythe arching above it. The inscription was still clearly legible.

FREDERICK WILLIAM MESSENGER
Born April 19th, 1837
Died March 4th, 1884

'On the laconic side, don't you think?' Hudson cocked his head to one side, mirroring the listing of the gravestone. 'Perhaps he didn't want the orthodox pieties on his gravestone.'

'Are you sure this is where the hand was found?' David said suddenly. 'Absolutely sure?'

Michael shook his head. 'We've only got Howell's word for it. I –'

'We've got more than that,' Sally interrupted. 'I think those trousers on the left are a pepper-and-salt tweed like Maxham's. And Sergeant Carlow wears a pinstripe suit.'

'Why have the police kept this quiet?' David asked.

'For the same reason that they didn't release the news that Lucy's tights turned up yesterday,' Michael said. 'To give them a chance of winnowing out the hoaxes.' He rubbed his forehead and stared down at the photograph in Hudson's hand. 'It's macabre, isn't it?'

Hudson peered at the print. 'I don't suppose the chap's name has any significance?' As he spoke, he glanced up at David Byfield, who shrugged and turned away to light a cigarette.

'I don't understand,' Sally said.

'A messenger usually brings a message, that's all. So perhaps the hand should be interpreted as a message. Don't you agree, David?'

Byfield nodded, his eyes on the glowing tip of his cigarette.

'The Greek for "messenger" is "angelos", of course,' Hudson went on. 'Which is where our word angel comes from. The Angel of Death? I wonder if someone might be playing word games?'

David straightened up and turned round. 'The important thing is the skull and the scythe.' His face was no different from usual, but at the end of the sentence his voice trembled; for the first time since Sally had met him, he sounded as old as he was. He stabbed the cigarette in the direction of the photograph. 'There's a pattern which links that to St Michael's yesterday and Paradise Gardens today.' He sucked in smoke. 'Whoever is behind this is probably Catholic, or at least has a nodding acquaintance with Catholic theology.'

'But St Michael's is an Anglican church,' Michael said.

David waved the cigarette impatiently, and a coil of ash fell to the carpet. 'Catholic in the wider sense. Not necessarily Roman.' The cigarette tip swung between Sally and Michael, and for an instant she glimpsed what David Byfield must have been like as a teacher. 'Do you know what the Four Last Things are?'

Michael glanced at Sally and shook his head.

'Death and Judgement,' Sally said automatically, her mind on Lucy, 'Heaven and Hell. In the Roman Catholic catechism, they are "ever to be remembered".'

'Precisely,' murmured Hudson. 'The *res novissimae*. Pre-Tridentine, aren't they?'

David nodded. 'The theological basis is a passage in the Apocrypha – in *Ecclesiasticus*. But the division into four isn't a formal one: it's a matter of popular usage. Long established, though. You find it in the catechisms of St Peter Canisius, for example. But I think it goes back further than the sixteenth century to the Gallican church.'

'I'm sorry,' said Michael, looking so young and vulnerable that Sally wanted to hug him, 'but I don't see what this is about.'

'It's about a great evil,' David said slowly. 'A perversion.'

'We know that,' Michael snapped. 'But what's theology got to do with it?'

'Eschatology, to be exact.'

Hudson blew a perfect smoke ring. 'I always found that a very difficult subject to get to grips with.'

'On a superficial level eschatology is quite straightforward,' David said, as if addressing a recalcitrant seminar. 'Technically it's the branch of systematic theology dealing with the ultimate fate of the individual soul and of mankind in general.'

Hudson leaned forward. 'David?'

'What?'

'Would you get to the point, please?'

For a moment, the two old men stared at each other. Sally held her breath. She knew there was a struggle going on, though not why, and she sensed both the authority flowing from Peter Hudson and David's obstinate anger. And there was another, less predictable emotion present: David was scared.

At last David nodded slightly, an unconditional capitulation. 'As you say, the name Messenger suggests that the hand wasn't left on that particular gravestone at random,' he said quietly, no longer the lecturer. 'It's a hint to the effect that there's a message for us, that there is something to be read into the symbol, a transference of meaning. And the bas relief makes it quite clear what that meaning is: the grim reaper, Death.'

'There was the painting.' Sally needed to pause because it was suddenly hard to breathe. 'The one over the high altar in St Michael's. Did you see it?'

David turned towards her, and to her astonishment she saw that there were tears in his eyes. 'Yes. Rather an unpleasant version of the Last Judgement. After Giotto, I suppose.'

Sally nodded. 'A long way after.'

His face almost lightened into a smile, then became grim again. 'So St Michael's would give us Judgement.'

'Michael's name is in the church's dedication. There might be significance in that.'

'Come off it.' Michael scowled impartially at the three of them. 'Isn't that the logic of paranoia? Selecting the facts to suit the theory?'

'Perhaps.' David stubbed out his cigarette and immediately shook another from the packet. 'But I rather doubt it. Too many facts fit. There's another possible link between St Michael's and Judgement. While we were there I happened to notice that the first incumbent was a Reverend Francis Youlgreave.'

'Youlgreave?' interrupted Michael.

'Yes.'

'But they used to live in Roth, didn't they?'

'That's how I know the name.' David stared at Michael and then turned back to Sally. 'I was Vicar of Roth for a few years, before I went to America. I don't know whether Michael has ever mentioned the place. It's a village in Middlesex, a suburb, really.'

She stared blankly at him. Miss Oliphant had lived, or at least stayed, in Roth. *Small world?*

'Francis Youlgreave is actually buried in the church,' David was saying. 'In his spare time he was a minor poet, rather

255

in the manner of his namesake, Francis Thompson. One of his poems occasionally turns up in anthologies. It's called "The Judgement of Strangers".'

Michael was frowning. 'But that's quite a coincidence, isn't it?'

He looked at David, and David looked back. The old jealousy twisted inside Sally: they excluded her automatically from their shared past.

'In my opinion, coincidence is a much overrated idea,' Hudson said. 'It often seems to be the norm rather than the exception.'

David's lighter flared. 'True enough. And then, of course, there's Paradise Gardens, which gives us Heaven, the third of the Last Things. What do you think?' He was looking at Hudson.

'It's plausible. But will the police agree? Will you tell them?'

'We can try,' Michael said. 'I can't guarantee that Maxham will listen, though.'

'He must,' David said. 'He *must*.'

At that moment the doorbell rang. None of them moved.

'And what about the fourth Last Thing?' Sally stood up, scattering biscuit crumbs. 'Have you thought what your precious theory means for Lucy?'

3

'Yes,' Sally said, her throat dry and her stomach fluttering. 'I'm quite sure.'

Sergeant Carlow rubbed his long, clean hands as though trying to warm them by friction. 'It was the crucifix, you see. That's what made Mr Maxham wonder.'

'I don't think many churchgoers would encourage a child to wear a crucifix in that way.'

They were standing in Bishop Hudson's hall – Carlow and DC Yvonne Saunders, Sally and Michael. The two old men had remained in the living room, and their voices rose and fell in the background. Michael's face had a green pallor. Carlow was wearing the same pinstriped suit; the trousers were so short that when he moved Sally glimpsed pale, hairless skin above his black socks. A wave of dizziness hit her and for a moment she thought she was going to faint.

'And you can confirm that Lucy's ears weren't pierced?'

'Of course I can.' A thought occurred to her, driving away the dizziness: 'The ear couldn't have been pierced recently?' She held her breath, waiting for the answer.

'We think the piercing was done a long time ago, and not very well. There's what they call a keloid on the lobe, sort of raised scar tissue. The ear was probably pierced months ago, if not years.'

Sally let out her breath. Her heart was still pounding uncomfortably; news of the temporary reprieve had not yet reached it. She swallowed convulsively. Michael gave a dry sob.

Yvonne smiled nervously, exposing the flawless teeth, and patted Sally's arm. 'Do you want to sit down, love?'

Sally allowed herself to be guided towards a chair that stood beside the wall. 'Not Lucy. Not Lucy.'

'No, love,' said Yvonne with the bright sincerity of a housewife assessing a washing powder in a TV advertisement. '*Definitely* not.'

'I'm sorry this has been a shock,' Carlow said mechanically. 'But Mr Maxham thought that we'd better check with you right away.'

Underneath the mass of black hair – Lucy's hair? – the police had found another, much smaller package, shrouded in clingfilm, at the very bottom of the padded envelope. It contained a small ear, roughly severed from the head. From the lobe dangled an earring with a silver crucifix attached to it.

Michael touched Sally's shoulder. Sally raised her hand and clung to his.

'Could the ear have come from the same body as the legs or the hand?' Michael asked.

'Definitely not the hand.' Carlow was patently happier

257

talking to a man. 'The skin's white. Don't know about the legs. But if I had to put money on it, I'd say not.'

'Why?'

Carlow shrugged. 'I don't know – the legs were sort of big and clumsy – whereas the ear's rather delicate. Just a guess, but I'd say they come from different kids.'

'Had the ear been frozen too?'

'We don't know yet. Quite possibly.'

Three victims, Sally thought: one for Death, one for Judgement, one for Heaven. And for Hell –

'There was one other thing,' Carlow went on. 'You know the tights we found yesterday?'

Sally nodded, thinking that this must pass for tact: not mentioning that the tights were Lucy's or what they had contained.

'Forensic found a hair clinging to the wool. Natural blonde. We should know more by this afternoon.'

'Man or woman?' Michael asked, his fingers tightening on Sally's shoulder.

'At a guess, a woman's: it's about twelve inches long and it's fine hair, too.'

'I need to talk to Maxham.'

Carlow looked blankly at him. 'Oh yes?'

'For God's sake!' Michael shouted, moving away from Sally and towards Carlow. 'We've just found what might be a pattern. If we're right, time's running out.'

'OK, OK. What sort of pattern?'

'The one the killer's using.'

'Tell me.'

'I'd rather tell Maxham. It supports what we already thought, that there's a religious nutter behind this.'

Carlow clamped his lips together. A muscle twitched above his big jaw. 'If you insist.'

'Of course I insist. And I'll need to bring someone with me.'

Carlow glanced at Sally, raising his eyebrows.

'A priest,' Michael said. 'David Byfield – you met him yesterday. He can explain the technical side better than I can.'

'The technical side?' echoed Carlow. 'I'm sorry, I don't – '

'We'll all be sorry if we don't get moving.' Michael turned back to Sally. 'You could stay here if you want, or take the car back to Inkerman Street. Up to you.'

'I'll see. You'd better take the mobile. You can phone me here or at Oliver's.' Sally was upset that he did not want her to go with him but was unwilling to insist; she could add nothing but emotional complications. Besides, she had an overwhelming urge to find somewhere private so that she could cry without interruption or well-meant sympathy.

Carlow tried again. 'I'm not sure there's any advantage in this. If you've got any information, I can pass it on, of course. But Mr Maxham may be too busy to actually – '

'I know,' Michael said in a voice that climbed in volume and wobbled towards the edge of hysteria. 'He's got a full-time job. It doesn't leave him much time for socializing. But let's see if we can persuade him to make an exception.'

4

In Inkerman Street, Sally carefully reversed the car into an empty space. Unfortunately, she forgot to brake. The back of the Rover collided with the front of the dark-blue Citroën. The engine stalled.

Sally rested her forehead against the top of the steering wheel. *Your will be done.* Could God really and truly want something as stupid as this to happen? The red oil lamp on the dashboard winked at her, red drops on a dark background, blood on a floor. She closed her eyes but the blood would not go away. More than anything, she would have liked to pray for Lucy. When she tried, her mind filled with her daughter – not with her name or her face, but with the essence of her. In Sally's mind, Lucy expanded to such huge proportions that there was no room for anything else, even God.

Gradually the image of Lucy contracted. Like a departing aeroplane, the image grew smaller and smaller until it was no longer visible but still there. *I am not worthy to be a priest. I have no room for God.*

The sound of tapping forced itself to her attention. Sally opened her eyes, resenting the intrusion. Oliver was standing in the road outside, bending down so that his face was level with hers, just as Frank Howell had done. She rolled down the window.

'Are you all right?'

Dumbly she shook her head.

'Come inside.' He put his hand into the car and unlocked the door. 'You've had news? Is it –?'

'No. They haven't found her.'

'Then she may still be alive. She may still be all right.' Oliver opened the door. 'Out you come.'

Moving like an old woman, she struggled out of the car and clung to Oliver's arm. With his free hand he turned off the ignition, took out the key, rolled up the window, shut the door and locked it.

Sally stared at the front of the Citroën. It was this year's model and the paintwork gleamed. Now there was a dent in the front and one of the headlights had lost its glass. It was surprising how much damage a little knock could do. She had not realized that cars were so vulnerable.

'Look what I've done.'

'It doesn't matter.'

'But the owner –'

'I'm the owner. You can drive into it as much as you like. It's only a car.'

Oliver led her towards the house. He took her into the kitchen and put the kettle on. Sally put down her handbag on the table. She picked up a tea towel and began to dry the mug on the draining board.

'There's no need,' Oliver said after a while.

'No need of what?'

'No need to dry that. It's been draining there since last night, and even if it were wet, you would have dried it four times over by now.'

Sally stared at the mug and the towel in her hands. 'I don't know what I'm doing.'

'That's not surprising. Why don't you sit down?'

She watched Oliver making tea. He poured two mugs and added three spoonfuls of sugar to hers. He gestured towards the kitchen table.

'We'll sit there.'

She sank into a chair, grateful to have the decision taken away from her. 'We must do something about your car. Shouldn't I ring the insurers? Or report it to the police?'

'I told you: forget the car. Do you want to tell me what's happened?'

In the midst of everything, she noted his technique: asking questions rather than advancing propositions or making statements. In that respect, policemen were like priests and psychologists. She told him what Maxham had shown them in Paradise Gardens. Gradually, his questions prised out the rest: the meeting with Howell, David Byfield's theory and the arrival of Sergeant Carlow.

'So what does it add up to?' Oliver said at last. 'If I was Maxham, I'd be thinking that the blonde hair probably belongs to one of the victims. As for the rest, it's largely speculative, isn't it? But I suppose it supports the theory that there's a religious crank behind this.'

Sally wrapped her cold hands around the warm mug. 'It does more than that. We've got two patterns now. One's obvious – the geographical concentration in north-west London. The other's religious, not just vaguely anti-religion but specifically tied to the Four Last Things.'

Where hell is, there is Lucy.

Oliver went out of the room. A moment later he came back with a London street atlas. He turned to the index.

'Michael's already looked,' Sally said. 'There's a Hellings Street, but that's in Wapping.'

'Way out of your geographical frame.' Oliver's finger ran down the printed column. 'But that's the closest match to hell.'

'It wouldn't be that simple. The connection will probably be oblique, like using that church in Beauclerk Place to represent Judgement.' Sally looked across the table at Oliver. 'Michael's trying to make Maxham take it seriously.'

'You must admit, there's not much to go on.'

'What else have we got?' With sudden violence, she pushed aside the mug. Tea slopped on to the table. Neither of them moved. 'Time's running out. Can't you see the schedule? Friday, Lucy was taken. Saturday, the hand was found in Kilburn Cemetery. Sunday was St Michael's, today was Paradise Gardens. So tomorrow –'

'Why?' Oliver interrupted. 'What's the purpose of it all? Have you thought of that?'

There was a silence. Then Sally said, 'Revenge, of course. Against the Church, authority, parents – who knows? But I think there's something else as well.' She shook her head, trying to clear it. 'The Four Last Things – in theological terms they're meant to represent what will happen to us all: death, then whatever lies beyond. And if there are four victims, each representing one of the stages, one part of the possible destinations of an individual soul . . .' She looked at Oliver, trying to gauge his reaction.

'Someone who wanted to be a priest but was turned down?' he suggested. 'This could be a way of –'

'No, I don't mean that, though you may be right.' Sally sat up. 'It's as if the killer wants to die by proxy. His victims are dying for *him*.'

'But what would be the point of that?'

'To cheat death and be reborn? To have a second chance? To escape from a private hell?'

His face had turned in on itself, like a house with curtained windows. 'You may be right.'

'I'm not sure. I'm not sure of anything.' Sally shot another glance at him. 'Anything at all.'

Except that where hell is, there is Lucy.

Oliver sipped tea and said nothing.

In the silence high above her she felt rather than heard the sound of wings. It was vital not to stop talking to Oliver, and yet so tempting to surrender, to let the wings overwhelm her.

'Pain is very dreary, you know,' she said hurriedly. 'I never realized that before. It's like a desert. Nothing grows there.' She hesitated. 'You don't go to church, do you?'

'Not now. My mum and dad were chapel people. When I was sixteen, I decided all that wasn't for me. Not just the chapel. The whole lot.'

'Lucky you.'

'What?'

'It sounds so simple. So comfortable.' She saw the disbelief in his face. 'A lot of people think religion's a prop. It isn't. If you believe in God, it's as if you're facing a constant challenge. He's always wanting you to do things. You can never relax and get on with your own life.'

'And you still believe in him? Now?'

'Oh yes. After a fashion. Not that it helps. Not in the slightest.'

Oliver raised the teapot and held it out towards her. Sally shook her head.

'I have dreams, too,' she heard herself saying. 'Waking dreams sometimes. I wish I didn't.'

'That's a common side-effect of stress,' Oliver said briskly, topping up his own mug. 'We know there's a relationship between stress and suggestibility. That's been clear since Pavlov. And there's also a link between stress and the seeing of visions. If you apply the appropriate stimuli to the appropriate bits of the brain, you get hallucinations.'

'And waking dreams?'

'OK, and waking dreams.' He shrugged, telling her without words that he personally did not see any distinction between a hallucination and a waking dream. 'Stress is just another stimulus. It can cause the sort of electrical activity in the temporal lobe that makes you see things. It's as simple as that. There's nothing mysterious about it.'

'Isn't there?'

He was instantly apologetic. 'It's a bit of a hobbyhorse, I'm afraid. Don't take any notice. I'm reacting against all those sermons I had to listen to when I was a child.'

'This is a watershed,' Sally said. 'Whatever happens, however it ends, this is a watershed. In Paradise Gardens, Michael said that nothing would ever be the same again, and he's right. There will always be a gap between before and afterwards. It's made a break in the pattern.'

263

Oliver nodded as if he understood, which of course he couldn't. But it was nice of him to go through the motions. She wasn't sure why she found him so comfortable to be with, to talk to. If she talked like this to Michael, either he wouldn't listen or, if he did, he would engage passionately with what she was saying, agreeing or disagreeing.

He glanced up at the window. 'Why don't we drive down to Hampstead Heath and have a walk, and then have a pub lunch?'

'Now? I couldn't.'

'Why not? It will do you a lot more good than moping around here.'

'But what happens if – ?'

'I'll let Maxham know where we are, and I'll take my phone.'

'I don't know. I – '

'Come on, the exercise will do you good. It's a lovely day.'

She lifted her head and stared out of the window. 'It's not.'

'It's better than yesterday. It's not raining and the wind's dropped.'

'I don't call it lovely.'

He smiled, and for an instant the plainness of his face dissolved. 'All right. But I still think we should go out.'

She shrugged, suddenly tiring of the discussion; it was easier to give in, and safer to be with Oliver than by herself. It took her much longer than usual to get ready. Everything distracted her – not the fact of Lucy's loss but little, unnecessary things. Twice she counted the money in her purse but she still could not remember how much she had. She hesitated over which of two jerseys to wear, her mind swinging restlessly between them, before realizing that it didn't matter because her coat would cover the jersey, and in any case, she wasn't trying to impress anyone.

At last she declared herself ready, not because she felt that she was but because she did not want to keep Oliver waiting any longer. He untangled the cars and they drove down to the Heath in the Citroën. They parked in Millfield Lane and walked south from Highgate Ponds towards Parliament Hill.

There were a few other people scurrying along the paths; the weather wasn't warm enough for sauntering. She eyed them warily as they passed, ready for hostility, ready to assume that they belonged to a different order of humanity from hers. In a world where they stole children, anything was possible.

She walked close to Oliver, partly because she was scared in this green wasteland and partly because she was terrified that they would not hear his mobile phone if and when it began to ring. At first they did not talk. Then Oliver said something which she had to ask him to repeat.

'I had a letter from Sharon this morning. She's met some-one else.'

'Do you mind?' Sally heard herself saying.

'I feel relieved. I think we both felt guilty when we separated, guilty because the marriage hadn't worked. If she finds someone else, it means the marriage wasn't one of those permanent mistakes that can't be put right.'

Like the death of a child.

'So as soon as you find someone else, it will all be sorted out.'

'That's the theory. There's a lot to be said for being able to start again, for second chances. But I suppose you wouldn't condone that.'

'Why not?'

'Isn't marriage meant to be for eternity?'

'Yes. But you know very well that even committed Christians get divorced.'

'Even clergy?'

The question took her aback. For an instant, Oliver's meaning – or rather a possible implication of what he was saying – penetrated the fog of unhappiness and fear in Sally's mind. 'These days even Anglican clergy get divorced. Their bishop may not like it, but it happens.'

She glanced up at his face, and on the whole liked what she saw. He smiled down at her. It seemed bizarre and inappropriate that they should be having this conversation, that she should be thinking these thoughts at this time. *Your will be done.* It was too easy to drown in the mess of your own life. You had to cling to commitments, like spars, and hope they would keep you afloat.

'Sally,' Oliver said. 'Have you ever – ?'

'Do you mind if we go back to Inkerman Street now?' she interrupted.

'What's wrong?'

The fear flooded back. Oliver loomed over her, his face wooden, the features suddenly seeming exaggerated to the point of horror, like a gargoyle's; she remembered thinking in that horrible little church in Beauclerk Place that David Byfield now looked like a gargoyle. David must have been a sexy man when he was younger. All her defences were down, she realized; she was vulnerable.

She shivered. 'We must get back. I think something's happened.'

Twelve

'I believe many are saved, who to man seem repro-
bated . . . There will appear at the Last day strange
and unexpected examples both of his Justice and
his Mercy; and therefore to define either, is folly in
man, and insolency even in the Devils.'

Religio Medici, I, 57

1

No time. No time to lose. No time to wonder about consequences.

Leaving Lucy asleep, Eddie ran upstairs to his bedroom
and pulled open the wardrobe door. In the bottom was a
brown canvas bag strengthened with imitation leather and
fitted with a zip and lock plated to look like brass. It had
belonged to Eddie's father; every year Stanley would take it
away with him on the Paladin camping holidays.

Eddie pulled out the bag, which had been squashed almost
flat under several pairs of shoes. He unzipped it and glanced
wildly round the room. He pulled a shirt from the wardrobe
and stuffed it into the bag. Socks and pants followed. He
opened the drawer where he kept his papers and riffled
through the contents. He couldn't find his cheque book so
he pulled out the entire drawer and upended it on his bed.
His cheque book and wallet joined the clothes in the bag. As
an afterthought, he also threw in his birth certificate and his
building society passbook. He returned to the wardrobe and
rummaged around until he found the thickest jersey he
owned. All the time he listened for the sound of the van
pulling up outside.

267

On impulse, he took down the picture of the dark-haired girl from the wall, the picture his father had given his mother. He would have liked to have taken it but he knew it wouldn't be practical. He tossed it on to the pillow. His aim was bad; the picture slipped off the end of the bed and fell to the floor; there was a sharp crack as the glass shattered in the frame.

Eddie carried the bag into the bathroom and collected toothpaste, toothbrush and shaving things. His legs were so wobbly that he had to sit down on the side of the bath. It was so unfair that all this should have come together – that he should have to cope with this while he was ill. He would need a towel. His own was wet so he took Angel's, which smelled faintly of her perfume. The smell made him feel nauseous, so in the end he fetched a clean towel from the airing cupboard.

He went slowly downstairs and into the kitchen, where he opened cupboards at random. He might need food and drink. He added biscuits, two cans of Coke and a tin of baked beans to the contents of the bag. He checked his wallet and purse and, to his horror, discovered that he had only a few pence. He emptied out the jar of housekeeping money into the palm of his hand. There was less than five pounds, all in small change. He pushed the loose coins into the pocket of his jeans. He would need more than that, he was sure. He couldn't rely on being able to get to a bank or a building society.

He remembered Carla's green purse. It was in the basement, along with the Woolworth's bag containing the conjuring set he had bought for Lucy on Saturday and had still not given to her.

Eddie went into the hall and pulled on his coat. He stood hesitating by the open door to the basement. He had not wanted to go down there. He peered in. Lucy was still asleep. Both the conjuring set and the purse were on the top shelf of Angel's bookcase, far above Lucy's reach. Eddie tiptoed down the stairs. He reached the bottom safely and, still carrying the brown bag, crossed the room to the shelves. He had to stand on tiptoe to reach the top one.

'Eddie.'

In his surprise he dropped both the purse and the conjuring set. 'What?'

'Is it getting-up time?'

'Well,' said Eddie, answering a question of his own, 'I don't know.' He bent down, picked up the purse and glanced inside the wallet section. There were at least three ten-pound notes.

Lucy wriggled out of bed and stared at the purse. 'That's Carla's.'

'Yes.' Eddie scooped up the conjuring set. He slipped it and the purse into the brown bag.

'What are you doing?'

Eddie stared at her. She looked enchanting in those pyjamas with the red stars on the deep yellow background; except that now the red stars made him think of splashes of blood. Everything was spoiled.

'I have to go out for a bit.'

'Stay with me,' she wheedled.

Eddie smiled at her. 'I wish I could.'

'I don't want Angel. I like you.'

'Angel's not here,' Eddie said, and then realized that this might be a mistake. 'She'll be back in a moment. She's just popped out.'

'Don't leave me.' Her face crumpled. 'Want Mummy. Take me to Mummy and Daddy.'

Eddie's legs gave way and he sank down on the bed. Lucy put her hand on his leg. He felt her warmth through the material of his jeans. None of the other little visitors had been so trusting.

'Nice Eddie,' she murmured encouragingly.

He found that he was staring at the door to the room of the freezer and the microwave. If he left Lucy here, she wouldn't be warm for much longer. In a very short time she would probably be as cold as ice. He couldn't leave Lucy to Angel. Yet he could hardly take her back to her parents' flat in Hercules Road or drop her in at the nearest police station. 'Hello, my name's Eddie Grace and this is a little girl called Lucy I kidnapped four days ago.' There must be a way round the problem. But his head hurt too much for him to find it immediately. He and Lucy needed time. They needed a place where they could go and where they would be safe from Angel, safe from the police, safe from Lucy's parents, safe from the whole world.

'Don't like Angel,' Lucy confided. 'I like *you*.'

Automatically he patted her hand. 'And I like you.'

Angel might come back at any moment. There was no time to waste. Lucy, the little coquette, was peeping up at him through her eyelashes in a way that reminded him of Alison all those years ago in Carver's.

Alison in Carver's. That was it: that was the answer, at least for the short term.

'We've got to get you dressed quickly if we're going out.' Eddie opened the chest of drawers and began to pull out clothes at random: jeans, socks, pants, vests, jerseys. All of them were new, all of them bought over the last few months by himself and Angel. 'Quick, quick. It will be cold outside so leave your pyjamas on.'

Lucy's surprise at this unorthodox way of getting dressed lasted only a few seconds. Then she decided to treat it as an exciting new game. The only problem was that there were no shoes. Eddie could not find the red leather boots which Lucy had been wearing when she came home with him. He had rather liked those boots. Then he remembered that in the cupboard in the basement there were a pair of lace-up shoes which had belonged to Suki. He got them out and tried them on Lucy. Lucy squealed excitedly at the idea of new shoes, partly because these were blue and decorated with green crocodiles. They were two or three sizes too large for her but she appeared not to mind. Eddie made up the difference with extra pairs of socks which would help to keep her warm.

'Going away?' Lucy asked as he helped her put on the second jersey. 'Never coming back?'

'That's right.'

'Never see Angel again?'

'No.' Eddie hoped he was speaking the truth. He ruffled her hair.

'I'm hungry. What's for breakfast?'

270

'I've got some food in the bag. We'll have breakfast after we've left.'

Lucy's eyes widened with excitement. She needed a moment to assimilate the information. Then: 'Jimmy? Mrs Wump?'

'You want to take them? Put them in the bag.'

She squatted and pulled open the bag. When she saw the conjuring set, she sucked in her breath. 'Look – for me, Eddie? For me?'

'Yes.' Eddie added a few more clothes for Lucy. By this time the bag was bulging. 'We must go.'

'From Father Christmas?'

'Yes. Come on.'

In the hall Eddie hesitated, wondering whether to bolt the front door. It was already locked, but Angel would have taken her keys. He struggled to think out the implications. His head was hurting. Angel would come round to the back if the front door were bolted. She would guess that something was wrong, but not what. What if he bolted the back door too and if he and Lucy stayed inside the house? Would Angel break a window? Or ask Mr Reynolds for help?

Bolting the doors wouldn't be any use: either Angel would succeed in getting in, and be furious; or the uproar would lead to neighbours, even the police, coming in and finding Eddie with Lucy.

Better to go at once, to leave the house deserted and the front door unlocked. To his consternation, he found himself giggling at the idea of Angel walking into the house and finding that, in her absence, 29 Rosington Road had become the *Mary Celeste* of north-west London.

'What's funny?' Lucy asked.

Eddie took her hand and towed her towards the kitchen. 'Nothing important.'

'Where we going?'

He opened the back door and the cool air flooded in. 'We're going to my secret place. We're going to hide from Angel.'

Lucy did not reply, but her eyes seemed to grow larger with excitement and she jiggled up and down. Perhaps the absence of her morning dose of medication had made her

271

livelier. Certainly, Eddie could not remember seeing her so vital before, even on that first evening when he saw her in Carla's backyard.

'Coat,' Lucy said. 'I need my coat.'

'Where is it?'

Lucy pointed towards her feet. 'Down there.'

'Wait here.' Eddie dropped the bag on the kitchen floor and hurried back into the hall and down the basement stairs. The green quilted coat was at the bottom of the chest of drawers. It had a hood, which would be useful, and as he carried it upstairs he discovered that there were gloves in the pocket.

The kitchen was empty. Panic attacked him and he began to tremble. Lucy had run away. Lucy had tricked him. She, too, had betrayed him. In the same instant, his mind filled with an unbearably vivid picture of her running down Rosington Road, her legs a blur, towards a uniformed policeman.

Lucy appeared in the doorway to the back garden. 'I saw a bird. A robin?'

He lunged at her and grabbed her by the shoulders. 'Don't do that. I didn't know where you were.'

She stared up at him but said nothing. He wondered how many times her parents had said those words to her. He wasn't Lucy's parent – he was her friend. He helped her into the coat and did up the zip and the buttons. Hand in hand, they walked into the garden. Eddie glanced up at the balcony of the Reynoldses' flat. It was empty. They reached the belt of trees at the bottom of the garden. In the distance a train went by. It was very quiet.

Eddie had not been down here since the previous summer. A faint track wound its way between the saplings and bushes – perhaps made by the fox. At the fence, Eddie pulled aside the lid of a wooden packing case which he had leant against the hole, partially blocking it. On the other side of the hole was a piece of wood he had manoeuvred into position to conceal its presence from anyone in Carver's. He poked his foot through the fence and kicked the wood over.

'Funny forest,' said Lucy, very seriously.

Eddie had put on weight since his last visit over six years

earlier. The hole would be too narrow for him now. Lucy watched, fascinated, while he enlarged it. The surrounding wood had rotted still further, the damp creeping up from the earth. By pushing and kicking he managed to snap off enough of the neighbouring planks to widen the gap sufficiently for him to wriggle through.

'Angel cross?' Lucy suggested.

Eddie grunted non-committally, not wanting to frighten her unnecessarily. He wasn't sure whether she meant that Angel would be cross when she discovered the hole, or that Angel was already cross for other reasons. He picked up the bag and swung it through into Carver's.

'I'll go first.'

He crawled through the hole, making the knees of his jeans muddy. On the other side he turned, crouched down and held out a hand through the hole to Lucy. Without a moment's hesitation, she put her hand in his and stepped through. Eddie tried to conceal the gap in the fence with the packing-case lid. With a little luck, Angel would think that he and Lucy had left by the front door.

'There's a nice little shed through there.' Eddie pointed through the undergrowth. 'You can see the corner of it. It's like a house, isn't it? Let's go and explore.'

The fresh air was making him feel a little better. With the bag in his free hand, Eddie towed Lucy between the brambles and leafless branches. The ground was damp and mud clung to the soles of Eddie's trainers. Once he had to lift her over a fallen tree, and she floated as light as a feather in his arms, her face smiling down at his; and in that instant Eddie was as happy as he had ever been. They drew nearer to the shed.

'Is it a house?' Lucy asked, her voice full of doubt.

'It can be our house.'

Eddie hesitated in the doorway. Past collided with present. In memory it was always summer and the shed was in much better condition; he remembered it not as he had last seen it but as he had known it with Alison. Now it was winter and the shed showed all too clearly the effects of exposure to the elements for over fifty years. Only a third of the roof was now left. The two ash saplings towered above the walls like a pair of gangling adolescents. The floor was a sea of dead leaves. The window opening had lost not only its glass but its frame as well. There was rubbish, too – more than before, which suggested that people were regularly finding their way into Carver's. Eddie glared at the empty cans and bottles, at the crisp packets and cigarette ends; they were blemishes on his privacy.

Lucy poked her head inside the doorway and looked around. She said nothing.

'We must tidy it up,' Eddie told her. 'Make it more homely.' He noticed two tins which had once contained cement at the back of the shed. 'Look, they can be our seats. We'll put them under the bit with a roof.'

He set to work violently – pushing most of the leaves and rubbish into a heap against the wall underneath the window opening; setting the tins upside down so they could be used as seats; turning a wooden drawer on its side to serve as a table; and removing the worst of the cobwebs from the roof.

At first Lucy stood there, watching and sucking her fingers. After a moment, the magic of playing house affected her and they worked as a team. She fussed over the placing of the tins and the drawer, adjusting them, standing back to observe the results from afar, and then readjusting them. All the time she was doing this she hummed to herself, a made-up tune which consisted of three notes, monotonously repeated. He glanced covertly at her, marvelling at her absorption.

Lucy found a jam jar in the pile of rubbish, emptied out the brown water it contained and set it with a flourish on the table.

'It's a vase,' she informed him. 'For flowers.'

She darted out of the shed. There was a spindly mallow bush growing by the wall; it still had some leaves and even a few shrivelled flowers whose pink had rotted into a dark, funereal purple. She broke off a spray, brought it into the shed and stuck it into the jam jar.

'Lovely,' Eddie said. 'Very pretty.'

Lucy sat down on one of the tins and looked from the jam jar to Eddie. 'Is it time for breakfast?'

He sat down on the other tin, lifted the bag on to his lap

and unzipped it. The exertion had brought back his illness in full force: he felt very dizzy, his eyeballs too large for their sockets. He put the packet of biscuits and a can of Coca-Cola on the table.

Lucy stared at them. 'For breakfast?'

Eddie opened the biscuits and removed the ring pull from the can. He waved his hand in a lordly gesture. 'Help yourself.'

Lucy looked worried. 'Mummy doesn't let me drink Coke. It's bad for your teeth.'

'This is a special treat.'

'Like on holiday?'

Eddie nodded. While she ate, Eddie hugged himself and tried to keep warm. He knew that he should be using this time to make plans, to avoid the opposing dangers of Angel and the police. Lucy was such a complication. He couldn't leave her and he couldn't take her with him. He stared at her and she lifted her head. Little white milk teeth chewed the biscuit. She smiled at him and picked up the Coke.

He decided to explore the contents of the bag again. If he were by himself, and if the police weren't looking for him, everything would be straightforward. He had several thousand pounds in his bank account and his building society account. He had his driving licence. He could go anywhere in the country, even apply for a passport and go abroad, and Angel wouldn't be able to find him. He could hire a solicitor who would evict Angel from the house. His mind shied away from considering what she would do with the contents of the freezer in the basement; take them with her, presumably. If necessary he would leave the house and start a new life somewhere else. The prospect was unexpectedly attractive: a new Eddie, away from Rosington Road, away from Angel, away from all the memories; anything might be possible.

But not with Lucy. The police were looking for her. These days there were video cameras everywhere – in banks, building societies, shopping centres. He could not take her anywhere without the risk of being seen.

While he was thinking, his fingers dug restlessly into the contents of the bag. He came up with Carla's purse. He opened it to count the cash it contained. There were credit cards, too, but he couldn't use those. Carla was an untidy woman, he thought disapprovingly. The purse was full of things which needn't be there at all. There were old receipts and credit-card slips, some going back for months. There were books of stamps, now empty. There were library tickets and photographs of small children. There were scraps of paper with telephone numbers and addresses scribbled on them. The woman should have had the sense to buy an address book. He stared at one of the pieces of paper, smoothing it out, his mind elsewhere. Suddenly his eyes focused on the writing: *Sally Appleyard*. Underneath was the address in Hercules Road and the flat's phone number. There were three other phone numbers: one was Michael's at work, complete with an extension; the second was in Kensal Vale, judging by the three-digit preface and the third was for a mobile phone.

'Eddie,' Lucy said. 'Is it Christmas yet?'

'Not for about three weeks. Why?'

'Have I got to wait till then? For the magic set?'

'No – not necessarily. Would you like it now?'

'Can I? Won't he mind?'

'Who?'

'Father Christmas.'

'No, he won't. It's OK for you to have it now.'

He handed her the conjuring set, an oblong cardboard box. On the outside of the box was a colour photograph of a small, fair-haired boy in a long black cape; smiling broadly, he was in the act of tapping an inverted top hat with a wand; what looked like a pink rabbit was peeping coyly out of the hat. Lucy's fingers tore impotently at the packaging.

'Let me.'

Reluctantly she returned the set to him. The ends were held down with Sellotape, which he slit with his thumbnail. He eased the end out and handed the box back to Lucy. She did not thank him. He did not mind. He knew that her entire attention was focused on the conjuring set.

Lucy shook the contents on to the table. They looked much less impressive than in the picture on the box. There was a pink, long-haired toy rabbit about the size of a well-nourished mouse. The wand was cardboard and had a kink in the middle. There was a polythene bag full of oddments, chiefly made of cardboard and plastic. Among them Eddie noticed three miniature playing cards and a purple thimble. Finally there were the instructions, a small booklet with smudgy print on poor-quality paper. Lucy glanced at him and then back at the conjuring set. He guessed that she was trying desperately to preserve her excitement in the face of disappointment. How do you explain to a four-year-old that it is better to travel hopefully than to arrive?

'No hat,' she pointed out, her lips trembling.

'Perhaps we can borrow one.'

Eddie tried to think constructively about what to do next. He couldn't concentrate. He stared instead at Lucy's hands as they picked their way through the contents of the conjuring set. Her head was bowed. The strange rigidity of her position told its own story.

'Lucy. Shall I help?'

She looked up. Her face was bright and her eyes gleamed with tears. Wordlessly, she pushed the instruction booklet towards him. He picked it up and opened it at random. The words looked like little insects, flies perhaps. They were moving. Some of them took off from the page as if to attack his mind. Some of the words made phrases. *Astonish your friends.* Why should you want to do that? *Hold card in place with thumb so audience see nothing.* Eddie turned over a page and found more insects, swarming as if feeding from an open wound. *A simple but effective trick. . .* His eyes slid diagonally across the page. *It will be the Queen of Spades.*

'I want to do the card trick. Why is it so hard?'

'I don't know,' Eddie said, thinking that it was hard because things were always harder than you thought they were going to be. 'I'll see if I can find out how to do it.'

There were three cards provided, about a third of the size of normal playing cards; one of them was double-sided. Eddie struggled to match them up with the instructions and the accompanying diagram. The writer of the booklet seemed to be labouring under the delusion that there were five cards, not three. Nor was English the writer's first language. While Eddie was working on the card trick, another part of his mind was wondering what he was going to do. His hands were growing colder. They couldn't stay here indefinitely. It was winter.

'Hurry up,' urged Lucy.

She must have had a vision of herself as a magician, looking like the boy on the box and effortlessly astonishing her friends and relations. How could the reality ever measure up to the anticipation? Perhaps it would have been wiser to have made her wait.

'I think you do it like this.' Eddie fanned out the three cards in his hand, their faces towards Lucy. 'You see – the Queen of Spades is the one in the middle.'

She looked blankly at him and he realized belatedly that she did not know what the Queen of Spades was. He laid the cards on the table and explained what each one was called. She nodded, frowning. Then he made up a version of the trick. You showed your audience the three cards and then hid them under the box. Then you waved your wand and said *Abracadabra*. Next you asked the audience to tell you which of the concealed cards was the Queen of Spades – the card on the right, the card on the left or the card in the middle. The audience thought they knew – but you fooled them, because the Queen of Spades was a double-sided card, and you had cunningly turned it over as you slid it under the box. On the other side of the Queen of Spades was the Two of Hearts and you showed them that instead. You made them think that the Queen of Spades had disappeared.

'Is that all?' Lucy asked when Eddie had finished explaining.

'Yes.'

She said nothing.

'You don't like it?'

She wriggled on the tin. 'It's all right. Where's the toilet?'

'There isn't one.'

The wriggling became more pronounced. 'But I need to go.'

'You'll have to do it outside.'

Lucy stared at him, her face shocked, but did not object. He led her outside, and with Eddie's help she managed to relieve herself in the angle between the mallow bush and the shed. He worried continuously – that she would wet herself, that she would catch cold, that someone would see them. Because it was winter, there was less cover than he had expected.

When Lucy had finished, he hurried her back into the shed and then helped her to dress herself again. It was the hurrying rather than having to pee outside that upset her. She began to cry. Eddie gave her Mrs Wump and Jimmy and sat her on his knee and put his arms around her. He felt her trembling gradually subside. The only sound was the soft *click-click* as she sucked her fingers. He rested his chin gently on the top of Lucy's head.

'Lucy? What do you want?'

There was a long silence – so long that he wondered whether she had not heard. Then she said, very clearly, 'Mummy.'

'Yes. All right.'

'I can go home?' The joy in her face was almost more than he could bear. 'Now? To Mummy and Daddy?' She slid off his knee and stood up. The playing cards fluttered to the cracked concrete floor. 'Shall we get a bus?'

He took her hands in his and shook them gently. 'It's not quite as easy as that.' He could see what to do now – not a perfect plan, by any means, but the least of the available evils. 'I need to go and phone her. I'll ask her to come here.' Lucy's hands were cold too, even colder than his. 'Will you be all right here while I go and phone?'

'I want to come with you.'

'It's not possible. You have to stay here.'

He could not risk being seen with her in the street. She stared at him, her lip quivering, but said nothing. She did not ask for reasons. She heard the finality in his voice and accepted it. He stood up and took off his coat.

'You must stay in the shed while I'm gone.' He made her sit down and wrapped the coat around her.

'And them.' Lucy held up Jimmy and Mrs Wump.

Eddie tucked an arm of the coat around the two toys. Lucy lifted them both to her face, pushed two fingers into her mouth and shut her eyes. He picked up Carla's purse; the phone numbers were there, and also change and even a phone card. 'I won't be long – I promise.' He bent down and kissed the top of her head.

He left her, small and forlorn, in the shed. His problems began immediately. If he went back through the hole in the fence, there was a danger that Angel might have returned and he would walk into a trap. In any case, he could not use the phone in the house. The police would probably be able to trace the call. The wisest course would be to find another way out of Carver's and use a public telephone box.

He moved slowly westwards, keeping the fences of the Rosington Road gardens on his left. It would have been diffi-cult at the best of times. The further into the site, the more overgrown it became. Nature had partly masked the hazards of brick, concrete and rusting iron. Brambles slashed at his clothes and tore the skin on the back of his hands. He missed his coat. It began to rain, fine drops of moisture which drifted like powder from the dense grey sky. As he walked, he searched in vain for a gap in the fence on the left.

After what seemed like hours he stumbled on the main gates, which were in the south-west corner of the site. They were surprisingly narrow – two sheets of metal mounted on a cast-iron frame, surmounted by rows and rows of barbed wire. On either side were brick pillars topped with spikes. There was a wicket in the left-hand leaf of the gates, secured by bolts and a large padlock.

Eddie wondered what to do. Nowadays there was no other way into Carver's. They had torn up the railway tracks inside the works and fenced off the lines to the north. The place was like a fortress or a prison. He ran his eyes along the western boundary of the site: this was a high brick wall, similar to the one that divided the eastern side of the site from the council flats but in less good condition. It might be possible to climb it. But on the other side was a terrace of shops on Bishop's Road. Presumably there would be yards behind the shops. Even if he managed to get over the wall, he would then have the problem of getting from a yard to the road.

His eyes on the top of the wall, he stumbled on a loose brick and almost fell. His head swimming, he bent down and worked the brick out of the mud into which it was impacted. There was a colony of woodlice underneath. His skin crawled. He dropped the brick and most of the woodlice clinging to it fell off. He scraped the remainder away with a stick. Perhaps brute force was the answer.

Eddie carried the brick carefully towards the gates. It felt cold, hard and heavy, and its jagged edges hurt the skin of his hands.

He stopped beside the wicket. If there was no one on the other side, it might be all right. The sound of banging during the day was not in itself suspicious. He raised the brick in both hands and brought it down on the padlock. There was a dull clang. The brick twisted painfully out of his hands and fell to the ground. Just in time, he jumped backwards before it dropped on his feet. Flecks of blood oozed from a graze on the side of his left thumb. The padlock was hardly marked.

Steeling himself against the pain, Eddie picked up the brick and tried again, this time more cautiously. The brick did not fall. Once again, the padlock was undamaged. But the rusting staple to which it was attached was now bent at a slight angle. He hit the padlock again and again, building up to a rhythm. Air laboured in and out of his lungs and the pain seared his hands like flames.

Finally the staple gave way. The padlock fell to the ground; apart from a few scratches, it showed no signs of the ordeal to which it had been subjected. Eddie opened the hasp and then worked the bolts to and fro until they too moved back. He lifted the latch and the wicket gate opened.

He stepped warily into the alley beyond, half-expecting to find a squad of policemen waiting for him. He closed the wicket behind him and walked away. Both his hands were bleeding now so he stuffed them in his pockets. Brick walls reared up on either side – to the right was the yard belonging to the end shop of the terrace in Bishop's Road; and to the left was the playground of the infants' school on the corner of Rosington Road and Bishop's Road.

The mouth of the alley was on Bishop's Road. Eddie hesitated on the corner, feeling extraordinarily conspicuous. The pavement was crowded. Cars, vans and lorries rumbled up and down the road. He feared that everyone was looking at him.

He took a deep breath and began to hurry along the pavement after the bus. Ahead of him the road rose towards the railway bridge. There were two public telephone boxes beside the bridge. As he walked, Eddie kept his face turned towards the windows of the shops in case Angel passed by in the van. The cold made his eyes water.

At last he reached the telephone boxes. One was in use but the other was empty. He hurried inside, relieved to have some shelter from the wind, relieved not to be exposed to the curious eyes on the street. The box took phone cards, so he fed Carla's into the slot. He dialled the Hercules Road number first.

The phone was answered on the second ring. 'Hello.'

Eddie said nothing. He wasn't sure, but he didn't think that the voice belonged to Sally Appleyard: it sounded higher-pitched.

'Hello. Who's speaking, please?'

It definitely wasn't Sally's. There was a hint of a Welsh accent. He put the phone down hastily. A friend? A police officer? He tapped in the Kensal Vale number.

'St George's Vicarage. Derek Cutter speaking.'

Once again, Eddie broke the connection. He felt foolish. Of course Lucy's mother wouldn't be at work at a time like this. He wanted to cry. Why were they making it so hard for him to help Lucy? Why was it so difficult to do a kind action? If there were a God, you would think he'd make it easy to be good.

Slowly he pushed the buttons for the mobile's number. While it was ringing, he allowed himself to think for the first time what would happen if he could not get through to Sally Appleyard. The problems multiplied. Then the phone was answered.

'Appleyard.'

Michael Appleyard, not his wife. Eddie said, 'Is Sally there?' Panic made his voice sound even higher-pitched than usual. 'I want to speak to *her*.'

'I can take a message. Who is this?'

Suddenly the future seemed inevitable: it swept down on Eddie like a tidal wave. 'I know where Lucy is.'

'Where?'

'It's all a mistake,' Eddie heard himself saying. 'Lucy mustn't be hurt.'

'Why should I believe you? How do I know this isn't just a hoax?'

The injustice took Eddie's breath away for a moment. He was only trying to help. 'She's wearing the dark-green quilted coat she was wearing at Carla's. I found this number in Carla's purse.' His voice sounded petulant. 'Now do you believe me?'

'I believe you. Is she all right?'

'She's fine, I promise.'

'When did you last see her?'

'Ten minutes ago? Fifteen? I left her playing with a conjuring set.'

There was a sound on the other end of the line which at first Eddie couldn't identify; a second later, he wondered if it might have been a sob.

'You can come and get her,' Eddie said. 'But don't tell the police. Don't bring them. Promise?'

'I promise.'

'If you do,' Eddie said as menacingly as he could manage, 'you'll regret it. Lucy will regret it. No police. Not if you want to see her alive.'

'All right. But where is she?'

'Do you know Bishop's Road in Kentish Town?'

'I'll find it.'

'There's a school just south of the railway. Beside the school, there's a lane leading to an old engineering works. It's called Carver's. She's in there.'

With a surge of optimism, Eddie slung the handset back on its rest. *I've done it. Everything's going to be all right.* The phone card emerged like a tongue from its slot. As he pulled it out he noticed that it was smeared with his blood. *Whose blood on the moussaka packet?* He would walk down to the bus stop, climb on the next bus and let other people sort out the mess that Angel had made. He was sorry that he would never see Lucy again, but this way was best for everyone.

He pushed open the door of the telephone box. The cold air hit him. With it came the realization that he had miscalculated.

2

Eddie ran all the way back to Carver's. As he ducked into the mouth of the alley, Mr Reynolds's van passed him, signalling left for the turning beyond the school into Rosington Road.

He didn't see me. Please God he didn't see me.

Eddie reached Carver's gates. Relief washed over him as he pulled the wicket closed behind him. Carver's felt safe. He took a few steps towards the shed and then stopped. He leant against the fence, bent over and retched unproductively. The stitch dug deep into his side. He was panting so hard that for a moment he thought his heart would pack up, just as his mother's had. The nausea came in waves. His head hurt. Entwined with the physical distress was the urgency of panic. He felt his forehead: so hot you could cook an egg on it.

He picked his way through the wilderness towards the shed. He hadn't been thinking straight. He couldn't walk away from Lucy and leave her in Carver's: not without the brown bag, not with Lucy just a few yards from the fence leading to 29 Rosington Road, not without his money.

With luck there should be enough time to do what he needed to do before Michael Appleyard arrived. Eddie planned to take Lucy and the bag away from the shed and lead her by a roundabout route to the gates. He would leave her there, just inside, with Jimmy and the rest of her things.

She would come to no harm: her father would soon reach her. There was, of course, the risk that Lucy would be able to lead the police to the back garden of Rosington Road. It was a risk that had to be run. The more he confused her about the geography of Carver's, the safer he would be. In any case, if the worst came to the worst, and the police raided 29 Rosington Road, then they would find Angel there, Angel and the contents of her freezer. He would be far away. Once he was better, once his temperature was normal and he had regained his strength – that would be the time to consider what to do for the best.

The journey back seemed shorter than the journey out had been. Eddie saw the silhouette of the shed looming. He glanced upwards, and for a moment he thought he saw movement on the balcony of the Reynoldses' flat. *I'm imagining things.* That was the trouble with a fever: the boundary between the world within your head and the world outside was not as effective as usual; it was still there, but it was porous. An event inside could become an event outside, and vice versa. Eddie tripped over a root and fell flat on his face. *Must concentrate. Must concentrate.*

Eddie picked himself up and hurried on. He was dimly aware that his clothes were wet and muddy. He wanted someone to look after him. Into his mind flashed a picture: someone large, kind and faceless urging him into a warm bath, making him a drink, slipping a hot-water bottle into a bed with Mrs Wump on the pillow.

The shed was very close now. Eddie heard a high-pitched wail. For an instant, he thought the wail was inside his mind – a sound of disappointment, because the bath, the hot-water bottle and the bed weren't real after all.

Lucy was crying. Eddie put on a spurt of speed. Tripping over tree roots, skidding in the mud, he flung himself towards the shed. The crying continued. The grief of children was unconditional, fuelled by the implicit belief that it would last for ever; for a child, grief was not grief unless it was eternal.

He stopped in the doorway of the shed. Lucy was sitting where he had left her, clutching herself, hunched over the makeshift table. Her tears fell on the conjuring set. The vase had fallen to the floor. Her face was white, tinged with green. It seemed rounder than usual, the features less well-formed, the eyes smaller. That was another effect of grief on children: it made them a little less human.

'Lucy, darling.'

He picked her up, sat down on the other cement tin and held her on his lap. Her arms clung to his neck. She rammed her face painfully against his cheek. The sobbing continued, violent surges of emotion that rippled through her whole body. He patted her back and mumbled endearments.

Gradually the sobbing grew quieter. As the crying diminished, Lucy went through a stage of making mewing noises like a kitten. Then the sounds turned to words.

'Mummy. I want Mummy. Daddy.'

After a while, Eddie said, 'I've just talked to your daddy on the phone. He's –'

'You left me alone.' Lucy let out another wail. 'I thought you weren't coming back.'

'Of course I was coming back.'

'Don't leave me. Don't leave me.'

'I won't, I promise.' He had spoken without thinking. Of course he would have to leave her. 'Your daddy's coming to collect you. He'll take you home to Mummy.'

'Don't leave me.' Lucy seemed not to have understood what he had said – either that or she had automatically dismissed it as meaningless. 'I'm cold.'

Still holding her, Eddie leant forward and picked up his coat, which had fallen on the floor. With his free hand he wrapped it clumsily round her shoulders. Automatically he rocked her to and fro, to and fro. Lucy's breath was warm on his cheek.

'I must go.' Eddie felt the arms tighten round his neck. 'We must go.'

Lucy shook her head violently. 'Want a drink.'

Eddie leant down and picked up the can of Coca-Cola from the floor. Judging by the weight, it was well over half-full. He handed it to her. Leaving one arm round his neck, she pulled away from him a little. She drank greedily, her eyes glancing at him every few seconds, as if she feared he might try to take the can away. He stroked her back.

Time trickled away. Eddie's head hurt. Part of his mind rose above the pain and the fear and surveyed his situation from a lordly elevation. Every moment that passed increased the risk he was running. But how could he leave Lucy before she was ready? She needed him. What would it be like if the worst happened and the police arrested him and he was eventually sent to jail? He knew that prisons were foul and overcrowded, and that sex offenders were traditionally picked on by the other prisoners; and that those whose offences had involved children were the most hated of all and were subjected to unimaginable brutalities.

'Eddie?' Lucy held out the can to him. 'There's some for you.'

He disliked Coca-Cola but on impulse he nodded and took the can from her. She rewarded him with a smile. For an instant the roles were reversed: she was looking after him. He drank, and the fizzy liquid ran down his throat and refreshed him unexpectedly. He lowered the can from his lips.

'Drink,' Lucy commanded. 'For you.'

He smiled at her and obeyed. When the can was empty, he rested it against his cheek and the cool of the metal soothed him. Lucy slithered off his knee and picked up the wand from the conjuring set.

'Let's do more magic.'

Eddie stood up suddenly. The dizziness returned. He leant against the wall to support himself. 'There's no time. We must go.'

'To Daddy?'

Eddie nodded. He bent down and pushed their belongings into the bag.

'And Mummy?'

'Yes.' He straightened up, his head swimming, with the bag in one hand. 'Come on.'

Lucy refused to be parted from Jimmy, Mrs Wump and the conjuring set. She clasped them in her arms and allowed him to push her gently towards the doorway. But as she reached it, she gave a whimper. Instantly she backed away. Eddie heard footsteps among the dead leaves. A branch cracked. Then he saw what she had seen.

'No,' Lucy whispered, retreating to the corner of the shed furthest from the door. 'No, no, no.'

'We'll go in a minute,' Eddie said to her. 'See if you can find the magic wand and learn another trick.'

He stood in the doorway. Angel had stopped just outside the shed. She was wearing her long white raincoat with the hood. Her lips were drawn back and her face was lined and old.

'And where are you thinking of going?' she asked, her voice soft.

'I – I'm taking Lucy away.' The words came out in a trembling whisper. 'She's going home.'

'I don't think so.'

Eddie stared at Angel, desperately wishing to do as she wanted. 'She's going home. No one need know.'

'About what?'

Eddie gestured towards the house. 'About all this.'

'You're a fool. Mr Reynolds saw you in Bishop's Road. He said you were coming out of a phone box. Who were you phoning?'

Eddie felt sweat break out all over his body. 'No one.'

'Don't be absurd. If you didn't phone from the house, it means you didn't want the call traced. So you were phoning the police.'

'I wasn't.'

'You're lying.'

Angel turned her body slightly. The full skirt of her raincoat had concealed her right hand. Now Eddie saw not only the hand but what it was holding: the hatchet, the one that his mother had used on Stanley's last dolls' house. He had not seen it for years. Most of the blade was dull and flecked with rust, as it had been before. But not the cutting edge. This was now a streak of silver. He thought of the joints of meat in the freezer and of the three lives, cut into pieces, wrecked beyond repair like the dolls' house.

Behind him, Eddie heard Lucy murmur, 'Abracadabra. Now you're a prince.'

'What have you told them?' Angel said, swinging the hatchet to and fro.

'Nothing. I haven't phoned the police. I promise. I just want Lucy to go home so I tried to phone her mother but she wasn't in.'

Angel hit him on the collarbone with the hatchet. He heard the bone snap. He heard himself scream, too. Then she hit him again, this time on the side of the head. He fell against the jamb of the doorway and slid slowly to the ground.

He wanted to turn to Lucy and say, 'It's OK. Your daddy's coming.'

Angel lifted the hatchet once more. Warm liquid trickled down Eddie's left cheek. There was a great deal of pain, which swamped the headache completely. Men were shouting in his mind. Were they cheering or condemning him? He heard cracking and rustling, the sounds of fire devouring wood. He burned. Angel was no longer beautiful, but an old, foul woman, a witch, an avenging fury. The blade was descending. There was blood now on the silver edge.

Two men were running towards Angel. It was all just a dream. When you had a fever, you had terrible dreams. A man was screaming and screaming. Eddie wished the man would stop. The sound might frighten Lucy. She had been frightened enough already.

A thunderbolt hit him. The force drove his body deep into the ground, into a lake of fire with flames streaking across the surface. There was a bubbling sound. He could not breathe. Someone hung a piece of red gauze across his eyes.

Finally, the flames died, the sun went down, and the grown-ups switched off the light.

Thirteen

'This is the day whose memory hath onely power
to make us honest in the dark, and to be vertuous
without a witness.'

Religio Medici, I, 47

'Do you think Michael's already there?' Sally asked. 'Oh God, I hope he is.'

Oliver turned into Bishop's Road. He was driving far too fast and the Citroën tilted dangerously towards the near side. 'Could be. Depends on the traffic.'

Michael had used the mobile to call Inkerman Street. He had phoned just after Sally and Oliver returned from Hampstead Heath; Oliver had taken the call. Michael had been in Ladbroke Grove with David and Bishop Hudson when the kidnapper phoned, because Maxham had sent him away with a flea in his ear.

'But Michael hasn't got a car,' Sally wailed.

'Hudson lent them his.' As Oliver drove, his eyes flicked from side to side of the road. 'It must be here. There's nowhere else.'

He swung the wheel round and the Citroën cut across the stream of oncoming traffic. A horn squealed. The car surged into the little alley. Sally registered the frightened face of a woman they had nearly knocked down. The woman's shopping bag lay on the pavement, disgorging tins and packets.

The car rocked and jolted in and out of ruts and potholes. Sally saw a school on the corner, its playground empty. Next came high brick walls on either side. The alley curved round a corner. Oliver braked hard.

Immediately in front of them was a small, white car,

parked at an angle across the alley, the driver's door hanging open. Beyond the car was a pair of high metal gates between tall brick posts.

Oliver pulled up alongside the other vehicle. Sally leapt out, pushing her door so vigorously that it collided with the open door of the white car. She noticed in passing that the keys were still in the car's ignition, and that on the back seat there was a black umbrella and a copy of the *Church Times*. She broke into a run.

'Where's Maxham?' said Oliver behind her. 'He should have got the local boys here by now.'

There was still a notice on one of the gateposts.

JW & TB CARVER & Co LTD.
RAILWAY ENGINEERING
ALL VISITORS MUST REPORT TO THE OFFICE

She raised the latch of the wicket gate. It swung outwards.

'Sally – let me go first.'

Ignoring him, she stepped through the opening into the wilderness beyond. Even in winter, the predominant colour was green. The remains of the buildings were barely visible. For the time being, nature had the upper hand.

'It's huge,' Oliver said behind her. 'We'd better try shouting.'

'No.' Sally pointed to the ground. There were footprints in the mud leading away from the gates on a course roughly parallel with the fence to the right. 'They're fresh.'

'Padlock's smashed. From the inside.'

Sally was studying the mud. 'There's such a jumble here.' Her voice rose. 'I can't tell if any of them belongs to a child.'

Oliver joined her. 'Looks like three people. One in trainers.' He pointed. Then his finger moved. 'Trainers go both ways, to and from the gate. Another pair of shoes with smooth soles. Size eight or nine.'

'David's? That one's Michael's, I think.' She too pointed, at a single footprint from a moulded sole, as crisp and

291

unblemished as a plaster cast. 'See? So maybe the trainers belong to the man who phoned Michael.'

'He said it might have been a woman.' Oliver straightened up. 'Or a man trying to pitch his voice high. They're small enough for a woman's.'

As they talked, they were moving, casting about, trying to find more footprints. They kept their voices low, almost at the level of a whisper.

'Here.' Oliver set off at a run.

Sally followed. She stumbled several times, and once she fell, bruising her shoulder against an abandoned oil drum. She was praying, too, if you could call the word 'please', repeated over and over again, a prayer.

They crossed a patch of open ground. For a moment Sally could see ahead. She glimpsed a high wall and beyond it grey blocks of flats, faced with weather-mottled concrete. A woman was standing on one of the balconies and Sally clearly saw binoculars in her hand. *A ghoul.* The woman was looking at something below her at a point roughly midway on a line between herself and Sally. Then the wall, the flats and the woman were gone.

Sally plunged after Oliver into a thicket of brambles and saplings. Thorns tore at her clothes, her hands and her face. Oliver tripped over a fallen branch and fell head first into a clump of nettles. He swore. Sally overtook him and struggled out of the embrace of the thicket.

She found herself on what once might have been a path. Crumbling concrete was visible among the mud and the puddles; so too were more footprints, including those of the trainers. In the distance was a small brick building, almost roofless. Sally ran towards it. She was almost there when she heard Michael's voice say, 'Drop it, please. Drop it on the ground.'

She put on a final rush of speed and burst round the corner of the building. Her first impression was of a bright, vivid redness.

Michael and David were five yards away. They did not look at Sally. Their eyes were on the woman in the doorway.

For an instant Sally thought that it was Miss Oliphant, the

woman who had cursed Sally and later killed herself; whom Sally had last seen on her deathbed.

But only for an instant. Then a form of reality took over, and that was even worse because this woman was so clearly a part of a recognizable world. Like Miss Oliphant, this woman wore a long raincoat and a black beret, but there were few other similarities. Sally had never seen her before. She was tall and slender, with long, pale hair. Her face was pinched, the skin glowing with angry red blotches, the teeth and the eyes unnaturally prominent. In her hand she carried a sort of axe with a tall blade which at the end curved into a hook.

Around the woman was a pool of blood. There was so much of it. Pints and pints and pints. It had sprayed over the wall of the shed, the jamb of the doorway and the long skirt and arms of the woman's raincoat. Those were not blotches on her face but splashes of blood.

Sally had not known there could be so much blood in this world, let alone in one person. Frozen with shock, she stared at the scene in front of her. It took her a moment to realize that a man was lying on his back in the pool.

He was at the woman's feet, one arm almost touching her left shoe, his legs across the threshold of the doorway and his body along the base of the wall. Sally's eyes travelled up the body. The man's head no longer fitted on his shoulders.

The blood had come from the side of his neck. It was still flowing, but only just: pumping out sluggishly over the ground. Carotid artery, Sally thought automatically. Far too late to do anything. Not that she really cared about the man on the ground or the woman in the doorway or even Michael and David.

'Where's Lucy?'

The woman, who had been staring as if fascinated at Michael and David, glanced at her.

'Sssh,' the woman whispered. 'She mustn't see.' She waved the hatchet in the direction of the body. 'It would inflict terrible psychological damage. With a child that age, the scar would remain for life. Surely you know that?'

'If you put down the hatchet,' Michael suggested, sounding

unbelievably calm and relaxed, 'we could cover it with my coat.'

Oliver stumbled round the corner of the shed. Sally put a hand on his arm.

'I had to kill him,' the woman said. 'He was going to kill the little girl, you know. It was the only way to stop him. He's done terrible things to little girls in the past. Terrible,' she repeated, in a slower, deeper voice like a clock running down, 'terrible, terrible.'

'How do you know?' Michael asked.

'I rent a room in his house.' The voice was middle class, rather musical. 'His name's Edward Grace. I've been there for five or six years. But until today I hadn't the faintest idea what he was up to.'

Sally knew that the woman was lying, that she was talking not to convince them but to gain time. 'May I see Lucy now?'

The head of the hatchet swung in Sally's direction. 'In a moment.' Her eyes slid down to what lay at her feet. 'The pervert – do you think he's dead yet?'

The blood was no longer flowing.

'Almost certainly,' Michael said. 'And if he isn't he soon will be. Now – if you put the hatchet on the ground –'

'You.' The woman pointed the hatchet at David Byfield. 'You can see her if you want. Come here.'

For the first time Sally looked at David. His face was extraordinarily pale.

'Yes,' the woman said to him in a flat voice. 'I want *you* to see her.'

He looked steadily at her but did not move. The pair of them reminded Sally of wrestlers studying each other in the few seconds before the fight began. And when the bell rang, the false stillness would vanish and everything would change.

God does not change. But we do.

The words came from nowhere. Time once again was paralysed. The silence was total. As time could not move, all time was present. This is where it began, Sally thought, with Miss Oliphant in St George's; and in the beginning was this end.

She saw David's face and saw behind it to the pain and

the guilt beyond. Why all that guilt? What had he done to deserve it? She saw the woman's face and saw that it was almost a mirror image of David's, except that there was no guilt within her, only pain streaked with anger, and more pain beyond, dark, dense, impacted like a seam of coal.

'Your will be done,' Sally said, or thought she said. 'Not mine.'

As if the words were a signal, time began to flow once more.

'*Mummy.*'

The tableau broke into pieces. Lucy was standing at the far corner of the shed, on the woman's right. In her hand she held three minuscule playing cards.

'Lucy,' the woman snapped, 'did you climb through the window?'

Lucy stared open-mouthed at the stern face.

'I thought I told you to stay inside. Naughty girls have to be smacked.'

Sally thought: *Lucy mustn't see that man on the ground.* The desperate importance of that overrode everything else: all the blood and that horrible body – it wasn't something for a child to see.

She flung herself at Lucy. Somehow she found the time to hope that the woman herself would be a barrier between Lucy's eyes and that terrible, ghastly mess on the ground.

She was aware, too, of a flurry of movement behind her. Oliver, Michael and David were converging on the woman in the doorway of the shed.

The woman lifted the axe and swung it towards Sally. There was all the time in the world to notice the lazy arc of the blade. The shortest route to Lucy would take Sally within a yard of the woman, well within her reach. The need to be with Lucy was more important than the need to avoid a blow.

The hatchet slammed into Sally's left arm halfway between the shoulder and the elbow. She gasped, but as a moving target she missed the worst of the force of the blow. She swept her daughter into her arms. Lucy cried out as the air was driven out of her.

Sally threw her round the corner of the shed. Lucy lay on her back, her arms and legs wide, in a pose that mimicked the dead man's. Sally flung herself on top of her daughter.

'It's all right. It's all right. I'm here now.' Sally burst into tears. Between sobs the words continued to stagger out of her mouth as though by their own volition. 'It's all right, darling, it's all right. Mummy's here. It's all right . . .'

Lucy lay very still and said nothing. One of the playing cards, a Two of Hearts, had fallen beside her head. People were shouting and crying, but they did not matter. Lucy smelled different from before, impregnated with the aromas of strange people and places. For an instant Sally was on the edge of despair: perhaps all this had been in vain; perhaps she had saved not Lucy but some other child.

After a while, the shouting and the screaming stopped. For a few seconds the world was quiet. The tears ran down Sally's face and splashed on to the shorn, dark hair.

At last Lucy stirred. She looked up at her mother and said, 'Mummy. I can do magic.'

EPILOGUE

'There are wonders in true affection: it is a body of
Enigma's, mysteries and riddles . . .'

Religio Medici, II, 6

The chapel was little more than a room full of chairs with a
crucifix on the far wall. The Reverend David Byfield lowered
himself slowly on to one of the red, plastic seats. The chaplain
sat down nearby, angling her chair so she was at right angles
to him.

'There's no change.' She touched the pectoral cross she
wore. 'She spends most of her free time either praying or
reading the Bible.'

'How does she behave with the others?'

'She has as little to do with them as possible. It's not that
she's rude or difficult about it. She simply ignores them.
Some of them call her "Lady Muck". But not to her face.'

'I suppose the question is whether the repentance is
sincere.'

'It's very difficult to tell, Father.' The chaplain was meticulously courteous. 'The psychiatrist isn't convinced. As you
know, there's a history of manipulation, and he feels that
this may be one more example of it.'

'He's probably right.' David stared at his hands, knotted
together on his lap, the fingers like a tangle of roots. 'But
we have to bear in mind the possibility that she means it.'

'Of course.'

'Another point that concerns him is that she still won't
use her own name. She insists on being called Angel. By
everyone.'

The silence between them lengthened. It was restful, not

297

uncomfortable. David thought that the woman was probably praying. She was in her fifties, he guessed, short and stout, swathed in shapeless clothes. Before ordination, she had run one of the larger children's charities.

At length, he stirred and asked the question he had wanted to ask on previous visits. 'Does she ever mention me?'

'Not that I know. She mentions no one from the past. It's as if her life began when she came here.' The woman leant forward. 'Would you like us to pray?'

'No.' David looked up. 'Don't think me rude. Perhaps after I've seen her.'

The chaplain nodded.

After a moment, David said, 'Sally tells me that you and she were ordinands together at Westcott House.'

'Yes, though I didn't know her well. How is she? And the rest of the family?'

'Things have calmed down a little.'

'And Lucy?'

'It will take time. She's changed.'

'We can pray for healing, but not to turn the clock back.'

'Just so.' David shrugged. 'When Lucy prays at night, she wants to pray for the man Grace. She adds him to the list, along with Mummy and Daddy.' He paused. 'And Father Christmas.'

'Why does she pray for him?'

'She liked him. He gave her a conjuring set and some sort of cuddly toy. She's still got them. She's very attached to them.'

'It must be hard for Sally and Michael to accept.'

'That and the uncertainty. No one really knows what was happening in that house. No one knows how it's going to end. Michael's leaving the police. Did you know?'

She nodded.

'It's his own choice.' He knew he must sound defensive and was mildly surprised to discover that he did not care. 'There's no question of his being forced to resign.'

'What's he going to do?'

'He hasn't made up his mind. Sally's still on leave. But they can't go on like this for ever. They're in limbo.'

'At least they have Lucy.'

David was tempted to pass on the news he had heard the previous evening: that Sally was pregnant. But it wasn't his news, and in any case, it was a long step between conception and birth. For a few moments neither of them spoke.

'It's almost time,' the chaplain said at last.

David followed her out of the chapel and along a corridor that seemed to stretch for miles. The place smelled like a school. Summer sunlight streamed through high windows. The security was omnipresent though unobtrusive. The chaplain led him to the interview room they had used before. She conferred with the warder on duty.

The warder stared blankly at David. 'You can see her now.'

Angel was sitting at the table, examining her hands, which lay palms downwards on the metal surface. She looked up as David came in. He thought she might have put on weight. She wore no make-up. Her face was pink and unlined.

With sudden clarity he saw the child she had once been. In his mind he saw her running down the path towards the garden door into the house, saw her looking up at his face as he stood waiting in the doorway.

'Hello, Father,' she said, and smiled.

AUTHOR'S NOTE

The Four Last Things is the first novel in the Roth Trilogy, which deals, layer by layer, with the linked histories of the Appleyards and the Byfields. Each book may be read on its own as a self-contained story. The three novels are also designed to work together, though they may be read in any order.

The second novel, *The Judgement of Strangers*, will describe events which took place in and near the village of Roth, Middlesex, during the summer of 1970.

The third novel, *The Office of the Dead*, will be set in the cathedral city of Rosington over a decade earlier.